Text Classics

DAVID IRELAND was born in 1927 on a kitchen table in Lakemba in south-western Sydney. He lived in many places and worked at many jobs, including greenskeeper, factory hand, and for an extended period in an oil refinery, before he became a full-time writer.

Ireland started out writing poetry and drama but then turned to fiction. His first novel, *The Chantic Bird*, was published in 1968. In the next decade he published five further novels, three of which won the Miles Franklin Award: *The Unknown Industrial Prisoner*, *The Glass Canoe* and *A Woman of the Future*.

David Ireland was made a member of the Order of Australia in 1981. In 1985 he received the Australian Literature Society Gold Medal for his novel *Archimedes and the Seagle*. He lives in New South Wales.

PETER PIERCE is adjunct professor in the School of Journalism, Australian and Indigenous Studies at Monash University. He edited *The Oxford Literary Guide to Australia* and *The Cambridge History of Australian Literature*, and is the author of *Australian Melodramas: Thomas Keneally's Fiction* and *The Country of Lost Children: An Australian Anxiety*. His reviews appear regularly in Australian newspapers.

ALSO BY DAVID IRELAND

The Chantic Bird
The Glass Canoe
A Woman of the Future
The Flesheaters
Burn
City of Women
Archimedes and the Seagle
Bloodfather
The Chosen

The Unknown Industrial Prisoner

David Ireland

Text Publishing Melbourne Australia

textclassics.com.au
textpublishing.com.au

The Text Publishing Company
Swann House
22 William Street
Melbourne Victoria 3000
Australia

First published by Angus & Robertson 1971
This edition published by The Text Publishing Company 2013

Cover design by WH Chong
Page design by Text
Typeset by Midland Typesetters

Printed in Australia by Griffin Press, an Accredited ISO AS/NZS 14001:2004 Environmental Management System printer

Primary print ISBN: 9781922147066
Ebook ISBN: 9781922148148
Author: Ireland, David, 1927–
Title: The unknown industrial prisoner / by David Ireland; introduced by Peter Pierce.
Series: Text classics.
Dewey Number: A823.3

FSC
www.fsc.org
MIX
Paper from responsible sources
FSC® C009448

This book is printed on paper certified against the Forest Stewardship Council® Standards. Griffin Press holds FSC chain-of-custody certification SGS-COC-005088. FSC promotes environmentally responsible, socially beneficial and economically viable management of the world's forests.

CONTENTS

Unrefined
by Peter Pierce

IN 1928, the year after David Ireland was born, George Mackaness edited the anthology *Australian Short Stories*. The selections were drawn, he cheerily declared, from 'the cream of thousands of Australian stories typical of Australia and her "makers"'. Many of their titles focused on supposed distinctive national types. Here were 'The Half-Caste', 'The Drover's Wife', 'The Parson's Black Boy', 'The Emancipist', 'The Tramp'.

The title of Ireland's second novel, *The Unknown Industrial Prisoner* (1971), announced the discovery of another national type, hitherto unrecognised or without acclaim: the prisoner bound to have his individual identity suppressed by gaolers, in this case the managers of the oil refinery on the shores of Botany Bay owned by the giant British-European Puroil Company.

Each element of Ireland's title resonates. The workers are unknown, except to one another, and then they are known through a screen of nicknames, affectionate and abusive. They are deemed dispensable and unimportant, treated as though they are 'Men Without Qualities' (the title of the novel's seventh chapter). The cruel and newest manager, referred to as the

Wandering Jew, muses: 'now individual man is detached from the earth, from others, even from basic life itself.' Worse, the men acquiesce in their own abjectness: 'the Sumpsucker knew that though they were tall, bronzed, rugged Australian individualists, more or less, they would end up doing exactly as they were told.'

They are workers in an urban, industrial setting, not a rural, agricultural one. Thus their labour is of a kind that had seldom been depicted, let alone anatomised, in Australian literature.

Finally, they are prisoners. Notionally free to come or go, or not to work, they are self-imprisoned, whether by domestic demands, by habit or by fear of freedom. Figuratively, most of them bear 'the inch-wide residual scar of chains passed on from father to son, from ankle to ankle for half a dozen generations'. Their many small acts of rebellion neither reform nor overthrow the system in which they toil.

The cover of a previous edition of the novel showed a detail from a Geoffrey Smart painting, *Factory Staff, Erehwyna*, in which workers huddle at the base of the towering fence of iron that encloses them. *The Unknown Industrial Prisoner* is, among much else, Ireland's brilliant and eccentric intervention in the long history of Australian convict literature. He has diagnosed the pervasiveness of a prisoner's habit of mind and a new kind of imprisonment for the modern era. The novel's first chapter, 'One Day in a Penal Colony', makes a blunt announcement and analogy.

If each of the workers at Puroil—whether trade or clerical, blue collar or white—is an unknown industrial prisoner (despite glimpses of the lives outside that some of them lead), this is paradoxically reinforced by their bestowing of nicknames on each other, welcomed or not, that submerge their previous identities. These nicknames are metaphorical and particular, rather than literal and generic.

They can be endearing. The Good Shepherd is a kind and considerate boss, albeit hampered by his position. By contrast, and as their epithets uncompromisingly denote, the Python, Captain Bligh, the Black Snake and the Whispering Baritone are bosses of an altogether different stamp. Some nicknames, such as that of the would-be foreman the Sumpsucker, are plainly disparaging. Others are nostalgic and winsome. One of the prostitutes who works at the Home Beautiful, the refuge in the mangroves created for the prisoners by one of their own, the Great White Father, is known as the Old Lamplighter.

The rich mingle of other nicknames evokes worlds elsewhere: Glorious Devon, Two-Pot Screamer, Oliver Twist, Bomber Command, the Volga Boatman (who ferries beer and bodies to the Home Beautiful), Blue Hills, Far Away Places, the Wild Bull of the Pampas, Gunga Din. They refer to past times and other lands, speak at least of unrepressed memory and reverie within the fences of the Puroil refinery.

Nicknames are closely related to stereotypes: they may be hidden behind, lived up to and embraced, or allowed to diminish those to whom they have been fitted. The two main dissident characters in the novel do not object to the names that they go by within the confines of the refinery. The Great White Father actively resists the ethos of the company. The Samurai, whose name connotes his solitariness and power, does so philosophically.

They join a small band of literary troublemakers from this period that includes the titular anti-hero of Peter Mathers' novel *Trap* (1966) and Monk O'Neill in Jack Hibberd's monodrama *A Stretch of the Imagination* (1972). The Great White Father is reconciled to the prisoners' condition: 'we're no one, just whites marooned in the East by history.' Born, he believes, 'from a dream of strong drink and several campfires', the Great

White Father knows that he is 'no frustrated missionary like the Samurai. He was teaching these poor wretches, trained to captivity, to make life bearable.' The Samurai takes a more pessimistic view: 'the place was full of personnel...and short on men.'

Soon there will be fewer of either at Puroil. The refinery is in 'a transition stage' towards automation. Men are still needed during the change, which is bungled because of rundown inventory and demarcation disputes. Ireland, who worked in an oil refinery, observantly and no doubt disobediently, writes in acrid detail of backyard improvisations and the consequences when calamitous months-long shut-downs inevitably occur.

> String holding the governors, solenoid trips wired up, blocks of wood holding in key compressors by blocking mechanical trips, drop-shut gas valves jammed open with bits of wire, buckets and tins placed under oil drops on plants operating at high temperatures, contract labour brought in to do quick and slapdash maintenance jobs on equipment they'd never seen before just to keep the labour establishment figures down to the maximum prescribed from elsewhere. Cutting costs.

He spares no one. If management bears the heaviest indictment—'just as silica-alumina was the catalyst in the company's industrial production process, so hate was the catalyst in the company's industrial relations process'—the unions are not excused. 'They'd never been to the plant to look at it. They lived off prisoners' wages just as industry did. Their organisation was the same pyramidal hierarchy as Puroil.'

Although it takes place in a disturbed and angry present of fruitless industrial anarchy and petty bureaucratic tyranny, Ireland's novel brims with historical references and resonances. The refinery is located on 'the spot where Cook first stepped ashore, two hundred years before'. That is, the east coast of the country was 'discovered' in 1770, at the site where the Caltex refinery at Kurnell (the basis for the novel's Puroil plant) would be established. Within two decades of Cook's visit the penal colony of Sydney would be proclaimed. Not far away 'the first Australian factory, at Parramatta, was a place of correction'. The habits of servility, revenge and resentment abide into the modern era at Puroil.

The novel is also instinct with more recent history. Several characters are veterans of war who have exchanged one strict, if more dangerous, disciplinary regimen for another. The connection is explicitly made in the title of the thirteenth chapter, 'Tomb of the Unknown Industrial Prisoner'. Others are refugees and migrants from post-war Europe: the Kraut; Herman the German; the Pole called the Plover-Lover; the Italian man (as yet without a nickname) who implores the Glass Canoe ('a large and formidable man with a history of mental illness'), 'Break the arm. I go hospital, get compensation. No work for six week, my wife sick, I look after. Please. Not be frightened.' In a novel replete with them, this is one of the bleakest scenes.

Ireland's prose register is formidably capacious, his handling of it adroit. His ease with demotic speech has rarely been matched in Australian fiction, but this is also a novel full of literary and biblical allusions. He ventures arresting images: 'because of the magnification of their size and speech on the walls the shadows seemed to possess more life and vigour than the men who made them.' The natural world around appears despoiled by Puroil: 'the sunset was magnificent, but it was butchered by a few malicious minutes, and fell in ruins to discoloured cloud.'

Such eloquence prompted a reviewer in the London *Times* to praise the novel's 'ferocious satire'. Yet Ireland is no dour and programmatic social-realist decrier of industrial capitalism in a tradition that includes Judah Waten and Alan Marshall. As the Great White Father remarks, 'the whole world is Puroil Refinery, Termitary [the offices] and Grinding Works.' Ireland is indicting institutional and personal cruelties, exposing the decay of the will to resist them, but the nature of dissent in his book is more quietist than revolutionary, a counsel of resignation if not of despair.

The Unknown Industrial Prisoner is imbued with an exultant pessimism. There had been nothing like it in Australian literature before, and the only thing like it since was Ireland's second great proletarian fiction, set in a pub in western Sydney: another microcosm of, or satirical counterpoint to, the world outside. This was *The Glass Canoe* (1976), and it too won the Miles Franklin Award.

The Unknown Industrial Prisoner

1
ONE DAY IN A PENAL COLONY

LOWER DEPTHS It was the same every morning. At ten to six reveille sounded. Mostly a broom handle was applied to the green dented side of a locker, one of sixty to hold the clothes of the men of the four shifts. This time someone with a sense of humour had taken a length of two-inch plastic hose and used three or four lockers as a gong, producing a deafening, heart-stopping crash. This was a bad thing to do; it split the hose used to get hot water from the taps over the handbasin into the mop bucket. Finances didn't run to another tap or to the employment of cleaners. The echoes died quickly into the concrete.

'Spread out!' roared the Glass Canoe. His voice was throaty and rich and greedy as if his words were cream. He'd taken his wake-up pill. 'Stand aside or lose a limb!' He was always nasty when it wasn't his turn to go down on night shift. His face smiled when he bashed the lockers with the hose, but that smile was for the Glass Canoe, not the other prisoners. He advanced into the narrow floor space between the rows of lockers with mop and bucket of hot water. Red-eyed, faces puffed and pouchy, hampered and confused by early morning horns, the sleepers were up, desperately scrambling to get hundreds of pieces of scrap rag—their beds—up off the concrete and back into the rag carton before the Glass Canoe could spill hot water on them with the legitimate excuse that the cleaning roster had to start on time. He was a large and formidable man with a history of mental illness; his head full of ambitions, his pocket full of pills, his mouth full of other men's words. He had no trouble getting past Doctor Death when he came up for his medical. Doctor Death, who would pronounce a prisoner fit for work if he could stand unaided, breathe and had a detectable pulse, was a paid company man in the best understood sense of the word: he knew what his modest two hundred dollars a month was worth and gave service to that amount, making three short visits a week. Six hours. Put out your tongue. Drop your tweeds. Cough. He wasn't paid to look for nervous disabilities, just cripples and dead men.

This was shift 2 at the cracking plant. Friday morning, the last of seven consecutive horror shift mornings. Pay day. The normal visible life at the Administration end of the refinery would proceed for the rest of the day and close down at four. Three other shifts would keep the revenue-producing end going—the refinery itself, whose columns rose spirelike into the distance—and shift 2 would come back at seven Monday morning for another seven days. In this place no day started. Nothing ended or began, things just went anonymously on. Morning was a start for some, an end for others.

They were more than half asleep still; only the fear whipped up by the Glass Canoe's savage voice got them moving quickly. And the heart-thumping shock of his way of waking them. They were demoralized, cold and cramped and stupid and something less than men. This was due to night shift work; no reflection is intended on the economic circumstances they had been allowed by the wise and benevolent workings of an almost planned economy to attain. Strong young men who'd never been tired in their lives were stopped cold by night work.

Night shift was sleeplessness, it was an upside down stomach, bowel movements back to front. It was waking up in sunlight at home after two hours sleep to the sound of motor mowers, children, pneumatic drills, door to door salesmen. It was trying to sleep through summer days drenched in sweat, eyeballs grating in sandy sockets, and waking not knowing what day it was. Or where you were, or who you were. And it stretched before them for the rest of their working lives.

Dust and silverfish dropped from overalls and hair and boots back into the rags from which they came. Look back at the title of this chapter, it has saved me an explanation.

Most stooped unthinkingly to scratch the inch-wide residual scar of chains passed down from father to son, from ankle to ankle for half a dozen generations, their legacy from the bloody and accursed empire which, to the amusement of its old enemies and its powerful pretended friends, had since died a painful, lingering death. Though you would not know this if you examined the laws of the colony: all were promulgated in the name of the sovereign of another country.

Somewhere beyond the refinery's dome of dust and gas the sun shone splendidly golden.

GENERAL COMPULSION Dutch Treat eyed the glare of day with annoyance and prepared to put his earphones away and pack up his crystal set. Daylight was no time to be contacting God. Night, when stars shone and the impediment of light was removed, was the right time. God dwelt in impenetrable darkness and could only be contacted by radio.

Blue Hills, who usually had a better hideaway up on the structures, pulled the beanie from his head, the woollen cap decorated with concentric circles of red and white. His only contact with the society about him was that he was a one-time verbal supporter of a metropolitan football side and grew orchids in his spare time. A shiftworker now, there was a time when he wasn't; he could still remember going to see the football every week; the yell of the crowd, beer-flushed faces, men selling doubles, ferocious women barrackers, the sly pee into empty cans. It was a long time ago. He had been in for eleven years.

He had fifteen years to go to retire at sixty. It was a long time. A lot of orchids opening and falling and one year less of life for each few years on shift.

The country towns had nothing to offer, no new cities were being developed or dams built in the country's dead centre; prisoners were allowed to drift jobless to the few large coastal cities from all over Australia as soon as they left school, to choose their place of detention. Since wherever they looked the land was owned by someone else, the only place they were not trespassers was on the roads and there were laws about loitering and vagrancy. You had to keep moving and you had to have money or else. There was an alternative. Without alternatives there can be no democracy. There was an infinite freedom of choice: they could starve sitting, standing, asleep or awake; they could starve on a meat or vegetarian diet. Any way they liked as long as they didn't bother anyone. Unemployment payments weren't meant to be lived on. They weren't compelled by others to apply to any one place of labour, but they understood that once accepted for detention their boss or commandant had power over them just as great and far more immediate than the government of the country. To all intents their employer was more powerful, for he was the main point of contact between government and prisoner: he deducted the government's tax. Apart from this he prescribed how and when men should come and go, how they dressed, when they ate, the movements of their arms and legs, the words they spoke. There were accepted facial expressions, compulsory signs of loyalty, accepted opinions, desirable morals, compulsory attendance on pain of loss of food money, and the rule, made by employers, that the prisoners must not refuse to work no matter how unfairly they considered they were treated. This had once been relaxed and the right to strike obtained, but this right was being eroded away and soon would be no right at all. Employers simply applied to a Court and a strike ban was written in to prisoners' Awards: no one consulted the prisoners. The days of five hundred lashes were gone but in their place were strike penalties of five hundred dollars a day. The word Democracy had been heard for centuries on political platforms but was nowhere to be seen in the daily earning lives of citizens. They knuckled under or they got out. As for having a say in the running of the enterprise that repaid their support by rigidly controlling them...

The funny thing was that with all this power, employers were not the State, they were free men. They could come and go out of one industry into another, they could employ or dismiss, make new rules and change old ones. No responsibility beyond the elementary one of providing themselves with a workforce able to work. If they didn't want to pay an extra cent in wages, they appealed to the prisoners' patriotism—think of the economy's good. The economy's good consisted of each employer maximizing sales or profit or both: there was a maximum wage but no maximum profit.

However, these considerations didn't bother prisoners. Fifteen-odd years to go. All Blue Hills had now were the orchids and his beanie—it kept his head warm at night—and the extra money from the shift penalty rates prescribed under the provisions of the Industrial Service (General Compulsion) Bill.

Penalties? Who was penalized? At the best of times any of them could have made only a confused answer to this question, but now all were numb, too numb for thinking, including those who had stayed up almost reading, almost sleeping, almost listening for the phone, almost alert for the steps of inexperienced foremen who did not know the ropes and might come stumbling in on those who had gone down. A Commissioner of Conciliation ruled once that a man was less than fit on night shift, showing a greater understanding of refinery working conditions than any other person who sat in judgment on prisoners' grievances. He was preparing to reduce their shift loading percentage and in fact did, but the fact didn't register, they thought of him as their champion. But no amount of money makes up for lost sleep.

What was Puroil? In Australia it was a few gardens in which distant proprietors planted money and after a while tangled masses of plants grew, though with no fairy princess inside waiting to be wakened with a kiss. Their financial budgets were larger than the States in which they operated. What was Puroil? At Clearwater it was a sprawling refinery, an army of white shirts, a fleet of wagons, a number of apparently separate companies, dozens of monolithic departments protected from each other by an armour of functional difference and jealousy. On the refinery site it was two hundred and fifty shabby prisoners, a heavy overload of foremen, supervisors, plant controllers, shift controllers, up to the giddy height of section-heads (popularly miscalled Suction Heads, a metaphor deriving from pumps) who were clerks for the technologists; project and process engineers and superintendents who were whipping-boys for the—whisper it!—the Old Man himself, the Manager, who was actually only a Branch Manager and a sort of bum-boy for Head Office in Victoria which was a backward colonial outpost in the eyes of the London office, which was a junior partner in British-European Puroil its mighty self, which was the property of anonymous shareholders.

Did these people know their humblest prisoners were asleep on the job? Could they have ridden easily on their magic carpet of dividend cheques if they had known the foundation of their empire was missing? Would they have suffered attacks of vertigo, thinking the whole edifice was tottering? Not at all. For not only was their investment spread over dozens of countries so that whatever tariff barriers were erected Puroil could get underneath them and whatever upheavals occurred Puroil would survive and only people would suffer, but with real ingenuity the humble prisoner was being replaced as the foundation on which the structure was built; machines were to be the foundation. Machines that ran day and night; machines that ran for years. Why imprison these men? Why not free them?

This was a transition stage. The refinery processes were more automatic and needed far fewer men than a manned assembly line, but were far short of automation.

On the job, it was not necessary to do anything about it unless a transition man was caught sleeping. If no one actually tripped over a body there was no need to find one, for owing to the many sudden, strange shifts of Puroil industrial policy, it was not always clear which body was going to be in the soup: sleeper's or finder's. If there was some industrial advantage to be won by turning a blind eye perhaps on the eve of a wage agreement, an eager foreman might easily find himself caned severely and with a bad staff report. It was demonstrably bad to be one of the lowest bodies, a part of Labour, but being on the Staff wasn't all beer and kisses either. It was a one-way ladder suspended over the cruel sea of separation.

BOOKS VERBOTEN 'What's this!' the Glass Canoe exulted. 'Books! Papers!' He had spied the poor, torn Westerns, science fiction novels and *Reader's Digests* left lying about, and the sheets of newspaper that Bubbles had used to insulate his sleeping rags from the cold concrete.

Books were forbidden to prisoners. Even when the plants ran well for twelve months and there were hours between alarm buzzers on dreary night shifts or between routine checks and instrument readings, the men were expected to sit and stare at the concrete floor; and, to give them their due, most did. Puroil preferred zombies. Standing instructions expressly forbade reading during working hours, or the bringing into the refinery of books or newspapers.

Yet there they were. The company guards in their smart field-grey uniforms and peaked caps—if you took the stiffening wire out of the crown you could have a real Rommel cap, and they did—the guards realized that operator bods could cause them a lot more work if they chose, so they went easy on them. When the men's bags were opened under their noses on the way out each shift, they were blind to little things like paperbacks. They looked mainly for 44-gallon drums. In return, the men obligingly failed to report them when they neglected to open the boots of certain outgoing cars.

The Glass Canoe picked up the reading matter, pocketed a war novel he hadn't read and shot the rest in with the rubbish.

THE HOUR OF THE PEARL The frightful noise made by the Glass Canoe in the locker-room woke the foreman, who sat in the far corner of the foremen's room, his back to the door, apparently gazing down at his hands. He had dozed off. He, too, observed the rule that you didn't sleep obviously. Man is a day animal and

Stillsons was very tired. He got his name from a habit of trying to do fitters' work: this led unfailingly to Union trouble but he couldn't kick the habit. Supervisors were not to do operators' work. Operators were not to encroach on tradesmen's work. This was the custom of years—without it where would they all fit in?

When Stillsons pulled himself together and tried with cold water to splash the sleep from his swollen face, he found from the Western Salesman, who volunteered the information and asked for action, that the Glass Canoe had damaged the men's lockers. He didn't mention he'd been cruelly wakened. He was one of those at Union meetings who sat well back on the outskirts of the crowd and hurled comments, like grenades, into the centre. Then ducked. Stillsons was on the point of tackling the Glass Canoe about it when some of the others came after him into the amenities room where the Glass Canoe was mopping. He mopped with such vigour after his pill, backing out of the room as he worked, that Stillsons was in danger of being impaled on the mop handle. Those behind pretended they couldn't see him and had him in a squeeze. They turned their backs and wouldn't move, pretending to look at the coloured nudes on the wall. To make clear his position you need to know that the amenities room, where fourteen men had their meals, measured fourteen feet by eight; a large part of the space was taken up by three tables, a cold box, oven and sink, all decrepit trade-ins from a dealer's yard; it was half the size of the foremen's office, which accommodated three. Like every building on the refinery it was designed somewhere in Europe. Stillsons was rescued by the Samurai, who came to the door of the amenities room and said, in his cold voice that was never loud but always managed to silence everyone, 'The Enforcer'.

The Samurai never allowed himself to be awakened by reveille, he was up and about before the cleaning roster had to start. No one ever surprised him, but then no one was eager to tangle with him either on the job or outside the massive blue steel gates which so impressively guarded the entrance to the works. The first thing he was told when he started on shift was to keep out of the Enforcer's way. 'Tread on his toes and he'll get you if it takes years.' The Samurai had met men like this before.

Stillsons, however, was made of different stuff. He turned and brushed his obstructors aside and scream-whispered, 'Where is he?' The mention of the shift superintendent's name was enough. He darted around, his head sinking down into his shirt as if he were an animal retracting its vulnerable parts, as if his body remembered the flogging past, his face white from night shift and blank with fear.

'Where? Did he come in? Did he ask for me?' In his anxiety he made to touch the Samurai, perhaps by the shirt, but even this human support was denied him. You didn't casually touch the Samurai. It was very hard to touch him. You didn't see his feet move, he simply slid out of reach. Now he kept after Stillsons.

'Time you went up to report to the Enforcer. There's nothing for you to do here.' Stillsons hesitated. Thank God the Enforcer hadn't seen him asleep. He'd dob his own mother. 'Unless you want to help with the mop.' The mob laughed heartlessly; no one wanted to side with a foreman, not in a crowd. They would sneak into his office later one by one and square off.

Since this specimen of Puroil management still hesitated, it was necessary for the Samurai to put out a greater effort to get rid of him. To be without a foreman in this part of the morning was a good thing. Once the evidence of the night had been safely stowed and the floors of the amenities, locker-room, toilets and hundred-foot control room had been swept and mopped, and this latest day marked off in scratches on the cement walls, there was time for leisurely dressing and, if you got in early, a shower. There were two showers among the fourteen men, but one wouldn't work if the other was started first. Bubbles was first showered. He wiped a pore closing stink repressant over his armpits for that fresh cool carefree feeling. It kept the sweat in. Choking clouds of baby talc surrounded him. He loved his body and overhauled it for the girls. His tongue was still cocky-caged from the night before, his huge pink belly tight as a drum. He'd had his six hours down. All he had to do now was order a new pair of boots, his present pair were slightly worn at the heel. They'd be worth three dollars at the pub.

The Samurai was quickly dressed and had the next hour to himself for thinking or just picking over the laundered overalls to see if his friends had left him one of his own pairs. He enjoyed this one hour of the shift. At seven they would be out the gate and gone. He had never worked on the better sections of the refinery—pump-houses, utilities, bitumen, distillation, platforming plants—where, on night shift, if the plant was producing and running steady, the men waited for the visit of the mobile canteen at midnight, then for the foreman's visit soon after, then half went straight down, taking their turn in a civilized manner and were wakened at six by the foreman ringing their phone. Yes, that was a better reveille. There were no vacancies on those sections. Months ago, when the Good Shepherd was telling them of the European owners' expansion plans, he'd said 'The honeymoon's over.' With the new investment would come a more rigid control. The cracker was the first big complex needing its own on-the-spot supervision. On all other plants supervisors were visitors; the men kept the plant steady so there'd be no visits.

BIG DADDY The Samurai sat watching the rest of his shift come dressed from the locker-room. Technically they were citizens, allowed to reproduce at random. A place had to be found for their children, too. As he watched, something like a fine despair seemed to spray up from somewhere inside him and shower his organs of concern with a set of patterned words, the same words that had often risen to his tongue when he saw them attacking each other openly or in secret. It was man against man at every level and the company suffered from the situation's wastefulness, but no one saw it as a blot that should be published, condemned, eradicated. Poor devils, you can't take care of yourselves, you need a father to watch over you and fight the battles you should be fighting against the false and the unfair, the cruel and the oppressive...And, as usual, he knew that although he had heart and ability for such a fight and many wanted him to be their delegate, to stand in the front line and take the company's first shots, he had never convinced himself that he had the basic inclination. Mostly the Union attracted men looking for an excuse to get off their plants when they felt like it. Those with ideas, energy and initiative got a second job outside. The Union knew only one thing: how to go for money. But what was the use of a wage increase awarded because prices had risen and industry could afford it, when as soon as the increase was awarded prices rose again because industry couldn't afford it? If the Samurai had been a man of ambition, self-seeking could have carried him through and he could have built a career on serving them, but not from love. He did not—he could not—love his brothers.

And yet he had no inherited ankle scar to scratch.

Official, pompous things amused him. He chuckled still over the name Puroil Refining, Termitary & Grinding Works painted in large letters on control block walls. Every so often it was painted out, but it always reappeared. He repeated the name aloud to the others. Few laughed. Only the Great White Father, who had written it. He met this man on his first day at the plant, as he started on afternoon shift, just before the day workers went home.

He said, 'There's our termitary', as they passed the administration block in the company bus, and sure enough there were the little ant-people running up and down stairs, on view behind plate-glass, arguing silently with each other or sitting impassively for hours in offices equally on display. A glass box, completely enclosed except for tiny ventilation holes. He had worked there himself before transferring to the works, but he had never seen the building this way before. A great manorhouse watching over its feudal fields and wage-serfs.

'What about the grinding works?' he asked the Great White Father, who was exceedingly tall and bony and good-natured.

'The whole thing is a grinding works. Each man, if he lets it happen, is ground down a little each day until, finely and smoothly honed of all eccentricities and irregularities and the originality that could save him, the grinding suddenly stops at sixty. Then they shot you out. You wait five years to qualify for the old age pension, and when you qualify you make your choice: whether to take the government one or carry on with the company pension. They're pretty close to the same thing, in cash. Under our beneficent social system, one disqualifies you from the other. Most of us won't have to worry, we're all specially picked and processed so we peg out within a year or two of retiring. The system is further safeguarded; in the last few years of service they down-grade you so your pension won't be much, anyway, in case you escape the health hazard. You see, your pension amount is tied to your earnings in your last couple of years service. Demote you, pay less. You're just an item of cost. The bigger the organization, the smaller the value of each man in it. And this one's huge.'

The very tall man's sea-blue eyes sparkled and danced so much during this short lecture that the Samurai kept listening attentively so as not to miss the joke, which he felt sure was coming. But no, the Great White Father was serious. He seemed to enjoy talking—the sort of man who enjoyed everything. Laughter patterned his deeply creased face, lined with the scars and lacerations of a varied, reprehensible, non-respectable, wholly enjoyable past.

'You said, if a man lets it happen…'

'If you let them grind you down, yes. You don't have to.'

'What else?'

'Fight 'em! Every step of the way!'

'They've got the whip hand. What do you fight with?'

'Smiles, a quick wit, sex, alcohol, and never say Yes to the bastards. Once you recognize the place is a prison, you're well off. The best that can be said is everyone draws an indefinite sentence. The final horror of a life behind barbed wire is mercifully withheld.' He glanced out at the high wire fence they were passing then, topped with several strands of barbed wire. 'You see, the battleground where they beat you is in here.' His long, friendly brown hand lay relaxed on his own high, resonant chest.

But just where the Samurai was expecting him to go on, he suddenly stood. The bus stopped. Their crew was decanted like a carelessly handled bacterial culture outside the host body of the low grey control block on their growing plant. Drawn by a power unseen, the human bacteria quickly made their way inside and were apparently devoured. Gunga Din, lean, brown, small and dry, went first to the urn to check the water level and turn it on ready for the first cup of tea.

The Samurai tried to catch up with the Great White Father, and did succeed, but all he would say was: 'That's where your Gallipoli is, in there.' And a long, bony finger prodded his chest, then was gone, busy with locker key and bootlaces.

'What do you mean, an indefinite sentence?' He felt foolish as he persisted, but this seemed to be a man worth talking to. The rest talked interminably of second-hand cars and overtime.

'Indefinite? You don't know when you'll get the bullet, do you?' And turned away to sniff his boots, then to scratch his right ankle. When he had his boots on, he went to wipe some dried mud on to a pile of rags in the corner, but stopped himself in time. The Glass Canoe didn't, and was busy rubbing his feet on the rags before the Great White Father tapped his shoulder.

'Humdinger,' he said. The Glass Canoe looked down. The rags stirred and stretched, yawned and looked up.

'Is that what you think of your fellow workers?'

'Christ, I'm sorry, mate,' said the Glass Canoe and everyone gaped. Perhaps he was getting sick again.

On the job, events moved slowly. On the drawing board in the Admin block though, for eight hours a day, the pace was frantic until four, when the white-shirted multitude suddenly went home. Their effort might have been more wisely spread over the twenty-four hours to take advantage of the quiet of the dark hours, but white-collar men don't yet do shifts.

The tall man had another word for him when he was dressed for work. 'No one enters those blue gates only to make gasoline, bitumen or ethylene from crude. Oil *and* excreta, that's what they fractionate here. Us and oil. With foremen, controllers, suction heads, superintendents, managers and all the rest, there's maybe forty grades. Forty grades of shit. That's all any of us are. White shirts, brown shirts, overalls, boiler suits, the lot. Shit. The place is a correction centre. The purpose of giving you a job is to keep you off the streets. It's still a penal colony. All the thousands of companies are penal sub-contractors to the Government.'

Puroil's land included a stretch of what had once been park-land. Residents' petitions, questions in Parliament, real estate developers' organized, agonized pleas, no amount of democratic pressure was able to beat a foreign oil company. A few words were altered on a piece of paper somewhere, the parkland was declared industrial land and Puroil had a foothold in New South Wales. The total of 350 acres included, on the river side, some of the swampiest land this side of Botany Bay, but mangroves were cleared, swamp flats partitioned and drained and filled until only a few dozen acres on the river bank were left in their natural state. Another hundred acres of mangroves still stood on the other side of Eel River, just down from the gasoline depot of a pretended rival of Puroil: Puroil supplied them from a nice fat silver pipeline that nuzzled into the slime of the river bed and came up again out of the ground handy to their shiny white tanks.

Puroil supplied the depot of another company too, with a line that ran half a mile under cleared clay. Wagons of rival companies that ran out of their own brand, simply called in and gulped down a load of Puroil, went out and sold it as their own. Even Puroil sent out grey unmarked wagons—they had brother companies with different names. The rival companies fixed the price between themselves in the first place, the Government approved their figure then made a big deal of getting them to reduce half a cent a gallon when crude went down a cent. Then they all advertised like mad and called it competition.

At Puroil, the largest vessels of the new cracking plant were in position and complicated mazes of pipelines were being lagged with glass wool and aluminium sheet. Turbines, pumps, compressors, heaters, coolers, columns were assembled from many parts of the world, there were even a few girders and pipelines from Australia. Puroil never gave out the usual unctuous bumph about the refinery belonging to the Australian people; it was very clear that whatever faceless people owned it were a long way off. They were clever faceless people. At that distance they were able to persuade Australians to pass an Act of Parliament subsidizing their search for more oil. Even with retained profits and the help of liberal depreciation provisions they didn't feel able to bear the full cost themselves. They even persuaded Australia that Puroil's increased wealth was good for Australia. The way they put it was that it was Australia's wealth.

The plant was a new design, the first of its kind; there was a power recovery system hooked in to the catalyst reaction and regeneration cycle. Integrated, vulnerable, but designed to save half a million dollars a year on fuel bills. This one complex of twelve plant units cost forty million dollars. Even so it was an economy plant, as it said in the operators' manual. The overseas owners weren't willing to provide enough standby equipment. On two thirds of design feed-rate the cost would be recovered in two years, after which the profit was enormous. And in seven days of twenty-four-hour running, the wages of the sixty men operating it would be paid for one year out of profit on gasoline alone, aside from sales of steam to neighbouring industries, top gas for the ethylene compressors, gas and slurry oils to the gasworks, low pressure gas for bottling, cycle oils and furnace oil to the many little oil processing factories that sprang up round the refinery. The normal cracker, they were told, ran continuously for eighteen months to two years before shutting down for inspection and repairs.

WONDERS OF THE WORLD While the Samurai and the rest of the troops were down in the control room waiting the last half hour for the bus that would take them up to the blue gates a thousand yards away, other bipeds had come out of the structures. One of these was Far Away Places.

Far Away Places had been standing on a metal grating two hundred feet up, looking west into the light mist lifting from the distant Blue Mountains. His night had been quiet and solitary, with no nightmare awakening, on several bags inside one of the top walkways in the reactor vessel. Until the plant started there would be no regular work for men like him, and in the absence of intelligent operator training courses, he and the rest had nothing to do but learn the plant, which meant study flow schemes and walk over the structures. On night shift, it meant melt into the darkness and keep out of sight. There had been a course, but the instructors had only been able to talk about cracking plants they knew in other countries, and this one was different. Neither instructors nor men had ever seen a power recovery system.

As he looked down at the squat control room with its flat roof already scarred by well-aimed bolts and metal droppings from the welders, Blue Hills and little Gunga Din came out to empty rubbish from small tins into large tins. He saw how like rats they were, darting about outside for a space, then ducking back to shelter. The air was gauzy with gas.

'Look at it,' he said aloud. 'Air. Running with crap. Call that air. We breathe that shit in.'

If only a man could get away. A small farm somewhere. A man could produce all he needed to eat, you'd never need go near places like this, never be herded on to an assembly line or a process and never have to muck in with people you hated. Other people. Keep to yourself. A few sheep, fruit trees, bit of a garden. Christ, it was a glorious dream! It was freedom.

Freedom? It was isolation and that was better. Feel of the wind on your face, the sun warming you, the grass growing the same as it had for millions of years. Mending the fences. Enough food for you and the dogs. A dream. A man wakes up one day, realizes the world was made for other people and knows he's going to be at the arse end all his life. Nothing here for a man to live on. A pay packet stops you from dying, it doesn't teach you to live.

Far Away Places, from his perch on the lift-top landing, spat. Meditatively he fingered his private parts under the loose khaki overalls—he wore no underwear—and watched the little white gob of liquid as a few drops broke off and moved away from the main mass. Like a big bomb and little bombs. A piece of paper will float away, down and up in the warm draughts round the columns and, when the plant is running, above the coolers with their waste heat shimmering and rippling, but spit goes straight down, like bombs. He fingered, in his pocket, an old trumpet mouthpiece. He amused himself by playing strangled tunes on it way up on the structures, alone.

On the rail near him a large battered moth rested, its wings frayed.

'Poor bastard,' he said to it. 'Knocked about. The wind pushes you around, doesn't it? Yet you're supposed to be at home flying in the air.' He picked it up and dropped it over the side. It fell straight down. He followed its fall till he lost sight of it. Did its wings open? If they didn't, he'd killed the poor thing. But it had wings, why didn't it fly?

'You stupid bloody moth!' he called after it, guilty. 'If I had wings I'd take off, tired or not.' But would he? Perhaps the thing opened its wings and saved itself a few feet from the concrete. Anyway it was only a moth. His guilt remained. The moth had a life and would never have another.

Far below another of the rats, or of the three thousand million wonders of the world, scuttled out into the propane laden air with the slops bucket and from a spot five yards short tipped its contents in the direction of a drain. Far Away Places felt unaccountably that the earth should tip a little in response to this sudden violence. The Glass Canoe was back inside about the time the slops landed. Far Away looked away from the humans across the altering air to the tall gas flares, north to Sydney, east to the sea, west to the Blue Mountain range, south to the eroding headlands defying the Pacific. All round him the tiny houses seemed to bow down, performing the kowtow to tall industrial plants. He came reluctantly downstairs.

At ground level, under the concrete skirt of the largest vessel, the Rustle of Spring was stirring under his heavy tarpaulin. He was young and Italian and worked for a construction contractor. Camping on the job saved him money; he could send more home to Italy after he paid his debt to the company that brought him out.

Far Away Places trod on him as he stepped exploringly under the fat regenerator. Rustle of Spring sat up with a jerk, not awake. When he saw it was an overalled prisoner, he lay back, thinking sadly of Italy in another ocean. Far Away left him there, covered in thick dust. Rustle of Spring was too young yet to start coughing.

Far Away was late getting down. With any luck he could creep in unobserved. The rest of the boys had ways of not understanding anyone who always went off alone. Even Blue Hills spent some nights with the rest of the crew.

LIFE BY ORDEAL 'Look what the cat shat on the mat!' roared the Glass Canoe, hooked a finger in his overalls and flied his every button from neck to crutch. The rest of the men laughed, but not too loud. They had felt that big brown finger in their own overalls. Or in other places when they were bending incautiously. The Glass Canoe had a great sense of humour.

My silence will always protect me, thought Far Away. But the Glass Canoe had the bit between his teeth. 'What've you been doing all night, Far Away?' And to the others, grinning his brown sleek smile, 'I think we ought to take a look at the old love muscle. Whadd'ya say?'

They said nothing. Their own long since gone High School and National Service initiations rose up before their eyes as the big man fished for the muscle he spoke of.

If you say nothing and do nothing and feel nothing, no one can hurt you, said Far Away to himself. Perhaps. The Glass Canoe brought it out. It was quite small from fear. Mercifully his tormentor did not crush what was crushable. Years before, when he was conscripted into the service of an overseas crown and dumped into Asia to help fight somebody else's undeclared war, Far Away had had a ritual sex experience—miscalled harmless initiation—in which unresolved perverts like the Glass Canoe had extracted from his body, by cunning application of oil, fingers and feathery grass, that which he was shyly reserving for his first woman. Now here was the Glass Canoe about to make him play the same game. With all his concentration he tried to resist the Glass Canoe's insidiously gentle treatment, but he failed. His member had a life of its own to live and once erect had no conscience.

Not one of the audience was game to butt in. The Samurai was outside, the Great White Father visiting some of his old mates in another plant. Stillsons was gone to see the Enforcer; only the Sumpsucker was on hand to speak up for Far Away.

The Enforcer was partly human: he wanted no Stillsons rubbering up behind him in his office at 0615 hours to report job activities that didn't exist. He knew there was nothing to do, so did those above. But reports had to be written in case someone from Head Office got nosy. He had written his fictitious reports already. He got rid of the visitor with two coarse words. 'Piss off!'

'Chee!' Sumpsucker said harmlessly, as he got beside the Glass Canoe and saw what he was doing.

'Chee...' The Sumpsucker was a senior man, expecting his dust-coat any day.

'What d'you want?' bullied the Glass Canoe, working steadily. His hands smiled up at him with approval and love.

'Some day someone'll hang one on you,' Sumpsucker said mildly. 'You can't do what you like to people.'

'He won't hit me. Will you, Far Away? Or I'll wear his guts for garters.'

Say nothing, said Far Away over and over to himself. His own heftiest punch wouldn't have dented the Glass Canoe's skin, but if he ever tried to throw that punch it would be the end of him.

THE ADVANTAGE OF FLEXIBILITY He found a thing to do. Many of the prisoners had been so corrected in their way of life that they looked for work in their time off. Far Away Places had found something to kill time and bring in a few dollars. He helped his brother-in-law in his big black shiny meat-wagon. When there was a death round about, Half-Cup was called and if Far Away was handy, both went to pick up the body. While the Glass Canoe was doing his worst, Far Away re-lived his first pickup.

There was no father in the family. The mother died sitting up in bed and the kids, seventeen and younger, didn't know enough to lay her out. She had half-stiffened in a sitting position. Here was the point Far Away went over in his mind so many times and which helped him now.

Half-Cup shooed the family out of the room, shut the door, turned up the radio on the bedside table, walked up to the corpse and BLAM! His fist took her fair in the breast bone and she flattened out on the bed. Now she would fit under their sheet on the stretcher and in the coffin later without the mortician having to cut anything to make her more flexible.

ORDEAL RESUMED Far Away Places concentrated so hard on this trivial incident that the Glass Canoe had to work very hard to bring on the end result he wanted. Not only that, but Far Away's face contracted in a dreadful grimace of disgust and fear at the thought of such violence being used on the corpse of somebody's mother. He didn't reflect that the majority of lady corpses would be somebody's mother and nothing out of the ordinary. This expression of disgust had taken complete possession of his features at the moment that the Glass Canoe's efforts bore fruit.

'Looka that!' yelled the Glass Canoe delightedly as Far Away's body shuddered in natural spasms. 'Ground glass and razor blades!' Ever afterwards this casual, inaccurate reference to Far Away's grimace was to label him as a case of urethritis. Far Away grimaced; the Glass Canoe said he was in pain: the others did not reject the connection so easily made for them. They swallowed it whole. They had no particular love for anyone that they should look for reasons in his favour. It was easier to take someone's word. 'Make sure you don't go pissing in there with us,' he added with relish.

'What about the floor?' asked the Sumpsucker.

'I'll mop it up,' said Far Away Places, replacing everything. 'It's all right. I'll clean it up.' His face was part white, part pink; his mates couldn't say if he was angry or ashamed and since no one gave them an opinion to swallow they were without one.

I'll just act as if it's something that might happen any day, thought Far Away Places. I can see the funny side of it though. He mopped the floor, his mates watched vacantly. Stillsons returned, the Sumpsucker followed him into his office.

'Hey Sumpy!' chipped the Glass Canoe. 'You're always chockablock with sex and dirty photos. How come you've never dropped it out for us? Come to think of it I've never seen you have a pee. Or take your clothes off to have a shower with the boys. Is it true you get a horn every time you take it out, so you can't pee, only by accident?'

The Sumpsucker's head retracted into his carapace of sweat-stiffened shirt—his body, too, remembered the lash of the past—his hands clasped themselves over his bald forehead to push his head further into his clothes.

'You'll get yours.'

'Not from you.'

'Some day.' The Sumpsucker feared heights and freely admitted he was a coward, but he was the only one there to talk back to the Glass Canoe.

'What you following Stillsons for? You after a dustcoat?' The position of foreman was an eminence few would reach but most hoped for. A permanent carrot before them. The Glass Canoe himself had a dustcoat in his sights. The waiting men snickered, but even the Glass Canoe despised their support. He grinned broadly at their group as if at one man.

Far Away went in the locker room to change. Dutch Treat was sealing his precious carton and stowing it in the false bottom of his gladstone bag.

'Did you make contact?'

'Not yet, no. What frequency do you think He'd use?'

'He's God, isn't He? All frequencies at once. Tune it anyhow you like—you'll get Him. But why don't you try it up on top of the plant? You won't get much reception down here. You can see the sky from up there.'

SOMETHING FOR THE BOYS Out in the dawn the Samurai came across a square of light-gauge welded guardwire left over by a construction contractor. Without thinking very much about it, he brought it inside, bent down both ends and had a toastrack. There was a small battered electric stove in the amenities room, the rack fitting neatly over the hot coil. Gunga Din was filling the urn so the next shift could have their cup of tea first thing.

With more satisfaction than he had felt about anything he had done for Puroil, the Samurai threw the old chicken-wire rack away and substituted his.

He had done something for the crews, it was a good feeling.

MATES Fifteen minutes later they waited—pale, blank-faced sheep—for the company bus. They stood in line on Road Nine on the edge of a huge ditch ten feet deep, eighty yards wide and hundreds long, like prisoners on the lip of a mass grave. Behind them was a three million gallon tank floated into position in this ditch.

Since it was a refinery, Puroil allowed no matches within its gates. Or lighters, though the smart ones carried them. Matches had to be smuggled in. The smartest thing was to smuggle them out, for Puroil matches came in boxes of 1200. This was a real service for all ranks. Some jokers liked to throw empty match boxes about the refinery to nettle the brass, but the best joke was to plant them in someone's bag or coat then ring the guards at the gate to report the breach of rules.

Each man checked his bag for prohibited articles that might have been slipped in by a practical joker and gave his socks a last pull to hide the scar.

THE SURVIVAL OF WEEDS The Samurai waited in line for the bus with the rest of the crew on the lip of the great ditch. Idly he speculated on methods of defence against an attacker from all eight directions. He had been a formidable player in his judo days and it was second nature to him to consider his position at any time in relation to any possible opponent. Since his training from childhood by his peculiarly unworldly mother was away from any show of aggression, he considered only defence. Ambition was a sin, and had been submerged so far under layers of studied inoffensiveness that now this potentially dangerous man had drifted into a job as a shiftworker, a nominally unskilled man, one of the deprived, subhuman mass on whom our rich civilization so tentatively seems to rest.

The soil he stood on was dead. On its surface miniature mountains rose above pink plains; canals and lakes formed from wheel-tracks, footprints. It was dead, waiting to be torn about by explosions, bulldozers. Inert, plastic.

There was little talk in the bus and it was confined to aggressive or defensive noises. He considered this soil from the window. Here and there on the mixture of pink clay and shale a tough weed made a way for itself and for a brief lifetime sucked up enough water to go on living. But only the most tenacious, only the toughest lasted through a Puroil summer.

Here and there was a weed of a different kind; spiky, symmetrical, strange. He had seen it often when he walked among the tanks and bent once to pull out a specimen. Its roots reached as far underground as its leaves did above, but as well there was a penetrating aromatic smell from it and everywhere he touched it his fingers felt sticky so that hours later he was reminded of it. As if it belonged to a different planet. It grew in oil-soaked sand surrounding the tanks. The Samurai was not self-conscious enough to see that something like this was the impression he made on all who came against him.

BURYING GROUND The Two Pot Screamer's rumour said right from the start the new plant was Jonahed; it was built on an Aboriginal burying ground and the spirits of the dead would never allow it to go right.

There was something in the Australian temperament that rejoiced in thinking the odds were against them. They liked to start behind scratch. The Two Pot Screamer, amateur columnist of the house journal, was aware of this. He'd written a short story on it, just to collect more rejection slips. He persisted in thinking of himself as an artist and only submitted his stuff to arty magazines and what did they care for factories? The first Australian factory, at Parramatta, was a place of correction.

ACROSS THE RIVER The Great White Father wasn't on the bus that morning. No one knew who clocked off his card; maybe he didn't bother.

There were some mangroves grew aslant the creek and he was waiting under one of them for Cinderella who was standing at the foot of Boomerang Street, waiting for the Volga Boatman to ferry her across to the Great White Father's refuge from the Termitary and Grinding Works. He touched the leaves of those trees. Barely warm. They'd sucked in all the light they could get and were greedy for more.

On Saturdays and Sundays you heard the roar and echo of the power boats using this end of Clearwater Bay for their derisive turns. On the smelly mud green crabs slid under the blanket of water.

A LARGE DOB Volga dipped the oars in without a splash, the muscles on his neck strained, the oars bent. He sang, she whistled; both in perfect time. You could hardly hear the sound of his strokes.

Far out on the bay, mullet rippled the skin of the water. Water slapped the boat with little chuckles, the rowlocks made hardly a creak. Volga had them lined with cord and smothered with Puroil grease. The inshore blade bit mud and blacked the water.

The Great White Father watched the Volga Boatman's thick back coming nearer, and Cinderella in the back of the rowing skiff. Volga's coming on well; he had character enough to have nothing to do with the company, but he's only happy when he has a boss to look up to. Poor sods—thinking of the men herded inside the high cyclone wire fence topped with tight barbed wire—they have to be told they're human. Where had they all got off the track? Was it when they were children, forced to knuckle under in the schools, made to leave their humanity outside the well-drilled classroom with their lunchbags, hanging on a nail? Why did they have to be taught again later that their humanity could be brought inside the classroom and the factory fence? Sooner or later someone has to teach them freedom. He smiled. Not a secret smile. When he smiled it was for all to see. He was no frustrated missionary like the Samurai. He was teaching these poor wretches, trained to captivity, to make life bearable. It was a shameful and unblessed thing to take the scum of people and wicked condemned men to be the seed with which you plant a nation.

The sun was hot. Trees shook out their shadows like skirts to keep the soil cool. He slipped under one, touching its naked trunk.

He'd get them pining for the natural state of man. Where they would start to do what they wanted when they wanted; acknowledge no man's orders simply because they were orders; where women were easy, as they are if you treat them right; and where you can always get a drop to drink when you're dry. For my jokes are dirty and I travel light.

He had no misgivings about freedom. He knew you could never get so much of it that it became a kind of death. He knew, too, that you can always squeeze out a bit more for yourself than you think.

He thought of Far Away Places who had broken his glasses at two in the morning on a rod welded to a stanchion just where it would poke your eye out. Being the sort he was, he put the compensation papers in but didn't make a nuisance of himself at the office, pushing his claim and asking questions continually. He had some idea there was a system and if you did your part others would do their part and justice would bring you a new pair of lenses eventually. That was the law, wasn't it? He didn't realize justice has to be pushed and teased and prodded and reminded, that the system won't work without your efforts. Your push is what makes the wheels turn. Without your shove there is no system.

He thought of Dadda, who had slipped on the polished corridor of the testing lab. Fell sideways, putting out an arm to break the fall. No one else in the corridor; none to see him fall. Hurrying to get done an extra test they put on him at the last minute. Men like the Sleeping Brute or Big Bits were never asked to do extra tests; they always argued. Why should argument exempt a man from work? The answer was built into Puroil; the foremen had to be men with no guts. If they did their job fairly, their own superiors said of them, 'There's always trouble wherever he is. Arguments. Complaints. Fuss.' Superiors wanted quietness and peace, and thought an absence of noise indicated a smooth-running machine.

Dadda's wife worked and was changing her pants at work, as they say; he was full of troubles and moody, and when he got into a fight outside a shift workers' pub one morning a week later, he found his arm was broken from that fall. Fractured radius.

'Where's your accident report?' they said.

'It didn't feel broken then. I didn't know it was broken. Do I get the foreman to write out accident reports every time I bump something?'

They said yes. He did that until they told him to stop it. He tried to explain that he fell trying to get an extra test done quickly, but the people he explained to were personnel people—couldn't care less about lab tests. He told the lab boss, but he couldn't do anything about compo claims, he wasn't in Personnel. There was no one to listen. He got nothing. They even told him to go off work and not come back until he had a certificate to say he was fit. It didn't pay to have pride, like Far Away, and it didn't pay to be big and tough, like Dadda. It paid to be weak, cunning and gutless, like the Slug. The Slug was in business outside and although slimy, amoral and a foreman, was always lucky. He won a 16,000 dollar house in an art union, but still collected other men's empty soft drink bottles for the deposit. He shuffled about with his face rigged in a full, meaningless smile. As if he carried it in his hands and constantly made adjustments.

When the Slug had a backlog of orders and instructions for his three outside business enterprises, he would equip himself with an audience of white shirts, cause a panic somewhere, have it announced, then run up steps with the white shirts, working himself into the lead. A dramatic collapse, a clutching of the shirt front and there he was breathless and pale, a dead ringer for a heart attack. Good for five days off with pay while he caught up with his outside work.

The Great White Father eased the bow of the skiff expertly into the bank of the river Eel with a carelessly extended foot. He shoved the boat about, headed it upstream and stepped aboard.

'How many?' kicking the sacks of beer.

'Four dozen,' rolling the words against his palate as if he could taste them.

'Gold Label?'

'Half and half.'

'Good man.' He kissed Cinderella on the nearest strip of bare flesh that presented itself, her cheek. Too late she turned her lips to him; he was looking away across the water through a gap in the oil-coated mangroves. It was an interesting view. A foreman called Samples was creeping along slowly on a motor-scooter looking keenly westward. He was shifted from distillation work to tankage and knew nothing about his new job, but instead of asking questions he would tell an operator to get him a sample of something, then follow discreetly to see where he got it. The Great White Father smiled. The world was normal.

Volga aimed the skiff for a spot on the eastern bank where a large overhang of branches hid the stone-slabbed landing-place. There was a narrow canal dug into the bank so the boat could be hidden. The tide ebbed miserably, baring hydrocarbon stains. Muttering rose from the oil-dark waves.

As he lifted Cinderella on to the stones, the Great White Father got a powerful whiff of talcum powder undoubtedly applied on top of yesterday's layer. Looking into the blue iris of his eyes that contained the dull black pupil she felt warm and close as if his arms were round her and after uncounted anonymous embraces treasured the touch of his surfaces on hers. He kissed her again, this time on her smeared, shiny mouth. As he did so, his eyes were held by a large dob of sleepy dust which she had moved from the inside corner of her eye on to her dry, thickly coated cheek. His lips must have narrowly missed picking it up when he kissed her before. It seemed to have a hard end of a light brown colour, like a head. And a greyish-white body and wet tail. Almost as if it were alive and had crawled out from her eye.

FUNCTIONAL MAN Cinderella walked ahead on the twisting secret path to the hideaway. The two men carried the beer.

'What's all this about making the shacks bigger?' she asked tactlessly. Shacks! In reproof, a branch whipped back on her face and neatly cleaned her cheek of a patch of make-up.

'The hideaway is going to be extensively redecorated, remodelled and so on,' said Volga, injured. 'I like the idea of ranch style,' he added, lobbying for his own view.

'I like the white look,' said the Great White Father. 'Spanish hacienda. White for purity and human buttocks.' Cinderella waggled hers. 'But we'll have it green to match the mangroves.'

The mangroves grew thicker and thicker, the path made sharply angled turns. It was the only solid ground into the mangroves, all else was wet mud flats. The water reached it at high tide, enough to keep it swampy. There was another entrance from a little spur road off Boomerang Street; only these two men knew it.

Some of the equipment for the buildings had been brought in the secret way, though most had been carried piece by piece from the banks of the Eel River. Certain contractors' corrugated iron and timber frame sheds had been left out in the open too long. They disappeared overnight one Christmas Day and were re-erected facing each other deep in the swamp where the mangroves were tallest. Three large sheds, with a courtyard in the centre. One for drinking and eating, one for comfort and one for rest.

Cinderella went to the comfort shed. It was her day on duty and up to ten men would be deafened if she felt super. When she felt super she hooted triumphantly like a great liner leaving port. When she was normal she hooted like a cheeky little tug. When she was off-colour she could only manage an owl hoot and perhaps this was the most nerve-racking of all. The hoots started when the men started and continued till they finished. Right in the ear. She didn't know why she did it. She would make about forty dollars today, maybe fifty. The Great White Father had experimented with giving the girls a guaranteed wage, but it didn't work. The Sleeping Princess slept too long, and there were complications with the others. He let them earn what they could, five dollars a throw. The men wanted a straight go, mostly. No frills, not too much fuss and quick as possible. He tried to liven things up by suggesting variety but they were in such a hurry to get it off their chests they settled for the usual.

'You've just come off the plant. Why don't you have a snore?' said Volga kindly, watching Cinderella climb the step into the shed. Her heels were dirty as usual. Never mind, the legs were a beautiful shape and clean shaven.

'I might do that,' said the Great White Father obligingly, seeing him eye Cinderella. Volga liked to be first. Even so, he'd worry that she might have stopped on the way to work. He had a puritan streak:

it accounted for his weightlifting, his diets, his regular routines. He was as proud of his strength as Uncle Tom of his master.

The Great White Father of his people entered the empty sleep hut, threw himself miserably on a stretcher, said, 'Hell, do I have to die again?', then slept for two hours, two hours in which the course of life revived at the hideaway. Volga visited Cinderella, who kept her shoes on all the time and hooted like a departing liner into his right ear. He opened a can in the drink hut, then rowed back to the Puroil wharf. He was on duty.

The refinery opened its mouth and swallowed 750 more people. They were day-workers who sat at desks or maintained equipment or stored spare parts so that our 260 heroes of labour could operate the production end. Unfortunately for our metaphor, the refinery took in its crude oil and production supplies at the other end, so that if its true mouth extended down into Clearwater Bay, the employees must have entered the other end of the refinery's alimentary tract, for that was the end that discharged the company's products, suitably refined, into the waiting arms of the public.

Men came and went, the number of cans dwindled, Cinderella racked up more customers and her hoots diminished to the tortured sound of a weary owl, while at the Refining Termitary and Grinding Works man was alienated from his true essence; he became functional in the service of a handful of far-off anonymous shareholders. His labour, his opinions, his family were for eight or more hours this day, depending on his local status, owned as a means of wealth by someone not himself. It would have been no use to tell him that instead of serving a few shareholders of great wealth, he might be privileged to serve the common good of millions. He would still be serving someone not himself. He would be constantly at war within himself; his deepest instincts of self-preservation, selfishness, greed and hate constantly at loggerheads with his collective, anonymous, meaningless duties to a society too large and varied to be intelligible to him.

Those who took time off from this servitude to visit the mangroves, their energy went into talk and drinking, and when even this got too much for them and the spectre of lifelong bondage to an enterprise they couldn't understand rose up terrifyingly before their eyes, they retired to Cinderella's shed for comfort in the eternal soft arms, between the everlasting breasts and bore with fortitude her continual hoots.

Let us not heap reproaches on Puroil Refining Termitary and Grinding Works. No matter who owned the labour and the life of any of these workers and no matter how many times they switched owners, they would be in the same position. The whole world is Puroil Refining, Termitary and Grinding Works. Except for little outposts of a better order, hidden away from official eyes. Outposts like the Great White Father's.

We know man is alienated from his true function, but what is he? What is his true function? That is the hardest question. What should he do? What should he try to be?

ONE DAY AT A TIME Late into the morning, the Puroil men spoke of what seemed to them to be the past, but which swirled in great gusts around them as the present.

The Outside Fisherman, with his prominent drinker's lip and long silver hair always covered with a hat, was amusing Cinderella, who could be persuaded to spend some of her money and have a beer now and then, with a little story of the nearly finished cracking plant.

He was close to sixty and had been looking forward for years to getting his gold watch. His thirty years' service would be up two days before he was due to retire. There would be a regular slap-up feast attended by three or four long-service men and forty to fifty office staff to make it look well attended. The decaying prisoners would be presented with reliable gold watches and the freeloaders would clap. He would just make it.

'There's the phone inside and here's the wall. Like that. So? You couldn't get at it. What did I do? I says to the Good Shepherd, why not make a hole in the wall, nice and neat and put the phone on a little ledge in the middle and you could get at it from both sides? OK. The Good Shepherd always sees sense where there's sense and he gets the contractor to bash a hole in the wall. Comes knock-off and a new shift, we pass the information on about my idea, but the maintenance men are in a different division. They don't get any messages, so they wall it up again nice and neat. Night shift does nothing. Next day we bash the hole in again, maintenance patch it up. Three weeks that went on.'

Cinderella shook her head, finished her can, went to the toilet and back to the comfort shed, open again for business.

Who will condemn them for trying to imitate their leader and be earthy, loud, mean, generous, shifty, gay? For being sometimes fascinated by being alive? For wanting to be alive in no other age than this one for the simple reason that they were workers, slaves from time immemorial and therefore at home in all ages.

Once they stepped ashore on the stone-slabbed bank and made their pilgrimage through the thick mangroves and entered the magic circle, they couldn't help enjoying each day as if there had been no fall.

SILVER BELL The Great White Father experimented with special calls on the Puroil steam siren, but the management was alerted by an ill-disposed prisoner, so the prince of prisoners commandeered a bell from a museum. It was once ship's bell on a pleasure craft plying from Sydney to Broken Bay the century before.

It was a beautiful thing—its tone like highly polished silver—and rang clearly but not loudly from the dense mangroves over the river and on a fine day could be heard at the blue gates. It was rung when a new girl came on, and in emergencies. So far there were no emergencies.

It reminded some of the prisoners of a church bell and the Two Pot Screamer suggested the hideaway be called The Church in the Wild Wood or The Refuge of the Latter Day Saints, but the Great White Father didn't want his underground movement contaminated by association with religion, which was famous for making men kiss and polish their chains.

THE STINK OF SLAVERY At nine o'clock the Great White Father woke and it was a new day. He strolled into the drink hut and swallowed a can of Gold Label.

'Had a dream about atoms,' he announced. 'Some with single bonds, some with double and others, like carbon, with four bonds. I was just on the point of making a tremendous discovery that would tie up the behaviour and the future of man with the theory of chemical bonding, when what d'you think stopped me?' He stopped impressively, standing at the head of the trestle table with one can of Gold Label high in the air.

'You got up for a wee-wee,' ventured Desert Head, aiming a crack at his own skull to disperse his constant halo of mosquitoes.

'No,' said the Great White Father. 'I remembered this is Animal Week and I've got to take the ferret for a run!' He bounded outside and flew in at Cinderella's front door, his long legs only touched the ground twice between the two sheds. Thump! He descended on the bed, there was a second of quiet, then he came crashing back into the drink hut with a fine disregard for his limbs and years.

'Who's been eating salmon and onion sandwiches?' he bellowed.

A small voice piped up, 'Me.' It was the Angry Ant, squatting quietly in a dark corner of the shed after visiting Cinderella. He loved the hoots, he thought she pretended with the others and he was the only one who actually forced the hoots out of her.

'Got any left, Angry?' asked the Great White Father.

'Half a one,' said the Angry Ant. 'Here, take it. I'll starve.' The Great White Father accepted the sandwich, shoved it all into his cavernous mouth, chewed a couple of times, then swallowed.

'Must fight fire with fire' he said, and bounded back to Cinderella singing at the top of his voice the first two lines of the Workers' Anthem,

He who works and does his best,
Gets bugger-all just like the rest,

to the great hymn-tune Aberystwyth. The hooting revived immediately. Urgent, vibrant, triumphant.

Humdinger amused himself by creeping up on each of his friends and shoving his fingers under their noses. They had all been at the same girl but there was something objectionable about being reminded of it.

But even in these surroundings, where the better life had a chance to flourish and where their souls had a chance to grow fat to resist the daily grinding at the works, even here, out of sight of industry, seemingly so safe from the pestilence of work amid the pleasures and luxury they brought with them and renewed daily, even here they took the smell of death with them. Death by plague. They thought the Great White Father was joking when he came back from Cinderella and told them that while he was on the nest he had conceived more ideas for improving the hideaway; naming the sheds properly, painting inside and out and putting a roof over the little courtyard between the sheds. The work would be pleasant because it was for themselves, but it was still work and the smell of it had followed them even here.

'Well, home to Mum and into bed!' yelled the Humdinger, confident someone would supply him with the reply he wanted. Sure enough. The Sumpsucker poked his head round the door and called, 'Home to bed and into Mum! If you're lucky you'll get home before she gets out of bed. That's what I do with my widow!' He would also take home a non-returnable polymer catalyst drum—empty—as a present for her. She had no use for the drums, but felt he should pay something for the use of her facilities. The drums were black and three feet high and filled half her backyard.

His widow was not offended, like many of the younger wives, by the sour gas smell that penetrated the prisoners' clothing. Sumpy got a warm reception no matter what his personal condition. Many men, though, whose wives were unwilling to accept the fact that they, just as much as their husbands, were employees of a foul-smelling refinery, were compelled by the boss in the home to keep their street clothes separate from their work clothes, which were denied entry to the family wardrobes. They changed for work in the laundry. As if the fact of their subordination, their dependence on a large industrial enterprise, was something not to be admitted in private.

CHRISTENING 'Prisoners all!' intoned the Great White Father. 'All of us were born in this industrial prison. Maybe not in the Termitary and Grinding Works, but in suburban wings of the same complex. It is safer for most of us to be shackled in our chains than to be free to fend for ourselves.'

He punched a can.

'What we have to do is make our little hole in the barbed wire and creep out now and again to our hidey hole where we can forget we are born prisoners and will die prisoners, a little place where there are no bosses and no commands, where nothing we say is taken down and used against us.'

He finished the can.

'This is our hole in the wall!' Cheering and a great opening of cans. Another can was slid along the table top. It stopped near his great brown bony hand.

'With the Home Beautiful to come to, life can be made bearable!'

He had christened his hideaway and headquarters.

'The Home Beautiful!' The flimsy hut vibrated to the toast. They drank gladly.

ANARCHY AND ALCOHOL 'Friends and fellow crabs nestling in the warm armpits and other smelly crevices of Puroil, I have news for you! I am at the end of a period of psychic research, under the influence of an old miracle drug.'

He held aloft a can of Gold Label, solemnly drained it. Cinderella hooted ten yards away like a busy tug in a fog.

'Those who have gone before us are malicious, waiting above our heads to destroy us. You see, they have arranged the world so that we are more closely prisoned than they were. Every year the screws of supervision pinch us tighter. Even to those of us who are more free than others, they have given an awareness that sharpens our sense of confinement. Everything that spreads this human influence wider over the earth, spreads wider the net that meshes us in. It's our pleasure to escape from this net as often as we can—through the cyclone wire or off the end of the wharf—to our glorious Home.'

'What if they pull down the mangroves?' piped up the Ant, quoting a rumour.

'Get behind me, Satan. You smell not of man but of machines. To help us survive the coming machine age we must cultivate our peculiarly human abilities and attributes. Machines can't be beaten at their own game, but the bigger governments and organizations get, the more escape holes there are. We'll never go short of a Home Beautiful even if we have to burrow underground! In the last resort democracy or dictatorship, freedom or slavery are in here.' A hand on his stomach. 'No matter who's giving the orders. They can't beat us—' he moistened his voice passages briefly '—while our aim is to drink till the bald moon's hairy. You know the ones the system finishes off? Those who rely on foremen and show an obedient spirit, those who show initiative in their work, those who make suggestions, those who step back and let others go first. And those who think the company's fair dinkum and will reward those who look after its interests.'

The people he was speaking to nodded, but they were the very ones the Great White Father described. To a man they felt in their bones merit was rewarded, that the company could see into the heart and was a just parent who handed out appropriate rewards for nice conduct and for sucking up to its petty officers. None of them had a clue that the higher ranks, though their technical knowledge was greater and their shirts white, were the same sort of people as themselves, scrimmaging for scraps that fell from richer men's tables, dobbing their lifelong friends as soon as they imagined they were in the slightest danger of disapproval from above.

His few hearers settled further into their places; listening and not listening. The words were enough, the deep, penetrating voice and the great man's concern for their tiny fates. The hooting came slower. It should have stopped. Someone was holding out, getting his half-hour's worth.

'When I was a boy I first woke up to our sort of economy when I saw string being wasted. If I'd rescued it from the waste bins, that would have been stealing. It had to be burned in the proper way. Like the overalls and boots. Burned and written off. Take one out the gate they dismiss you for theft. Built on waste. Why all the records at the top office? They burn 'em in a touching little ritual at the tip. Why keep 'em in the first place? Why make all this colossal mess in the first place? Why the gasoline? So a few million motorists can burn it up going from nowhere to nowhere, then come back and buy some more. We can't even say, Look! I made this! I'm proud of it! The damn stuff's gone up in smoke.'

He sat down, his eyes glazed with alcohol and anarchy. He continued from a sitting position, legs sprawled. The hoots stopped, then started again after half a minute. Cinderella was coining money.

'Beware the evils of temperance and sobriety and embrace the worship of the bottle! Beware the dangers of isolation from your fellow man in haunts of coot and hernia! Every man needs homoeopathic exposure to germs and windy ideas. The temperate man sees the same world always, the proper inebriate finds the world never presents the same aspect twice. The bottle keeps a man away from his family, preventing over-exposure and low ratings. Stops him working about the place. Diminishes self-esteem which is a good thing, the world of keeping up with appearances and neighbours is a world well lost. Be not led into the wretchedness of right conduct. Temperance drains off surplus money into the maw of commerce. Without the bottle there's women always hanging around for wrong reasons; you become a victim of intolerance, covered with the bruises of respectability, narrow and evil-minded. Compare this with our present seclusion with the eternal bottle as god. Let me give you an example of early man's lead in the matter. One of my ancestors was a missionary in Northern Rhodesia—grog forgive him—and he found the noble savages in obedience to custom everlasting had grain for bread and grain for beer and every year or so they endured a cruel shortage of food rather than touch the grain set aside for the beer. With such a magnificent lead from primitive man, what else can we do but drink? Drink! And the deliverer from this bondage and the refuge to which you fly are in you!'

The hoots stopped. A quickie.

TENTACLES Prison sounds followed prisoners wherever they went. Sleeping by day, off night shift, the scream of motor mowers and power tools brought the life of the factory into every backyard; and radio and television with their howl of advertising extended the market place into every private house.

CORROSIVE PRAYER The man next door to the Samurai was a fireman, also a shiftworker. His wife was working and he was alone with his dogs, for he was a great lover of dogs and of what they could do for him. His dogs were greyhounds and provided they had the best of care they were very little trouble. One had become sick with distemper before he could arrest the disease and although to his wife and relations and anyone who cared to listen he was overpowering on the subject of his love for dogs and the money they won in races, he was at the mercy of a disastrously quick temper. The Samurai was also at its mercy. He had a sleep of perhaps five hours to look forward to and had enjoyed only an hour, so that at nine o'clock, when the Great White Father was bounding amorously from shed to shed at the Home Beautiful, the Samurai was wakened from the deep, dreamless sleep of the shiftworker by sounds of terror and hysteria under his window. The man next door had despaired of the dog's recovery and reacted with his usual speed.

There he was, unselfconsciously wielding a hammer. He got in a good blow on the dog's head, having thoughtfully taken the precaution of muzzling it, though if you asked him point blank he would have been surprised if you suggested one of his dogs might bite him. The dog's legs gave out and the howling beast was reduced to dragging itself along on its underparts. The man was upset by this time and ended by dispatching the dog with several dozen poorly aimed blows with an axe, weeping all the time. He buried the dog behind his outside lavatory—an unsewered area—and because he was fond of animals and had a special love for that dog, he sliced off one of its ears and kept it in his pocket in a matchbox.

The man went to bed and slept soundly, but sleep was gone for the Samurai. He was tortured by the man's cruelty and by the inaction that his own private principles of conduct bound him to. First it was the other man's dog and second, the man was smaller than the Samurai. The Samurai would have been less frustrated if he had been a smaller man: the range of his adversaries then would have been so much greater. He could with honour fight only an equal or larger man. Such a man might beat him, but defeat was honourable.

A prayer on his wall, written on a piece of cardboard, consisted of three words: Help, Care, Listen. Confronted with a situation that did not call for violent action, he found that Help, Care, Listen often fitted well. Since he was a man of action, he had no fretful thoughts about the corrosive effect on himself of his short motto with its suggestive initials, HCL, which he repeated to himself as he tried to find a way to help the man next door. This good intention kept him awake for the remainder of his sleeping time.

PRIVATE MORALS Back at the plant by three, working a love-shift for a man who'd run out of sick-pay, he moved among the men of a strange shift like a man apart. His week of seven night shifts weighed heavy on him. Several of the shift, noting his dazed condition and because of it moving in for a quick thrust, taunted him with being hungry, believing he was called in on overtime. Many left their phone numbers prominently displayed so they might be called in on days off. He wouldn't bother to correct them. The trouble with a private system like the Samurai's was that others had to learn, over a period, where the boundaries were they could not cross.

He walked out on the plant at sundown, checking over his plant knowledge, following lines. The cracker was a graft on to a patchwork of old plants. Puroil expected men to acclimatize to the old, the feeble, the makeshift, but this was new. It should work.

The sunset was magnificent, but it was butchered by a few malicious minutes, and fell in ruins to discoloured cloud.

There was a little flurry after dark. The Good Shepherd visited the wharf while girls were there; not everyone took advantage yet of the privacy of the Home Beautiful. These girls were rowed from Clearwater Bridge directly to the wharf.

Quick Tip, quick on the uptake, barred the doorway with his thick body and racing conversation—he had been a bookie's penciller in real life—while the others got the girls into lockers. Since you could open all the narrow-shouldered lockers with a paper clip, this took only a few seconds. The Good Shepherd left after they had given him a cup of tea. Part of his saintliness was in accepting their tea in mugs tasting of mouth and brewed in their urn. Socks were washed in it. After he left, the gallant seamen of the wharf continued their exercises.

'Back to navel manoeuvres!' shouted Quick Tip joyfully. It was a phrase coined by the Two Pot Screamer, who delighted in making up words for others to say.

But the time was ripe to take the women off the job. No consultations were held, no meetings arranged, the general trend of thought moved naturally and gratefully in the direction of the Home Beautiful.

DIGNITY OF LABOUR The Samurai was eating. He found a neutral seat to occupy and this was important. There were invisible priorities to the tiny patches of seating space available in the amenities room; special places for sitting and staring at certain spots on the floor. Some sat and stared vacant and unseeing at the floor for seven days till pay day. A few adventurous ones ascended to the top of the structure and followed the movie at the Jerriton drive-in.

Out of the night came Mogo, famous for making rude signs at every refining plant he passed. He knew work was a curse.

'All you fellers got books?'

The prisoners looked up from their humble pursuits. It was night, they were disoriented, their minds focused uneasily, unwillingly.

'Good. Stick your noses in them. I'll have a cup of tea but no talk.'

The rebuff was unnecessary. Their heads swung down over books or patches of floor; in a few seconds they forgot he was there. Lovers in the locker-room made noises.

'How are you, Mogo?' said the Samurai.

'Stop the gush. You don't care how I am.'

'Love job?'

'Love. The Elder Statesman caught me for this one. I'll take the last day off next shift. Suits me.' Mogo was also a soft touch for love jobs.

'Want the paper? There's a good story on the struggle for leadership among politicians in Victoria.'

'Politicians are arses. I don't read anti-Labour papers. I don't recognize Victoria. The only good thing about Victoria is they fought on our side in the war.' The other prisoners gaped.

The low control block shot beams of light defiantly out the windows at the dark, which was a live monster crouched hugely above the hemisphere trying to leak darkness gently in at the cracks.

On a peculiar impulse, the Samurai got hold of some scrap paper and began making notes of the things he saw about him.

POOR HANS 'Jesus!' exclaimed Quick Tip, returning from a session with the girl he had rowed across Eel River.

'Christ!' roared the Sandpiper antiphonally, 'the same yesterday, today and forever!' She was the girl. There were sandpipers out on the flats, real ones, little stick legs propping too fast to follow; they called her Sandpiper because she got the boys to take her out of doors. Paddocks she liked, open spaces, anywhere under the stars. She was born in Balmain in its dingy days but always wanted to live on a farm. The mangrove flats were the nearest she got to the sticks, and they were further east, back toward the sea, toward the spot where Cook first stepped ashore two hundred years before.

'Take me, lover!' she would bellow at some skinny shift-worker. And when he gaped she would add 'For a walk!' in a burst of healthy, gum-showing laughter. 'You get electricity through your feet from the ground,' as she took off her shoes and expected her companions to do the same. They never did, though, and if you kept your eyes open as you went by the water-cooling tower you could often see a pair of boots tangled up with two bare feet. Usually facing opposite ways.

'She's an eye-opener, this one,' said Quick Tip to the Samurai, belting the Sandpiper affectionately on the left buttock. The Sandpiper would have preferred the Samurai's hand on her rump, and since she was direct by nature she seized his hand where it rested on the table and applied it to her bottom in an imitation of a slap.

A small robust fly, Hans to his friends, fresh in from the black filth of the river and the unprocessed sewage which found its way there, was making a meal of a large, monolithic grain of sugar on the table near the Samurai's other hand. It had been a good life, born in shit and with sugar and stools to lick, sweat of humans to drink and the runny eyes of dogs. The Samurai's hand, with the Sandpiper's still attached, returned from her buttocks and killed the small, vigorous fly named Hans.

HUMAN BACTERIA He took a walk after tea and went near some of the other plants on the site. But not too near. If you went to some of them unannounced, you could be hosed from the doorway by someone pretending to be cleaning the area; you could collect the slops bucket or the tea leaves.

There were no barges at the wharf, so the Samurai climbed a finished structure back at his own plant, went through his pockets for something to read, found nothing and settled down in the bed of the empty regenerator under the air spider on two cornsacks hidden there for the purpose and went to sleep.

He slept soundly while life went on in the refinery and outside. Just as operators' work was part of a digestive process in the body of the company, so they themselves were germs within that body, in much the same way, if you like, that the bacteriophage attaches itself to the bacteria—hanging on and feeding—and the bacteria, in turn, attacks the host body of society at large.

When he woke up and went down to the control room they were kicking up a fuss. The man who pissed purple had struck again. There was purple dye all over the stainless steel wall.

'It must be someone from another plant. Not game to have a pee where he belongs,' they said.

A mile away on a corner of Highway One an idiot sat on the concrete footpath with strips of filthy rag knotted thousands of times, old stockings, pieces of soft rope grey with age—all knotted. The whole mess was somehow tied in the middle so that the hundreds of knotted lengths could be reached one by one like the spokes of a wheel. Each strand had dozens of knots along its length. Tying, untying, over and over. Most days he was there: his people put him out every morning. Some days they forgot to bring him in. Pedestrians walked round him.

2
TERMITARY

UTOPIA, 1852 The head sherangs wrote nasty little notes to the lower bosses every time they saw it, and the little bosses protested as reasonably as they could to the office staff—the shinyarses—but the notice kept appearing, glued on walls and windows with uncut Puroil resin adhesive that couldn't be dissolved, burnt off or cracked with an axe. The Two Pot Screamer had a great supply printed.

RULES FOR PUROIL STAFF. BOTANY BAY 1852.

1. Godliness, cleanliness, justice, punctuality, prudence, diligence, continence, fortitude, honesty, faith, temperance, hope, obedience, charity, loyalty and chastity are necessities in a good business.
2. On the recommendation of the governor of the colony, this firm has reduced the hours of work and the staff will only have to be present between the hours of six and seven Monday to Saturday. The Sabbath is for the worship of God, but should any work require to be done, work will take precedence.
3. Daily prayers will be held each morning. All staff will be present.

4. Clothing must be sober and of uniform colour. The clerical staff will not disport themselves in raiments of bright colours. Long socks must be worn—no ankle scars must be visible at any time and undue scratching is forbidden.
5. Heavy clothing may not be worn in the office, but neck scarves and headwear may be worn in inclement weather.
6. A stove is provided. Coal and wood must be kept in the locker, not in desks, filing cabinets or pockets. Each member of the staff will bring 4lb of coal each day during cold weather.
7. No member of the staff may leave the room without permission. The calls of nature are now permitted and the staff may use the garden. This area must be kept in good order with the rake provided.
8. No talking is allowed, except after business hours. Movements of the lips will be viewed with suspicion.
9. The craving for tobacco and alcohol is a human weakness and as such is forbidden.
10. Now that the hours have been drastically reduced, the partaking of food is allowed between 11.30 and noon, but work will not on any account cease.
11. Staff will provide their own pens.
12. Forty minutes before prayers and after closing, cleaning work will be done. Brushes, scrubbers and soap are now provided by the management.
13. If in chains, staff are held responsible that their irons are perfect and not ovalled or too large.
14. If any person shall feel himself -aggrieved by any order, he is to obey instantly, but may complain, if he shall think fit, to the manager.
15. The manager must never be addressed directly.
16. A Record Book will be kept of the conduct of all staff.
17. The management will expect a great rise in output to compensate for the Utopian conditions.

MORNING SONG OF THE TERMITARY Take any Monday. The Black Snake was first in the office. A man waiting patiently for attention asked him about the 1852 notice freshly stuck to the glass door. The Black Snake sniffed; there was a nasty smell coming from the man's overalls.

'How would I bloody well know?' spat the Black Snake. He hated Mondays. He hated the other days, too.

A fat typist came in, but the man waiting patiently for attention could not catch her eye before she parked her bag, opened her desk and departed for the ladies' rest room.

The Colonel entered, having parked his old Rolls carefully. He was a clerk now, still with moustache and bar but in '45 was a colonel. He knew one of the Directors and this kept him employed, but he had no hope of promotion after he called The Whispering Baritone a refugee from a male whore shop in one of his grander moments when he was training officer. His papers were marked 'never to be employed in any higher capacity'. He drove a Rolls for the satisfaction it gave him to have a bigger car than the Wandering Jew.

The Colonel sniffed as he passed the man and marched up to his desk at the back of the office and took out little cards with cost formulas on them for the supervisor to see, then busied himself with his art gallery. He was a sculptor. His 'Mother and Child' was his finest work. It was constructed from two straightened paperclips, a spring, a disc of metal with three holes in it, a twig, and a short bent thing. The child was the twig. There were long-legged creatures and twisted wire faces: he spent most of the day on them. His phone trilled. He listened.

'What does Procedure say?' He listened again.

'But what's laid down?' He lost patience and took a firm stand, gambling on the other's ignorance of the rules. 'No! International Puroil Procedure says it must be countersigned by three officers, none in the same department. I don't care how many signatures you have to get. Three counter-signers, O'Grady says. Goodbye!' He hung up. The man waiting patiently for attention sighed. If only he had a job where you could play children's games instead of the boring business of staring at the floor or furtively reading stale newspapers.

Soon the rest of the staff were in. They would rehash till midday Wednesday the sporting events of the past weekend. From the half-way point of the week they would anticipate the coming weekend. All sniffed something peculiar in the air.

At eight o'clock industrial music started. Now and again a huge payroll machine chewed into a lump of silence and crunched it up with a frightful racket. Shortly after it started—and if the man waiting patiently for attention had been there every day he would have noticed that one followed the other—three whistlers started too.

They began with 'Drink to me only'; their whistles were nearly a semi-tone apart, though this was sometimes increased to a full tone or decreased to a precarious quarter-tone. And sometimes, just before the end of a phrase, they would all be dead on the knocker, all in triumphant harmony; then on the last note fall into a tableau of dissonance and hold the dissonance until breath gave out or until their supervisor, the Garfish, rubbered his head round to look over the partition separating him from them, in which case they would stop as if they had never whistled in their lives.

When the machine got a go on and looked like carrying all before it, they began to whistle deafeningly. The others frowned on the whistlers, not on the machine whose noise they took to be inevitable.

The man waiting patiently for attention nearly got served when a tall, redhaired clerk bounced in and asked, 'What can I do for you?' but the man took more than a second to answer and by that time the clerk was gone amongst the tables and chairs, singing. He was the only one who didn't sniff the air.

The working class can kiss me tail
A bludger's job will never fail!

Everyone stopped work to talk to Should I.

'Did you fellers read the latest?' chattered Should I. He held up a sheaf of eight-by-five pamphlets.

'Epistles from the Apostle Lewis,' he orated. This was the Puroil Chairman of Directors, Australian Board; another bum-boy to the distant owners.

'Puroil and the Credit Squeezes!' he declaimed. 'During the past twenty years, Government-inspired credit squeezes have had a marked effect on the Australian economy.'

'Where'd you get 'em?' sibilated the Black Snake.

'They're everywhere,' Should I declared. But the Black Snake's question was rhetorical. He was making notes, watching to see who said anything against the company.

'Severe competition has been encountered, the monthly increase in sales is getting less, new oil companies coming in, higher wages bill, caught in a cost price squeeze, major internal reorganization, economy drives, disastrous effect of the lifting of import controls.'

'Let's have one, friend,' said the man waiting patiently for attention, in a hard voice. Should I, in surprise, gave him one and went on reading. The Colonel fiddled with a new work, Diversifications, as he listened.

'The avoidance of waste, waste of human resources which carry a high cost factor, management of expenses, banish inertia, the disinclination to move or act. Inertia is the product of prosperity, we should not hesitate to depart from our traditional ways, constantly strive for better and safer working conditions, the Puroil Team, shaping the future of Australia, tremendous future, it is up to each of us to give of our best!'

Should I paused for breath, his chest heaving, a prominent Welsh vein throbbing in his right temple.

A phone rang and broke it up. Should I went away. A worker had gone to hospital with a back injury and his wife was asking for food money.

'Can't be done,' rapped the Colonel. 'He'll have to call and see Calamity Jane the nursing sister and fill in the compo papers.' He listened a bit. 'Madam, your husband might be on night shift, but Calamity Jane isn't. He should have reported to the sister and then seen the company doctor. Two in the morning? Then he should have waited outside the casualty room. Couldn't stand? What sort of wound was it? Did he lose much blood? No blood? No wound? I fail to see, Madam, how a man can be incapacitated by an invisible injury. Madam, his pain is no concern of ours. There is no claim until he fills these papers in. How do you know he suffers, Madam? Can you prove pain? Can you measure it? We have no pain-gauges, Madam. He could be fooling you, the doctor, everyone. Our rules are laid down. We can't take anything on trust. We don't make the rules, Madam. You can talk to a dozen Unions, Madam. He must call and see the sister, see the company doctor and fill the papers in. With back injuries, he'll need all the witnesses he can get. He was alone? That's bad. A man should never be alone when he has his injury. It's not doing him any good delaying this way. It's not my problem, Madam, I'm only here to help and I've done my level best to give you all the information at my disposal. Goodbye, Madam.'

He put the phone down quickly and his fingers flew as he put the finishing twists to Diversifications. He listed it in a little notebook along with a drawing of it, in case barbarians destroyed his art in a forthcoming invasion of the pay office, smiled at it, then placed it on the shelf behind him.

'Was that 1444?' slimed the Black Snake and the Colonel nodded.

'He done his back in the other day,' said the Black Snake.

'That's what that woman said.'

'He did that once before. Walked like this.' He got up and did an imitation of a bent man, putting an agonized expression on his face. The office laughed and laughed.

The thermostat reacted to the warming office, and the tone of the air conditioning system altered, filling the large room with a deeper hum. The air vents in the ceiling showed black patterns round them; the air they breathed was the air that circulated outside, with a high soot level. The system had filters to keep out rocks. The man waiting patiently for attention shifted from buttock to buttock on his chair and fiddled with something in his overalls. The tea-lady trundled in with her mobile urn and morning tea was on. The Garfish came out immediately to get his cup, trying to set a good example. Too much time was wasted if the woman had to go round with each cup. But the woman was against any limiting of her functions, she started to take cups round immediately, she wanted her job to fill all the available time. If the Garfish had his example followed, there might have been no Mother and Child from the Colonel to enrich our heritage, no Communication, no Will to Progress, no Encounter, no Diversifications. And worse still, no Unknown Industrial Prisoner, a work whose grandeur of conception took the Colonel's breath away when he thought of it and made his fingers tremble as he bent his potent paper-clips.

AMBITION The Garfish had his head down, ignoring the hullabaloo outside his cubicle; busy on his ideas for putting the labour force in its place. It was crazy that a man so far above the Colonel, the Black Snake, Pork Chop and the Mountain Cat, was despised by them. They took no notice of him at all.

If we can get a big shutdown of the plants after the cracker gets going, we'll have the operators, he ruminated. We'll start putting off the deadwood, get a pool of operators, make their jobs interchangeable, get a no-stoppage clause into their agreement, then apply somehow for an oil industry Union, to dodge the chance that the GWU will ever step in and split the operators down the middle by claiming it covered their jobs better than their present Union.

Yes, if he could get company Unions, or even the no-stoppage clause, he could ease out the Brown Snake and take his job. Industrial Relations, that was the job he wanted. He reckoned he had a talent for industrial relations. Above his desk, neatly framed and hung, was a pyramid-shaped diagram like a family tree. It represented orders of responsibility, starting at the base with many minor members of the hierarchy and ascending through the upper levels occupied by fewer and fewer functions until at the top the lines met at the word Manager. It was only a local chart; the Garfish's function was on the bottom line, but he had a place on the money tree and the faceless people he supervised didn't. He was actually on the tree: they were the ground on which the tree rested, the soil in which it grew.

THE DAY THE TEA-LADY The Brown Snake slithered through the door.

'Hey, Colonel! The Brown Snake!' hissed the Black Snake, who despised the Brown Snake although he was his superior officer.

The Colonel was miles away, head down, bent over the Unknown Industrial Prisoner. Easy meat.

'Take him out and shoot him!' murmured the Colonel, just loud enough for the Brown Snake to hear, which was what the Black Snake wanted.

Just then the tea-lady, dithering behind the urn, shot a gigantic fairy. The Brown Snake stood stock still, the Black Snake looked directly behind him at the poor soul without turning his head—he had Picasso eyes, on stalks, nothing was safe from his eyes—the Garfish ricked his neck looking over the partition that protected him from his subordinates, Pork Chop clattered the space bar on her machine aimlessly, waiting for someone else to laugh.

The Mountain Cat broke the tension. She gathered her considerable bulk together and leaped for the door, but just as she got it open she started to release the choked laughter that was pressuring up her vast interior and screamed all the way over the courtyard to the Ladies' Rest.

'That was a bit titter,' observed the Prohibited Import in his penetrating Scots voice. The room roared.

DOWNFALL OF EMPIRES The Brown Snake got his laughter under control quickly and by the time the others stopped, he appeared never to have been laughing. He was Puroil Industrial Relations Officer, and had a duty to the company to see nothing funny during working hours.

'Who paid 1554 last week?' he asked, knowing this number was in the Colonel's section.

'The Colonel,' said the Black Snake promptly. The Colonel braced himself and put the Unknown Industrial Prisoner aside.

'I'll tell you what I'll do!' he announced loudly. He always said this when he had to think about something. It was his way of gaining time. Then he decided to duck. 'What did he claim on his card?'

'Item 11,' supplied the Brown Snake. The man waiting patiently for attention got to his feet, the better to hear them. He knew that number.

'Not on the list,' said the Colonel smugly. 'We don't pay 'em if it's not on the list. Gotta be on the list!' He waved a list of special claim rates which had lain idle on the desk while he fiddled.

'How does it get on the list?' interrupted the man waiting for attention. The Colonel did not readily talk to the crap—workers without white shirts—but he welcomed a diversion. His booming parade voice filled the office. He had been a good wartime officer; it was peace put the mockers on him.

'I'll tell you how! This—this sort of complaint'—waving at the time card in the Brown Snake's hand—'happens enough times and they'—he meant the overalled crap—'make a squeal and see a delegate and he sees the Industrial Relations Officer and he sees the Accounting and Office Procedure man and the head Union man sees the management and the management sees the men and while this is happening the men threaten to strike and the company threaten to go to court over illegal stoppages. Every stoppage is illegal. And they face up and threaten some more, then the management might grant the new rate.'

'What happens in the eighteen months the men do the special job and don't get the special rate while they're waiting for all this to happen?' asked the man waiting patiently for attention.

'Put that down to experience!' He turned away. They all turned away.

SUDDENLY 'What's that man doing there?' asked the Brown Snake loudly. He meant the man waiting patiently for attention. His question did not register properly, as he knew it wouldn't, but it served to get the attention of the whole office, including the Garfish, who stood up. The Brown Snake had seen the Whispering Baritone approaching—the head of Administration—and timed the repetition of his question to coincide with the Whispering Baritone's entry. The Baritone was uncommitted in the green and orange war and might be influenced against the Garfish.

'Why hasn't that man received any attention after all this time?'

The man waiting patiently for attention got up suddenly just as the Whispering Baritone came up to him. The Baritone reared back. Sudden movements of prisoners often panicked executives. The days were gone when prisoners cowered into corners at their approach. And the Whispering Baritone himself was a prisoner only a few grades higher than the man beside him. Not just a trusty or guard, but lieutenant to the camp commandant, no less.

The man who had waited patiently for attention now allowed himself to think of the reason he had presented himself there and in a moment was raging.

'We were told by the Good Shepherd that Item 11 was twenty cents and I've been claiming sixteen hours a week of item 11 for sixteen weeks now and where is it? It's no use telling me it's not on your list! When we're told by management down there that we get this money then we expect management up here to know about it and pay it!' He beat his breast. 'We're not the communicating links between departments in this detention centre, it's not up to us to be on your hammer reminding you all the time: you should pay the right money off your own bat. So where's my twenty cents an hour?'

The Garfish struggled to the counter separating the man from the rest of the office.

'Is that all you're here for? Twenty cents? You've been here since 7.30!'

'I've waited on that seat for hours for someone to come up to me and say What do you want?' thundered the man with dignity, 'But everyone passed by on the other side.'

'Why couldn't you knock on the counter for attention?' shrieked the Garfish.

'Why should I? You mob know I don't work in this office. If I'm here I must want something. Why don't you come and ask me? Why rely on me to push in and get attention? I don't care if I wait. Something doesn't get done down on the plant, that's all. Or don't you care about that?'

'Well, that's Operations Division,' said the Black Snake and the room murmured approval. 'It won't show up in our figures. They'll have to look after themselves. We've got our own work to do here in Admin.', cunningly including the Whispering Baritone in the argument. 'If you want something, just get somebody's attention in the usual way.'

'How, by throwing a fit or smashing your windows or sticking up a Puroil 1852 poster?' barked the man. 'I came here for my money!'

'We'll have a look into the matter and if it's OK we'll pay you next week,' said the Garfish.

'You'll pay me now! I'm staying here till I get my twenty cents!' said the man very loudly.

The Garfish stuck his hand in his pants pocket and pulled out a twenty cent piece. Flipping it on the counter he sneered, 'Here's your twenty cents! Take it!'

The coin slid along the counter near the man's hand.

'It should be paid in the proper way, through the payroll.'

'It's money, isn't it? Isn't that all you want?' He turned to the Whispering Baritone, without caution. 'All they ever think about is money. Money rules their lives. Don't know the meaning of gratitude. Where could you get a better employer than Puroil? They don't know when they're well off. They'd never get conditions like this anywhere else!'

'Neither would you,' said the Whispering Baritone, who had a lisp and avoided talk as much as possible. Wary of the latest Luxaflex manoeuvres. He picked at his finger ends, flaking. The Garfish blinked, swallowed, shut up. The man picked up the twenty cents, held it high, turned it over and flung it to the farthest corner of the room. It tumbled off the brick wall and fell to the floor. Everyone looked round, anxious that it shouldn't be lost.

'I'll have my money in the proper way. I've claimed it on time cards for sixteen weeks. And when I say twenty cents I mean twenty cents an hour for sixteen hours a week for sixteen weeks. And it better be in my pay this week!'

'Why do you come here smelling this way?' demanded the Whispering Baritone.

'Because to make your rotten gasoline I have to get soaked in stuff you shiny-arses would run a mile from. Everyone down there has to put up with the same stink.'

'Ridiculous. We don't have it here in Admin. You people are always making out you're hardly done by.'

They were convinced he was lying, so he walked out under the large safety graph on display to all who came in the works. TOTAL DISABLING INJURIES FOR THE WEEK. He took from his pocket a Puroil 1852 poster, licked the gum on the back and pasted it to the door behind under the pretext of bending to tie a bootlace.

Far Away Places was moderately happy. If he took knocks and insults from his fellows and injustice from Puroil, he was determined to cause a little commotion where he could. He would never mention his broken lenses, so he'd always have something against the company. There was no one person to hate, just the vast vague company. It made a big target. He walked slowly back to the plant, his left hand touching himself, his right playing with the trumpet mouthpiece. His wheel spanner, held in a low slit pocket, slapped against his right thigh. He swaggered like a movie cowboy. Nothing was as satisfying as revenge.

3
THE HOME BEAUTIFUL

ONE GOOD TURN The Great White Father scrounged a collection of beds and lounge chairs, strips of carpet, kitchen tables, steel sinks, plumbing connections. A chain of men carted these things from the stone slabs at the river bank along the covered trail to the clearing. Painters were at work on the outside of the buildings, painting so that not even from the air could the Home Beautiful be discovered. Places had to be marked on the floors for the overflow from the old furniture when the Home Beautiful was crowded; that would not be necessary now. The Great White Father impressed on them that those who were on duty must present themselves at regular times back at their plants. Those who were really busy on the plant were not to leave until things were slack again.

One Eye was one of the helpers. He'd been in for eight years and wanted to get out. This was unusual. Mostly young ones wanted to get out. However much they hated it, the older ones, over thirty, wanted to stay on, hoping that by the time they were sixty and retired from Puroil the means test might be abolished, the retiring age lowered and they would be able to collect the old age pension as well as the Puroil pension. All their lives they had paid for their pensions in the Social Services segment of their pay-as-you-earn income tax, but any income after retirement, over a certain amount, such as a pension from their employers, would disqualify them from the pension they had paid for.

One Eye had his reasons. He was going into business and needed his proportion of eight years' long service leave as well as his pension fund money, to finance him. But he could only get his long service leave proportion if he could get a dismissal or a doctor's certificate that he was unfit to work any longer. Since he could both stand upright and breathe, he knew Doctor Death would never give him a certificate, so somehow he had to get a dismissal, but it must not be for misconduct. According to mysterious laws to which he had no access, misconduct disqualified him from the long service proportion. Nor could he get it if he resigned. One Eye had tried being found sleeping on the job, but the foreman who found him wouldn't identify himself and kept a torch on him while he gave him a little lecture.

'This shift is never all down. We have a reputation, so get on your feet. Everyone else is missing, someone has to be up.'

One Eye got back to the river bank in time to meet the Volga Boatman and buy a few cans. This was not allowed usually, but One Eye had done a good job, so Volga gave him a ration. Even here One Eye missed his aim, for when he took the cans back to the plant to drink them where he would be found, the Beautiful Twinkling Star, who wouldn't drink on the job, hid his empty cans and stood guard over him while he drank so that he wouldn't be discovered.

One Eye, rabid, quicktempered football supporter, was so infuriated by this goodness of heart that he planted the empties in the Beautiful Twinkling Star's locker.

LUST FOR COMFORT The Great White Father slept while they worked. When he showed signs of stirring, the Humdinger went over and held two fingers under his nose.

'Sandpiper,' said the great man, waking up immediately. He had never been known to make a mistake. The Two Pot Screamer got up from a corner of the drink hut and in a voice moist with warm emotion and cold pilsener, said,

'This new era of comfort and escape and sexual freedom has meant a lot to me and my mates. I move a vote of thanks to the Great White Father and each and every one that helped him in this magnificent new conception.'

'No conceptions, Two Pot,' murmured the Great White Father.

'Magnificent new erections, then.' There was no dissent. 'Only a short while ago a man was reduced to disgraceful attempts to get a bit of snooey. The Lady of the Lake—up there living in a shack near the tip—she was down at Mack the Knife's and when I come in looking a bit lean and hungry and under-privileged, what does Mack do but pretend to the Lady of the Lake that I been in boob two years and in great need. "Will you fix him up?" he says. "Sure," she says. And she lays down on the floor and her not a day under 65. Well I ask you. "While you jokers are looking?" I say. So there you are. All that's changed now. I know we're not British or European—we're no one, just whites marooned in the East by history—but we have the Home Beautiful, plenty of beer and a fine bunch of girls and all I hope is the British mob doesn't tear down this fine patch of mangroves and make us move elsewhere for escape from our industrial prison.'

There was moderate applause; most of them suspected the Screamer of sitting there quiet all the time, thinking it up. The reference to the British mob—another overseas-owned patch of Australia, just as their refinery acres were European-owned—didn't go over their heads. They took it as quite the natural thing that this patch belonged to Britain, that to France, another to America and so on from one valuable patch of Australia to the next. Yet if you referred to them as natives of an underdeveloped colony with not enough guts to toss the foreigners out as the Indonesians did, they'd look at you.

The Great White Father revived, unfolded himself to his full height, and got into top gear.

'My friends! We now have the blessings of electric light. Put forth the right hand of fellowship and flip the switch, Volga!'

Light smothered them.

'I am a light in the mangroves. Whoever believes in electricity will never fear darkness. We took the leads under the river, so take care you don't displace any stones on the banks. The stone you displace may darken this place.'

There was clapping of hands on the timber table and ceremonial lifting of cans.

'Another important project is also under way. When winter comes, we'll have no need to rely on our animal heat and the warmth of alcohol to keep out the cold. We have tapped the gasoil line. Our modest offtake will never be noticed. The lines won't be all connected till winter, the heater is here already. Don't forget, if you have any suggestions for our comfort, pin them on the new notice board.'

'I thought I recognized it.'

'They don't need another safety notice board near the office block. There's two dozen already.'

AND INTO THE TREES YOU CAN BE SURE OF PUROIL was the advertising slogan stencilled on the four-gallon drum holding up one corner of the bed on which the Sandpiper performed her indoor duties. Many wits made reference to this slogan when they boarded the bed. But the Sandpiper enticed her men or compelled them, depending on the strength of their characters, out into the clay paddocks beyond the mangroves, sometimes in among the tangle of mangroves, balanced in the forks of trees, playing ape.

The Two Pot Screamer had had his two pots and sank a third before his half-hour with the Sandpiper.

'We've never had it so good' he remarked to the Sandpiper, sprawled on the bed like a mongrel dog. As he prepared himself, he tried to get the Sandpiper to talk. Some small prideful weakness in him, left over from a life of defeats, resented her professional indifference. All the jokes he'd ever made about his most prized possession and about the action that gave him his one spiritual consolation, where were they now? Coition was the only bit of heaven he had ever tasted, unless you count the oblivion of alcohol. He had a bad start in life and could never forget it.

'Wish we had beds like this on night shift up at the plant. Rags has a dunlopillo for the concrete. Blue Hills has bags; he puts his feet in one and the rest on him and underneath.'

'Get a move on,' exhorted the Sandpiper. 'You've only got half an hour. The Sumpsucker's next.'

'You can take him in your stride, can't you?'

'I'll handle him.' The Sump would recount endlessly his previous adventures, the odd demands he made on his widows, his victories over stubborn housewives. Physically he was amazing, though. Soon as his pants were off, up it came.

'Do we have to go outside in the bush?' he asked.

'Suit yourself. It's your dough.'

'You won't go dead on me?' plaintively. He didn't really care. Talking to a woman in a bedroom atmosphere was as much to him as the mechanics of it.

'Who's after Sumpy?'

'Sea Shells. He just does the one thing.'

'Who?'

'Sea Shells. Never on Sunday christened him. The missionary position always, and blows down your ear the whole time.'

'What missionary position?'

'Missionaries to the heathens taught converts there was only one Christian way to do it. The man on top. In some American states any other position is illegal.'

Two Pot whipped out his pencil and made notes.

From outside, the Sump sang 'Rock of Ages, cleft for me, Let me hide myself in Thee' in a kidding tone of voice.

'Shut up!' called Two Pot. 'Wait your turn!'

'Muggy in here, isn't it?' mentioned the Sandpiper to hurry him up.

'Let's go, Sandy!' insisted Two Pot desperately, grasping her broad hand and rushing her outside. Sumpsucker watched them trot into the mangroves, with a gently superior twist to his mouth and his tiny eyes bright—kept apart only by the top of his long pliable nose.

He didn't see the accident. The pair in the paddock stood face to face in a tiny clearing where the ground was firm. Two Pot straightened up just as the Sandpiper lifted her knee. It caught him. The pain took his voice away. He cut off her apology—none of the women wanted to incapacitate the sources of their cash—and surprised her by going ahead with the business in hand.

'I've never seen a man do that before. Not when he was hurt.'

'And not when he's paying, I'll bet. Can you keep something to yourself? If you wouldn't mind, next time, just give me the knee there or a smack with your hand. When I'm not expecting it.'

'If you like it.'

'Like it! Christ, I've never felt anything like it. Makes me feel I'm suffering a bit in return for the pleasure. Sort of paying for it. Properly. Not just with money.'

'Suits me,' said the Sandpiper sensibly.

THROUGH A SNOTTY RAG The Sumpsucker clasped his hands behind his head in his normal attitude of thought. The Great White Father was a gentle man, guided by moral scruples. He had a respect for the wholeness of others. The Sumpsucker changed his hands, still clasped, to a position on his forehead from which the hair had tactfully receded. His head retreated downwards into his chest cavity. Usually only the oldest operators pulled their heads in like this, being closer to the convict past and the days of a thousand lashes.

'You on probation yet?'

'No. Never be a foreman while my arse-hole points to the ground.' Every prospective foreman said it.

'Your boys will help you with the heights.' Sump was terrified of heights. He couldn't climb a stepladder.

'I'm a coward. A cowardly custard,' he said happily.

'The whole population is,' soothed the Great White Father.

'Except the Samurai and you,' amended the Sump. You only need a uniform to be a field-marshal, he thought, looking into the Great White Father's sea-blue eyes and equating courage with the bearing of arms.

'I'll do my trick for you,' said the Father, rising on his toes and falling flat like a tall plank. Sump gasped.

'That'll put you in hospital some day,' he said unhappily. 'Proves you're not a coward.'

'It proves nothing. I do it because I'm just as much a moron as any prisoner. We're the same anywhere. Prisoners of our own moronic mental patterns. Body mechanics who leave gauze pads in stomachs, electrical operators who blow fuses in power stations, medical students braining each other with cadaver legs in dissection rooms, prime ministers who terminate the careers of competent successors. Morons.'

'You could be prime minister yourself if you weren't in the grip of the grog.'

'Get thee behind me, Sumpy,' intoned the Great White Father. 'Don't tempt me with the splendours of power or the riches of public office. I see no riches. I see no splendours.' He put an empty can to his eye for a telescope. I see no ships, only hardships. As for the grog, I'd drink it through a snotty rag or a baby's nappy.'

A howl floated in from outside.

'Was that Adam and Eve discovering a maggot in the apple?' declaimed the Great White Father.

'More like a cat howling,' enviously. The Sumpsucker didn't like to think anyone else could rouse the Sandpiper to frenzy or make her howl in the bushes.

'Then bring it in,' said the Great White Father grandly, 'nail it by the ears to the table and let it howl inside. I'd rather live in a swamp amongst friends and howling animals, than pay rent and instalments in a suburban shed.' He stretched. The beer made him sleepy.

'Being cowardly runs in the family,' the Sumpsucker returned to his permanent subject. 'My brother got tricked into a paratrooper unit. They keep having to push him.' He was happy when he could make the Great White Father laugh.

'Perhaps they shouldn't have put an experimental plant so far from civilization,' the Father ruminated. 'The start-up's six months late already.'

'The cracker?' Sump was amazed. 'I didn't know you ever bothered about Puroil!'

The Great White Father turned away to open two cans and pushed one across the table.

WIND IN THE WILLOWS 'Thanks,' said a gummy voice. It was Sea Shells. Sumpsucker was gone. Sandpiper must have come back. Two Pot was still pulling himself together in the mangroves.

'Hullo, Shells,' the Great White Father welcomed him, but had no further chance to speak. Sea Shells was a constant sound in the ears. He suffered from razorback gums, his teeth had been out for too long before his dentures were fitted and the gums had thinned so his plate couldn't get suction. He still lisped, his top set dropped continually, clattering down noisily inside his mouth. Often food stuck the two dentures together, they might be both up or both down, depending on the way they bounced, revealing large spaces, steppes, ranges and prairies of tongue, palate and gum.

'Having trouble with the new stepfather, you see Mum got a divorce shortly after I showed the stepfather into the house while Mum was taking a shower, he's a cop—the stepfather not the old man—he brings home watches and bracelets and dollar bills every week, he's a better provider than dear old Dad and he gives Mum more sex, not that she'd take it from Dad she was always knocking him back, but she still says Dad never showed her any affection I guess she likes a change, anyway the old bed creaks night and day now, Dad's applied to come back and live as a boarder because he's used to the place and Mum's cooking he must be nuts, it's a sickening thing to discover your father's nuts, so now he hits the grog, he's a case of alcoholic remorse every day round two in the morning, the only time he was sober for a week was once on pay day he called in at the Corroboree Hotel and had his pay snatched, he tried to run after the bloke that took it but was tripped before he got to the door by a bloke standing there reading the paper, accidental, of course.'

He paused for breath. His top teeth had dropped, his appearance was ferocious for a second or two, a vast Jenolan cavity became visible above the hump of his fallen plastic palate.

'How did you get off the plant today?' asked the Great White Father firmly. Sea Shells sucked his top teeth back to a more convenient position.

'Went to get some keys cut, the keys to the tool store the stationery locker and the main warehouse, you know everyone in the place has keys to all the things that are supposed to be secret, security, why Slug has the biggest collection he has a key to everything, no one gets into strife unless something goes wrong and you get caught, remember the Fallen Idol? How he rose and rose then fell and fell raising the company flag one minute, ass-holed the next? Well they wanted him out of the way and they finally got him over keys, not many know that, I may be deaf from the turbines but I hear things I'm not supposed to hear, it's all in here'—tapping his head above his ears—'and it'll stay in here until I can get even with this rotten company, you know they wouldn't get me compo for going deaf around their stinking turbines and compressors and I had to pay all the doctors' expenses myself, there's lots of blokes in Puroil going deaf but they know from my experience they won't get compo so they shut up about it, if they find you're deaf they get an excuse to hoist you, I wouldn't spit on Puroil land, talking about spit did you hear the joke about the full spittoon?'

'Yes,' said the Great White Father, 'I heard it.' Sea Shells didn't mind.

'There was this bet in the pub. Ten dollars to swallow the contents—'

'Never mind,' said his listener. 'I heard it.'

'—but it was so difficult to swallow, not because he was a piker—'

'Shut up! It's filthy!'

'—One lump!' He laughed loudly so he couldn't be interrupted. 'That's why it took so long, one lump!' And in the same breath, 'You know what the secret is to beat this company? How we always have the wood on them? It's the fantastic unity amongst the men that has this company on its knees!'

The Great White Father swallowed hard.

'They know about the heads going down on night shift, the management knows all about it, the Union knows but no one ever says anything about it, but you know what I think? The amazing thing, the fact that really amazes me is that there isn't more crime against the company, not that there's so much but that there's so little, take that compressor with the pump and the stand and the mobile generator and the pump went last weekend, the whole thing could have disappeared, that's if there was a real criminal element here but there isn't, somebody had a use for them that's all, they even took them out the main gate that's how good the security is, just hook them on behind your truck or even your car and the guards don't know you didn't come in with it, you've got to be cheeky with this company and you can get what you want, the squeaky wheel gets the oil, they'll treat you viciously if you look as if you'll take it, the one that doesn't complain always gets the crap, you take a sick pay query up to the Brown Snake and get treated like dirt but if you start to fight back and look as if you mean it he'll back down and end up giving you your money and he does this to everyone that stands up to him not only lodge members—'

The Great White Father tuned out. Later he took his eyes from his hearer to open two cans and passed one across to—the Two Pot Screamer. Sea Shells was inside with the Sandpiper, she wouldn't go out playing ape with him, she couldn't stop his patter. The Sumpsucker was just behind the Screamer, he didn't need twenty minutes to pull himself together. As soon as his pants were on and the job done, he had it under control.

'It's all right for you, Sump,' said the Screamer, while the Father opened a third can.

'Why better for me?'

'You got her when she wasn't so fresh,' complained the Two Pot Screamer, guarding his new warm painful secret.

'You're too old,' jeered the Sumpsucker. 'Age tells.'

'Besides, I heard Sea Shells performing. I wasn't going to come back into a blast from him.'

'Never mind Sea Shells. She'll stop his yap.'

'I wonder,' said the Great White Father.

SANDPAPER Forget all your other troubles—wear tight shoes, her father said before she went out into the world to earn her living. Now, she sat on the edge of the hut bed and in the few seconds left to her before Sea Shells was ready, she drew on her face a red mouth, with the lips unfortunately slopping over on to her face.

After working an hour or two she felt gummed up in her throat passages from kissing men with differently constituted saliva. Perhaps one had a cold. Strange how swapping spits thickened up your own.

'Just a minute,' she said and turned away to do out her nose and throat into her wash-basin (by courtesy of Puroil welding shop change-rooms) with a mixture of salt and bicarbonate dissolved in water. It was one of Dad's hints, he used to do this in the bathroom each morning and she was so used to the sound it never disturbed her. Sea Shells didn't like it, it turned him up.

'What's the matter?' uneasily.

She hawked and spat like a man. 'Just swapping spits with you men does this. Gums me up.'

'Do you have to talk about it?'

'Not talking won't make it go away.' She would rather have been out in the paddocks.

'Would you like to go for a walk?' she asked, but her heart wasn't in it. 'You're very quiet. For you.'

'Why don't you put your grass skirt on?' Usually he talked from go to whoa: what was the matter? She had to do something to get his full attention. She wiped her face carefully on some scraps of paper tissue and let them flutter to the floor. He watched, fascinated. Covered with germs and here she was spotting them on the floor.

She stretched her arms behind her head, clasping her strong hands; the muscles over her shoulders pulling her breasts up. Nothing dampens a man's spirits so much as sagging breasts. The strong black hairs—three days shaved—under her arms slanted out of her pores like arrows. Around the base of each hair was gathered a thick white crust of powder cemented by deodorant.

She should have gone to the lav, too, but it wasn't so easy for a female. All she had was an old pot, to be tipped down a hole in the floor boards. Like on a train or in a plane.

She swung her legs up on the bed.

'Remember that time in the winter?' It flattered a man if you remembered a particular time with him.

'When?' He tried to recover some of his spirit by pretending he needed prompting.

'When we were out in the storm. You know. We were both a bit full and it was like a love affair before the honeymoon.'

He remembered. The furious wind, the needles of rain driving into their flesh, stinging their skin. They had been bare, standing up in the sticky clay.

'Making one shadow,' he said, letting her know he remembered. Of course there was no shadow. If he held out too long she would curse him and still take his money and tell nasty stories about him.

'When the lightning flashed.'

She was pleased. Orphans in the storm.

'I was new here then and you called me Sandpaper, not Sandpiper.' She tried a small laugh. Thank goodness he responded. She didn't know the boys had told him that name in reference to the texture of a certain stretch of her anatomy. He felt a bit above her now. He had something in reserve, an edge, he could afford to be generous. He stroked the broad, thick-toed foot she extended toward him on the bed. She had shaved her legs and the tops of her feet and toes where the hairs grew, but some had escaped the razor and this struck him as faintly pathetic. He felt better now, the nose sounds were forgotten. He kissed her knees.

She thought back years ago to the little joke her father had made with her older sister, the chance remark that had set her on the game. They had been watching tennis on the television. Deuce was called. Her sister and father had their heads together, talking. Suddenly he had said, 'After deuce comes advantage.' She corrected him. 'After juice!' They laughed till match point. Trying to find out what this meant from the boys in the church fellowship got her an introduction to a girl who persuaded her to leave home and live with her in her flat.

Since then she had been entertained by the smells of over three thousand men, from the unsupported to the jockstrapped, from the perfectly clean and fresh to the two-singlet brigade. Like the Sumpsucker.

The girl had let her go; some of the younger boys complained they'd seen her weeing in the bath. She got to know the Great White Father. Once when she lost her little bag out on the mud flats, he had gone out and found it and made a speech when he got back to the shed.

'Think! If this had not been found, a thousand years from now archaeologists might have unearthed the remains of our rude civilization, to find what? To find the poor little feminine things we have here: mirror, pins, hanky, lippy, contraceptive pills, calendar with X's in red, cigarettes, a few coins. It's all so inexpressibly sad.' He stopped just short of making her cry.

Sea Shells was finished. She passed him a fresh piece of paper tissue and didn't forget to smile at him. Now she was a moral to be able to go.

LIGHT-SENSITIVE Night. And Knuckles was in the bed hut trying to persuade the Old Lamplighter to turn off the light. He was sensitive, and the boys knew it. They peered through old nail holes in the corrugated iron sides of the hut to watch him, and made plenty of noise. He would have been on his feet swinging his fists if she didn't have him in such a grip. The lady had entertained them all many times, she felt no inclination to be embarrassed. It was all as natural as breathing to her; perhaps that was why her own husband took no pleasure in her. When the youngest went to school she announced that she had a job and might have to be out any time day or night. He worked at Puroil, too, in the warehouse. He came down once a week—that was all he needed—after dark and looked in at the nail holes. A watcher from the corrugated iron balcony, masturbating as he watched.

Knuckles ended up arguing loudly with her, shouting, 'Damn the light! I don't like the light!' She wasn't bothering to soothe him. He couldn't get away.

'Shut up, little boy! You have to do it in the dark, don't you? Like a thief!' But something was happening. Suddenly Knuckles arched his back and got out of control like one of the old steam trains that puffed and panted up a long hill, then got to the top and raced down the other side, piston flying and hot breath whistling. Mechanically, she tried to help—they expected it—but in regaining her grip she swung her arm and scraped his eye with a fingernail. The whole thing was ruined. Still, it was money in advance. While he was cursing, she looked sideways to see if the dollar bills were still there.

Her husband never went there to watch with the other regulars. He liked to feel alone.

4
START-UP

OPEN HOUSE To find how Puroil was going, opposition companies sent a man once a month to park his car in the employees' car park, walk through the gates like the rest—there was no employee recognition system—carrying a dilly bag with his foreman's disguise and change in one of the unused huts. With a white safety helmet and a biscuit coloured dustcoat, this man wandered everywhere with notebook and pen, looking at new construction, listening to men talk, examining pumping logs and product transfer sheets and generally getting the drift of things.

He would go away smiling, for the drift continued.

18 YEARS OF ASH One of the things he found was that job-creativeness was well rewarded. Men with imagination could put pen to paper and rough in the outlines of a new job any time.

For eighteen years Ashpit Freddie, a sort of clerk, collected details of various heaps of rubbish and ash, wrote reports and supervised them in a far corner of the company's land, tended them with a long-handled rake, kept them in order so they were a joy to him to behold, and occasionally moved them a little farther on.

Sometimes he would amalgamate two or three, make the ground in between shipshape, and even requisition a helper or a new rake. He dressed neatly in a pair of overalls that were a credit to him, and made trouble for no one. At his presentation nice, wise things were said about the dignity of labour and the beauty of a labourer going to his retirement.

After he had gone, some fool cleaned up the yard with a fleet of trucks. No new ashpiles accumulated, no heaps of any sort replaced Ashpit Freddie's. The rubbish and ash tended by Freddie were eighteen years old, the same heaps at the end as at the beginning.

THE HAND THAT SIGNED THE PAPER High up in a tiny office in the very alps of the Termitary, a man drew a sheet of paper from a tray of start-up instructions on his desk, casually read through a list of typewritten words, casually lifted his company issue (intermediate supervisory grade) pen and wrote:

Delete Area D. Insert Zone 5.

A mile away and a month later Zone 5 golf club, chess club, picnic and children's outing, cricket and keg club, were all going, formed and instituted. The shifties formed their own clubs, they wouldn't have a bar of the Puroil social club. Zone 5 became a legend to its members inside three months; the starting place and point of reference for everything they did during their daily detention. On this they built their working dreams and constructed their plans ahead for trapping that elusive animal, pleasure.

JUST LIKE EQUALS With a man of such eminence as the Python, the Glass Canoe was quiet and meek. He knew the Python's reputation for smiling at you, licking you all over then swallowing you, but man to man and face to smiling face it seemed a different thing. If you treat a man as a sort of father, he'll soften and come your way, won't he? The Glass Canoe always did this when he got into trouble and it had always worked so far. It seemed to work with the psychiatrists. He felt better, talking with a real engineer, a man who'd been educated. Not like the shit you had to mix with on the plant.

‘I got my boy a model car outfit—he’s very interested in anything mechanical.’ You could never tell what good this sort of private chat might do you. Or your son. The Python might have some advice for his education. The skin of his brown, sleek face grew relaxed and shiny. Men of his education like you to look at ease, they clam up if you’re edgy.

‘It’s more than a toy,’ said the Glass Canoe. A grotesque smugness was the nearest he got to a relaxed manner. An ingratiating hangman talking to members of the supporting cast.

‘They have clubs, they tell me,’ deigned the Python.

‘We’re in one! I’m the secretary and timekeeper of the Toy Minicar Club!’ the Glass Canoe eagerly supplied.

‘I respect a man who gives time to local activities.’

‘Four days a week. There’s so much work and so many new members I often find myself doing a bit here. In slack times, of course. I map out a few circuits, change them every night, adds variety to the racing.’ He fished in a pocket. Out came a piece of grey paper covered with the loops and whorls of car racing circuits. ‘You get a bit of time on night shift to nut these things out.’ He didn’t see the men making tactful signs to button his mouth.

‘Jove, they’re pocket Grand Prix!’ enthused the Python. ‘Have you been able to interest some of the others in this?’

‘It’s hard to get them going on something new.’

‘Well, keep up the good work.’ He escaped. The Glass Canoe was on top of the world for five minutes and in that short time winded several prisoners with huge pats on the back and kidded Far Away Places about his venereal disease. What a decent lot the bosses were! They talked to you just like equals. They didn’t have to.

IN AND OUT When there was a dispute at the cracker about the safety of the top firing platform of the vertical down-draught boilers, where men had to manhandle forty pound gas guns at shoulder height under pressure on a narrow platform with a hip-high railing suspended over nothing, the Glass Canoe saw his chance of improving his position. A clear stand against his fellow prisoners might make the management favour him when they handed out the next dustcoats.

First he agitated to have the Union represented on the Safety Council. The company splashed the Administration and visitors' area with free safety notices distributed by the State Government but would baulk at any more positive or costly action on the plants. The Union had withdrawn its members, who after all manned the plants, so the remaining members were office bodies who never went near an oil-splashed vertical steel ladder or a slippery grating a hundred feet up at three in the morning in pouring rain, and who didn't know what a manway was.

He succeeded in this and got himself elected operators' representative. The men working the plants had one representative, the rest were other trades, white collar men, drivers, storemen, clerks.

'In the name of Christ, what are we?' pleaded the Glass Canoe passionately. The Wandering Jew made no objection to this intrusion of the Christian religion. He only attended the Safety meetings every three months.

'Are we children, that we can't trust ourselves to look where we're going? Do we have to be hemmed in by barbed wire and railings everywhere we go? I can understand the attitude of operators who want this work done, but I can't sympathize with it. It's childish; and expensive.'

They were impressed by his concern for cutting cost. The thing went to a vote amongst office workers, draughtsmen and storemen and majority rule established that the top landing was safe.

The operators' Union got nasty and withdrew again from the Council. This freed the Glass Canoe from having to attend meetings. Most of the time they were not represented: majority rule came up with such ridiculous decisions that all they could do was resign in protest. There was no one outside Puroil to appeal to.

THE FASCINATION OF WAR The Glass Canoe was a sailor once and read avidly every book he could lay hands on that told of the war in which he had been a number. Now he was perched aloft a gas-burning Peabody heater. His duty was to watch the flame through a peephole in case it went out and to give the fire more gas each time the order came. If the fire went out, and he didn't notice it in time, there would be a build-up of gas in the heater and when it was lit again the lot would go up, the Glass Canoe with it. The Peabody was heating air, which in turn was heating the regenerator. Now and then he swallowed a tranquillizer so he could pass the night feeling nothing. In order to crouch against the warm flanks of the fat regenerator and read his book, he had a scrap of polished aluminium propped on the sight hole. He could see the reflected flicker of flame at the end of each sentence as he glanced up. He talked to himself continually.

He looked up, grinning at the nothing in the sky. 'God pulled the chain, the doors of heaven were opened and all the piss pots in heaven were emptied,' he shouted and made a two-finger sign at the rain.

He had scrounged a huge slab of cardboard from the sides of a carton in the catalyst shed, bent it in the middle and held it propped on his head in an inverted V shape to keep off the driving rain. There is no shelter on a refinery plant. He was soaking wet.

The Glass Canoe had been away in hospital for treatment and was discharged with a paper to say he was sane. Picked for promotion and ambitious not because of overwhelming interest in refining but rather out of an overwhelming idea that he was better than the next man, he was sent away to study to be a senior man on this new cracker, but the strain of holding tightly to his conviction of superiority was too great and he started to do wild things in the control room. They took him away, strapped him down and dug away at his insides with pentothal, electrodes, drugs and group therapy, but all they did was get him to talk interminably about himself and accept new ideas quickly. He flitted from interest to interest, hobby to hobby. He was never without an aim. They didn't touch his sense of being better than other men. Sport? He could be a champion. Business? Could have made a fortune. A week after the Python got his guts on the subject of toy car racing, someone casually enquired after his hobby. He was lost. What hobby? He'd forgotten all about model cars.

He read nothing but war novels. He was mad on war, a fitting representative of the island race which suffered less than any European combatant nation. Here he was in the open at 3.30 in the morning, soaking wet, reading of Hitler's glorious panzer divisions grinding across the face of eastern Europe and people dying like flies in a storm. Small areas of wet decorated each corner of his mouth.

THE EFFECTS OF ENCLOSURE It had been raining for days. The world smelled like a diseased lung. The high wire fence enclosing the Refinery, Termitary and Grinding Works dripped freely in the driving rain.

Why was there no one to investigate the harm done by this high barbed wire? Sometimes it was as if the wire stretched from one side of the 350 acres of rich industrial land to the other at head height, the rusty barbs constantly threatening to furrow vulnerable human skulls. Those that were once men, and still often were when they had gone outside the blue gates, walked about with bowed-down heads as if in a vast, intimidating cathedral.

Would it be inquiring perhaps too closely to ask whether the fumes from the men's slowly corrosive discontent were not making thinner and more brittle the wires caging them? But it was only an experimental plant; there would be more plants built and new and tougher wires extruded to hold and cage more securely these men who came daily to the blue gates offering their lives in return for the means to continue them.

FEAR OF NUMBERS When the Samurai left the Termitary for the larger and more exhilarating life of the works, his former fellows felt the first breath of uncertainty about their earning future. They were comfortable prisoners of the trusty class and looked anxiously beyond the Samurai's leaving for a sinister reason. They saw not far off the computer processing of the work they did, and were afraid. Within three months the staff which previously had 2 per cent Union membership, added 93 per cent. The boys of the personnel office gracefully refrained from paying Union dues out of a nice feeling to those above them that as they knew many secrets of the company's industrial dealings, they should not be thought to share them with the rank and file of an industrial Union. They thought of this as loyalty. The cashier, a Unionist, refused one day to handle pay dockets prepared by non-Union labour, the company ordered the 5 per cent into the Union, and that was that. They were amazed the company didn't need their loyalty.

The Samurai was happy to hear the first result of the landslide. Most increases in pay had been absorbed into their above-award wages for some years until they were back on award rates; entry to the Union changed all that. The threat of a white-collar strike—unheard of—put the next wage increase into their pockets. The Samurai smiled when he thought of the distaste with which most of those trusties would have approached a defiant attitude to almighty Puroil, and of the wonder in their struggling hearts when they saw Puroil back off from all its righteous protests and offer five dollars it didn't have.

The Samurai was a little ashamed he hadn't stayed with them to fight, but had the good sense to realize that his action in leaving their ranks spoke more eloquently than words.

The two things were of course not connected, but shortly after this, in the interests of economy, white-collar prisoners were denied the use of their separate dining-room and were obliged to eat the company lunch in the larger mess-hall, rubbing reluctant white shoulders with storemen and packers, fitters, electricians, riggers, drivers, gardeners, drum-rollers—anyone. Khaki overalls, boots, ragged shorts and buttonless shirts, grease on the chairs, chipped tables; there was a lot to put up with. The trusties were no longer separate. The staff dining-room was no longer. And for those whose lives were bounded by Puroil and felt a glow when they saw its advertising on television and who used to feel they were dining out in society when they sat elegantly at the staff tables with no roughly dressed prisoners in sight, this was bitter punishment. To sit and lunch at their work desks in sight of the depressing evidence of their indeterminate sentence of industrial imprisonment brought on feelings too heavy to be borne and thoughts too sharp and offensive to be allowed to become conscious. There was only one place to eat. Nibbling a packet of sandwiches in the sun was no solution, for trespassing on the attractive lawns was forbidden, they were only to be looked at. Only employees saw them, and salesmen trying to get favours from the company, but the principle was the same.

The energy tensions that create the illusion to our eyes of a solid substance, in this case a group of persons and a demarcation of one group from another, had broken down. Molecules of fitter and administration officer were seen to mingle. Nothing was the same again.

The only consolation left to the trusties was they were not branded as lower grades were. They didn't punch a card under the eyes of Heels or Hanging Five or the Prohibited Import or the Black Snake: all they had was Luxaflex peeping out through venetian blinds. They had no numbers stencilled on chests and backs or on the foreheads of their safety hats, although they learned gradually that they did have numbers. The new machine payroll system required a number inserted as a key-figure on their monthly salary entry, but so far they avoided the indignity of being addressed directly by number and the self-destructive habit of thinking of themselves as numbers rather than persons.

NEW DEAL The Wandering Jew, the newest manager, altered office working hours, came down hard for punctuality and saved money on plant maintenance. Even more privileged prisoners were not exempt. One fine morning the Whispering Baritone arrived at five after eight to find the Manager in his chair. Their conversation was reported by a typist talking to the Manager's secretary in the next office.

'Where the hell were you at eight o'clock?' chattered the Wandering Jew in his inadequate voice.

'Ah—I must apologize for being a trifle—er, late!' stammered the Whispering Baritone. He twisted his head quickly sideways, his collar had become tight. His thin face grew red. His fingers picked at the tips of his other fingers, the dry skin flaked and came away. He was temperate and ate sparingly; he had no buffer of alcohol or surplus of good food to fall back on in emergencies. Glorious Devon, the previous Manager, had never done this to a man of his status. The Baritone was a devout supporter of the new economy cuts but had never considered that he might be cut.

Just in case he thought of leaving Puroil in a huff, the Wandering Jew took away his big title of Admin Superintendent and gave him a smaller one to reduce his bargaining power with other employers.

The maintenance bill was reduced by the simple expedient of taking men off shift maintenance work, cutting regular maintenance programmes and reclassifying fitters so that expenditure on their wages could be charged elsewhere. Managers who saved the company money were rewarded: the Wandering Jew wanted rewards. The crew left on maintenance shrugged, tore a few pages of reports out of the loose-leaf maintenance book and drifted on as usual. Breakdown maintenance became the order of the day.

RELATIVITY Pixie, a Puroil man born and bred for obedience, now stationary in about the middle orders of the local hierarchy and with little hope from ability, connections or cunning to get any further, first heard of the ructions that followed these economy cuts on a day when he had a Credit Union meeting. They were standing around waiting for the rest of the nine directors. He was full of the ingratitude of the hard-case prisoners who complained bitterly about their maintenance overtime being taken away and the wickedness of their transfer from shift to day work with its consequent loss of penalty rates.

'If anyone complains about conditions at Puroil you feel like taking them by the scruff of the neck and shotting them to the shouse!' This last word was indelicate, an indication of powerful feelings.

'Tossing them anywhere!' said Luxaflex mildly. He tried to turn the edge of Pixie's speech by his tone of voice; there were bottom-of-the-barrel prisoners present who might resent a meeting of a common interest society being turned into a forum for orthodox Puroil doctrine.

'It's everywhere!' said the Garfish, also a member.

'Why, over at Aluminium,' said Pixie, 'the telephone operator walks six hundred yards to a toilet and makes her own tea. Yet our lazy buggers of girls here only have to turn a corner to find a toilet and have their tea brought to them. They get it too easy! They don't know when they're well off! The more they get the more they want!' He kept an eye on Luxaflex, to see if he was on the right track.

'And at Pax,' said the Garfish, mentioning a nearby refinery, 'the Manager himself is often up on the pipelines wielding a pair of stillsons, yet here they walk off the job if a staff man so much as touches a set of tools.' He, too, watched Luxaflex keenly. Alert for any reaction.

The Two Pot Screamer, the operating prisoners' representative, took out his notebook. He was elated by the stupidity of their remarks, and copied them faithfully. He knew they had been down to the plants at least once a year and knew nothing of the processes.

Another man, looking round a corner of the building from outside, grabbed the opportunity of reminding his fellow prisoners of the eternal verities. He wrote the word Eternity in yellow marking crayon in odd corners of the refinery, imitating a famous Australian who for many years did the same thing on Sydney footpaths. Or perhaps consciously carrying on his good work, for the other man had died and was even then tasting his beloved or dreaded Eternity. He stooped and wrote carefully on the concrete.

THE DISEASE OF WEAKNESS The Samurai was aware most strongly of his own desire always to have the power to do to others what they did to him. But a little beyond that feeling there was another. It was on a little prayer he had copied out from the writings of an uncanonized nineteenth-century saint and carried in his pocket. The Samurai was a natural equalizer, but there was in him a calmness and strength that could find the ring of these words echoing quietly in his own mind. He took out the prayer and read the words half-aloud.

I think I could turn and live with animals, they are so placid
and self-contain'd,

I stand and look at them long and long.
They do not sweat and whine about their condition,
They do not lie awake in the dark and weep for their sins,
They do not make me sick discussing their duty to God,
Not one is dissatisfied, not one is demented with the mania of owning things,
Not one kneels to another, nor to his kind that lived thousands of years ago,
Not one is respectable or unhappy over the whole earth.

He had to go out in the rain and check a series of valve positions before the power recovery boiler was brought on line. The night was dark, without purpose, mindless as rags flapping in the air. The rain wet his strong jaw and splashed unnoticed down his thick neck and up into his boots; his mind went over the pathetic letter he had in his pocket. One of the men, young, vague and poorly educated, as most of them were, had written a plea to the Samurai. His young sister of twelve had been raped, but being genuinely frightened of the mess the newspapers would make of the affair, he had not gone to the police, some of whom made a lucrative sideline of selling news tips in cases where the victims didn't have money enough to object. The man, known as Pigeon Post for his interest in racing pigeons, had found the rapist from his sister's description of him and of the car in which she was raped, but he didn't know what to do.

The Samurai knew exactly what he would have done in Pigeon Post's place, but Pigeon Post wasn't the Samurai. What could he do for this man? He checked the gas lines from the liquid gas tank back to the boilers—without waking Blue Hills who had insisted on going out into the rain—and went over his answer to Pigeon Post. He would have to do something himself. Revenge was the obvious course: the law would let the rapist off after a few years. Sentences were light for rape and killing, and heavy for stealing, destroying property, shooting at public figures, prison warders or policemen.

He could call on Pigeon Post. No, better not. Say nothing. Delay the answer until he had done what was necessary, then answer Pigeon Post with a counsel of mercy and forgiveness.

'I could turn and live with animals,' said the Samurai aloud. He shouted it, filled with a sudden access of rageful energy. 'I could turn and live with animals!!' to uncomprehending concrete and uncomplaining steel.

Walking about in the rain in the floodlit dark, he looked like a burly threatening priest, a contradiction. His heart encompassed mercy and pity and a large capacity for revenge and hate. The falling rain glittered with the fluorescence of the blue tubes all over the structures.

What was the remedy for his pitiful seekers after help and advice, who from their very natures leaned on stronger men? Should he give Pigeon Post the idea of extending his hobbies, taking up weight-lifting or judo to give himself the illusion that he was not weak and dependent and indecisive, but quick, masculine, strong? Perhaps there was no remedy for weakness.

Snaking after him on the ground and slithering over pipes and vessels, even his shadow was wet.

AN ARM, WAVING When he woke Blue Hills took a dawn walk out to the battery limits, ducking past gas leaks from flanges and valves that wouldn't shut, to get a view of the slopes on the other side of the river where Riverditch rose from the water towards Jerriton and away to Cheapley. He had spent a little time relieving the Glass Canoe on the heater, a little time reading vacantly through year-old newspapers though reading was strictly forbidden, and a little time sleeping in the reactor, sitting on a four-gallon drum.

There it was again. From a house set apart from its neighbours, with just such an array of trees and shrubs as Blue Hills liked, a waving. Like an arm waving, almost every time he looked that way. Was it a wave of distress? There might be someone in need of help. Or a friend looking at him, disappointed at receiving no answering wave.

Timidly, he waved. Looked round, to see if any of his fellow prisoners had seen. No answering wave. Maybe it was a free man, retired from industrial or military service and on a pension, someone who didn't have to spend ten hours a day a prisoner. Ten hours allowed for an hour each way getting ready for work and getting home. It would be great to be like that, not having to clock on and clock off. Naturally, it might not be for long—retirement freedom was a quiet anteroom before the crematorium, but at least it was a little freedom to look forward to.

Could the waver perhaps be a man his own age, fond of trees and green things, the mate he had always wanted? Blue Hills had acquaintances: no friends. And there was his heart. He didn't complain at home when he had a mild flutter, as the doctor called it; his wife made life hell for him with her form of sympathy, a great, oppressive cloud of worry. Worry attacked her only when he was present. He found it increasingly difficult to ask if she had taken her pills; this question he considered sufficient indication of his desire for a spot of intercourse. And that's all it was, a spot. He had to work like a slave to bring her to orgasm.

They had moved from further north than Cheapley, from an old house surrounded by Blue Hills' specially loved trees; bottlebrush, liquidambar, pistacia, citriodora, snow-gum, even turpentine trees with their dull grey-green leaves, silver underneath, and stringy bark. Orchids in the greenhouse and paperbarks on the wet patch. Moved into a more modern house closer to the works, with no trees: developers flattened the lot. He had gone back many times past the old house, just to see his trees. The Lebanese who had bought the old place left most of them standing. But even their way of waving in the coastal airs, and their leafing shape, had something now that was alien. The thing he couldn't get over was they were doing just as well for a stranger's touch as they had for his.

He turned east, hoping for a sunrise. But the rain still hung about. Morning lay in a coma, flat out for miles, as if it might never wake. He walked over to his little hideaway under the fuel gas tank. There were leaks there, too, but he liked the propane smell. He lay down.

He was a simple man. He treasured one magic moment on night shift. Once he had gone out a little after four in the morning, twenty minutes before sunrise. Sunrise over Clearwater, that's how he thought of it. Mauve clouds, Conrad Martens clouds, low in the sky and the silvered tanks magical with reflected violet. Nothing moved but a few early workers' cars arching over Clearwater bridge. He brought the mob out to look at the sunrise—he was so excited, rushing about in the dawn dark, desperate for them to see the vision splendid—but they rubbished him and went back to sit miserably in the smoke-filled amenities waiting for seven o'clock.

THE ACHE OF FRIENDSHIP The Samurai bent over his control panel desk in concentration on the masses of paper work connected with the start-up. As usual, he couldn't keep his mind off the prisoners round him. How far could he keep going, how far could he take his fight for the helpless prisoners who, but for him, had no one to turn to who would be content to help without wanting to imprison them further?

'Wakey, wakey!' called the Enforcer from his office door.

'They won't let you sleep here, Samurai,' said the Elder Statesman, protected by the controller's presence. 'What you need is a blanket or two behind the panel! Doesn't he?' directed to the Enforcer, who pulled his mouth wide open in a hefty grin, showing the Samurai it was a joke. He was British. What he really wanted was a line of men standing at attention.

The Samurai said nothing. They thought of sleep when they saw a man sitting still. Was it a reflection of their own inability to concentrate? He went back to the problems of the helpless. He could scare off the Enforcer any time by asking him a question on the plant. The Enforcer had been promoted when the refinery was tiny—hadn't expanded his knowledge to keep up.

The open trench under the panel console for air lines and electric cables was full of water from the drain system. Prisoners threw rubbish there hoping the tide would take it away. It didn't. The trench stank.

He remembered Blue Hills had been gone a few hours. It was half past six. He walked over to Blue Hills' little gunyah and looked down on his face which was yellow in the grey morning. He stood there, looking at Blue Hills closely. He could not have told you why. The sign of life was one plume of breath; a sinus blocked the other.

It was a high forehead, but not wide. Pitted with large pores and the skin supplied with fine light down. Many grey strands grew among the curly black hair. His ears red-brown and very large, standing far out from the head, coming in close towards the lobe, curving out again. The lobe pink-red and full of blood, the skin uneven under the beard, rising to small hills near each sturdy spear of stubble; outside the borders of beard the skin was smooth. He looked at Blue Hills' nose with its enormous pores clogged with black and the oil from his body giving it a gleam even in this light. A small black ant struggled in the forest of hairs on his calf. Lower down, the dull inherited scar. He was wearing Puroil socks—scrap rag wrapped round the feet inside the heavy boots. He looked away. Again he could not have explained why he wanted to look no further but he felt rising in himself all the pity he felt for his fellow prisoners. Granted they may have been conceived casually, brought up lazily, educated carelessly, but they were here. On earth. Why? To feed the appetite of industry and work to foolish regulations for the sake of the few free men in the world? And they had been kept ignorant of the fact that they were slaves. They thought slaves were some other people, in another time, and probably coloured.

It was cruel. They got no joy from their lives, only the respite of oblivion in alcohol, dreams in drugs, relief in sport or in the Great White Father's underground movement which was intended to undermine the whole synthetic fabric above them, which might as well be quite different for all it mattered to those beneath.

Blue Hills couldn't even give his blood to the bloodbank and tell himself he could help others live. He was anaemic and couldn't spare blood. It was too much for the Samurai. He felt himself equal to anyone in the great pyramid above him, but Blue Hills didn't even have that frustrating consolation.

'Hey, Blue!' he said. 'Wake up!'

He shook the sleeper. There was a peculiar ache in his upper right arm. Someone had punched him on the muscle, where it crossed the bone. Playfully, of course. He bent and stretched the arm. The ache stayed. Fifty yards away a shadow flickered on the sides of the catalyst shed. A man running head-down like a rat darted into the tool store. The amount of equipment knocked off bore a direct relation to the size of the men's bags. The guards looked in the bags but could not put their hands in or unwrap anything. All you had to do was wrap your loot or toss it over the fence like the Thieving Magpie did with his electric motors. Gently, on to a prepared pad.

The Samurai had his own worries. He had allowed himself to drift into association with a girl, had even thought of marriage, then with a suddenness that surprised him he broke it off. She made quite a fuss. In one of her outbursts she told him she had lied about using pills. She said scornfully he wasn't a man.

'You can't even make babies!' she screamed at him in a crowded street. They had been having intercourse for months; he left precautions to her; as far as he knew his seed might be dead. He had no other children that he knew of. On the other hand his young brother, who was married, only needed to look hard at his wife and she was pregnant.

He took a small bottle of it to a doctor. The neatest thing he could lay hands on was a small jar with a blue plastic screw cap, previously containing a deodorant jelly. Remarkably like the real thing. In a quiet voice he told the receptionist who he was and what the doctor wanted. He wasn't a vain or over-sensitive man, but when the woman, hardened to years of sickness and dying, enemas, catheters, and specimens, asked loudly: 'How?' he was confused.

'What do you mean How? It's a specimen of—'

'I can see that! How was the semen produced?' she roared.

'What's it to you?'

'Mister, there's a routine here!' she shouted. 'I have to put down how the semen was taken: masturbation, ordinary sex, coitus interruptus, electric shock or the special method for Roman Catholics.'

'Masturbation,' he said quietly. The woman wrote down the horrible word. Her writing was uneven, she broke off after every few letters and repeated them aloud. He thought she would never finish. The waiting room was full of patients all either bowed over in a reading position or looking the other way.

'What is the special method for Roman Catholics?' he asked obstinately.

'Listen, sir! I won't be part of any conversation of that sort, thank you. Ask the doctor.'

Put in his place, he tried to walk erect to a chair in the waiting room. But he knew he was slinking.

VOLGA BOATMAN As he got ready for the shower, baring his forty-five-year-old bones, Blue Hills wickedly sang:

Down in the valley where nobody goes
Lives a little old lady without any clothes,

and proceeded to chuckle politely as he thought how like a little old lady he looked without any clothes.

When he had taken out his teeth and left them to soak in a glass of detergent, he tip-toed into the shower cubicle; he didn't like the feel of cold concrete on his naked soles. As soon as the Volga Boatman heard the noise of water, he sneaked in and pinched Blue Hills' teeth, his truss and the arch supports from his shoes, all nicely powdered and ready for him when he was washed and dried. It was a stupid joke on poor Blue Hills—toothless, crippled and unslung.

Volga made a neat parcel of Blue Hills' effects in a paper bag the showering man had his sandwiches in. He took the bag with him to the Home Beautiful. For the last six hundred yards before the wharf there was new work on the road. He traversed a plank path and the tops of pipelines with the ease of a man who trusts his muscles. He passed the new cooling water tower in which river water was exposed in drips to cold air from fans. It was a marshy area, low. When humidity was 95 per cent as it often was, it simply didn't work. Another puzzle. The design worked well enough in Europe.

From his boat Volga could see the Old Lamplighter's car parked in Boomerang Road near the children's swings and seesaws and slippery dips. He tied up and walked to the refuge of the Home Beautiful. The Great White Father met him with a welcome can of beer.

'Take a look at the latest comfort, Volga,' he said. 'Something to gladden the heart of men.'

'What?' asked Volga, swilling beer.

'We have an outside header with a slope downwards, and inside we have individual tubes with bell-shaped funnels on the business end.'

'Who installed it?'

'The Angry Ant. He was a plumber in real life.'

'Where is it?'

'Sit down.'

When Volga sat on one of the new chairs—things appeared overnight, mysteriously—the Great White Father swivelled him round and there, under a tray newly installed round the wall to hold beer and ashtrays, was a round funnel and a pipe from it going through the wall.

'Have one on me, Volga,' he said kindly.

'The beer hasn't gone through me yet.'

'There must be some tea there. Or some water. You must have had a drink.' He felt Volga's stomach in the region of the bladder. Volga pulled away.

'I'm ticklish. Not on the stomach.'

'I think you're virginal, never mind ticklish.'

'It's no good. I'm all dried up.'

'Tell that to the Old Lamplighter.'

'That's different.'

'OK Volga. If you can't you can't, but when you can it's right there. No more stumbling over feet and chairs and upsetting beer to get out. Once you sit you stay till you're full. That's our motto.'

'Sure is progress.'

'No such thing as progress, Volga, but I know what you mean.' He lifted his own blue and gold can. On its sides was a fur of dew pearls.

ASSEMBLY LINE LOVE Ambrose turned up, a youth of twenty. Just old enough for adult pay.

'Welcome, prisoner!' said the Great White Father as he stumbled in.

'What prisoner?' asked Ambrose, lost. They passed him a can. His eyes crossed as he watched its rim approach his mouth.

'Us.'

'We're not prisoners,' he said stoutly. 'I go home when the shift ends.'

'What do you do tomorrow?'

'Come back here.'

'Why not go away somewhere?'

'I'd get the sack.'

'What then?'

'I'd have to get another job.'

'And you're not a prisoner?'

'I can work some other place.'

'Why not just stay home?'

'Cut it out. You've got to have a job.'

'Then you're an industrial prisoner.'

'Then everyone is.'

'What difference does that make?'

'Everyone has to work for a living.'

'Do they? Read the social pages.'

'Working for a living is the right thing to do.'

'You're crazy.'

'Work is good for you.'

'A good crap's better.'

'I'm free to starve.'

'Freedom to starve! That's it. The clause they forgot to put in the Atlantic Charter. Declaration of Human Rights. Freedom to starve.'

'But if everyone—'

'—Not everyone, son—'

'—Practically everyone has to work, then it all cancels out.'

'It doesn't cancel out, it adds up. We're prisoners.' He could see Ambrose was excited and confused. He changed the subject.

'Reminds me of my wife when she was young. She was beautiful, I had to chain her up. But they still got to her.'

'What you want out of life anyway?' demanded Volga. And the Great White Father answered for Ambrose.

'All he wants is meat three times a day and knock-off time.'

He was due for holidays in two weeks and the Humdinger and Big Dick had recommended that he visit the Home Beautiful to prepare him for his trip north to Surfers Paradise with some mates and their girls. He was nervous. The Old Lamplighter would treat him right, but she had to do everything in plenty of light. Once her business had been men in suits, appointments and all; here it was first in best dressed. Shorts, muddy boots. The other girls would never be in her class, they could only go down. She never forgot that once she had been a respectable middle-class prostitute. Ambrose couldn't have managed the Sandpiper with her yen for paddocks and sandflats and bare feet. Or the Sorcerer's Apprentice with her dazzling repertoire and scholarly approach, recording every new sensation in a little blue notebook.

The Old Lamplighter loved to listen to the Great White Father. She loved the bright patches of twinkle in his sea-blue eyes and the rough, chesty voice. When he got around to her in his regular test of the girls she tried to keep him talking so she could see the movement of his firm, dry lips and feel the vibrations of his voice against her chest. She never listened to what he said, she was unshakeably convinced that whether they talked of cars, government, life or death, men never said anything important.

She splashed her bottom with gin to stop bedsores.

'Come in, son,' she said to Ambrose. 'You're next.'

The Volga Boatman finished dressing in a hurry and made way for Ambrose. He knew the Old Lamplighter had been thinking about the Great White Father all the time. It didn't bother him.

'You're a funny boy,' came the lady's voice clearly. 'Not many men dress on the right.' The answer from Ambrose was inaudible.

'What's the matter? Lose the string?' The taunt came to the drinkers' ears.

'String?' They heard him this time.

'If you're not particularly well hung you should tie on a piece of string. Helps you find it. Good in cold weather, too.'

'Take it easy in there!' called the Great White Father. 'Don't forget this next one's his first!'

Ambrose had gone in expecting to come out triumphant, brandishing his experience. Volga took the paper bag and crossed the river back to the refinery.

YOU HAVE TO BE A BASTARD Anyone else would have had a bad moment meeting the Good Shepherd—guilt and suchlike—but not Volga.

'Hullo Volga.' The Good Shepherd knew every sheep by name.

'Great day for it.' Volga knew, as everyone knew, that the Good Shepherd was being gradually outed. His superiors reasoned with him and threatened him to make him change his attitude to the men, but how did you reason with a man whose actions were controlled not only by what Puroil asked, but modified by outside, abstract things called principles?

'You have to be a bastard,' they told him piously. Church members with a lifetime of worship of the gentle Jesus behind them in their cold stone churches, all thought like this. For the sake of the Company you must be a bastard to the humans in it. It was taught as gospel in Basics of Supervision.

'I get more out of the men my way,' he answered.

'We don't care what you get out of them. When Puroil says Jump all you have to do is say How High.'

'My way leaves them a little human dignity.'

They shook their heads. He was not an Oxford or Cambridge man, not even a proper university man. He had gone through—the phrase appropriate to a degree factory—on a part-time course. Working his way through, taking jobs as a waiter by night to pay his fees. They despised this. All the regular engineers were equipped with parents who could at least afford a university. Puroil preferred men with a solid background and when top appointments were made they went to men from the best universities.

'I won't ask what's in your little brown paper bag,' the Good Shepherd said archly.

'A pair of false teeth, a truss and an arch support,' said Volga matter-of-factly. He couldn't help noticing the frayed cuffs. The Good Shepherd gave a tenth of his salary to his church.

The Good Shepherd folded his arms and laughed immoderately. It was a good joke, there wasn't much room for laughter in Admin. Volga walked on, the Good Shepherd got into his car and drove out of the blue gates, but not before he opened the boot of his car. Somehow, vertebrates like the Python could take home scrap paper and foreign orders, and slimes like the Slug could drive humbly out with jacks, oil cans, aluminium sheet, greaseguns, spanners, instrument fittings, ladders, cement bricks, cups, urns and supplies of tea, but men like the Good Shepherd were always stopped by the guards.

The Volga Boatman pressed on to the Elder Statesman's summer residence, giving his tremendous calf muscles a thorough workout by striding through and rising on his toes at each step. His boots had cut-down heels to give him more movement of the ankle and to make his calves settle to a natural angle when he stood still.

'Volga!' called the Elder Statesman. 'What do you think of this? This is a new pressure vessel from the States'—he indicated a twenty-foot erection on which clambered several visored and helmeted men—It's got a quarter-inch hole in it, but not a soul in this country can fix a quarter-inch hole in cast aluminium—they have to fly out Yanks to do it from the firm that made it!'

Sure enough, the men on the vessel made the monotone drawling noises that denoted use of the American tongue. There was a confidence about them, the manner the English used to have. And these were only welders. Now and then they looked down at the watching natives. They were proud to be Americans and didn't hesitate to show their pride, even if it meant not speaking to second-class citizens. After all, they were members of the club, they could only be easy with other Americans. The rest of the world were foreigners.

Volga got away long enough to go in to the amenities room and hide Blue Hills' teeth, truss and arch supports in the Elder Statesman's large gladstone bag, then made a sly phone call to the guards at the gate.

The Elder Statesman had dobbed him in to the screws—to Captain Bligh—for being off his plant when something went bang.

It was true, but the Elder Statesman was in no danger of getting blamed so why put him in? Luckily, Volga had seen Captain Bligh tipping sample bottles full of gasoline into his car—parked near the plant—so the foreman didn't want to know about Volga.

Volga had no trouble being a bastard and he'd never even had the benefit of Basics of Supervision.

BIG BROTHERS The Samurai was watching the aluminium welding. Some of the men who passed thumped him gently on the arm in rough affection. Everyone liked the Samurai, he was like the bigger boy in class, who shouldered the responsibility for other kids' adventures and, if need be, stood up and swapped punches with the teacher. The men who thumped him playfully took care to move into his field of vision, though, before they showed their affection.

Even the Good Shepherd came by to watch the American welders. They worked fast, Americans had a name for having the finger out. The prisoners were grudgingly impressed. Only the Good Shepherd and the Samurai realized they worked fast because their system of payment was different from the Australians': they were paid for the whole job. The sooner they got home, the sooner they earned more dollars. Australian welders were paid for their time; they saw to it their jobs took time. The Good Shepherd would have been more impressed if the vessel had been cast without the quarter-inch hole.

He was depressed. He knew the company should not do provocative and cruel things to the detainees under its control—the ban on books was absurd: it penalized the brighter prisoners—and yet he knew there must be a hierarchy of control in the camp and felt deeply that the equality that was supposed to exist between high and low was a dark, shadowy thing with no substance. His mind swam away from the clutches of these irritating thoughts as a tiny fish glides past the gently waving fronds of the anemone. Not into safety, but away from immediate danger.

A DEDICATED MAN The Great White Father called in at the wharf at six one morning, just the time the nit-keeper should have wakened those who were down. All were asleep. There was only one barge in and it was discharging steadily with three hours to go before it was empty. They had transgressed the unwritten law that you didn't let yourself go to sleep while you were keeping nit for your mates, and they'd had a clancy. The Corpse had been about to have a shower before waking the others: he liked to clean up early and walk to the gate without waiting for the bus, to be out of the place at the earliest possible moment. It was a mile to the front gate. He had dozed off with the water running, there was water slopping everywhere.

This was not an important clancy except for the sleepers, who had water lapping round their rag beds on the concrete. The Gypsy Fiddler was doing a shift at the wharf—they spared him from the cracker start-up because someone had to make up the number at the wharf, they didn't want men back on overtime. He'd never worked at the wharf before and he missed learning how to start his own unit, but it saved money. He woke thrashing sleepily about with his arms, splashing the water. Blue Hills was down there, too, exiled from the hateful cracking plant for the same reason. He'd never worked on the wharf before, so he had to be guided every step of the way. He received some of the cold splashes from the Fiddler's waving arms. Blue Hills rarely spoke up for himself, so he was often sent away to other plants.

They looked up, wet, at the same moment.

'I just work here for tucker money,' said Blue Hills, stupidly. He'd been dreaming of a five day a week job.

'We're afloat!' yelled the Fiddler, waking everyone. The Corpse was the last to come round. He had gone to sleep sitting in a chair: only his boots were under water.

'She's sinking!' he roared, leaping for the door. They held him down so he wouldn't go over the side of the wharf. Men did funny things if they were suddenly awakened.

The Great White Father looked around and told them how to get the water away so the next shift wouldn't dob them in for the spill. He was organizing his system of look-outs for the Home Beautiful for the following week, but wisely decided to have no part of this lot.

The distant noise of the starting-up cracking plant beckoned him. He left the wharf and walked up the road towards the gas screaming in the forty-eight-inch lines, the shattering roar of banks of compressors and blasts of steam.

The Sumpsucker was on deck, pacing the concrete floor of the control room, hands clasped on his forehead, pushing down into his chest cage his small bald head on its retractile neck. He always had two T-shirts under his shirt; he let the bottom one rot off from inside, then put a fresh one on. That way, one was always warm. Decomposing, if you like, but warm.

The Father knew the Sumpsucker's ambitions for a dustcoat. The company had recently cut out overtime payments for foremen; an operator with overtime got more cash. The white shirt made up the difference. The Father decided to use Sump as a lookout; the more he had on him now, the better.

'It's your turn on lookout.'

'I was there last day shift.'

'You're there again this day shift.'

'Chee!' He was thinking.

'You want club privileges?'

'Yes, yes! I'll do it! Who's on today?'

'Sorcerer's Apprentice!' He could have added that she had a new trick, but it wasn't necessary. 'Plenty of beer, too.'

'As long as she's there, you can have the beer.'

'You're a dedicated man.'

'I don't care who knows it!' He was joyful, he would have a stop on the way home before he saw the widow. That would make two today, if he could get the widow to send her daughter up the shop for half an hour. He took no notice of her complaints that the backyard was full of black catalyst drums, stacked two deep. Higher than the fence. They stopped the grass growing, didn't they?

THE BASIS OF OBEDIENCE The Good Shepherd saw the Great White Father from a distance. He knew he was not on shift today: he knew where he had come from, but was capable of turning his eyes away from little irregularities. A confrontation with the Great

White Father was not always comfortable for a man who served an organization; the Great White Father could call on all the resources of his originality when he argued, but an officer of the company had to use borrowed words, and the cause for which Puroil would have a man lay down his integrity was usually long dead and putrid. He often wondered if his sense of loyalty was stronger than his personal faith in honesty, truth, purity and organized religion. Organization again. Was it a purer thing to serve your religion as God gave it to you personally or to uphold the tradition of your fathers? He wondered if he was as out of date as he sometimes felt in a world where one out of every two people on earth lived under rulers who openly condemned religion. It was a lonely feeling. His father had never known it.

At least he wasn't on the lookout for the men's badness and transgressions all the time, neither did he dob. But the thought of the Great White Father returned. Why did such a man continue to work here? Did he think every alternative as pointless as every other? Could he do without public respect as easily as he could do without God? He never displayed his financial power, yet it was said he was well off, much better off than the Puroil officers who mistook their continued dependence on the company for loyalty. But where was the place for a man who believed in the old things, God and good, sin and guilt and eternal life?

Once, when he went to see a man sick for weeks and was let in humbly—as if he were a bishop or a doctor—he was surprised at all the gadgets this family did without. That was how he put it to himself—did without. As if they had a choice. It was common enough in Sydney to have no sewerage—he had none himself—but this man and his wife had no sink in the kitchen. When he went down the back steps—he could have got the water in the bathroom, but didn't like to open the shut door in case he embarrassed them—there was no washboiler even: only a fuel copper. He was surprised, too, at the weight of a water-bucket. Downstairs, he could smell the black tin in the little house down the yard.

As he looked in the kitchen at the sagging window and nail-scarred linoleum and the whole room not so clean as to make you praise poverty, he thought: I couldn't live like this. But as he moved around helping and both smiling at his talk as if at jokes, he was surprised to find he was getting used to the place.

Only a step away, it was. And made a mental note not to say this to his wife, whose life balanced on the possession of every material thing as soon as it became available. Was he no better, for all his good intentions, than the most abject of the spit-lickers? Worse, was he loyal to a shadow and obedient to the shadows of shadows for no better reason than to maintain his wife's gadget-differential over the poorer classes?

TINY DIFFERENCES The Great White Father was in his natural element. Wherever he went, clouds of witnesses gathered round him. Some worked. The start-up was proceeding. Few took it seriously. Only those standing up on the turbo-expander landing, putting one by one the machines into the system, rooted with fear and the terrible scream of the turbines to their action stations, their hands welded to the inlet valve winders, trembling on the butterfly valve that opened the discharge valve in one hit, waiting for the metal fragments to blast them all like shrapnel into infinite retirement.

'We don't want anyone neglecting Mum because of the Home Beautiful, so we have a suggestion from Pommy Bill here that we issue books of coupons to all married men,' he announced.

Pommy Bill, a small cockney sparrow, stood flushed and pleased as the debate started. But just then a merry ex-Bomber Command pilot came up behind Pommy Bill, inserted a claw between his legs and grabbed joyfully and vigorously at his genital cluster.

'Gotcha!' he roared. Pommy Bill had his own private ascension.

'Jesus!' he screamed on the way down.

'Christ!' came the antiphonal from the faithful.

'The same yesterday, today and forever!' added Bomber Command solemnly.

'Amen!'

The coupon motion lapsed with the arrival of Bomber Command who was a plant super. He was eager to get in with the Great White Father and enjoy the superior amenities of the Home Beautiful but he had not been given the invitation. He had a collection of bad photos, yet showing these round, which he did often, was not enough to gain him the acceptance of the mob. He persevered, the world could be conquered by goodwill. He wished they would continue with their previous conversation, but they didn't.

'Did you hear about the escapees?' he asked. There had been another break at a State detention centre, one of those where men couldn't bundy out each day.

'They'll be holed up in some warm spot by now,' remarked the Great White Father. Bomber Command was relieved. Getting him to speak relaxed the mob, they were more likely to tolerate his own presence.

'How about some coffee?' Bomber Command asked Loosehead, who was standing around hoping there was nothing to do. Loose-head was glad to go. He could hang around inside, out of the weather, safe from the foremen.

Loosehead brought the coffee, the Great White Father tasted it.

'This isn't coffee! Take it away!' Loosehead took it, walked outside, three times round the amenities room and brought the same cup back.

'Ah! That's better. Why couldn't you do this before?'

The Great White Father found himself loving smoke and heat, the metal of vessels, pipelines, pumps, valves. Because they were there and had, or seemed to have, an existence of their own. The fact that they were fabricated out of anonymous masses of mined metal and shared a common form with multitudes of similar manufactures, did not deter him from seeing something unique in each one. And if you looked you could find the tiny differences that made each one separate from its neighbours. It was comforting to find these differences. He would round his big warm hand over a piece of bare metal, feeling a wonderful affinity with it for no other reason than that it shared with him an existence on the planet he loved so well. In his earlier days at the refinery, he often slept sitting against a giant electric boiler feedwater pump, feeling that it was a large warm animal with comfortable sides. He imagined its vibrations to be purring.

He loved life, whatever shape it took, and was eager to extend the privilege of life to objects and creations not usually thought of as living. He could pick up a stone and ask it about the things it had seen in the millions of years since it was formed.

A scuffle in the lavatory. Canada Dry and the Humdinger emerged dragging an overalled prisoner, a stranger.

'Here he is! The man that pees purple!' called the Humdinger.

'Caught him in the act,' said Canada Dry triumphantly.

'Let's have a look,' said the Great White Father, striding in towards the stainless steel wall they peed against like dogs.

'How can we fix him up?' they asked, when the great man came back.

'Fix him up? What do you mean fix him up?' bellowed their leader. 'If a doctor treats this man he'll be different. Leave him alone. He's magnificent! Purple pee. I've never seen the like! You come back whenever you like,' he said to the man. They let him go. He ran out like a dog used to kicks. He wasn't used to tolerance.

THE FACE ON THE LAVATORY FLOOR 'Phone for Terrazzo.'

'Anyone seen Terrazzo?'

'Probably in the shouse.'

'With his pencil.'

'Who's Terrazzo?'

'If he's in the shouse, he'll be sketching.'

'The funny thing is,' explained the Humdinger to the Great White Father, 'every time he goes in he takes his notebook. Finds faces in the terrazzo floor. In the patterns of the little bits of stuff they gum together to make it.'

'Is he looking for one particular face?'

'Hey! That's a thought! The lost face on the shouse floor!'

Terrazzo approached, worried.

'Lost it.'

'What?'

'The spitting image of the Colonel. You know, up in the pay

office. The one that called the Whispering Baritone a male whore. Probably never find it now. I had a girl's face there once, the most beautiful face I ever seen. You think I can find it? Say, are you the Great White Father?'

'Yes, that's him!'

'Why?'

'Don't drink Loosehead's coffee.'

'Why not?'

'After he cooked his frankfurts in the urn, he boiled up his socks.'

'Too late now,' said the Great White Father, making a face. 'Answer the phone, you might have won the lottery.'

He hadn't. One of the clowns had rung Dial-a-Prayer and Terrazzo listened, stunned, to '...all we like sheep have gone astray, we have turned every one to his own way, and the Lord hath laid on Him the iniquity of us all.'

BIRD-LOVERS 'Did you see in the local rag,' said the Great White Father, 'where some poor lame devil applied for a job and the Garfish said, "We're not employing any bloody cripples here."'

'Wouldn't put it past him,' said Canada Dry. 'Some of our blokes are worse than any Wop-whippers, boong-bashers or Kaffir-kickers!'

'Who wants to buy some racing pigeons? Nice pets for the kids,' asked the Western Salesman, seeing a profit in the crowd.

'Don't buy 'em,' advised Canada Dry and the Western Salesman thumped him playfully. He would like to have been admitted to the privileged circle of those who thumped the Samurai, but he never made it. His eagerness for overtime and promotion cruelled him.

'You're spoiling my pitch!'

'They fly back home to his place!'

'Shut up! Let 'em buy if they want to!'

The Western Salesman would have sold pigeons to his own mother, knowing they would fly home to his coops the minute they were let out.

'Did I tell you about last Sunday morning at the flats?' asked

Bubbles, taking out his lighter to smoke a cigarette. Bubbles was a contraction of Bubble-guts; it referred to his impressive chest which he carried low, and the unkind called a brewer's goitre. 'Out the back Sunday morning in the sun minding my own business and all of a sudden this count appears with an old army rifle on full cock, waving it about. "Was you whistling at my wife?" he yells. "No," I said and it was the truth. I was watching her though. She weeds the garden every weekend, always bending right over in these little skimpy shorts; everyone's on her. He goes raving round asking all the single blokes, but it turns out two old people have a canary and it was whistling. He poked the rifle at the cage and blew the canary to bits. Lucky the windows were open and the doors; the bullet went right through the house without breaking anything. He didn't even apologize to the old people for shooting the bird and they were too scared to say anything. Feathers everywhere.'

'Did the bullet hit anything on the other side of the house when it went through?' asked the Great White Father.

'Only the bakery wall,' answered Bubbles righteously. 'In the afternoon the same bloke took a few of us up the Leagues Club—I didn't take the car, I knew I'd get tanked—and we were choofing along Highway One about forty-five or fifty when all of a sudden we see this wheel going past. Just slowly, as if it only wanted to overtake. "Somebody's lost a wheel!" this joker yells and he doubles up laughing at the stupid wheel sailing along with every now and then a little bump over the seams of the concrete. You shoulda seen the oncoming cars scatter. The wheel finished up in the showroom of one of the big car saleyards. It cleared the traffic, bounced over the gutter, hurdled the ornamental garden and through the plate glass. It was Sunday and no one came out to see who belonged to the wheel. We got to the club and it wasn't till we turned in to the car park and slowed down that the car heeled over on one side. It was our wheel. The car was so evenly balanced with our weight it didn't tip over till we turned sharply.'

'Did you get the wheel back?'

'Not a chance. He wasn't game to go back for it. He put the spare on. We waited for him inside. You should have heard him laugh when we left him. He was still laughing when he got inside for a beer.'

'That reminds me,' said the Great White Father, 'of a time I was in bed with the wife of a friend of mine, when all of a sudden, just on the vinegar stroke, I heard her husband's car come up the drive.' He had their attention. 'My luck held. His nearside front wheel came off just as he put the brake on. He changed the wheel then and there and I had time to have a shower and get dressed and wait outside the bedroom window for him to come inside so he wouldn't see me leaving. What do you think he did? I was still outside the window when he raced right in—she was still naked in bed—threw the covers off her and started to kiss passionately what I'd just left. He thought she was waiting naked for him and it inflamed him. You should see him go to town! Tied in knots on the bed, wriggling like snakes, sweaty skins slapping and sticking. I had to leave.'

STONE WALLS Far off, a sound of singing. Some clear voice lifted itself from its prison floor and overcame all barriers to dance out on the moveless air of the control room. High and tremulous were its top notes, full-throated its descent into the lower registers. It was a moment of beauty. Even the few working stopped to listen.

'Hullo,' remarked the Sumpsucker. 'Humdinger's singing. He must be on the throne.'

'Let's wish him a long reign,' murmured the Great White Father loyally, and brushed dust from the Puroil 1852 poster fixed to the wall with Puroil resin. Each time someone took it down another appeared. The resin was so good the concrete had to be chipped away to get the notice off. Luckily it was diluted by the paint makers who used it. It was so tough that undiluted it would have lasted a thousand years. No paint maker wanted that.

Our friend the moon, with no blood staining her image yet, rode high in the daytime sky. Men looked up and wondered at her white laughter.

VIEW FROM THE TOP Unfortunately for this pleasant group of prisoners the start-up work was proceeding and the Sumpsucker wanted to get near his control panel and had to screw up courage to ask them to move away. Naturally they refused. He went away and came back with Stillsons, who pleaded with them to hold their conference somewhere else. He had no other or higher members of the hierarchy to back him up, so they grabbed him and locked him in his office.

When the Humdinger came back he said, 'Want to see my flower arrangements?' and disappeared behind the control panel. Presently, from a round hole left vacant by an instrument scrapped before it could be used, came a large stalk. Loosehead was mystified, but grabbed it and pulled.

'Let go!' yelled a voice urgently.

'I can't understand it,' said Loosehead to an appreciative audience. It's wilting, yet there's still sap in it.'

'You boys have the wind in your tails today,' said the Great White Father approvingly, but their get-together was spoiled by a crowd of visitors stumbling through the door. Loosehead let go. A roar of disappointment came from the tea-drenched throats of the prisoners, who stood round gaping at the neatly dressed prisoners out on a holiday from other detention centres. They couldn't resist glancing in at the men peeing up against the stainless steel. The lavatory was on view to all who came in the door. The Spotted Trout led them in, they trotted along behind him as he waved casually at the few hundred instruments on the control panel, then took them along to look at the one-way radio system no one used. Since the man on the job couldn't send a message back, no one knew if he received the call or not. For the operators it was quite satisfactory, unless they were being warned something was about to blow up. The visitors gaped and laughed when the Trout brought out his usual joke.

'We have this sort of communication system so we can tell the operators what to do and they can't answer back.'

'That's why we scrapped it, son!' called the Great White Father. The Spotted Trout had no answer. No one told him the radio didn't work: the Section Heads made noises of agreement when he referred to it. It was the only thing he understood about the plant.

The visitors didn't even snigger at the discomfiture of the Trout. Since they were in their suits and ties and best shoes, and the working prisoners in overalls, they had that glorious holiday feeling of freedom so rare in the life of an industrial detainee, though they wore that insignificant look men get when they're dressed alike. As soon as they had looked at the defunct radio and perhaps at the television screen showing the condition of the gas flare they would go out to the main reactor structure and ascend two hundred feet in the lift cage, get out on the swaying landings and be pleasantly giddy looking at the view from the top.

It wasn't to be. A cloud of hydrogen-sulphide gas blew from the gas-treating plant; the Congo Kid was draining a tank and had opened a valve wide; he had the wind behind him and was quite safe. In concentrations of over a thousand parts a million this gas was odourless and fatal almost immediately, but luckily the concentration was much less and the rotten-egg smell much greater and thirty-five visitors and one guide were sick on the gravel outside the control room. All the operators had tossed their stew at one time or another, they had no sympathy for the visitors. Some even laughed. The Trout bundled them on to the company bus as soon as he pulled himself together, and got them out of there, apologizing. As they left, Stillsons was awkwardly emerging from one of the metal-framed windows, covered in greasy dust from desk tops and sills. Despite their collective sickness, the visitors stared from the bus windows, fascinated. They were even more fascinated later when they looked at the money in their pockets. The gas was so penetrating it tarnished all their silver brown.

CHEAP AT HALF THE PRICE Bomber Command, waving books of tickets, entered from the southern end, making a noise some distance away as you do with animals to let them get used to your approach. But they saw the tickets and were enraged.

'Men, I've come to liberate you!'

'Toss the bugger out!'

'Beat it!' His familiarity made them contemptuous.

'What's he selling?'

'What're you selling?'

'For the price of a few cents a week, we can all have a ticket in hope. There's money to be won, one chance in twenty and the extra chance of a jackpot. Dob in, men! Liberate yourselves from the hopelessness of working for a living. Buy a ticket in sunshine and sport and twelve months holiday a year.'

'He's selling freedom. I'll take one.'

But not all the men parted with their cents. Many of these gallant prisoners, detained as soon as they were freed from school-prisons and conscious always of the tremendous debt they owed the country of their birth, kept their heads and did not go about wasting their substance in riotous living in a spirit of despair or irresponsible hope. Some, indeed, had never spent a penny in anger.

THE HOLLOW MAN 'Hey, Far Away! You got a job?' The Glass Canoe had gone out on the job for once and now was back in the control room, covered with the golden stains of slurry oil. The pump seals were bad, there were leaks everywhere, waxy oil was inches deep on the concrete. The palms of his hands were black with grease. Whoever was on the cleaning roster wasn't game to chip him about the stains he trod into the floor.

'Yes, over on the reactor. Won't be long.'

'That's all right, don't hurry back.'

'Won't be long.' Eager to get away.

'Don't hurry back: hurry both ways!' roared the Glass Canoe for the benefit of the bystanders who sniggered uneasily, putting themselves on side with the bigger man.

'You bastards tell me if he pisses in there with us. I don't want the jack.'

Far Away shot out the door, propelled by the venom in the voice of the Glass Canoe, whose arms hung down, slightly bowed, from his great shoulders. His brain teemed with the echoing, strident voices of the men he imagined himself to be. He glanced round the mob faces confidently, not seeing them. He didn't know what he would do next.

The sheen was bright on his forehead, the skin tight on his face. He grinned. There was no health in him.

A FIRST INJECTION 'This little talk is designed to assist you at the present stage of your training.'

Luxaflex had called up the Sumpsucker for a first shot of Puroil serum. A foreman at last.

'Your progress depends on many things.' The word progress was meat and drink to the Sumpsucker, though once he was a foreman where could he go? The next level called for degree men. 'Among which is the ability to get things done. To do this you need, among other things: Knowledge, Energy, the Right Attitude! To help you gain number one, you have to rely on yourself in on-the-job training. Learn as much as you can, it's no weight to carry. Numbers two and three, I recommend the Basics of Supervision, paragraphs 1011 to 1271 and 14001 to 14090, and the Staff Guide, and put into daily practice the advice and instructions you find there.'

Suddenly Luxaflex broke off. 'I didn't employ you, did I?'

'I don't know what you mean.' The Sumpsucker was lost. Was this a threat? Did he know about the widow? Or his penial disability?

'I mean when you first came here to the Refinery.'

'No, sir.'

Luxaflex was relieved. The man's singlets, peeping out brownly under the V of his open-necked shirt, bothered him. I wouldn't have employed a man like this, he told himself. He felt powerful, niched in his personnel job. You didn't have to be an accounting expert; you didn't have to have technical knowledge, yet you had a say in who went into what jobs, if you said yes or no when you were told to. He would just last out till sixty; young graduates were yapping at his heels, but he'd hold them off for the six years with his excellent grasp of the complicated ins and outs of Puroil procedure, a grasp it had taken him thirty years to acquire. They couldn't possibly do it in six.

'Remember, when you're handling men, be consistently courteous and businesslike. If you can make the bodies who come under your control feel the job they are doing is important and appreciated by you, you will be well on the way to getting the best out of them.'

He was proud of that sentence. It gave him a feeling of fulfilment. Like seeing his function listed half-way up the genealogy chart above his head. The trunk of the tree started below his line; he was just above ground. Below him the tree put its roots down into the soil. Beneath the bottom line, unmentioned, was the dense subsoil of operators, clerks, fitters, drivers, draughtsmen, storemen, machine operators, cleaners. He never allowed himself to dwell on the feeling that assailed him when he was off-guard: of being a helpless minor executive in a tiny branch of a vast company more powerful than governments; caught between the vicious, wanton, ungrateful pressure upward of labour, and the grinding pressure downward of the juggernaut called shareholders and capital and successive boards of directors reaching upwards and beyond in an Everest perspective to the ultimate World Board of seven.

He was proud of his methods of selection of job applicants. A good man is so in tune with company policy that he can rely on a sort of instinct. But he couldn't guarantee Sumpy's success. It was up to the individual to learn how to get in the queue to pass the buck and keep his mouth shut, waiting for others to make mistakes.

'Another thing,' he went on with no sense of transition, 'you must be a bastard! I remember when I first had my foot on the bottom rung of the ladder.' It was now on the second, miles of ladder towered above his head, though he was on an eminence Sumpy could never reach. 'We had some high brass coming to visit. The men in my section were good, they did their work perfectly. The OIC of my department came round to inspect and I didn't bawl the men out for anything, so he bawled me out. "You're too soft!" he said. "Not fit to command!" "But there's nothing wrong with their work. It's perfect," I said. "You must be a bastard!" he repeated with great emphasis, and I've never forgotten that lesson. With a little effort you can always find something wrong.'

'But,' said the Sumpsucker, and got no further. Something didn't fit.

'I know,' said Luxaflex. 'You're thinking of the tact and courtesy guff. Never forget even the best horse slackens and the time to find him slacken is when you have a superior officer watching. Nothing else shows them—us—that you're on the ball.'

WHITE NEGROES Somehow the forty-million-dollar plant staggered off the ground. The power recovery had been started, the vessels of the reactor and regenerating section were up to temperature, catalyst was circulating and feed in. On the surfaces and in the pores of the silica-alumina catalyst marvellous things happened. Waxy distillate that was once used as furnace oil became high-grade gasoline. Steam supply wasn't sufficient: to help out, Puroil had bought an old boiler from a battleship sunk at Pearl Harbour. If they could get enough steam, and could weather the power dips that tripped the electric pumps, the plant might stay up. Every six hours the air driers serving the pneumatic instruments changed over from cylinder A to cylinder B with a roar that could be heard above the process din. It was hard to get used to: faces still went white when it happened.

Twenty assorted men were gaping at the control instruments or filling out the dozens of sheets of paper recording pressures, flows, temperatures, and the Sumpsucker was darting from place to place, when in walked the biggest brass the men had seen. Instantly the Samurai yelled: 'Quick! On your knees! They might chuck us a dollar!' Several lowered themselves to this position immediately.

Groaning Dykes, the foreign brass in charge of construction, could get away from Australia now the thing was going. It was officially handed over. Suddenly, without introduction, from the far end of the room, he burst out:

'This is a great day! I gratulate you all! We've got it going, let us keep it going! And KEEP ON CRACKING!!'

Twenty men gaped in his direction, then he was gone. Back to Europe, or Brazil or the Sahara. Anywhere but here.

'Whaddid he say?' asked a few voices.

'Who was that log?'

'Groaning Dykes.'

'Where's he gone?'

'Went for a crap and a sniper got him.'

'What did he say?'

'He said the thing might go.'

'Yes, but who is he?'

The Wandering Jew came in next, with a great retinue of Suction Heads, engineers, process superintendents, manufacturing managers, planning engineers, design draughtsmen and a full team of Senior, Advising and Junior technologists. All clad in white raiment. The effect was spectacular. They outnumbered the gaping prisoners ten to one.

'We have a good team,' announced the Wandering Jew.

'Britannia rules the waves,' came a voice from the crowd. It was impossible to tell who spoke; white shirts and cacky overalls were in a tangle. It came from the side of a prisoner's mouth, in the manner learned when his forebears dragged ball and chain.

'More chiefs than indians,' said the Samurai. The visitors towered over the Wandering Jew. Many of them had been athletes and sportsmen at University and had the idea they were leaders of the country, but here, after their glorious youth, they were congregated obediently round this risen weakling. The Samurai thought it was funny.

He looked around at the lowest prisoners. Fitter Dick was there, one of the bravest amateur aviators still living, full of reckless deeds outside the blue gates, but here strangely weak and bowed down. And the Mad Bloke, a shell-shock case, who took fits and could bend iron bars: he stood bent and deflated merely at the sight of the white shirts. What was it that so quickly burst the bubble of a man's pride? Was it the eight-foot wire fence, the white shirts, the senseless labour? Was it that those not dressed in white were the new negroes—the submerged mass on whom the edifice of society pressed most heavily? Or was it the humiliation of knowing that their occupation behind barbed wire was only to keep them off the streets? That Puroil and the other agents of the world owners could afford out of vast profits to support even more men when they became available from school or from redundant jobs rather than let them clutter the streets and become the new political menace. Instruments were available and being used in America that could have run this plant with two men and an instrument mechanic: the balance of the men—and the foremen with their crisis-producing orders—were superfluous.

In the high corners of the control room, spiders went about their age-old business of making safety nets for flies.

SHADOWS IN THE CAVE In the drink hut at the Home Beautiful, the Great White Father prepared a sketch to hang on the wall. He planned to get Terrazzo to draw some faces later.

'I'm sorry, did I tread on your foot?' he repeated aloud, reading the caption of the sketch. It showed the Good Shepherd apologizing on a scaffold to the hangman—the Python—for having stepped accidentally on his toe. The Great White Father laughed at his invention.

He wondered if his men would find it funny. He knew it was prophetic; bad people always drive out the good and men like the Good Shepherd die disgraceful deaths, apologizing.

Cinderella was in the bed hut with the Count. He was peeling at her blouse, looking as if he expected the white-green flesh of a young gum-tree to appear from beneath flaking bark. Or perhaps he was apprehensive about the hoots.

The afternoon proceeded, sunset dreamed away and died, the silence in the sky stiffened into night and darkness was there. The girls—shiftworkers too—came and went, shameless as dreams.

'Lend me your ears, prisoners,' orated the Great White Father, 'and listen to my general theory of civilizations, and how every generation inherits the worst of everything. Every conqueror that ever made a successful takeover bid destroyed the things the conquered were most proud of, and left the things that would be a reproach and a mockery. All the good buildings and statues and paintings and plays were torn down, ripped up, and thrown on the tip. The crap was kept; that's the stuff we idolize. Just imagine what the good stuff was like. All this shows the gradual deterioration of man; you won't hear it at your schools. Remember the fuss they used to make over finding inscriptions and marks and drawings on buried columns and tablets and tombs? Well, those were only the lavatory scribbles of louts like me. And the elderly louts that dodge work and go looking for them just pretend they say nice, stupid things; when all the time they're finding the worst the ancients could leave us. Look at me. Riches to rags. A living example of progress in reverse. Once I had a string of gallopers, a stable of trotters, and gym full of boxers and a house of ill-fame with twenty girls. What happened? I went bad. The gallopers started to trot, the trotters started to gallop, the girls started to box and the boxers started to—well, they started, too.'

As they drank and spoke and moved about the hut, their shadows played fantastic games on the walls, for all the world like shadows in a primitive cave deep in the earth, safe from monsters outside. And because of the magnification of their size and speed on the walls the shadows seemed to possess more life and vigour than the men who made them.

5
CRASHDOWN

QUITE EARLY ONE MORNING Before the break of day in the Puroil mental asylum run by its inmates, as the inmates described it, before the day's batch of dayworking industrial prisoners had awakened in their suburban and Sullage City huts, a group of sleep-hungry prisoners were taken outside by a foreman to try to keep them awake. He told them it was to be a lecture on the operation of the steam let-down valve and was surprised they did what they were told right away. Most foremen would never realize the men often wanted to work as long as there was some sense in it; they honestly didn't know when the orders they gave were senseless and certainly didn't expect the men to know. The normal pressure in the upstream line was 700 pounds a square inch, the temperature of the steam over 400 centigrade. As they stood there a square patch of inch-thick steel blew out of the high-pressure line. The group dispersed.

INSTANT PUDDING Land of Smiles, the foreman, ran seventy-five yards on his knees deaf with terror, sick in the chest, his mind paralysed. The others were in full flight before their knees had a chance to jelly. When they stopped, each man had a small patch of wet in the fork of his overalls. They knew what it meant to go to water.

Two hundred thousand people in surrounding suburbs woke immediately, sprang bolt upright and cursed Puroil from their beds.

AN INTEGRATED SYSTEM The plant collapsed. Turbines tripped, the power recovery system was dead, the pressure dropped, catalyst was siphoned from the pressured regenerator over through the power recovery boilers down through the turbine blades, out the vents and feet deep in the stack.

The refinery collapsed. Everything collapsed. Refinery plants of all ages were hooked up to the new plant's steam system. Fortunately for Puroil's compensation insurance premium rate no prisoners were cut in half, as they would have been if they were standing in front of the escaping steam.

AN EMERGENT OCCASION Sea Shells, that constant sound in everybody's ears, was in the lavatory when the metal blew. He ran out starkers. He always sat on the seat naked, but kept his boots on.

MIXED EMOTIONS Down at the wharf in the darkened locker-room, the Grey Goldfish sat up straight on his concrete bed, shedding rags. He had no shirt or singlet under his overalls. He strapped his hearing aid to the skin of his naked chest, switched it on. The blast came through clearly. He smiled. He could hear things, he wasn't completely deaf yet. He switched the thing off, no sense wasting the battery. He slept with his glasses on; his grey eyes swam lazily beneath thick lenses.

CAGED ANIMAL Blue Hills, on eight hours overtime, had found refuge on the flat top of a floating roof tank after having decided against a slanting bed on a fixed roof tank. He looked wildly round for the violent blast of sound that woke him. Something shivered inside his chest, something that seemed no part of him, a live, fearful animal darting about looking for something to attack. He checked his ears, to make sure his earplugs were in—they were—and lay back down, put his palms over the earplugs and shut his eyes. The sound was like a strong wind blowing inside his rib cage. The animal within shivered with fear, but gradually quietened as Blue Hills breathed more heavily.

AN INQUIRING MIND Stillsons had left his office and bent over a drain to investigate the source of an apparent water leak. Was it a broken cooling water line? If so, the water should be salt. Or fresh condensate. He scooped his hand along a shallow break under the concrete surface, where the water calmly rippled and slid along. He lifted his hand to taste the water briefly, but came to no conclusion. He scooped again and straightened up just as the noise took his legs from under him. He knelt then by the stream, transfixed, his paralysed hand squeezing out through thin fingers the components of a giant turd.

COMMUNICATION The blast continued. The Grey Goldfish turned on his hearing aid again and started phoning all the plants to find where the noise came from. To speak on the phone he used the mouthpiece first, then clapped the other end of the phone to his chest, round which his mechanical ears were strapped. His mates usually laughed at this, but not while his eyes swam at them under glass. He held grudges tenaciously and cherished them tenderly for years.

RAPPROCHEMENT Humpy, a young man who had never been young—he took to shift work at sixteen—was in bed with his wife when the blast broke loose. He lived handy to the works in a soot-covered house. For miles all the houses were soot-covered. He married at seventeen without realizing double beds were only four feet six inches wide and that his habit of sleeping with his knees up in a foetal position would not give his wife enough room in bed. Sometimes he kicked her, sometimes just kneed her in the back. All night they pushed and prodded each other. She was glad when night shift came, except that then he wanted sex during the daytime.

When the high pressure line blew they did opposite things—she involuntarily doubled up and he straightened out.

The funny thing was, they stayed like that. It was the start of a new understanding. That night they planned a honeymoon weekend and bought a new supply of contraceptive pills out of Humpy's overtime. He could always get overtime; he wasn't too proud to ask for it, and after all, the Sumpsucker was his brother.

POINT OF DEPARTURE Some contract prisoners—migrant welders, fitters and their mates—were smoking in the pig-pen just outside the amenities room. They were on night shift, too. The pig-pen was a barred enclosure in the open, set aside for contractors' eating and smoking. They were not admitted to the luxury of the control-room amenities, but often leaned in at the window to get water. When the line blew, they froze in sitting positions because of their jellied knee ligaments until someone yelled behind them out of the amenities window, 'Run for your lives!' They took off then, all nations united in flight, wearing bits of fence.

SOUND The Glass Canoe, who yelled at the scared workers, loved sound. He could lose himself in something more powerful than he was. The noise filled him, swelled him up so that he sang. At the top of his voice he roared, singing. The sound deadened his limbs: he felt he could smash steel with his fists. He could have charged across and butted the regenerator with his head. He ran out on to the gravel area round which was spread the plant in a huge incomplete rectangle and laughed and sang all the time the blast continued, waving his heavy arms and beating his chest.

INTERFERENCE Up on the reactor top Dutch Treat was tuning his little radio, ready for the signals he expected. He was getting a few beeps when the plant exploded beneath him. He clapped his hands over the earphones, pressing them into his skull. It didn't help. He stood up, outraged, cursed Australia and everything Australian. As a good European he didn't curse his distant masters.

THE LAST TRUMP In another part of the mangroves, near the rival oil installation which Puroil supplied from its under-river pipeline, someone had taken an old and once-loved Plymouth to let it decay in peace. The Great White Father found the Plymouth and hired a man to live in it. He picked the man up around 6.30 one morning in a shiftworkers' pub, thinking he would be glad of a job and a home. Surprisingly, the man had a wife. They lived in odd lanes, parks, gutters, backyards, under bridges. They moved in, did up the car, the wife put curtains in the windows, the man bricked up the car, put oil round the bricks to keep out the wet and discourage ants and weeds and in a short time they were settled in. The watchman's duties were simple; as soon as he heard someone going through the mangroves in a northerly direction he was to blow the whistle the Great White Father gave him. It was an Acme Thunderer with a plastic pea for longer wear and blew a beautiful fluttering, piercing note. Just like a football referee signalling a penalty. He could blow and whistle, too, if he wanted help with marauding kids, or dogs, but he never did. He liked being alone. He didn't even want to go to the post-office for his pension cheque, but sometimes had to when his wife got sick. She liked to dress up and go out once a fortnight. When the blast came they huddled together on the cushiony car seats under their war-disposals blanket. Maybe it was the end of the world. With a sudden access of life in their aged limbs they connected, just in case it was their last night on earth.

THE CONSOLATION OF RELIGION The Beautiful Twinkling Star was first back to the broken line. He isolated the broken section by shutting a block valve upstream in the high-pressure side, then the downstream side to prevent the medium-pressure steam escaping after the desuperheater. Neither valve shut off properly, but that was normal. As he did these things he sang heartily—but couldn't hear himself sing—'Jesu, lover of my soul'. The Welsh surge and pathos of the tune gave him extra strength. 'While the nearer waters roll, O receive my soul at last!' As he closed the huge valves, he felt faith had overcome the frightfulness of the stormy blast.

SOMEONE ELSE The Great White Father rolled over in the drink hut. He'd slept on the table.

'You hear something just then?' he asked Volga, who was wearing shorts and doing one-leg squats. He watched the exercises with surprise but no envy. Exercises on night shift? The man's heart must have been as big as a watermelon.

'They've blown her up,' was the calm reply. The calf muscles bulged, lengthened, bulged, lengthened, bulged.

'Thought I heard something. Glad I had that operation.'

'What operation?' He hadn't stopped his squats. Up, down.

'I had a little window put in my ear ten years ago. I was so deaf in those days that when I felt like singing I had to put my hand up to my ear to channel the sound round from my mouth. I tell you, I was a shocking mess.'

'When were you deaf?' asked Volga.

'Didn't I tell you I was deaf once?' Volga's legs grew thicker.

'Never.'

'Strange. Perhaps it was someone else.'

'Who else would you have told?' His calves had blown up with the exercises, big enough for several men.

'No. I mean someone else deaf.'

HEADLESS CHICKENS Steam was still coming from the hole, the emergency had brought down all available supervisory staff, engineers, security. Most of them weren't used to plant noise and escaping high-pressure steam and in their worry they moved round the valve and ruptured line in a circle, hands over their ears. Gradually they speeded up until they were doing a war dance round the spot.

Prisoners had come back and now watched this reaction of their superiors.

'What the hell are they up to?' asked the Humdinger of the Beautiful Twinkling Star, who shook his head.

One of the engineers, a tall blond foreigner, probably an Englishman, detached himself from this industrial dance and bravely approached the hole, lowering his head to look inside.

'Why don't you shove your melon right in?' roared the Humdinger and ducked behind his mate. The dancing circle slowed but didn't stop. In ducking for cover, Humdinger nicked his forehead on steel plate welded to a stanchion. The Star took him back to the locker-room—first aid was half a mile away—and anointed the cut from a little bottle of red rye. The label was long since gone, but everyone swore by the Beautiful Twinkling Star's red stuff.

THE GARDEN OF FORKING PATHS After this unscheduled plant crashdown there were the usual jokes about turning the place into a nightclub, using its reactors and strippers, or selling it as junk to Simsy, the scrap-iron merchant. At each plant upset the future lay before them unknown, at the mercy of metal behaviour as well as human conduct. And myriad random influences: a bird's dropping, a foot slipping, a valve knocked, a stray curse, an argument, a stupid order; and so on. Supplies of gasoline were imported, to make up production loss.

The Beautiful Twinkling Star casually picked up the broken piece of metal sundered from the line. In one hand. He thought nothing of it. Several prisoners and guards tried to do the same thing a little later, but the metal fragment weighed about eighty pounds and they needed two hands to lift it. The Star saw this. It was the first time in his life he realized his physical strength was above average. Why had he never noticed it? He began to wonder if he was so riddled with spiritual pride that he couldn't see others and what they did for his massive concentration on his own doings. Why had he never used this strength to subdue the wrath of fiercer men who overawed him with violent appearances?

JUSTICE The Dobber took an early look at the break. Most men spat only when he'd gone past. Some spoke to him, feeding him casual words that he might be grateful for. Those who prize chance information find people keep feeding them chance information, and that was all the Dobber got. He would like to have pinned the blame to some person, because persons bleed and he liked blood. All he got was stress and metal fatigue.

He tried his luck with the Sumpsucker who came on day shift at seven.

'All I know is I heard a bloke say he saw a fitter belting the line with a fourteen-pound hammer one day. Where? Well, near the place it bust, of course.'

The Sumpsucker's idea was that there was always a grain of truth in any charge made. Any smear overheard by him was a real smear and by the time he sent it on its way, swollen and loud, it became a reason for arson, lynching, and the burning of wooden crosses. Engineering promptly rapped the fitters over the knuckles by limiting their overtime.

EFFLUXION OF TIME That afternoon the X-ray technicians should have been busy for four hours round the section of line that burst: instead, it was five days before they were seen.

It seemed as if everyone wanted to stop the plant. The fitters, in the sulks, went off the job till they got their overtime back. The company floundered about looking for someone to blame. The operators started fishing around for openings on other, softer plants, approaching the Good Shepherd as the softest touch with an almost maiden shyness, the shyness they showed when it came to filling in transfer application forms and showing their ages. Just as women know that their market value as sex prisoners is affected adversely by rising age, so these industrial prisoners were in deathly fear of being led out of their prison without the means of surviving in the cruel world outside as their bodily strength was starting to fail, the frequency of their sick days to increase and their confidence to evaporate.

PAID TO POTTER Why didn't Puroil put them off for a few weeks while the plant was down? That was the question the white shirts were asking.

Their degree of mechanization prevented it. The plants needed very few men to run them, but without these few they couldn't run at all. If they were put off, those most likely to get another job were the brighter men. If the brighter ones were kept on and the others put off, the others would call them all out, since the brighter ones on the job were rarely prominent in the Union.

Puroil had to keep them lounging about or run the risk of having no competent men to start the plants. Of course if all the men were on the staff and paid enough to exempt them from trade union coverage, they would need fewer men. And if such men were trained fitters and instrument mechanics, the maintenance problem would be solved. High-salaried experts, no foremen: the future. In Puroil's English refinery it was the present: unlucky refugees from this system were being taken on at Clearwater. And what would the redundant men do? That was not Puroil's worry. In the meantime, fourteen men a shift were paid to keep out of the way.

TRENDSETTER From the back window of the locker-room the Samurai saw the Mercedes of the Wandering Jew stop and decant the great man himself. As he watched he pulled out his notebook.

The Wandering Jew was hailed by a group of second-level management bodies. Reluctantly he changed course. A dozen alert men were grouped round the spot visited earlier by Stillsons, who had not notified his find. Water was still coming up through the ground, but nothing tangible found. All in the group were bending, putting fingers in water, putting fingers in mouths, tasting and pronouncing. With gravity.

'Brackish.'

'Fresh.'

'Salt.'

'Salt.'

'Fresh.'

'Salt to brackish.'

'Salt contaminated with fresh.'

'Brackish.'

It was the Wandering Jew's turn. He tasted. 'Fresh,' he said.

The remaining men took their turn.

'Fresh.'

'Fresh.'

'Fresh.'

'Fresh.'

THE EXPERIMENT The Boy Wonder, risen from the ranks in the laboratory to be an engineer, buttonholed the Samurai. The Samurai enjoyed his nonsense; he was bright enough not to take Puroil seriously. He often passed on little items of news from the Termitary.

'Did you know the universe is a gigantic lab?' he said in his casual, unemphatic way, a refined management version of the old convict manner of speaking from the side of the mouth. 'And our earth is one small wing of the lab for training the Maker's research students. A viewing station for their sightseeing visitors from other planets. You know what they describe as one of our outstanding characteristics? I'll tell you: "The subjects perform in the machinery, sometimes, but their most revealing actions are first that they make no concerted effort to destroy the apparatus on which they are forced to perform, and second they accept their prisons as part of nature, surroundings perfectly natural to which they adapt themselves and which become part of them."'

The Boy Wonder prudently silenced himself as men of higher status approached, asking for Stillsons. The Samurai grinned at his prudence.

PRUNING No one ever got up and said, 'Okay. We're cutting you down. You'll do the work with half the men.' Instead, they let rumours do it, in a refinery complex whose individual plants were in all stages of newness, and whose star plant, the cracker, hadn't got going beyond a few days.

The men themselves helped, carrying rumours to their own men, trying to be important with something new to tell, trying to chip little bits off each other. The rumours were never happy, they always hurt.

On the heels of the pruning of maintenance men and instrument mechanics came rumours of plans to reduce plant manning figures. They were convinced they could earn more money by spending less. And someone thought the rumours would show up the men's reaction. An experiment on live animals. The Samurai made several phone calls to local Councils, Progress Associations,

Ratepayers' Protection Associations and newspapers, telling of these reduction plans, mentioning the size of the plants and the number of gasoline tanks, and inviting guesses as to the extent of any fires and damage resulting from processes that got out of control because of the lack of a few men in an emergency. The rumours of manning cuts stopped. Nothing more was heard.

THE CURE The Wild Bull of the Pampas had got thin suddenly and started doing funny things in the lab. He went to a doctor, asking for a sedative. The doctor went to another room and rang the police. They took the Wild Bull away. Now he was back from hospital after three months' treatment—electrodes, needles, the works. His wary cat-stepping walk was gone, he blundered healthily in to work, yelling cheerfully to people he thought he knew, drugged to the eyeballs and three stone heavier.

THE JUMP Slackie in a ferocious temper crashed a great three-foot wheel key against the sides of the regenerator.

The foreigners had it in for him, did they? Well, he'd never kowtowed to foreign bastards and he wasn't going to start now. Trouble was, when you got out of the ranks there was no Union to protect you. Granted the Union was weak as piss, but it was some protection. Without it, this rotten mob could do as they liked. Anyone who thought they wouldn't was crazy. It was night shift and he couldn't be seen; the process noise drowned the sound of his fury. The plant was getting back up again. He kept up his hitting for a good five minutes. He had used an axe in the bush once and acted now as if he wanted to chop this metal giant down.

The foreigners said they wanted the Sump in and Slackie out. He couldn't become an operator again: the company wouldn't allow it, he might spread things he'd come to know, the way bosses spoke about operators. The men wouldn't have him back now he'd been on the side of the enemy. Promotion was a one-way ladder. You had to jump off: you couldn't climb down.

A few tears of self-pity came into his little screwed-up eyes as he bashed and bashed. He was a big man, but he had no buttocks.

His trousers fell away behind him straight down from the small of his back to his heels. Slack-arse, they called him.

INCENTIVE Two months, and the plant was up again. Day time. From the top vents the usual five tons a day of fine catalyst spread over the suburbs. There was a ring of white shirts up one end of the control room.

'What's the panic today?' asked the Samurai, just in from ducking round the redhot glowing catalyst flowpipes.

'Remember the pressure balance valve? And how we told them it was crook while we were shut down?' reminded the Humdinger. 'I reported that every shift for three weeks. What's up now?'

'It's the fashion now to worry about it jamming.'

'We know it sticks. You can work it from in here while she's not going, but when the heat gets to it it won't move.'

'Why don't you write to the shareholders?' said the Humdinger sarcastically. The Samurai smiled his smallest smile.

'I wonder who they are.' No share registers disclosed the names behind the holding trusts or even the trusts themselves.

These men conveniently forgot Australia was being developed by overseas capital; the country owed its position to the greed of foreigners. But the Samurai couldn't leave it at that. He advanced on the group of white shirts. These jokers know so much more than I do of the theoretical work behind a catalytic cracking plant, he said to himself, it'd break the heart of anyone who really cared about the total effort here to see things like this happen. What they needed was one man to give his paper work to a stooge, then go out and control the plant. The trouble was, paper was so powerful that paper stooges became bosses. No wonder, in a place that said 'The memo is the lifeblood of the organization.' He detached Bomber Command from the ring and asked if the conference was about the pressure valve.

'It is,' said Bomber cordially. 'And don't forget to let us have any suggestions you have. The more we have thinking of these problems the better. You could even make a few dollars out of it if you put your suggestions up to the PRO.' There was a scheme by which a prisoner might be rewarded with cash if his suggestion was adopted. Trusties and higher were expected to give their suggestions free, so there was often a staff brainwave put on paper by a slave and the reward halved.

'Forget the dough,' he growled. 'Why not shave an eighth of an inch off the butterfly, all round, next time we crash?' He was about to go on when he saw the eyes of his superior officer glaze. He wasn't listening. Nothing the crap suggested could be good. Stop talking, the Samurai commanded himself. Don't think. Shut up. Forget it. He walked away.

A week later, when he got over it, he approached one of the engineers, a little higher up the ladder, with the same suggestion.

'Sorry.'

'Why not?'

'You don't understand. I have to go through channels. I'd like to be able to go up to the Wandering Jew and say, Look, I know how to fix it. But if I go over my superior's head, the Python, I'll get arseholed to some crap job. He'll have the knife in forever after.'

'Why not tell him, then?'

'Tell him? I'm not a fool! Any suggestion I give him goes up as his suggestion, he takes the credit and next staff meeting he hauls us over the coals for having no brains. If I get up and say he pinched it I'll get an even worse posting. And the others won't support me or they'll get the same. Besides, they'd be glad to see me downed. We're competitors.'

'God help us.'

'Don't tell anyone I said this or I'll deny every word. But it's a relief to get it off my chest.'

'With no kick coming, too.' The Samurai stared at him in disgust, but the man felt no shame and didn't lower his eyes. His livelihood was at stake, he had to be gutless to survive.

'I can't even tell these things to my wife. She might spill it to the other wives. They all listen to try and pick up something for their own husbands to use against each other. And the joke is, we have to mix constantly. Anyone who stays outside the circle is suspect. Not only that, he gets behind in the gossip.'

The Samurai laughed. This man had spent six years getting a degree from a qualifications factory and he was on a treadmill as shameful as that trodden by the lowest prisoner. At least they could go home and never have to see their workmates till they came back to work.

'I won't tell your secrets. You've got enough to worry about.'

Eighteen weeks and three crashdowns later, an eighth of an inch was shaved from the butterfly inside the valve. The Python thought of it himself, he said to the Wandering Jew, and the Good Shepherd squirmed. Silently.

THE ANGRY ANT The Angry Ant was practising a few tricks on the Foxboro instruments that controlled the boilers. He was changing the flow instruments from automatic to maximum flow on hand control, to automatic set point control, to manual set point control, then the level instruments to manual. Back again. Level instruments to auto, flow controllers from manual set point to auto set point, to hand control to auto with the over-rider limiting maximum flow.

The plant was wide open to any man who wanted to learn. True, you had to teach yourself, for chemical engineers wouldn't speak with authority on instrument functions, and instrument engineers didn't want to be quoted on plant operation. When new instruments were installed no one higher than prisoners—or Sump—was game to ask how they worked: the installing engineer might mention who had asked. When that happened everyone would jeer at such ignorance, though no one in the jeering group knew either. But no one knew they didn't know. But for the men there was always the Sump. It was a toss-up whether the other foremen despised him more for his steamy morals and his widow stories or because he would tell what he knew of process, instruments, emergency procedures, past failures, suspect valves. Most behaved like transplants from the closed communities of the Old World. Tell 'em nothing. Don't let 'em get your guts. Clam up. Speak Welsh when strangers come in.

The Ant was teaching himself, as the Humdinger had done, with the Samurai's help. These men were exceptions. Back and forth the Ant went, from auto to manual and back to auto; again and again. The Samurai and Humdinger pretended not to look; they were pleased someone was interested. The more men knew all the jobs, the better plant it would be. Of course, Ant wanted to get away from the turbo-expanders, too. Most ran past those machines, just in case.

When he had had long enough at the panel, Humdinger suddenly grabbed Angry from behind and bit his ear passionately. Angry's chemistry was not upset at the time and he responded mildly, wriggling free. Humdinger was playful, bit the other ear, licked his neck, fiddled with his overalls and grappled with him, trying to tickle him into a girlish fit of giggles. He worked his hands round the lips of his pelvis, digging into the pelvic cavity.

'Beat it, Dinger,' said Angry, but couldn't shake him loose.

'I'll fix you, Ant!' said the Humdinger, and squeezed out a sound.

'What was that?' shrieked Angry fearfully, trying to tear free.

'The mating call of the lost tribes of Israel.'

Slug suddenly appeared through the door and made for the Humdinger. 'Come on! Today you go to the flare!'

There was such venom in his voice that the Humdinger burst into tears and pretended to wet himself. For a moment young Angry thought the sobs were genuine—until he shoved two fingers of his right hand under the Slug's nose and said, 'Guess who?' Humdinger was selected because the others couldn't be found. They were out hiding on the structures or on their backs somewhere.

'What's up you this morning?' Angry Ant walked after Slug. He followed him into the office and bailed him up against the far wall like an Alsatian bailing up a postman.

'If the Enforcer gets down here and Humdinger's not on his way to the flare, where will we be then?'

'Where will we be?' asked the Angry Ant.

'I'll tell you where I'll be!' Slug screamed hysterically. 'I'll get the kick right up the arse! That's where! It's all right for you blokes, you got the Union to look after you! I got no one! No bastard'll help me. I give up Union protection to take this job and do in six hundred dollars in the first year and what for?—'

'To wear that dustcoat. You'll sell your mother for a white collar. And if ever you slimed your way into a Shift Super's job you'd think your shit didn't stink!' He walked out. The Ant was small and shiny, sharp and fierce. He knew Slug couldn't be insulted.

Five minutes later Slug was back, handing out notebooks and pens to try to get on side. The notebooks were slightly used, he needed a lot of stationery for his business records and wrote on anything handy. The Ant refused. The Slug's hands were pawing each other, both limp; his head set well down inside his shirt and those bright senseless eyes staring unwinking. He looked as if he might perform his heart attack stunt just for the sympathy of one man. As he shuffled away, he left on the ground a shiny track.

McONAN EFFICIENCY When the high-pressure steam line relieved itself by blowing up, the compressor which relied most heavily on this steam was at a loss to know how to carry on. Its job was to compress gasoline vapours from the top of the fractionating column from one to twenty kilos.

When the supply of steam dropped, the machine's speed slid ungracefully down and came to rest unnoticed on the higher of its two critical speeds, between 4800 and 5300 revs. Here it stayed for a few minutes. Next it felt faint and moved on down to the second critical speed, between 2800 and 3100 rpm. The machine knew no better, but when skilled operators were handling it, they contrived to hurry the machine through these two speed ranges, otherwise damage might be done.

Since most of the men were outside during the emergency, and those in the control room were provided with only two hands per man, some things were not noticed in the panic. The machine surged badly, sucking and blowing and grinding like an other-worldly beast landed on an alien shore and dying hard; unheard because of the greater noise made by the high pressure steam. The rotor was bent. The ordinary operators blamed the total lack of maintenance. The engineering boys, safe behind their dividing wall, blamed the operators for carelessness and inefficiency.

The Boy Wonder, trying to do himself some good, suggested a spare rotor be drawn from the warehouse. Right away. A group of lowest-grade prisoners heard this suggestion and laughed raucously, derisively, triumphantly.

'Spares!' roared the Samurai with unfamiliar gusto. 'Don't kid an old digger! This mob won't carry spares.'

'Why not?'

'Because they might not use them! So what happens when catalyst eats through a valve? Or a pressure drop gets rid of half the catalyst out through the turbo-expander vent valves? You shut down and lose forty thousand dollars a day profit!'

'It can't be that high,' said Canada Dry. 'They told us that was gross.'

'It's one hundred thousand dollars a day gross. After excise, overhead, cost of production and distribution and so on, it's forty thousand a day on a one thousand ton a day yield of gasoline out the ass of the debutanizer.'

'Yes,' agreed the Boy Wonder. 'But. Take today. Forty thousand dollars, you say. Then there's wages, cost of machinery, maintenance, advertising, cost of construction, all of which is over forty million dollars. Therefore there's no profit today. Take tomorrow. You say forty thousand. Take off the forty million and there's no profit tomorrow. Same the next day. And forever. You can't argue with figures. They keep the figures, they'll never let you into their private ledger. They bump up artificially the landed cost of their crude so there is no profit. Every day that forty million has to come off. They only stay in business to keep us in a job. You just don't realize how good-hearted they are.'

'Why don't you see someone about the rotor?' Canada asked the Boy Wonder.

'Who?' He spread his pink and white palms not yet soiled with work. With reasonable luck they would stay that way all his life.

'Someone high up.'

'There is no one high enough up to make a decision like that. They have to refer everything to AHQ or Europe. And *they* mustn't be bothered with details. No one's responsible.'

He didn't believe these men, though he appeared to agree. Their words were the vapourings of the lower orders. Why did they worry, anyway? They were collecting their pay each week. He followed up his own idea and made a personal appearance at the warehouse so he wouldn't be fouled up by some office Jack on the phone.

There were no spares. A sixty-dollar clerk in the warehouse determined, on rate of usage, the spares held in stock. None had so far been used, so he ordered none. There were far too many brands and countries of origin and makes of equipment used to make it economical to have spares for everything. The engineers had heard of standardized equipment, but they had no say in the ordering of materials. That was another department. There was no central materials pool that each oil company could go to.

Several years before this—before such a large addition to the old ramshackle refinery as the catalytic cracking complex had been built—an efficiency team had been through the company. It was imported from the country acknowledged the most powerful in the world for the eight years from 1945 to Sputnik. The McOnan team went round the Puroil world and came up with one important directive which had a great bearing on all subsequent Clearwater disasters. They saw money tied up in materials stored in warehouses and out in paddocks, so they worked out a magnificent simplification of materials policy. First, anything not used in two years had to be scrapped. Second, only essential spares were to be kept.

The people who had the say on what were essential spares were bodies high up in the Termitary who knew that the working, dirty, grease-covered end of the refinery existed and had even been to visit its more civilized parts once or twice, but this was the extent of their knowledge of the way the refinery actually limped along. A turbine rotor had a life of many years, certainly more than two, so there were no spares. When one was needed for the German machine, it had to come from West Germany and delivery took six months. There was no spare rotor for the air compressor—that took four months to be ordered, made, and delivered from Scotland. No bearings for the German turbine or compressor.

When one rotor was bent, it was straightened and another ordered, then the straightened rotor used till the new one arrived. It packed up three months before the new one arrived, so the place was down for a major overhaul. The new one came, was bent inside a month, the old bent one re-installed. Then that was bent. Meanwhile, old bearings were continually being put back in this magnificent machine, with predictable results. Only one new set of bearings could be ordered at one time and Materials Division were enjoying a new surge of strength at International Board level, and made it hard for Engineering to draw the new set. After all, it was an economy plant. For some reason it was easier to lose money on production hold-ups than to change a blanket policy on spares.

SEVENTY TIMES SEVEN Everyone forgives a large organization its mistakes, but forgiveness should not extend indefinitely.

Instrument fittings for pneumatic instruments last a long time, so there's not much turnover, but when they do pack up, it's desirable to have a replacement ready; that is if it's desirable to keep the process going. Some instruments, however unfortunate this may be, are key instruments. One such part went phut; the stock minimum was eight; since there had been no movement in those parts for two years, the lot had been scrapped according to policy, which at stock control level had the force of regulations. Since this was an emergency—a plant process halted—a part was brought in by special messenger, but materials division objected: there would have to be eight parts bought in addition, to keep the stock requirement up to minimum since there had been movement in the stock. At the end of two more years, these hardy parts had shown no further movement, so the eight parts were scrapped again. Because of the vertical division between materials and operations departments, the stock boys didn't care a hoot, didn't even know what the part was for; the operation laddies didn't know when the two years commenced or whether or if their parts were in danger of scrapping. They had no access to the records or the warehouse. After all, that was a different department. What did they expect, exceptions? Policy must be uniform, or something might get tangled.

At night the prisoners' talk turned naturally to these matters of high policy.

'I used to work up in that rathouse,' said Stretch. He meant the warehouse. He'd had to go because of an earlier redundancy policy when the clerks were easier to manage. I'll tell you about the turkeys. Did I ever tell you about the turkeys? You know the Spotted Trout—the PR boozer—well he was providoring a tanker and made a blue on his order form, this was before he was promoted to PRO; he got three thousand turkeys for their Christmas dinner. He put thirty on the order form. He meant thirty, but the stock unit was a hundred. They ate turkey for three months at sea, you should've seen the refrigerated trucks arriving at the wharf, there was a line of them half a mile long but it was too late to turn them back. The drivers wouldn't have gone, anyway. That's when they sent him up to this heap of old iron.'

'Three thousand turkeys!' snorted one of the Europeans, opening up a bit while no bosses were about. 'That's nothing!' Then the man, only a fortnight off naturalization, let loose with his conversation stopper.

'I was in a small refinery inland from Buenos Aires and we have to run some lines from the refinery to the new well-head booster station, and with the new lines go the telephone. So. We need thirty thousand telephone poles. You know where they get them? Eh?'

'Tell us, Aussie!' said the Humdinger. The Two Pot Screamer took out a piece of paper at this point and loosened his pencil in its holster.

'They get them from Sweden!' bellowed the man. 'Across the Atlantic Ocean, thirty thousand telephone poles forty foot long, the best pine from Sweden! Then they take these thirty thousand poles out to put them in the earth, but there is no earth. It is ground. Hard as rock. Rock-hard ground! You know what they do then? They get thirty thousand concrete poles forty foot long, and put the concrete poles in. Good! Fine! Beautiful! Then they think what is going to happen if one of the bosses comes out and sees thirty thousand pine poles forty foot long hanging round in a field and nowhere to go. So they take them out and dig a pit and burn them in the pit and cover them over. But one of the materials bosses comes. He looks up the stocks and the stock-code numbers and he can't find thirty thousand pine telephone poles in stock so he orders thirty thousand more! He didn't bother to ask and no one was going to chip him or he'd have got them arseholed for insolence and insubordination, so they finish up with another thirty thousand pine telephone poles from Sweden and they're still there!'

GO BACK, DAVID The Old Lamplighter took over duty in a blaze of light. The bed hut was inclined to be dark even in the day, so she switched on all lights.

'What I won't do with the lights on I won't do at all,' she said.

It was a puritan thing, this insistence on seeing what she did and making others see what they were doing. Fortunately for her, she had never been pushed into the excesses of feeling that were explored by the Sorcerer's Apprentice. Neither her men nor her own occasional lusts had put her in any danger of self-revulsion. Not even the newly acquired skills of the men who were led by the hand into the magic garden prepared by the Sorcerer's Apprentice and who took to it well. Some did not, of course, and went away scared and ashamed, too bemused to notice her take out the blue notebook and write up her sensations.

But the usual effect of the light on men who were accustomed to sex in darkness—with wives, maybe, who didn't want their faces and filled the dark with faces from the movies or the past—was a bracing, tonic one. They felt no need of refinements beyond the stark surroundings of the bed shed. The bareness of the corrugated iron, the one mirror, the Dettol dish, the nail-holes, these made the women's bodies softer and more lush to prisoners whose hands daily patted the throbbing sides of pump bodies, searching out vibrations that hinted that machinery had been run nearly to destruction, or wrestling in six-man teams with crowbars and levers on hot valves that didn't want to move.

She went to the door and yelled. 'Who's lucky?'

'Sump's first!' a voice came.

'Tell him shake a leg!' There was a sound of beer cans thrown into the wire crate the Volga Boatman brought home one night. Just standing there empty in the park, he explained. No use to anyone there.

She turned her back on the light, as if she had company, and cleaned some lettuce from under her top denture. There was something more; she explored, pushed with her tongue, it was not enough. Irritably, she took both dentures out and tongued her gums. Several tomato seeds and half a peanut. She finished the peanut.

The Sumpsucker. Him again. She had been a model at his old camera club, where most of the members had no cameras and there was a big turnover in models. He was married then. Keep her barefoot and pregnant, was his motto, but his wife got sick of both and left him after only two pregnancies, one of which she aborted. The first pregnancy was at high school now.

She applied a little gin to her bottom, and spread the jellied poison over her diaphragm which was the largest size. She was a big woman, whichever way you looked.

There was no knock, but the Sumpsucker was in the room suddenly, undoing buttons and reciting.

How does the little prostitute
Improve the shining hour?
She rinses out her diaphragm
But never takes a shower!

His eyes flashed narrowly either side of his long, lumpy nose. He sniffed at the gin.

She recoiled, in spite of her vast experience. She never liked chirpy customers; she preferred to have them approach diffidently and with scruples, then encourage their good spirits herself. Motherly inclinations.

'You still use that thing? Get with the strength and use the pill!'

How would he understand? The pill brought on her fits again.

'This is the strength. The pill costs too much.'

'You got the cash, spend some of it!'

'I put on too much weight with it and it turns me off the job.'

'Well?'

'Well what?'

'Put it in! Let's commit spermicide!'

'I hate gabby men.'

'Do you hate money?' Crinkling the dollars in his trousers, which he threw on the floor. He was very crude about money.

'I believe the widow's house is chock-a-block with big black drums.' She couldn't resist having a shot at him.

'Only the back and sides. There's room on the front lawn still.'

Through the Sumpsucker's performance she talked incessantly. She always refused to co-operate with him exactly—she said he hadn't paid enough money for what he wanted—and there was his smell.

'It's funny when I'm home and I have to tell the kids to wash their hands after they play with the dog. Here I am with you dirty dogs all day and half the time I eat my lunch with no wash.'

Her words came down from her mouth and through the mind of the Sumpsucker like trains through an empty station.

'Is the Samurai on today?' she asked, but getting no answer, pulled away from him until he answered.

'Yes. He's in,' said the Sump, and fastened on to her again. Why had she said that? she wondered. What did she care for men? Just the same, why didn't the Samurai come down to the Home Beautiful for the girls?

Sumpy let her talk.

'It's funny. The family knows I do this. Remember the cruiser at Bobbin Head?' She grabbed his ears and shook his head.

'Sure. I remember.' She was a big woman, six feet tall and very strong. If she had been a man the Sump would have been afraid of her. 'You don't still have fits, do you?'

'No. Only a couple a year, now. Do you really remember Bobbin Head?'

'My back remembers it. We were having a tread below decks and your son David comes looking for you. Where's Mum? he yells and instead of waiting for an answer he jumps down the hatch right in the middle of my back. Hullo, Mum, he says. And you say, Go back, David. Do I remember? Neither of us could get our breath back. "Go back, David!"' He mimicked her voice.

She was gratified. Her son had been worried she might go into a fit, but the strange thing was the fits had come less often after he had seen her at it. Strange how you feel your children have a hold on you, forcing you to put on a good front.

'I'll have to have a shave soon.' She glanced at her legs, black with stubble. Her armpit patch was long. A woman has so much maintenance. Men were lucky. Just their faces. Forgetting the Sumpsucker was there, she eased up one buttock.

'Sorry.'

'You won't take the Humdinger's crown. He can clear a room.'

Reflectively she picked her nose with her little finger. The other fingers enlarge your nostrils, her mother told her. You don't want to look like a native, do you? Mentally, she consulted her calendar. The twelfth. Should be on the twenty-fifth. That meant five days off work. If she could make sure of ten men a day until—that meant she wouldn't notice the drop in money.

'You finished?'

'I was finished back at Bobbin Head.'

'Why didn't you say something? I could be making a dollar! What do you want for five bucks, bed and breakfast?' She shook him off like a helpless puppy.

SITTING PRETTY   Cheddar Cheese was dying and it showed. Those who saw him mistook his leukemia colour for shiftworker pallor, but the Brown Snake knew. The man still did his work, which required effort only now and then. He tired quickly. There was no way to sack him that could ensure an escape for Puroil from the most ruinous publicity. Leukemia-pity was the fashion then and newspapers might conceivably have published a story of cruelty to a leukemia-sufferer despite the threat of withdrawal of Puroil advertising from the newspapers and the radio and television stations they owned.

He tried to have enough energy on hand once a week to visit the girls in the bed hut. This was his turn with the Old Lamplighter. She didn't know about his blood. The doctors called it leukemia so he would have a word for it, but really it was a rare and extremely interesting disease; like leukemia in that it was terminal. They had been very excited when he took his blood along to the researchers, and enthusiastic when he agreed to sell.

As soon as he was settled, he said, 'I'm sitting pretty! I sell my blood to a scientist!'

'You ought to keep some yourself.' He was a pale cheese colour; skin like wax fruit, almost transparent, not as shiny.

'I don't sell it all.'

'You're a bit yellow round the gills. I wouldn't sell mine if I looked like you.'

'I get ten dollars a pint. There's maggots in it.'

'Urk!'

'Little ones. Too small to bother you.'

'Still urk.'

'I'm going for fifteen dollars. Then twenty.'

'You just take the ten, never mind putting the bite on him.'

'It's a her. A research scientist.'

'You ought to give it free. I used to be a blood donor.'

'Give! Free! You're talking to a shift worker! Nothing for nothing!'

He was so put out by her callous attitude to money that he shot his bolt then and there just to get away from her.

6
TOP PEOPLE

THE MAN BORN TO BE BRANCH MANAGER A manager does his work by example; the way he looks is important. It was considered by the management midwives who assisted at the Wandering Jew's birth as a manager that the expression of the face was significant. It had been an article of faith in their own management training courses and they handed it down.

The Wandering Jew had been issued with a set of company masks for the purpose of setting his expression in approved patterns, and now set out to find the appropriate one. He knew the face gives no idea of what is in the mind and is a mirror of the experience and prejudices of the onlooker, but policy was policy.

'Let no one in,' he remarked to the secretary who was nominally his but whom in practice he shared with any other of the Clearwater executives that needed work done. Not even a secretary to himself. It would be different when he'd done his stint round the refineries, and was elevated to the Australian board. Then who knows? The London board? He was still young, there was always the lottery chance that he could make the world board. The lucky seven in charge of the second largest company in the world.

It was a tiny refinery by world standards, but one of his predecessors had made the London board. The Wandering Jew did not have his style; he'd been a gentleman, a man the prisoners trusted better than their Unions, who knew every man by name and not only knew but spoke each man's name. Actually took the trouble to speak to prisoners. A man who visited their homes if they were in trouble. They went soft at the mention of his name and spoke proudly for years after of this man they remembered as a man remembers a favourite schoolmaster.

The Wandering Jew took out his Convincing Worry-Earnest Application mask, pressed it into his features for the necessary minutes. It would last all day. One part of his preparation for this job had been an injection into his bloodstream of the main chemical additives to Puroil products: another was an injection of a plastic putty designed to help him retain whatever shape was moulded on him. It could keep his body in attitudes prescribed by top management, no matter what his own natural unregenerate urges dictated.

His ancestors had no connection with convicts and he was not a Jew but because of a chameleon component in his blood he began looking Jewish as soon as he was nicknamed and developed deep indentations above both ankles. Most Australians had the scar on only one.

The new plant was being started up again; it must go well. That confounded rotor had been straightened at Cockatoo dockyard. Why should a man's elevation to the Board rest on a rotor? Why couldn't manufacturers make their products sturdier? The thought of the recent recall of half a million new cars from several manufacturers on account of faulty material was a little help, but not much.

As he looked from his high window in the Termitary block he saw a thickset prisoner coming in the blue gates, clocking his time card, waddling down the concrete walk to his little change shed in the vast Puroil yard, coming out changed a minute later, eating his morning apple, making for a row of twelve-inch pipes under the eye of his foreman. He didn't know Herman the German by name, but he saw this incredible man lifting the pipes by the ends—surely there were cranes for this work—and moving them to new positions a little further on. Suddenly, as one of the pipe ends dropped near another (the man must have been careless) he lifted one hand stupidly and looked at his extended finger. The foreman looked away quickly; better not to see anything. The Wandering Jew couldn't see from this distance, but Herman must have hurt himself, for he put one finger in his mouth as if he had nipped the flesh. Old fool! He looked for a moment at his own fingers and felt a small thrill of pain as he imagined the same thing happening to him. Then Herman moved out of his line of vision, obscured by large projections on the southern side of the Termitary, designed to shield the offices from the direct rays of the sun. It was designed in the Northern Hemisphere.

He looked east to the wharf area, reached for his binoculars. There was an overalled prisoner standing on the wharf, casting with a fishing rod. Casting? Why would a fisherman cast on the greasy Eel River, where the eels lie down because they're gummed up with—not to be admitted—petro-chemical residues? He pulled over his binocular stand, laid the glasses on the felt supports, clamped them in position and focused again. After a few minutes he saw the reason. The man was fishing for seagulls with a floating bait. There was a white fluttering in the air, gone, rising into the air again, perhaps twenty feet, then the fisherman reeled the bird in, quickly wrung its neck and shoved it into a sack beside his feet.

Seagull stew. The Wandering Jew had heard of men catching ducks on a floating bait—casting along the surface—but never seagulls. There was no end to their inventiveness. If only it could be applied to Puroil business, at no extra expense, his own record would look much brighter.

He sheathed the binoculars and walked impressively round his desk, glanced at the pastel-painted walls. How cheaply the place was decorated. No better than any suburban box. At home he relished his marble stairs, urned flowers, shining cedar floor and sunken bath; the private trappings of power were exactly to his taste. It was all too easy for men without taste or means to pretend asceticism.

The man born to be boss. Before the mirror he practised a few expressions within the limits of today's mould. Situational Sensitivity. Style Flexibility. Openness—Candour. Change Readiness. He made his face darken with love, clear with pity, then redden with indigestion, his dullest passion. His features returned elastically to the expression fixed by the mask.

On the wall behind his desk was the refinery chart; his function was listed at the apex of the pyramid. But there was a difference. When he looked at it, it was obvious that only his name was above ground; the tree, invisible, was the line of responsibility above him to the Australian, the British, the World Boards. Below him the functions were a root complex gripping deep into the human soil of the Puroil community. Below that there was nothing: nothing but the anonymous earth and stones and clay—everything that was not Puroil. He looked away from the chart to the money plants outside his window, the plants the chart represented by magic means. The new cracking plant had to go well. It was the money-spinner of the refinery; his whole future was bound up with it. Damn their flimsy rotors.

He decided to make his rounds, went to the car instead of calling for the chauffeur so that no advance notice could be spread of his threatened visit, put on the safety hat marked 'Ref. Mgr.' and set off quickly for the cracking plant. He was not the type of manager who spoke freely to prisoners, so he needed the 'Ref. Mgr.' branded in large letters. No prisoner who insulted or bumped him could have as excuse the plea that he didn't know the Manager by sight.

THE HUMAN RUG As the Wandering Jew's foot hit the control-room floor, the Slug—though he hadn't seen the manager come in—lay sleekly prostrate. A group of sensory cells in that yellow greasy head enabled him to detect the approach of the species Boss at a great distance. One day the Wandering Jew had met him in the washroom and the Slug, keen for an investiture in the toilet or a whispered consultation in the confessional, said good morning, clammily. The Jew mumbled suspiciously, Morning. That brief contact had been enough for the Slug to get the wave-length of his hat. He could home on that wave-length any time and spread himself rug-like under the feet of whoever wore it.

Others saw the hat and sounded the alarm.

'Look out! Wandering Jew!'

Some scrambled, others shifted from one buttock to the other, some grunted, others didn't move. Terrazzo had found a face in some cracks in the cement wall and was filling in the outline. He didn't leave his work. Mogo said, 'I don't recognize bosses. When one man tells another what to do, that's not equality.'

Outside, he watched teams of fitters readying the last of the power recovery turbines for this start-up attempt. He crossed two fingers for luck. Last time they were delayed by a demarcation dispute. An operating man touched a wrench with his foot. The fitters claimed this was done on purpose and all engineering tools should be handled, and kicked, by engineering men only, for once this very thing had been done to deprive a fitter's mate of his employment. A scab had kicked some tools from one job to another, a quarter-mile away, to save the expense of having a fitter's mate carry them and to be able to say he didn't pick them up himself. Fitters didn't carry tools, they used them; they had assistants for the carrying. With luck there would be nothing like that this time.

And no more ball-ups with Workers' Compensation. A man from another plant, hungry for overtime, had worked his first night shift of the week at his own plant, then accepted a double shift on the cracker, from seven to three in daylight. He was last in bed on the Friday morning and by noon Saturday had been without sleep for twenty-nine hours. He stood watching several panel instruments with orders to give the alarm if certain things happened. Asleep on his feet, he reeled backwards many times, and recovered his balance. The time he didn't he fell back and fractured his skull. It was better to blame a slippery floor and get in a dig at the operators who mopped it than to admit the man had done too much overtime. It was like admitting the need to recruit more labour. The Unions were suspicious, but the company was so nice to the man in hospital that he maintained the floor was slippery. It was a close one.

Several drops of moisture fell on his upturned face as he took off his hat and looked with pride upward at the mighty structures. Rain? Probably a small leak, not worth mentioning. He didn't see Far Away Places, two hundred feet above, buttoning his fly. He had taken to peeing from the top rather than have the Glass Canoe on his back.

The Wandering Jew made for the dark blue gates in his dark blue Mercedes. The winter sky, too, was a merciless blue, flaming ice-cold down out of the sun. The flare, on its tall mast pulsing bright, low, bright low. The refinery's visible heartbeat.

BUILDING BLOCKS The Wandering Jew pressed a button, the door opened and the Whispering Baritone footed quietly over the carpet and stood at his right hand. He jerked his jaw so the skin right down to his neck lifted and sat more comfortably on his collar. His face was an even brick-red from collar to the roots of his hair. He wore heavy black glasses.

'What's this about the men putting up signs?'

'I get them taken down each morning.'

'Try leaving them there, they'll soon drop the idea.'

'They seem to be answers to the signs we erect, the signs for their protection; Look—Safety First—No Smoking—Think. Signs of proven value.'

'Why do they answer our signs with theirs?'

'They think our signs menace them.' The Baritone was a psychologist.

'Laughable.'

'They have the vague idea they want to be free. Sometimes I think the freedom they really want is the utter freedom they'd have outside our family circle.' He pointed dramatically outside the window to the blue gates. 'Out there they could be free of all our disciplines. Free to be hungry. If only they had the ability to see themselves as replaceable parts of an economy, instead of as individuals and mortal with one life to live.'

The Wandering Jew glanced out the window. 'You can go a long way in this organization while you think and talk Puroil.'

His tongue wedged firmly in his cheek. The Whispering Baritone knew it but was grateful for the gesture. 'But do try to get rid of any bitterness you may feel towards the rank and file. We want you to realize your potentialities, to attain the limit of your capabilities. We're training you for more and more responsibility.'

The Whispering Baritone beamed.

'We aim to put the round pegs in round holes and the square pegs in square holes. Remember my motto: Man's fate is himself!' The pathetic lectured man listened. He said the same things to his own subordinates, upon whose shoulders he sat squarely preventing their rise, as the Wandering Jew sat on his.

'We must always remember, though,' he continued, practising aloud, 'that we are mistaken if we feel that we alone are the company. We are composed of those who work for us and when we forget that, our own body turns on us and just as in the case of the human body slowly poisoned by what it takes in, so we are devoured by the individuals who compose our corporate body. We contain the seeds of our own defeat. Therefore—we must understand these individuals. You don't; I don't; but every day can bring its lesson to be digested.'

The Whispering Baritone found it impossible to break in at this stage in the great man's spiel.

'Once upon a time humans were the centre of the universe. Larger than life. But now industrial man is detached from the earth, from others, even from basic life itself. One's own body is replaceable, one's life. Property is disappearing, common to more people. Oneness with self is disappearing. The world is usable, therefore we will use it, bend it, break it, replace it. Man is usable. We must not fear to use up our human resources, for we have vast reservoirs of manpower. Remember: the earth is no longer sacred or to be feared. Let us play with it. Man is no longer sacred: let us use him. Religion's grip has relaxed. We—you and I, the managers of the world—we are the future; they down there are our building blocks. But when you feel too safe, in the words of the poet: Take a bucket and fill it with water, put your arm in it up to the wrist; pull it out, and the hole that's remaining is a measure of how you'll be missed.'

There was a ghastly pause. What had he meant?

'Thank you, sir,' the Baritone said nevertheless. He didn't know how to go on. He retreated from the room, head inclined, rump first.

THE UNKNOWN INDUSTRIAL PRISONER A court official called to see the Garfish to garnishee One Swallow's wages for a debt on a pair of wrought-iron gates he had ordered in a moment of drunken affection for his family. One Swallow was a chronic drunk who looked sober each day till he had his first drink, then fell over as if he'd just had twenty. Since the man wanted something—was a supplicant—the Garfish kept him waiting and while he waited he saw the Colonel's art gallery silhouetted on the ledge at the back of the office. Ignoring the stares of the office workers, which were enough to deter ordinary prisoners, the man marched up to the Colonel, looked at the gallery of sculptures and mobiles and pointed.

'What is it?' He pointed at the masterpiece.

'The Unknown Industrial Prisoner, chum.'

'I'll buy it.'

'Who are you?'

'Welding is my hobby.'

'What you want sculpture for?'

'Make a full-size copy and enter it in a competition.'

'Tell you what I'll do. I'll bring it out to your place Saturday and watch you work. What's the address?'

The man left his card. The Garfish hurried to fix him up once he invaded the office. His rule was push those who would yield and yield to those who pushed.

A NOURISHING MEAL The Python curled round in his low chair. He was so near the floor it seemed impossible for him to uncoil and strike from that position; so still, he appeared frozen or dead. But trickery gave him some life; he lived by it. He knew the impression of helplessness he gave from his low seat. He could feel rise in him, when a victim was within reach, the urge to crush the weak, hear them scream then whimper and finally swallow them whole. After all, how does a man stay alive but by killing his neighbour? Beating him for the best job, the nicest girl, was simply a modern substitute for doing him in. How does a man climb higher but by climbing on others' backs? Or how rich but by impoverishing his friend? How strong but by weakening his brother?

A man in overalls knocked at the door. Keep him waiting. The man knocked three times before the Python said, 'Come in.' He let him stand for a few minutes without inviting him to speak, then at last looked the man up and down, missing nothing. It was Blue Hills. The offensive smell of sour gas radiated from his prison clothes.

'I'd like to see about getting off shift, please. I want to get on day work,' said Blue Hills hesitantly.

'What's your name first.' He enjoyed putting them through the whole drill.

'Blue Hills.'

'You want to resign?' He sat back, twirling his pencil horizontally between his sharp front teeth.

'No. Day work.'

'Don't you like the money on shift?'

'Yes, I like the money—'

'Why leave it?'

'Money isn't everything. I want the wife—'

'Whose wife?'

'No one's wife! My wife! I want her not to have to wait up for me on the late shift and I don't want her going to bed without me on night shift. She gets nervous.'

'Nervous of you?'

'When I'm not there.'

'I wouldn't think you'd make much difference to her.'

'Can I get off shift then?' How could he say it was a day's work to climb several times up and down the 149 vertical steel steps on his plant structure? And on night shift...

The Python twirled the pencil and looked long and carefully at Blue Hills standing wretchedly before him. He noted the sweat beading the forehead just under the hair line and drops oozing out through pores on the upper lip. The eyes were piteous, an animal waiting to be killed.

But the Python's eyes were clear and bright. 'No.' And watched the man's face crumple and fall like the face of a man scalped, watched his body sag and shuffle out the door. The Python's eyes relished the sight.

Then he did a curious thing. From his pocket he drew a slip of paper on which he had written a passage from a French novel his daughter Nathalie had bought. He thought the book must have been written by someone very much like himself. Very softly he read, 'When the living get careless and come too near, I attack immediately their weak spot, the delicate unprotected fissure which pulses with life. I sink my teeth, the needle teeth of my intuition, into their warm flesh and soon I feel flowing from them the liquid that contains their nourishing life. It runs over my skin like water over dry sand and sinks immediately without trace. After a while all that remains of their warm and cheerful bodies is a heap of bloodless skin.'

He hummed a contented sigh. His tiny eyes glittered in the mottled, shiny skin of his face, and right round his head, from one ear to the other, reached his tight-lipped but cheerful grin. He sat perfectly still.

7
MEN WITHOUT QUALITIES

IMPROVISING Whistle Cock had more important work to do. He hurriedly adjusted the oil level in his interceptor, the oil-catching pit designed to stop oil getting into Eel River. Impatiently he added a half brick to the three bricks sitting one on top of the other, which propped up the long-handled shovel which supported the rusty pick-head which adjusted the height of the oil skimmer. Using equipment like this was like using a child's toy pedal-car to drive ten miles to work. The thing had been broken for years, but there was no money to spare for things like this: The Whispering Baritone's new extensions to the Termitary gardens came first.

Whistle Cock had suffered an accident west of Alice Springs seven years before: several wild Pintubis found him dazed in the desert sun when a front wheel came off his car. They gave him shade and shelter for three weeks while his gashes healed and bruises faded and during that time he found out about what he crudely took to be the traditional Aboriginal method of contraception. He was so grateful to the blackfellows and so taken with this discovery that he persuaded two of the least reverent of them to perform the painful operation on his own member. He used this operation often as the starting point of many of his conversations with women, as a persuader when women were obviously morally concerned about the risk they ran of conception.

He finished his makeshift job and sloped off to label the beer. Beer cans taken on to the job had to be properly re-labelled as soft drink; a rule made by the Great White Father so that foremen would not be embarrassed by the sight of the real thing and the men could enjoy their proper diet even on the plant. The Great White Father was negotiating with a backyard printer to put glue on the labels so all Whistle Cock would have to do was wet them and slap them on. At present he applied glue by brush. He went to the river bank, just outside the high wire fence, taking his glue pot and brush, and squatting in the shade of an old termite-ridden acacia on the bank, did his work on the cans, carton by carton. He took his working tools back and hid them in his locker, returned to carry the cartons up to the plant to be hidden in the ceiling of the amenities.

Next he brought out a gallon tin of turpentine and a long stick with a rag end. He left this equipment down on the river bank, the Volga Boatman would ferry it back; it was for the bands of wild dogs that occasionally committed a nuisance near the Home Beautiful. The dog laws had made them outlaws. The Great White Father didn't like using it, but if the barking of the dogs interrupted conversation, got the girls on edge and threatened to draw attention to the Home Beautiful, he would race out with the best of them, joyfully dabbing each dog's anus with the turps. This treatment was sufficient to take the dogs miles away, barking and howling and missing their footing in their earnest attempts to leave the sting behind. Their anuses maintained the usual distance behind, but the dogs always tried to run faster, just in case.

He punctured the can with the pig-stabber end of his pocket knife, swallowed the beer and hoyed the empty can far out into the water. It made only a little splash; no more than a seagull peeing in the ocean.

Round the nearest bend in the river came the Volga Boatman ferrying the Murray Cod over to the Home Beautiful. He pulled in to Whistle Cock's side of the river to pick up the turps and the applicator.

'Who's on?' said Whistle Cock.

'Sorcerer's Apprentice,' said the Cod with lust.

'He wants a marriage every time he comes,' said Volga.

'I want value for money and I want co-operation. I don't expect to bunk with logs of wood. I don't care how many notes she makes in her little blue book.'

'You don't think you'll give her a new sensation, do you? Anyway I didn't make up the marriage bit. The girls reckon that about you,' said Volga.

'Do they? I don't care. I'm paying and I'll have it my way. Which one said that?'

'All.'

'Oh.'

'You coming?' Volga asked Whistle Cock. 'She likes you.'

'Not now.'

'We could fit you in before the Cod here.' Trying to get the Murray Cod to bite.

'No you won't.' The Cod came in. 'I'm first.'

'Listen, Cod,' said Volga, 'the first was such a long time ago even she doesn't remember.'

'I mean first this morning.'

'She probably did a job on her way to work.'

'Some poor coot dragged off into the bushes,' chimed in Whistle Cock.

'What you want is virgins, Cod,' said Volga unkindly.

'Come on, Volga,' pleaded the Cod. 'I've got a barge pumping. I've got to be back inside an hour.'

The Volga Boatman pushed off across the black water and dipped his gleaming oars effortlessly into the slime.

A MAN WITH DRIVE The Glass Canoe was his anxious assertive self again. He was suffering a recurrence of the feeling that he must become something more definite than himself. He buttonholed the Samurai because he wanted someone to talk to who would treat his questions seriously.

There was a dream in his head, always only slightly out of

shape, that could have been a bridge between his great body and the place in the world that was really his. It was never exactly in that position between him and this rightful place so that he could step on it confident it would bear his weight. For if he fell. He was so vulnerable. He didn't want to step off into air. You have to be sure the ground underfoot is solid. Lately he had gone overboard about the new plant, surrounding himself with flow diagrams and product schedules.

'What are you hoping for?' asked the Samurai as kindly as he could. 'A dustcoat?'

'Hope?' beefed the Glass Canoe. 'Who cares about hope while he's got two hands and a quick brain? What you want out of life? First prize in the lottery? No prizes. If you work, you'll eat. And with a full stomach what else do you want?'

'You've gone off the track a bit, haven't you? I'm talking about all this guff.' Indicating the carpet of plans and diagrams.

'Eh? Oh. You've got to keep at it, get right into the study of new plants. The company's forging ahead, we should forge ahead with them. Their progress is our progress.' The man was sick.

'What progress? This isn't progress. This is change. Change is a law of life. Move or perish. Every change you make involves loss as well as gain.'

'I can't help that. A man can go ahead with Puroil.' He looked down for confirmation at the broad fingers of his brown hands. They shouted approval. He knew he was right.

'Loss as well as gain,' the Samurai repeated, 'and probably in equal parts.'

'Ah, bulls' pizzles. That's got nothing to do with me.'

The Glass Canoe turned back blindly to his flows and pressures, reflux rates and temperature controls. One by one he understood them all, but together they grew confusing. Too much. The plant was so rational on paper. And so clean. It didn't matter to him that the Samurai had to watch his plant and water-drain his vessels and bring his systems up to pressure while he sat inside reading. The foremen were weak and never chipped the Glass Canoe. He might do anything. The Samurai would never complain to a staff person about a fellow prisoner. The Glass Canoe had them by the short hairs.

The place was full of personnel, the Samurai reflected, and short on men.

A SCRAP OF PAPER He had come through the fractionating section, his boots carried the golden stains of slurry oil all over the floor. No detergent could touch it. Blue Hills walked in.

'I'm going for a hard hit,' he said, passing the Samurai.

'Did you get your day job?'

'No. That bloody Python.'

'Why didn't you see the Good Shepherd first? The Python'll never give you what you ask for. The way to get him to come good is make out you're happy on shift and hate day work. Then he'll break his neck getting you on day work. Like in the Army, remember? You put what you don't want as your first choice and what you do want you put second. They never give you your first choice.'

'I'm too tired of the place for all that. I just say my piece and that's that. Bugger 'em.'

The Samurai said nothing. Blue Hills went inside, then came back.

'What is it makes these nobs so much better than us? Why do we have to take what they dish out all the time?'

'I'll tell you, Blue,' said the Samurai quietly. 'They're given a little piece of paper. On this paper it says their name and Process Superintendent, or Suction Head, or Chief Assistant Technologist (Advising). Without that slip of paper, they're nothing. That paper's their life. And it's only good inside the blue gates. Outside the blue gates you can spit on them, because out in the world they're nothing. Just as much crap as we are. If they had no slip of paper you could spit on them here, too. Like they do on us and we do on each other.'

Blue Hills walked back inside for his hard hit and on the way called in to the amenities, filled the urn, turned the power to full and spat in the urn just for the sake of equality. The Samurai's words didn't reach Blue Hills; if he ever got savage, it would be with his fellow prisoners, not the higher members of the authority-pyramid.

The Samurai saw him spit in the urn, but still wondered what he could do to help Blue Hills' transfer to day work. He was human, though, and often had no solution for problems that cropped up. He did his few strokes of work on the Glass Canoe's plant and moved on to the others for which he had responsibility.

The world is dead, he thought, moving among the inert metal of pumps and lines and distillation columns, over the concrete apron on which the plants were constructed, over gravel brought from the Prospect quarries. It is a world of age-old stones—picking up a piece of gravel in which glinted minerals unknown to him—of basalt chipped from mountains ages ago, lying around on roads, lying under hills waiting to be plundered. And laughing at humans. These dead rocks were all of them older than the human race which trod them. Each fragment had an immortality. Humans rotted away into the soil in an instant of time.

What was the power he had that enabled him to lift this fragment of eternity in his hand and decide where to throw it? What had been breathed into his fragile dust that seemed for his instant of life to mock the inertia of rock? Was his own existence supported by a paper warrant somewhere?

He drew back from following these thoughts. There was a power in him, or rather a power came to him that made him stronger than he needed to be. A power that blew up certain feelings to an enormous size, a secret power. Was he so different from the men around him? What was the mission he had been born to perform?

He deliberately relaxed. As he looked about him with a new mood the whole world filled with love. Even the dirt underfoot was sympathetic and grateful. He could love these random stones, these heaps of inert, formed metal so far now from where they were mined. He could love the soil itself and everything that was. He needed, at that moment, no written justification of his existence.

In the control room the Western Salesman spotted the slurry stains and wanted to know what bastard tramped the oil in.

'They don't give a stuff that others have to clean up their mess!' he raved. It was his turn to clean up. He was still raving about it when weird noises were coming from his plant, still going to town on Blue Hills whom he had tracked in to the lavatory, while his own plant subsided and died outside. 'My name's up there on the roster. I'll get the kick up the arse for those stains!' There was no kick for a crashed plant. No one could know whose fault that was. It was all so complicated it was impossible to trace.

THE IMMORTALITY OF SPARROWS When he was seventeen Disneyland had his car paid off. The Samurai was disgusted.

'What's a kid that age doing shift work for? He should be out with his mates or playing a bit of sport or taking young sheilas out. The money should have gone on his education. Look at him.'

True, he was a nong, but according to democratic principles he had an inalienable right to be a nong. The Humdinger ran him round the Refinery to get him set for the Stawell Gift; had him walking across tank compounds up to his thighs in stinking black mud to help his muscles develop. It was just as good as running through soft sand on the beach or wading in the surf, the Humdinger assured him. And you got paid while you trained.

He got his name from the fact that America was the only country he had heard of and it was his ambition to go some day to Disneyland, its capital. He started as a sample boy at fifteen on shift work, working Saturday and Sunday three weeks out of four. He had never known sport. At twenty he was on adult rates.

'I'll show you how to hypnotize someone.' The Humdinger stood close behind him, put his arms round Disneyland's chest and squeezed in time to his breathing.

'Breathe in and out as fast as you like.' Disneyland blacked out after a dozen breaths. He slumped suddenly and the Humdinger lowered him to the floor. He made a fool of him but wouldn't injure the boy.

'They reckon an African scientist has found a way to double your life span.' Humdinger said once.

'What is it?' Disneyland was in. It was too easy.

'Eat sparrows.'

'Those little birds in the yard?'

'Spags. Little brown sparrows. There's something in their intestinal tract makes them live forever.'

'Go on.' Faint, uncertain derision.

'You ever seen a dead sparrow?'

'I've shot 'em with my BB gun when I was young.'

'I mean just dead. Natural causes. Old age.'

'No. Come to think of it, I haven't.'

'There you are!'

The Humdinger got him all set to buy another BB gun and make catapults to slaughter sparrows.

'Half a dozen a day will do. But you have to roast the whole bird. Guts and all.'

'Feathers?'

'Feathers, too.'

Disneyland went on a sparrow diet. His mother was waiting for the Humdinger one day outside the blue gates to have a piece of him.

'She was just as silly,' he said contentedly as he opened a re-labelled can in the Home Beautiful. 'I convinced her the whole thing was ridge! She went away thinking up recipes, how to get some variety into roast sparrow. I oughta been a salesman.'

The sparrow diet didn't stop until Disneyland's father got out of Long Bay gaol. He threw his first sparrow meal out into the street; plates, saucepans, the lot. He had been in for desertion and non-payment of maintenance. How he could remedy this in gaol was not explained. They never saw him again.

The whole shift followed the Humdinger's lead. They had Disneyland jumping off ladders on their promises to catch him, and when they let him thud to the ground said, 'Never trust anyone.' Or, 'Put your hands down by your side', then hit him in the belly. 'Don't trust a living soul,' they said piously and went away laughing. Disneyland seemed to accept it all as part of being at work. He did nothing else.

But it was fatal to be kind to him. When the Samurai went out of his way to help him with a little plant knowledge, Disneyland rubbished him. He thought he had come across someone weaker than himself. The Humdinger smiled as if to say, 'It's no use pitying this one', and persuaded Disneyland that the girls would go for him if he had a scar.

'Over the eyebrow, I think. Yes. Just work a blade over the skin there and before it heals up, open it again. Keep at it and you'll get a nice fat scar. Show the girls you've been in a few fights. They like that.'

Next day he came in with a great dressing over his eye, borrowed an old razor blade and opened up the two-inch cut. 'It doesn't hurt a bit,' he said and they believed him.

A MENTAL SYRUP   Ambrose was a different type of fool. Aware of more of the world but his failing was that he took as gospel the first thing he was told. He had been carefully nurtured in religious surroundings and never got over it. Some sanctified joker persuaded him to stand for election as leader of his church youth group and since no one else wanted the post, Ambrose got it. After that, he saw all situations as basic repetitions of church youth situations. He wouldn't tell a lie himself, but believed every one he heard. There were no corrections of first impressions with Ambrose.

Every newspaper comment, every joke and leg-pull were alike God's truth to him. One of the secrets of his certainty and composure was to be found in his habit of taking the tone of voice of the person talking to him as the substance of what was said. The Humdinger and even the Two Pot Screamer could be talking earnestly and kindly to him and interlarding their normal speech with the grossest insults: Ambrose heard the tone of voice, not the words.

He'd gone up to Surfers' Paradise with a few friends and their girls and came back married to one of the girls. The prisoners laughed at him.

'Why didn't you just find her, feel her and forget her?'

'She said she loved me.'

They roared.

When the Humdinger asked him one day, 'Should I be honest?' he replied, 'Yes.'

'Wait for it. I haven't finished,' said the Dinger. 'Now take my case. I'm twenty-nine and have two brothers—one in the Liberal Party and one serving six years for rape and arson. My sister Peg is on the streets and Dad lives off her earnings. Mum is pregnant by the boarder and because of this Dad won't marry her. Last night I got engaged to an ex-prostitute and I wish to be fair to her: should I tell her about my brother in the Liberal Party?'

'Well,' said Ambrose, 'I'll have to think it over. Would you be offended if I brought this up at our prayer meeting on Thursday?'

'Not at all!' said Humdinger joyfully. 'Bring it up all over the place.'

'Thanks. I will.'

'Now I know what Christian charity means.' He even had the effrontery to shake Ambrose's hand. The boy blushed with pleasure and pride.

Ambrose was puzzled. The Two Pot Screamer seemed to hang round him for no reason. Two Pot was listening for any gems of conversation Ambrose might drop, so that he could retail them happily to the boys in exchange for the ready cash of popularity.

Ambrose concluded he was queer. He went over to him one day and said, 'You hang round me too much. I think you're a homosexual.' He walked away. Two Pot was amazed and followed him back to the plant lab where Ambrose was stationed. This time he said it in front of others.

'Keep away from me, homosexual!' Two Pot kept away.

Later, Ambrose's ability to hold first impressions blossomed strangely. After he had first been persuaded to go to the Home Beautiful he appeared to go without hesitation or doubt that this might conflict with his church youth ideas. He seemed to hold both things—the church and the Home Beautiful—side by side in his mind in such a way that they didn't quarrel. There was no sort of correspondence between the ideas that settled in his mind: they floated in a mental syrup that isolated them from each other.

A SUITABLE CASE FOR TREATMENT 'The Glass Canoe's studying again.' Woodpecker was keen to keep the talk going in the drink hut.

'Hope it doesn't bring on another brainstorm,' said Angry Ant.

'They were packing the shits when he went off his head in the control room last time,' said Woodpecker. 'He's strong enough at any time, but he raced out on the plant swinging by his hands from some of the RSJs two hundred feet in the air.'

'I'd give my right hand to be able to do the things he can do when he's off his head,' said Congo Kid earnestly.

'He's left-handed,' explained the Ant to the Great White Father, who nodded to them both, watching the play of their tiny emotions across their faces, noting the progress the beer made in the flush of their skins and the merciful glaze of their eyes.

'You can talk to him about it, I'll say that for him,' said the Ant. 'Once you get him started he'll talk about himself all day.'

The Great White Father spoke. 'You never know what a word will do to him. He may pass it off or it may bunch up his guts and open his face like a hand and expand his heart and contract his muscles and the next thing you know he's wandering from girder to girder up in the structure like an ape. Or punching the shit out of you down here at ground level.' He still seemed to hear the sound of the Glass Canoe's voice as he was led away last time. Coming from his deep, powerful, protuberant, immensely resonant guts, that voice had a bone-jarring quality; the sound of it carried like the crack of a falling tree. There was a grandeur in his aimless violence, as if the man inside him that broke loose at such times was a hero whose nature it was to attempt the mightiest tasks.

And yet this same man, when the Father had gone to visit him, was flabby from sedatives, sexual indulgence and professional sympathy; he had this foldy neck and his collar too small; he was clean round the mouth but a bit wet. And they said he was better.

AN OBLIGING LAD Ambrose walked back to the cracker. A group of maintenance men brought in on contract to keep establishment figures down worked round the base of a huge tall thing. Was it the reactor? He thought it was.

'Hey son! You're an operator. We can't do this job with that valve turned on. Turn it off for us, son.'

'OK.' He closed the valve they pointed to. They were older than Ambrose. You don't just say no when people ask you to help them. That's like passing by on the other side.

It was the feed valve. The plant had just got to its feet. Inside the control room things had been going well. The panel room was clear. Humdinger was gazing, in a pleasant trance, at the feed instrument. Flow steady, pump pressure OK. Suddenly the flow pen slid gracefully sideways to nil. No flow. The alarm sounded. What? He slammed the emergency steam handle over and yelled for a man to go out and see if there was trouble at the feed valve. The automatic instrument was no good if the block valve had been shut.

Blue Hills ran out to investigate—despite their hatred of the company men ran in emergencies—and opened the block valve Ambrose had shut.

'You better come in. Don't touch anything here.'

'They wanted it shut.'

'Did one of our blokes tell you to do that? A foreman or someone? Was it Slackie?' then he remembered Slackie had gone. He jumped before he was pushed. One of the new mountains of ore in the west had swallowed him. But he hadn't got away from foreigners.

'No, those men with the tools.'

Blue Hills shook his head. The kid was an idiot.

'They wanted it shut.'

'Tell 'em they can't have it shut.'

'I couldn't do that.'

'Don't you know what valve that was? You just shut the rotten place down.'

Ambrose couldn't understand why everyone abused him. How could grown men ask you to do something wrong? He went inside to have a nervous pee. The trough was all over purple.

A MAN FOR ALL SEASONS The qualities of manager and worker were listed in a company manual. Far Away Places found a copy of this blueprint just before the Brown Snake lost it, and made sure the Glass Canoe got it. He had no defences against his own mind and the personal interpretations he put on the comparisons shown in the list:

MANAGER	WORKER
extrovert	introvert
cordial	reserved
gregarious	prefers own company
likes people	likes technical work
interested in people	interested in mechanisms, ideas
likes business, costs, profit and loss and practice	likes the sciences, mathematics, literature and principles
gets many things done	gets intricate things done
synthesizes	analyses
is fast, intuitive	slow, methodical
is a leader	is independent, self-sufficient
is inductive	is deductive
has the competitive spirit	wants to live and let live
bold and courageous	modest and retiring
noisy and aggressive	quiet and restrained
tough	vulnerable
impulsive	intellectual
vigorous	meditative
opinionated	broadminded
intolerant	tolerant
determined and impatient	adaptable and patient
enterprising, practical	conservative, idealistic

He looked down at his hands. They frowned at him. Poor Glass Canoe. Sometimes he thought he was a natural manager; sometimes he envied the qualities of the worker. He picked out combinations of qualities he liked. Next day the combinations were different. Most often he picked out as his own the greater part of both lists; he was modest and bold, impulsive and intellectual, aggressive and restrained, inductive and deductive, enterprising and idealistic. Yet he was uneasy. This was dishonest, trying to be on both sides. He should be on one side or the other. That's how it was on the list.

In his worst moments he was so tangled none of the words on the list fitted him. I got hold of it months later in an open locker. One that had become vacant suddenly.

NO COMPO From his window the Wandering Jew noticed Herman the German tramping through the blue gates, his left hand in bandages. He was late. Luxaflex too, from between venetian slats, saw the bandaged hand and checked the time. The Brown Snake saw it and rang the Union delegate for information. Oliver Twist, the Brown Snake's lodge brother, promised to find out why Herman's hand was bandaged. He rang back five minutes later.

'Herman's got something wrong with the bones of his finger.'

'Did he do it on the job?'

'Pinched a finger between two pipes.'

'That's not a disease. Did he notify it?'

'Herman's a hero. He doesn't notify a little thing like that, the boys would never let him forget it.'

'Is it serious?'

'The finger's off.'

'All of it?'

'Right up to the hand. Three joints.'

'Can he do his work?'

'He can do ten men's work.'

'But he didn't fill the papers in, eh?'

THE BIG BANG THEORY That night, near nine o'clock, the Volga Boatman hid the boat and ran to the Home Beautiful with alarming news.

'Going to raid us? What sort of raid?' asked the Great White Father mildly. He was sprawled in a chair, his legs taking up the room of half a dozen.

'It's on now!' said Volga wildly. 'They're patrolling the river. No one can come in.'

'But they're not actually attacking us. Is that it?' asked the leader of the revels.

'No, they don't know where to start.' Calmed by his leader's example.

'Then they'll have a roll call on the plants shortly. We'll just leave one at a time, those of us on duty. The rest carry on as usual. I've fixed up a ski lift. Our emergency exit.'

No one took him seriously till they got to the river bank. When he pulled on a rope attached underwater to an anchor, he brought to light two strands of cable reaching an anchor point on the other bank, and from behind a mangrove-tree nearby, a windlass and a pair of water skis. All took cover as the security patrol passed in a skiff powered by an outboard motor. When it was gone, they sped across the river one by one, the geared windlass pulled just fast enough to keep them afloat.

The patrol came back to investigate when the skiers' bow waves caught up with them, but with the rope dropped on the river bottom they found nothing.

'What do you think of it?' asked the Great White Father of the few who remained to keep the Home Beautiful going, and didn't wait for an answer. 'Let's have another beer,' he suggested. They delicately agreed.

'Whose turn to be barman?' asked the Volga Boatman aggressively. He was a little ashamed of his earlier panic.

'There was a young feller in the Nazareth branch of the Carpenters' and Joiners' Union once washed his friends' feet,' said the Great White Father. 'I think I can pull you jokers a beer. Where's the opener?'

When the beer was doing its good work, he sat back and prophesied.

'Their blasted operations would go phut! without the relief from boredom that our Home gives us. I've got a good mind to shut down for a few days and see how they like it.'

They protested bitterly.

'The whole place'd stop if the Home Beautiful stops.'

'That's what they're trying to do.'

'What they expect is eight hours a day from us, walking round pumps, watching pressures, doing all sorts of useless things. If only they'd get it in their heads that when we take it easy, things couldn't be better. The other day I saw an ad in a magazine—there was a panel room in a big refinery in some emerging country. The men were allowed to read—there was a bar of books, the operators were alert, they had a radio and a TV in the amenities.'

'What they need here,' said a worker slumped in a corner, 'is a real emergency. Something to go bang. Then they'd see which side their bread's buttered.' He was from a plant not likely to have bangs.

'Not so much of this bang business. I'm on the cracker; it could go bang any time,' said the Humdinger, digging Blue Hills in the ribs. Blue was lonely and had come for a beer. He wouldn't touch the girls. He had a wife at home. He loved her, he said once in front of other prisoners. He was never silly enough to say it again.

'I'll stay on the wharf,' said the Plover Lover. 'Safest place. Always go over the side if something happens.'

IT'S ONLY BLOOD 'Don't you worry, my fine boyos!' yelled the Great White Father in great glee. 'Somewhere in the world there's a big bang with our name on it. Dig as deep as you like, twist and turn like eels or greasy pigs, it'll chase us to earth. Boom. Little clouds of radioactive dust. But don't worry—it's a good clean death if it takes you squarely. You get the package deal—death, cremation and your ashes scattered over Sydney. All in one hit. Whatever life you've had up to now has been on the house. None of you paid to get here. It's only one life you lose. One death. No more. Blood's only blood. The human race doesn't stop 'cause you stop.'

Many there were who feared when they heard this speech and hid themselves. One such was Blue Hills who went home straightaway, refused his wife's offer of solace in bed—this was the way her conscience took her after her imaginary lovers had had their daily helping of love with her: she was lonely for sex, but it had to be more interesting than Blue Hills—and had nightmares all night about huge dragon-shaped missiles flying over thousands of miles of empty Australia to drop at last right on the refinery and Blue Hills. The thought of one dropping on to his own head, the nagging doubt whether he would feel pain before it killed him and if so, how much, these fine conjectures gave him the hot and cold sweats and made his wife wonder if she had been right in not insisting on twin beds, although when she got right down to it and remembered the lusty lover she imagined climbing through her window one fine day and the space he needed to do a proper job on her, she knew a double bed was best. For months after, Blue Hills looked up warily every time he went out into the open air. Daytime was the worst.

'Look, we're flooded with light from that damn sun and there's no roof on the world. They're up there. They'll get us for sure. They can't miss!' Sometimes he refused to go out.

One of the few who smiled at the threat of bangs was Cheddar Cheese. The Great White Father noticed this smile as it peeped from behind a blue and gold can.

'Hey, Cheddar, did you get twenty dollars a pint for your blood?'

'No, man.'

'Price too stiff?'

'I got twenty-five. Boy, I can choof out a pint a week sometimes. I've got it made.'

'Hard way to make a dollar.'

'Easy. It's only blood.'

'Only blood! Why can't you get them to fix you? So your blood won't be rotten.'

'What? And lose twenty-five dollars a throw?'

'What are they researching?'

'How to fix my blood.'

'Hope they find a cure for it, anyway, Cheddar.'

'You do, do you? What about my twenty-five?'

'I don't know, Cheddar. All my instincts tell me to get up and address the multitude. But I don't know what to say. Twenty-five dollars or good blood. No. I know what to say all right, but it would hurt your feelings.'

'I'll go away then and make it easy for you.'

'If I say it I'll say it to you, not behind your back. No matter what you say, I still hope they fix you up.'

'Well, that's nice and sentimental. You can give me a big kiss if you like.' Knowing he was going to die gave him the guts to stand up to anyone.

'Drink your beer, Cheddar.'

'I will. And I'll take one in later to the Sleeping Princess. She likes a nice little gesture.'

'She fell asleep on me last time,' said Humdinger. 'She didn't even notice my little gesture.' It was his turn. He went in. He couldn't make up his mind if he liked to look at her face or her back. He spent his half-hour spinning her round like a top.

SOMETHING FOOLISH In bad weather the Volga Boatman still rowed his little skiff across the river Eel, carrying miserable freight to the Home Beautiful for the blessing of the body and the satisfaction of the flesh. The Great White Father was there to receive them as they stumbled wet from rain, river and dripping mangroves.

Ambrose had been snared into painting the door of the bed hut. The Great White Father in his infinite wisdom had decided to give Ambrose some little foolish action to remember his Puroil youth by, and painting the door in the rain was foolish enough.

'Never forget that the man who puts most into the job gets the most out of it. The man working for a crust should be docile, content with low wages, poverty and a poor education, exhausted every day after hard toil and grateful to his employer. Promotion is the prize for hard work, energy, competence, enthusiasm, self-sacrifice and getting your nose brown up the foreman's arse. The rain's from the south, here's a pot of paint and it's for the good of all. Go to it.'

He settled back with another can while Ambrose, who didn't see anything incongruous in painting in the rain at three in the morning, lurched outside. You would have had to tell Ambrose particularly and carefully that painting in the rain was unusual before he began to think so. Three in the morning...

So Ambrose painted the door in the rain before he took another turn at the warm delights inside. He painted faithfully but not well. The light was understandably bad but he didn't appeal against it.

He didn't even ask what those two men were doing standing in the rain outside the bed hut, leaning up against the corrugated-iron wall. The Great White Father knew the force for Ambrose of the feeling that he was doing his bit for the common good, and let him have his head. When his turn came and Never on Sunday was on, he would approach her holding his head erect like a sturdy workman who has done a good job, bent on enjoying her facilities with a good conscience.

He wouldn't have made head or tail of her recital of domestic plans. 'Another yard of carpet,' she'd say, or linoleum, or new cupboards, or shoes for the kids, or a bedroom suite. Ambrose didn't think about what a married woman was doing at the Home Beautiful. For an extra dollar she'd tell his horoscope by the way it felt.

8
MATES

SHE'LL BE RIGHT, MATE The cracker was up again, with waxy distillate pouring in one end and high-grade gasoline flowing from the other; a seven-hundred-ton inventory of catalyst being circulated to reactor and stripper then regenerated merrily in the regenerator fire and the carbon-monoxide from the regeneration process burned in the twin power-recovery boilers and driving turbo-expanders to provide air for the regenerator and for the boilers. After four hours one of the boiler tubes ruptured, putting water into the fire space. The water expanded to steam, the header pressure rose like a rocket, the turbines had to be manually tripped before they blew to pieces, and the plant crashed. Black catalyst through the system, through the turbines—blades and bearings—on the ground, over the suburbs, everywhere.

They'd had to rush several of the boiler tube tests the week before; the tests seemed to bank up on to Saturday morning, the experts took their weekend off and the only engineer left had to take his wife shopping. The remaining tests were cancelled.

'She'll be right,' was the controller's answer to the Samurai's questions. 'They're engineers, we're not. You don't have to worry. Just start her up and collect your pay at the end of the week.'

Three days later the boiler tubes had cooled; two days after that the manways were off and the boiler tube bundles down on the deck. Another two days brought a report from the metallurgists: the wrong metal. The tubes were stacked to one side to wait for the scrap merchant and new tubes ordered.

This was one crash they couldn't pin on the operators.

WHERE THE WOMEN SAY YES Dadda was in the control room when the boiler tube ruptured; he was the first to see the header pressure rising and the first to press the cancelling buttons on the high speed alarms of the turbo-expanders. He got out of the way, of course, when the panic started: he had a few other matters to think of.

His wife had been changing her pants at work and Dadda found out. He cursed her and the man who had taken his place in her body, and cursed, too, the silence of all the people at the office where she worked. Surely enough people knew about it for someone to spare a phone call and tip him off months ago. The pain was no less if it was deferred. He only intended to go and talk to both of them, but his wife was very nasty about him finding out and one thing led to another; he found himself on a footpath around five o'clock in a back lane starting to swap a few excited punches with the man—who was bigger than Dadda and better dressed—when his wife stepped in to help the other man and collected Dadda's elbow on the side of the head and went down in a heap. Her head hit the edge of the gutter and that was that.

As the concrete stopped the fall of her body, her pretty dress fell above her waist and the two males stood looking down at the root cause of their differences.

The other man got very worried, he was only along for the ride. I never intended to let it go on so long, he said. I've got my wife to think of and the kids. What about your job, too? asked Dadda, who despised him for not loving her. Yes, my job too, the man said, the company doesn't like anyone to give the place a bad name. Listen, the man said, how about we both shut up and beat it? It wasn't your fault and there's no marks on her. They can ask us both questions, but we were never here. Were we? Dadda was so miserable by this time that he said no, we weren't here. They both left, going different ways and the woman had only stray dogs for company till a milkman found her. By then she had been assaulted by a middle-aged bachelor shy of live girls.

Dadda made his way to the Home Beautiful, where the Great White Father was putting down stone paths and garden borders and better drains for the various types of liquid effluent from the huts.

'I'll give you a hand,' said Dadda.

'If you feel like it,' said the Great White Father. 'But don't wear yourself out. We want you for the talent quest up at the pub tonight.'

'What's it worth?'

'Two hundred dollars and the boys'll be backing you to win. How's the cracker plant? Right down?'

'The works. See the smoke? We put the rest of the refinery down, too. Boilers and all.'

'Smoke, yes, and catalyst.'

'Lucky the wind was south-east. Lucky for you.'

It was a break, getting away from that stinking place to the Home Beautiful where any little thing you did was for yourself and the boys, and you could see it. It wasn't for some rich bastards the other side of the world. And the only women in the place always said Yes. As he walked inside, the sun lowered itself heavily on to its western bed.

The police came for Dadda later that night. The usual phone call was made from the guardhouse and every plant alerted. Police were not allowed past the gate, but the bun-truck was sent down to the cracker for Dadda.

The driver had a few cups of tea while he waited in the unproductive silence for the prisoners to come back from every part of the plant where it was likely a man would hide. No Dadda. The driver left and reported back; various foremen and controllers and even Suction Heads came down, but not even a great increase in supervision made any difference to the job of finding Dadda.

A man detached himself from a work party shutting valves, darted down over the nearest clay embankment and was unsighted for an hour. He headed for the river.

A CONTRAST Two men who spoke no English were working high up on the tenth landing of the prototype vertical boiler when the tube burst. They went over the side carrying a heavy metal tool-box between them. They didn't touch the rungs of the vertical ladders on the way down and when their four feet hit the concrete apron at ground level they ran, the box between them, for several hundred feet. The rumbling stopped. They broke step and walked, looking back. The rumbling and shaking started again, soot, smoke and flame spread heavily from the stack, and they ran on. They headed for the river and were never seen again. Their sponsors, an Italian construction company, waited vainly for them to come back and pay off their passage money plus the debt they owed for the privilege of working, but in the end had to take their names off the books.

Rumours of a primitive hut in another part of the mangroves sometimes filtered through to the pleasant atmosphere of the Home Beautiful, but as the reports were brought by men dazed and wandering in drink, no one took notice.

By contrast the Count, an Englishman of impeccable and ridiculous appearance, was still standing on the third landing taking pressure-tapping readings while the boiler rocked and rumbled and its guts fell down inside. An hour later, when all was still and everything going had been tripped out, he was collecting samples of flue gas from the stack and giving it the standard Orsat test for carbon-dioxide, carbon-monoxide and oxygen. He was surprised at the high oxygen content and rushed in to the foreman with the test results as if he'd made a discovery.

'What do you want? A Nobel prize? Get out, you stupid bastard,' said Captain Bligh. 'Do you have to see a notice on the board before you know it's crashed?'

LEADERS OF THE COUNTRY The Glass Canoe was still bent over plant manuals and flow diagrams up till the time of the latest crash. He seemed to be bewildered in the days following the break in Puroil profits, and when it was known the boiler tubes were made of the wrong metal he didn't seem able to take it in. As a relief to his feelings he took to long bouts of talking, with and without audience. The other prisoners would move near him now and then to see what he was talking about, but there never seemed to be any subject to his monologue.

'There's no need for this sort of thing; these men are trained for years, they know more than us, they're bent over books and calculus and things we've never heard of while we're out cat-shagging around and learning to get on the piss and even back in infants' school they start to get training to be leaders of the country. If you ever think you can do better than qualified men, I'll warn you: don't. Things they do always have a reason behind them otherwise why are they the bosses? They wouldn't be in that position if they were nongs like us. Their position deserves all the respect we can give them and if we co-operate and do our part properly and don't let the side down, the plant'll go for years and years like they told us. What right have we got to stand up and say they don't know what they're doing?...' And so on.

'He told us he was hypermanic when he got back from hospital: I reckon he's hypercomic.'

'I don't see how a big man like that can have such a small heart: he'll get down and lick their boots if he goes on like this,' said Oliver Twist when he had listened in to the Glass Canoe. It would make a good story to tell the Brown Snake.

'And while we're standing here rubbishing the Glass Canoe, the Beautiful Twinkling Star is outside doing his own work and four others',' said the Samurai, who drew on his work gloves and tramped outside, his valve-key swinging at his side like a six-gun. No one followed.

A FAVOURITE POSITION After losing forty tons of catalyst out the vents and over the rest of the equipment, and sucking out six hundred tons along the unloading line to the hopper, there was still sixty tons below the air inflow spider—15 to 50 micron silica-alumina dust. After three days the regenerator had cooled enough to unbolt the manway door. They sent the men in with stiff brooms to push the catalyst down the vacuum line. The men put the brooms in the dust, pulled them out. Puffs of flame, and the bristles were gone. A day later the welders had made up long rakes, with two-inch plates at the business end. Enough to push a cupful at a time. 'Bad workmen always blame their tools,' they were told when they complained. Two more days it took to get the latest means of clearing catalyst—the long-handled shovel and its mate the short-handled shovel. Vacuum hoses cost too much money. It was better to waste a week's production. After all, the Wandering Jew could sign only for 200 dollars' expenditure. Any more had to be referred to Europe.

When a few of the health- and future-conscious narks among the prisoners wondered aloud what sort of masks they were going to use, it was their own hardy and ignorant mates who gave the thumbs-down sign. In the face of men saying What's the matter with you? Worried about a little bit of dust? When can we get some men instead of these old women? the narks kept quiet and didn't press for masks. They objected a little to the heat inside the huge vessel until the same sort of mates said What's a few degrees of temperature? But even the self-confessed hardy prisoners drew back from the fierce heat when the first foot of catalyst was taken off the top of the heap. The following day they came to work with brown faces. Burn scabs. They asked Puroil for masks. The Python said 'You did it without masks before. You don't need masks.'

On the Samurai's shift they had been shovelling four days and it was the end of night shift. The Sumpsucker, who had never had to shovel dust and never had the vacuum line block and blow it all back in his face and felt sneakingly uncomfortable about this, and thankful too, leaned in at the open manway and said, 'OK. You can go down at three.' This was his bonus. There was a pretty picture below as the Samurai and two others froze in silence, covered in fine grey dust which filled their ears, penetrated boots and clothes, entered the nose and eyes and was spat out for days in their mucus.

They went down gratefully on rag-covered concrete in the darkened locker-room. The Samurai found himself a thick cardboard carton, collapsed it flat, piled a few dirty overalls on it for a mattress and had three hours in the land somewhere between sleep and waking. His heavy boots waggled awkwardly on the ends of his legs while the lay on his back, his favourite position, so he turned on his side in the narrow space between the rows of lockers. His back was turned on Blue Hills, his face towards the kicked-in, dented bottoms of the thin iron lockers. Like sleeping in a gutter.

A DREAM OF PRISONERS The Sorcerer's Apprentice beckoned him in to her flat. This was no sordid hut with nail-holes peeping in corrugated-iron walls: she lived well, her body was clean and smooth. The fingerprints of the men who had handled her body were not visible as they are on the skins of some prostitutes; rather her skin seemed to have absorbed them, perhaps as quicksands absorb what is thrown on them and appear smooth and innocent afterwards. She sat on her divan naked and laughed at him for some reason. Why should she look innocent and untouched and still laugh? Mockingly. She opened her mouth wide in laughter, her tongue writhed in her mouth, and presently it turned into a thumb and poked out at him. The thumb itself moved and jerked: it was a man's thumb, the skin stained and cracked, the thumbnail dirty. He noticed he was now naked and she was sitting in a live chair, which moved ceaselessly under and around her: the legs were live legs, the arms live arms, the back a human back, the seat two great convex buttocks.

A seven-foot blue book stood against a wall. He opened it, it was a door. He ran from there, grabbing his clothes as he went and trying to put them on. She chased him out into the gently undulating dairy country that surrounded her flat, which now stood by itself, one room in the countryside, while he tried desperately to dress. Out of sight of the house now, she was gone and he was lost somewhere in the breasty hills.

He was a boy again. Animals ran from him. The wooden sword he was using to behead cats and dogs in the fields was running red with blood. It wasn't human blood, he knew that; he was happy he hadn't broken the law forbidding the killing of humans. As if to approve his opinion, a great crowd of domestic animals attacked a sick man who had been lying in bed in one of the valleys between two suggestive hills, and the boy Samurai had great pleasure wading through the blood of these savage beasts to save his fellow man. In his frenzy he cut and slew and hacked until the last animal—a large tortoise-shell cat with expressionless eyes—was in small pieces and scattered over a wide area.

The man he saved was full of sores on every visible patch of skin, but instead of thanking him he abused him for being unkind to dumb animals. The boy Samurai protested that he had saved him from dogs and cats, but the man shouted the dog is man's best friend and cats never attack unless provoked. The boy Samurai had nothing in his vocabulary of life experience to answer this, and the thought came into his mind that he should seek forgiveness and possibly kneel down and kiss the sores of this poor man, when suddenly he became his own self—no longer a boy—and said to himself in a rage, Have I become a leper-licker?

Still holding his bloodstained sword in his hand he left the leper on the bed and tramped across the fields towards the nearest town. He went into the bar of a pub, hiding his bloodstained sword in the belt of his trousers, and accidentally knocked and spilled the beer of a small ginger man standing next to him. The man punched him about the body—he couldn't reach the Samurai's head and face—but he could not return the blows, for his assailant was smaller and he would never fight a smaller man. Finally the man struck his hand on the Samurai's sword and went away cursing and sucking his thumb, which moved and jerked; the skin stained and cracked, the thumbnail dirty.

Suddenly he was walking through the main square beside the Puroil Termitary block. Men were saying the Samurai hasn't been a superintendent for long, then presently he was in the centre of a hollow square, white-shirted clerks were lowering the Puroil flag and the Wandering Jew stepped up to him and stripped from him the insignia of his office—one biro pen, one white shirt, one dark tie, one pair of good trousers and the rest—and drummed him out of the blue gates dressed only in his jockstrap and socks, while a choir of typists and punched-card operators sang hauntingly *Naked I came into the world and naked I depart.* The guards on the gate peered into both jockstrap and socks for contraband.

HANG THE EXPENSE The Samurai slept soundly for the last two hours of his bonus break, and when he woke at six there was nothing to do but a little cleaning and to listen to a story of a recent disaster at another refinery. Some clowns had wired up a compressor the wrong way: it started, but couldn't be stopped. It was comforting to hear of disasters elsewhere. Several foremen were wandering about outside with work gloves on, but it was the end of seven days of night shift and the Samurai was too tired to make an issue of it, although they were undoubtedly doing operators' work.

When the day shift came on, one man went inside to the locker-room and went straight down and in five minutes was fast asleep in his good clothes. He'd been to a wedding and had celebrated all night. Some of the offgoing sleepers shook their heads. Fancy crashing in your good clothes!

PROTECTIVE CUSTODY Dadda turned up that morning; he didn't run a place in the talent quest, being a little down in the mouth, and the boys had kept him full in the Home Beautiful for ten days to hide him from the police, but he broke away, swam the oily, stinking river Eel and stumbled a mile up to the blue gates to ring off. His clothes were nearly dry then, but the river left them darker.

Pixie, seeing him bundy off, called the police. They found him in the cark park, sitting in his car, too stewed to drive.

THE PLOVER-LOVER A few hours after the crash-down of the refinery, a tanker in the Pacific took a radio re-direction to Sydney. It was low in the water with a full load of gasoline for a New Zealand refinery to bolster stocks during a planned shutdown. Several days later it was in Puroil's deepwater terminal to spew out its gasoline. Someone somewhere in the Puroil machine wanted the product to reach the market.

For some reason the pipeline to the refinery was not used for all the gasoline, some was barged up-river from terminal to wharf.

Loosehead was sent down from the cracker for a day's exile—day began at 2300 hours—and it was as an exile that he spent his eight hours there. He chatted amiably to the Plover-Lover who did the work. There were often plover on the clay flats, over the swampy areas. He preferred plover to seagulls when he made a stew.

'You're Polish, aren't you?' Loosehead asked. He was hanging over the short section of railing near the gantry which lifted up the fat heavy hoses from the barge decks. The Plover-Lover was opening and closing valves, getting ready to hook up. The river, innocent in darkness, was a picture of flickering surfaces, bright water and the slash of lights.

'I was,' he replied, grunting as he lifted the end of the hose. It was so heavy he could move it only a foot at a time. Loosehead watched, fascinated.

'What d'you mean? You a New Australian now?' There was no derision in his voice, only in the words.

'I have the papers. I am Australian.'

'Well, bugger me!' remarked Loosehead. He felt vaguely complimented. 'Hey, did I tell you the one about bricking the camel?'

The Plover-Lover grunted.

'No? Well, maybe you wouldn't get it anyway.'

The Plover-Lover knew the joke all right, but he had dropped a hose and coupling on his foot and had no spare breath to answer. He was wearing canvas shoes with rope soles. They made no sparks and didn't slip on oil as rubber boots slip, but they were not much chop when you dropped an eighty-pound weight on your instep. Loosehead laughed. Thinking of the camel-rider using two bricks on the camel's incentive.

'Remember the time we helped Volga get the beer in the boat at night and when we got back here to the wharf we passed it all up to a foreman standing there? We thought it was one of us.

And remember the time you went down in the rail truck to have a few hours' kip last year?' He laughed heartily, the sound carrying well across the black water of the river. Anonymous pairs under Clearwater Bridge stirred and peered anxiously about.

'And you woke up in the marshalling yards at Enmore on Good Friday morning and when they got you out on Easter Sunday your knuckles were down to the bone with knocking and all you could say was "Mess! Mess!" And the railway detectives agreed and said, "You're in a bloody mess, all right! Try and talk your way out of this!"'

He looked expectantly down at the Plover-Lover, waiting for answering laughter.

'It wasn't mess, it was Mass! I wanted to get to Mass. I always go to early Mass at Easter, like in the old country to St Lukaczewski's,' corrected the Plover-Lover.

'Well, Saint Lookawhisky didn't bail you out of that jam, the Samurai did, while the Puroil nobs were still arguing the toss about who was to go to the cop-shop. I was along with the Samurai; we went in my car and while I was waiting outside, this big copper came along and told me to move on. I'd been in the Home Beautiful and I was pretty right by then, so I up and told him to move along himself. And that mongrel copper hit me. Only once, but he hit me here'—indicating his lower ribs on the left side—'and I'll guarantee his fist went in about three feet. I couldn't speak for half an hour.'

The Plover-Lover started to heft the lower end of the hose; it was no use interrupting Loosehead and inviting disaster by getting him to work the gantry. He would have to run with the hose to get enough momentum to carry it over underneath the gantry. He would get up on the wharf and hook up himself. He started to run.

'Remember the time the Grey Goldfish opened the seacocks on Barge 56 by mistake and pumped the river up into tank 17? And the Whispering Baritone put up a yellow sign with big black letters: THINK! And next day the Great White Father added a word in big black letters to make it read: JUST THINK!' He chuckled. It was pleasant watching the lights on the river.

The Plover-Lover ran, came to the end of his rope, and sat

down. He came at it again and put all his Polish last-ditch courage into this run, for it was night shift and his stamina would soon give out. Loosehead thought to himself: he takes this seriously! The ex-Pole ran suddenly along the steel deck and triumphantly lugged the end of the hose over under the gantry. He gave a raucous cry of exultation even while his feet were slipping in the diesoline which came from the hose end and without interrupting his wild cry changed it subtly and with pure instinctual skill to one of alarm and then through the stages of alarm shaded his yell straight into terror. The black water closed over the sound but did not altogether cut it off: Loosehead heard it bubbling up from the depths. Each bubble that broke on the surface contained a fragment of yell.

'That steel sure is slippery,' remarked Loosehead when the Plover-Lover surfaced. 'Specially when it gets a bit of dieso on it.' He looked down for confirmation of his wisdom, but the Plover-Lover was struggling. Loosehead flipped over a length of rope which was looped on the rail and watched his mate climb up it on to the steel deck of the barge. The Plover-Lover shuddered when he followed the rope with his eye, up over the rail and down on the planking of the wharf where all that held it was Loosehead's large boot. If Loosehead had lifted his foot...The Plover-Lover climbed sadly up the iron ladder spiked into the turpentine poles and set about moving the barge downstream a little, for the hose wouldn't reach the connection. He slackened off the eastern rope from the bollard and re-tied it when he had another six feet. He came back along the wharf to the western rope. He slackened that off, but before he tied it again he had a thought.

'Hey, Loosehead!' and Loosehead had to smile at the cheerful voice coming from the soaking, clinging overalls. 'Remember the time you had to go and get a six-foot ladder to climb up on a rail truck and all you could find was a twelve-foot and you cut it in half with an oxy torch?'

'Sure. I remember,' said Loosehead with simple pleasure. 'And when they asked me why I said the other one was too big. And they had two ladders instead of one! When I told them they had a profit, the Good Shepherd didn't understand me.'

The more he chuckled and enjoyed this memory—which the Plover-Lover had felt sure would embarrass him—the more miserable the Plover-Lover became. As he turned back to the bollard Loosehead asked him, 'How did you get your name? Do you really go after the birds up on the clay flats?' He jerked a thumb in the direction of the land reclaimed from the mangroves but not yet sown with refinery plants. 'And cook them?'

But the Plover-Lover was too busy to answer. The barge had swung, unnoticed and silent, away from the wharf and the Plover-Lover was standing there with only another yard of rope to go before his end of the barge got away. Slowly the barge swung as he strained like Sandow to hold it back, bracing one foot against the ten-by-ten ironbark retaining plank.

As the last of the rope paid out and the barge went, he uttered a lost, despairing cry of 'Jesu!' with a Polish inflection and soft J and followed it into the black water.

When he surfaced, still holding the rope, Loosehead with commendable presence of mind threw him the rope with which he had accidentally saved him before and shouted to him to tie it to the rope he had. The Plover-Lover did this and handed himself back along this rope to the wharf. This time Loosehead fastened his end of the rope to the bollard. It was only a thin rope but it held till the Plover-Lover got a winch.

'You sure get into a lot of trouble,' said Loosehead. 'You ought to be like me. I don't do anything, so I can't make mistakes.'

As he watched the Plover-Lover depart in search of a winch, Loosehead said aloud to the bay and the distant lights, 'He's not afraid of the water, I'll say that for him. Wish I could spare him a bit more time, I'd teach him to swim for sure.'

A CHANGE OF COLOUR Before they started up, too many of the gratings were missing—not yet finished by the construction crews, and if finished, not yet erected—too many safety railings not installed on completed landings; the oil and gas guns on the top landing of the new boilers were so placed that when the prisoners removed them—under pressure, as they must—a forty-pound gun at head height and facing upwards nearly took the men over the hip-high railing one hundred feet in the air. Too many discrepancies existed between the safety posters papering the administration area and the actual conditions on the plant plot. Many valves, like the catalyst valves, were twenty feet in the air with no platform underneath, yet they required relays of four men with crowbars to open or close them. For want of a platform, men took up to eight hours to shut one valve.

There had been no bad accidents since the construction stage, but for some reason the men who worried about their own safety were shy of working the plant. Some, though, would climb out over the drop to an inaccessible valve, then come down and report it unsafe, though by their action in getting to it they demonstrated that it was accessible. That was all the proof the company required that they need do nothing about it.

The Good Shepherd took a risk by writing in his report book that the whole plant was unsafe in its present condition. Loosehead wandered in and read this. 'Six months behind in safety,' the Good Shepherd had written.

'Christ help him when the Python sees that,' said Loosehead, then wandered outside. He drifted by when Slug was being taken round by one of the faceless bosses and this man was having no difficulty getting the response he wanted from Slug: all he had to do was state his own opinion and wait for the echo.

The Samurai tailed these two in case a deal was being made. When he caught up, Slug, looking at a distant imaginary prospect of further promotion, said to the Samurai while the faceless one unsaw them both, 'Well, I think in the light of what this gentleman has said, the company will do all the necessary work we have asked for, so we can go ahead and start up now.'

The men had to threaten before they could get gratings installed, holes filled over hundred-foot drops, ladders to inaccessible valves or extensions to narrow firing platforms. If the company said it was safe, who was there to appeal to?

The Samurai said 'No.' The gentleman saw him then for the first time. 'Let the men look first at what's written in the instruction book.' Slug and the gentleman knew. They followed the well-known industrial relations principle that anything at all could be written in black and white under the noses of the prisoners, but the prisoners saw nothing and drew no conclusions until some agitator picked it up and waved it in front of their eyes and started to get angry.

The Samurai went back, taking the Slug with him, and in front of the dozen men he mustered showed Slug the Good Shepherd's instructions.

'There it is: Do nothing until that safety work is done.'

'No! That's right!' bleated the men. 'It's in the book!'

'Yes,' said the Slug, 'yes, I think that's best.' He blew with the strongest wind. 'We must get these safety jobs done first before we even attempt to start up.'

The plant was declared black. To protect himself, the Good Shepherd should not have written his instruction until after the plant had changed colour. It was better for all those above the rank of prisoner to appear to stick together and only to sanction a cease-work after they were forced to.

Loosehead gave the good old Samurai a friendly thump as he went his way, happy that the extra two feet of standing room and higher safety netting would be provided on the top firing platform before somebody took a dive.

THE CHRIST OF THE CRACKER Now Loosehead ambled on, one boot after the other. He climbed to the enclosure at the top of the polymerization plant and woke Bubbles, knowing he would be still asleep from the way his eyes looked when he came in the previous afternoon.

'Come on, Bubble-guts. Wakey, wakey.' Bubbles stirred, woke, roused himself, fell half asleep again, knocked his elbow on one of the empty drums of polymerization catalyst with which he had surrounded himself so that he couldn't be seen from the door; woke again with a start and a flurry, sprang to his feet still half in the horrors and scattered rags everywhere, looked down, fell down in a heap of ceramic balls, picked up armfuls of rags trying to hide them, found no place to hide them, and sank down again groaning.

'I'm crook. I'm crook. Crook. Christ, I'm crook,' he said with emphasis.

'Stay here another four hours, Bubbles, and you'll meet yourself coming on shift. You've been here twenty, stay for twenty-four.'

He couldn't leave him like this. 'What have you been doing to yourself, anyway?'

It took Bubbles a while to answer.

'I was in the pub at Cheapley. They told me about the haunted house. You know it?'

'Never heard of it.'

'I picked up this sheila, pretty old.'

'I thought you were fixed up with someone else's wife.'

'Yeah, but she was working last night. I'm in the pub, and this sheila—not real old, about sixty-five—she bets me I'm not game to take her to the haunted house.' Bubbles was twenty-seven.

'Was it haunted?'

'We get there—after she's sick in the car, but I don't worry about that on account of her age—she shows me to this old house with the windows broken and I go in. When I look round she's gone—turns out later she goes and hides in the car. Lucky I've got the keys on me.'

He took a deep breath and tenderly felt his side. 'I'm in there—it's dark as the insides of a cow—and I don't know whether to go on or go back—I feel this touch on my arm—"Darling," it screams, "you came!"—"I came," I said, "but I'm gone now!" But she fastened on to me. What with one thing and another I said OK, we get stuck into it on the floor and she was on!'

Loosehead let him rest before he went on. 'Go on, you're working me up, anyway.'

Bubbles went on grimly. In pain.

'Work? Work's the word. I didn't have to do anything. She did it all. She had this funny soft mouth—all loose—and there was something banging me on the hip. Whaling into me!' He rubbed it gently.

'This wet mouth was starting to give me the horrors—she kept sucking my tongue into it—and what with this thing hitting me on the side I tried to get away.'

'You must have been tanked,' said Loosehead.

'Pissed as forty arseholes,' admitted Bubbles. 'So I managed to get us to the door and open it and we got on the wooden veranda—it was a nightmare!—she must have been eighty if she was a day—no teeth—frightful!'

He shuddered violently. 'And she only had one leg—the other off above the knee—smacking me on the side Whack! Whack!—look at this!' He opened his overalls, displayed his hip.

'Black and blue from the stump—and I think I've ricked my neck trying to keep out of the way of those gums. Pecking at me like an emu! My head going from side to side to make her miss!'

Loosehead sighed. These young fellers.

'Better stay here the other four, Bubbles.' He left him. He'd gone a few steps down from the top floor and the story was gone from his head. His mind was always fresh. Nothing burdened him long. The Beautiful Twinkling Star was coming up the stairs fast. Even in a crashdown he worked as hard as he was allowed.

'Don't go up there,' said Loosehead calmly.

'What's the matter?'

'Something you shouldn't see. There's a bloke up there, you might report him.'

'Me? Report a man?' The Beautiful Twinkling Star was hurt. He would do the man's work, get rags for him to sleep on, but never report him to prison authorities.

'You would if you did your duty. The best way out is not to see him.'

'Is there something I can do?' Making to go up. Loosehead barred his way.

'Self-inflicted.' Significantly. The Beautiful Twinkling Star nodded wisely, forgivingly. An industrial saint. He took his own goodness seriously and was almost as understanding of his fellow-prisoners' weaknesses as the prisoners themselves. Loosehead thought to himself, irreverently, The Christ of the Cracker.

'I'll keep people away,' said Loosehead, 'or it might be outski for him.'

'God forgive him,' said the Beautiful Twinkling Star, with a look of prayer about him.

'He'll forgive himself, when he's better,' said Loosehead. 'No need to go dobbing him in to the Almighty.'

A GENTLE PUSH The Glass Canoe was the only man ever to report that he hit another car in the car park. Confessing belligerently. He wasn't afraid to face the truth of what he'd done. Now he was happy. He always knew when he was happy. The divisions between his moods were too marked to be missed.

If there were no happiness, it would be necessary to create it. It was good to have thoughts with a little depth to them. A man stopped feeling like a prisoner for a few seconds when he got a good thought floating through his head. Where do thoughts come from? Are they merely the mind manipulating the stock of words that a few years of life, listening and reading have pumped into your head?

His fears, his inabilities, his God-given incapacities encased him in an ever-hardening shell. The limits that originate within every man were conspiring to keep him a prisoner. Was there no way to break out of this shell that had grown round him since birth? True, it had been a protection at times, when he was unwell and unfit to cope with the persistent devils fighting and wrecking inside him, but when he felt better it always seemed to him this hard shell was a hindrance. He was isolated inside it. He could hardly hear or know what was going on outside. Often he longed to be without it, to feel, to mix—flesh to flesh—with his fellow men. In free communion. 'I want to be brothers with the whole world,' he said softly.

Yet when the generous mood passed, as it does with whole civilizations and empires as well as individuals, he wriggled his shoulders comfortably inside his tough, accustomed carapace and surveyed the world from a mere slit in his armour, a peephole, and felt safe.

The Elder Statesman was at his elbow.

'The men on the instrument panel need assistance. They should have approached their fellow shiftworkers. Instead, the four top-category men got together and saw the management by themselves. Instead of through the Union. The men don't like it.'

'Well,' said the Glass Canoe, sizing up the situation immediately, 'why not grab them by the throat and tell them?'

'Because that would look like coercion or intimidation. Standover tactics. We've got to slam them hard and have it look like kindness.' He laughed through tobacco-edged teeth.

There is no such thing as a joke, the Glass Canoe said to himself. When a word is uttered, someone is being fair dinkum about something, even if it's only about not being fair dinkum. That assistant's job would be a good one to go for.

The Elder Statesman moved on, searching the shelves of his mind for the next little capsule to place in the next pair of ears. He hadn't been stopped by the Volga Boatman's attempt at revenge. He couldn't change the way he was made. He was born a bastard and would die a bastard. The Glass Canoe heard him ask Canada Dry, 'Are there many workers get along to the businessmen's club? How much can a worker afford to lose on the poker machines? You can't hold your head up beside men in business who can afford to drop their hundred dollars a week, can you?' Then he moved off again. That was how he spent his day.

He had pushed the Glass Canoe away from shore, into the current. The rapids were still a long way off.

MAINSTREAM The Glass Canoe was shaken, though. The reference to the private deal with management had stirred him up, as it was meant to do, but the Elder Statesman's shot at Canada Dry about businessmen's clubs had penetrated down deep clefts in his confidence. He was not a member of that sort of club, but it was obvious he could and should be.

He looked up at the ceiling, closed his eyes in prayer and quoted:

The rich are more than mortal. What they do
Is precious, surrounded by an aura of worth
We do not understand. It is their due
To live up there, while we crawl on the earth.

He spoke quietly, his voice barely audible in the control room, but in his own head a voice of thunder.

'I'll write out a clear, concise statement of my aims, the amount of money I intend to get, the time it should take me, what I intend to give in return for the money, and a plan for getting it. Money is power. I'll read it aloud every day—morning and night—I'll see money in my mind's eye, then some day I'll see it in the bank.'

He spoke slowly as if he were receiving dictation from another mind.

'If I discipline myself, I will get what I want. Naturally, if I didn't have a wife and kids or if I had enough capital to start with, or a bit of pull in the right direction, things would be different. If I'd had a better education or times were more favourable. If other people understood me I might be able to get a job that would be more of a springboard to success than this one. If I could live my life over again I'd show everyone.'

His mind vomited up all the excuses he had ever used to keep him from action.

'No,' he said carefully, 'I must fight against this terrible lethargy that comes over me. Dreams are all right, but they won't buy the baby a new bib. It's time to get cracking. I'll write down the plan of my future achievements and read it aloud till I am burningly obsessed by it. Yes, obsessed. It's the only way to get to the top. I must know what I want and stand by it. I will not be deterred. I must not quit. No one is defeated until defeat has been accepted as reality. I'll develop an attractive personality by having a positive attitude, by being sincere, adaptable, prompt, tactful, courteous. With my emotions under control, just and fair to the workers, a pleasant voice and expression, tolerant, frank, with a sense of humour and a bigger vocabulary. Always showing myself to the best advantage. I must cultivate persistence, then the urge to escape poverty and hunger will stimulate my imagination into action. I must root out negative emotions like fear, jealousy, hatred, revenge, anger and replace them with love, sex, hope, faith, enthusiasm, loyalty, desire. I will organize my thinking. Successful men are always doing work they like. I must find the best sources of information, mix with other men who have good brains, read deeply and use my mind for good, not evil. I will become enthusiastic; nothing great was ever achieved without enthusiasm. My attention must be controlled, geared to the task in hand. I'll use the golden rule and opposition will fade away, I'll get willing cooperation, and happiness will prevail. Finally, I must remember certain principles. A good boss must be ruthless, not with his staff but with himself. He must be able to put aside the personal problems, ambitions and personalities of those around him and consider the company first. To stay in his position of authority the boss must be humble, capable of forgetting himself, capable of relinquishing friendships which may otherwise prove embarrassing.'

His voice was a booming sound inside him. It echoed through his whole hollow body.

Outside, a compressor surged, its waves of sound passing through the chests of everyone within a hundred yards of it, fluttering their internal organs. Sudden steam hammer in the 700-pound lines made noise like cannons in the operators' ears. The Glass Canoe dimly heard approaching, passing and fast-receding voices of those running to catch the emergent condition before it got out of hand. The spit and snort of steam traps. The high, tilting voice of a strangering young prisoner from otherwhere, a gravelled boot slip, fractional word, the solid air split with words and with the fractional distillation of words and human calls of terror and future pain. Emotions passed through the Glass Canoe like gases through a washing bath of reflux, and bubbled upwards, out to the great world beyond his mind. Men ran. The Glass Canoe sat huddled over the tiny dying fire of his own thoughts. The chemistry of his brain had changed, the mood of confidence and resolution was no longer possible. His religion of business success went backsliding.

'I feel sick,' he said. And he did, with weakness at the knees and various of the shaky ailments, certain orders of trembling, fainting at the stomach, aches within the head. He pulled a bottle of chlorodyne from his pocket and licked a dozen drops from his palm. 'The chlorodyne may help. At least a pleasant taste. If I relax completely and not use the eyes at all, the oppression of headache is gone. At such times it is easy to say: I shall think away this head; which is, however, full of bundles of words, of various sizes. Ah, there it is; the light around me hurting the eyes. This is disgusting. Filthy sickness. I am disgusting.'

The pain was high in the front of his head on the left-hand side; not a sharp pain but one that eased when he smiled and resumed its grip when his brow narrowed in concentration on himself. His voice, speaking of his sickness, was softer and strangely poetic. Brimming with sympathy.

'I remember when I was a boy crying myself to sleep after Dad had forbidden Mum to come and put me to sleep, he didn't want me to get any comfort and love for Mum. He asked me was that all I had against him. One other thing, I said. Don't say it isn't true: I remember you dropping me a great height out of a window. You said: Now try and save yourself if you can! And Dad laughed like mad. Even though I had a four-inch nail through each of his hands into the garage door. Now some nails through your legs, I said, since you always made out you're Jesus Christ. You fool! he yelled at me. You fool! You cried yourself to sleep because we woke up to your cunning. Time and again she would go in to see you were all right. We had to stand up to you or you'd have driven us crazy. The other thing you remember wrong is the time the car turned over. It landed on its side and I dropped you out the back window to save your life in case the car caught fire. He didn't cry with the pain and I got the nails out with the claw hammer. He told everyone he got some boils lanced, that's what made the scars in his hands.'

His mind switched tracks now as easily as it had before his last committal.

'That night a mouse crawled up my back and perched on top of my head. Way up high. I knew it wasn't there, but I went to the doctor and got some nerve tablets.

'They didn't help me with my own boy. He won't recognize me any more, even after I bought him the mini racing set. Just because I work as an operator in cacky overalls. And boots. He even says the car's too old. Don't come to speech day, he tells me. I don't want my friends to see that old bomb parked outside the school. Then I find he's only going there two days out of five.

'What can I do with him but send him to Surfers' Paradise? Pay his fare and ten dollars a week to spend, then when he gets through six weeks' money in three days he comes home on his return ticket. I wasn't like that when I was a kid. Then he rings up the wife's best friend one day and tells her there's an accident at work and her husband has his scalp lifted and he's in hospital. Come quickly! he says. Then the stupid little bugger ransacks the house—takes everything—calls a taxi-truck on their phone and starts loading everything on to the truck. Their neighbour races out and tries to stop him with nothing but a starting pistol. Front page headlines. Caught. And everyone says he's a good boy at heart. He was lucky to get off with a bond. All the stupid little bastard could say to me when I thrashed Christ out of him was "You always said what a colossal time I'd have when I grew up a bit and now I try and do what I want everyone says it's wrong and call the fuzz. I'd rather be a stinking kid again."'

He looked at his hands. They were weeping with compassion for him. Good old hands. Hands never let you down.

'When I got to the asylum they made me sit in the middle of the dormitory. The keepers looked the other way. Patients round me in a circle, shouting at me, and me too stupid with largactil tablets to bash their heads in. All I could do was sit and cry like a baby while they accused me of everything from raping babies to sniffing old ladies' pants. They set up a judge over me and tied me up helpless. Group therapy. I made a dash for the window trying to jump out and kill myself, but I caught my shoulder on the frame. They just let me lie there. So I got up and went back and sat down. When I broke down and confessed everything they wanted, they were happy and let me go. I couldn't even feel angry at them, I was so glad to get free. One of them gave me a tip about the tablets: next time I got them I drank four pints of water with them and they had no effect.

'Then they really started on me. The doctors. Strapped down struggling, needles, shock treatment, evil spirits, my soul leaving my body out through the bone of my skull—the top of my head was tender most of the time—I came to believe in the devil, I had strange and peculiar thoughts, terrible filthy words came into my head and stayed there for weeks. I could never remember the words and when I asked afterwards the words they told me were too silly and tame to be right. Words no one ever used before. Afraid to be indoors, yet the windstorms outside could have suffocated anyone, everyone was watching me and I blushed, which is something I haven't done for years, I had visions that told me I was born from a fire and sent here to be a special agent of God. I could hardly stop myself going to pieces.

'At times I think I'm no good at all. I haven't lived the right sort of life. I get urges to do shocking acts in public, as if I must injure myself or someone else. My sins are unpardonable. I brood over them until they hatch out into the light. I deserve severe punishment. They convinced me of that. They convinced me of everything bad about myself.'

He looked down quickly to see if his clothes were on.

THERAPY 'Now that I'm well and truly churned up inside I ought to try and get out of all this misery. I'll try to float these sharp thoughts off just as if they were little puff-balls bouncing off the top of my head. Or they might float out through the back of my skull under my hair. If it helps me I'll keep doing it—even in hospital next time they pull me in off the street.'

Day, which had remained respectfully outside, was blind as a madman with mist and cloud. On the turbine landing men sweated, working a foot from red-hot glowing 48-inch flue headers, their sweat drying quickly, faces burning; cursing the company, the process, themselves, and their mates who disappeared in emergencies or wouldn't get off their bottoms.

RATIONALE 'But why should I expect to be happy and comfortable all the time? Once upon a time a man could stare out a window or yell at people or have a fight or walk off by himself without all sorts of bastards rushing out to drive away your bad mood or lock you up alone with it. You've got to be desperate sometimes.

You've got to fight and be alone and have stinking things happen to you now and then. Anyone happy all the time is mad. I'm not mad: just nervous. If you're in good health you must get unhappy whenever you've got good reason. Without having to apologize or be anxious about it.

'Why should I try to adjust to the way everyone else is? Who says they're worth adjusting to? I'll be myself. Use my own brain, push my own talents to their capacity. What does it matter if I'm not popular with anyone?'

DREAMS Inside the Glass Canoe the weather changed again. In a sudden mood of elation he went straight on down to the river Eel and ferried across to the Home Beautiful. He was welcomed there only by the Great White Father, no one else would give him the time of day. He was not aware of this. If he felt like hailing his workmates cheerfully, he did so, and straightaway thought how cheerful everyone was. If he didn't, he was absorbed in himself and didn't notice others.

The Great White Father had got some small-leafed ivy from one of Puroil's ornamental garden walls and was training it over the huts. He didn't reject the Glass Canoe's offer of help, but allowed him to plant a few dozen of the rooted cuttings provided by the gardener. After half an hour the Glass Canoe had begun to remember vaguely that it was his own idea to use the ivy, and he thought out a few modifications to the Great White Father's plans. After an hour he was convinced of it. This renewed his confidence and from that point he lost interest in the actual work and was easily drawn into the clutches of the Sorcerer's Apprentice. He took her techniques and manipulations for flattery. He didn't mind what she wrote in her notebook. He was used to people writing down what he said and did. He jumped up the steps to the drink hut.

'Here's the Glass Canoe!' said Bubbles who was squatting naked in one corner of the hut ready for his encounter with the Apprentice. 'He'll tell you! Didn't Big Bits stay away on night shift?'

'Don't ask me,' said the Glass Canoe. 'I'm not the pay office. I don't keep a check on my workmates.' This was untrue; he was often seen going through the time cards, looking for workmates who had exceeded the overtime limit.

'Well, he did, anyway,' grumbled Bubbles. 'And he got his mate—I won't mention names—to clock him in and out. When the Enforcer kept coming in and asking Where's Big Bits?—they told him He's still out there.—What, still? said the Enforcer. He's been out for six nights now.—You keep missing him, they said. He had to go away, there was nothing else he could do. A whole seven days' night shift and he got paid!' He shook his head a long time, filled with envy. 'That's what I call a mate.'

The Glass Canoe bought some cans and settled down to drink, dreaming of promotion, efficiency, progress, greatness. The Great White Father would never be able to wean him from these dreams and Puroil would never dream of fulfilling them.

9
LIGHT ON A DARK NIGHT

GOING HOME IN THE DARK Going out of the refinery at night, hanging their heads, straggling like convicts loosely chained, the lowest grade of prisoners looked in on the occasional parties held in the dining-room where staff men and girls ate from buffet tables lobsters, roast beef and soft pink hams, stood around drinking from dainty glasses and talking of Puroil and its concerns and the details of their lives daily given for the company in return for monthly bank deposits.

The men passing by in the dark were conscious of their own badges. Their red necks, heavy hands and every word that proceeded out of their mouths, their lack of interest in office affairs, their partial interest in the actual messy business of refining—these were inseparable from them and an insuperable barrier to intercourse with the elegant creatures from the Termitary. It was another world in there. Office people didn't care what the process was on which they and the prisoners depended: their skills could be transferred to the refining of toffee or the manufacture of hearing aids with no significant difference. The less they knew about oil the cleaner they felt. The men down on the job never understood this—they sneered at accounting people for not knowing refining processes, never realizing that business people didn't need to know and certainly didn't want to know anything but through-put and production figures, sales and stocks on hand, costs and revenue, payroll-tax and salary. If there can be said to be a literary culture and a scientific, there must certainly be a business culture in which it is necessary to be able to define money, recite a selected passage of company law and to be inward with the Banking Act of '45. The men going home in the dark belonged to none of these cultures.

A GRIN IN EVERY GRAVE At the water's edge, waves muttered little asides and slapped the stone slabs in irritation. Out on the bay, the hop and splash of mullet swimming for their lives. At night the money plants of the refinery were covered in lights; for miles they were Christmas trees on the dark plains of industry. From cars and house windows people admired their fairy grace and pointed happily to them as sights to be seen.

Coming out of the dark it was heartening to see the light in the mangroves. At the Home Beautiful, Blue Hills came on the Great White Father talking to the Glass Canoe. He went past them to get a can of beer and the Glass Canoe dated him savagely, making him jump. He knew the man did this in order to interrupt the Great White Father so that a third person wouldn't hear him giving advice to the Glass Canoe. Blue Hills had left this sort of pride behind him; he waited frankly for the Great White Father to finish so that he could tell his own troubles.

The Glass Canoe's manoeuvre did not silence the Great White Father. 'You want me to continue this some other time?'

'No, no! There's no privacy about it. I have nothing to hide.' The doctors impressed on him that he must never again seek privacy, he must confess and be open about everything. With everyone. Privacy was unhealthy.

'Good,' said the Great White Father in his deep, dry, crackling voice. 'So you've got high blood pressure now. OK. Don't fight it. It is you.'

'Don't fight it? You mean let it kill me?'

'It is you. It's like Puroil. Take the kicks as they come. If Puroil toes you up one buttock, turn the other cheek. Same with life. You are a person with high blood pressure. Don't fight it. Be yourself, not a half-dead ninny trying to side-step death.'

The sting in the tail of the speech fought with the public nature of the advice, given in front of Blue Hills, to decide whether the blood should recede from the Glass Canoe's face or flood it with a shaming blush. Blue Hills won and the red started to glow behind the greasy brown of his cheeks.

'Whatever you are, you are you. Live with yourself and try to like it or lump it.' The Great White Father turned to Blue Hills. 'How are your tomato plants, Blue?'

'Not bad,' said Blue Hills and the Great White Father looked at him keenly. Poor Blue Hills, it was impossible to get him excited. 'I cut out the middle to make them spread,' he added, feeling that 'not bad' wasn't much of an answer.

'I cut mine, too. Always. Only I pick off the laterals, then at eight feet I pinch off the tops. They spread out like a willow and bear much better that way.'

'Jesus,' said Blue Hills reverently. 'I can't do that with mine.'

'I've got a very high fence. Makes it easier.'

The Glass Canoe laughed loudly, trying to break the spell embarrassment had cast around him.

'You don't have vegetables, do you?' asked the Great White Father, trying to include the Glass Canoe. 'You go for flowers, don't you?'

'Flowers?' Trying to remember what he might have said a week ago, a year ago—any time—about flowers. Mercifully he remembered the gardenia his wife had been trimming of its yellow leaves. It had wet feet. 'Yes.' What a load was lifted when he could qualify to be in the swim of the conversation. 'Yes, flowers. But I'm thinking of going in for beans and lettuce next.' Anything to keep his head afloat. 'With maybe a patch of strawberries, just for the wife.' Was he afloat? He didn't know. Perhaps he had sunk and didn't realize it yet. 'What do you think of cabbage and cauliflowers?' They say drowning is quite pleasant. You just float off easily.

'They're OK for the chooks,' said the Great White Father.

'You're not having me on, are you?' the Glass Canoe said with strain in his voice. He got to his feet uncertainly.

'Not to the point of physical exertion. Sit down. I don't fight with anything but words. Or, better—with grog.'

'I've got to go back, anyway. There's some blanks to be put in the lines, and the fitters have to be shown where they go.' He went, no longer afloat.

'You're lucky you can turn everything to a joke,' said Blue Hills. 'He can be very nasty.' Something felt wet in his underpants, perhaps the Glass Canoe's finger had made the blood come.

'It's hard to make him laugh,' admitted the Great White Father.

'Not many down here today.' If it was blood he could expect the place to itch later.

'Just you and me and the Sleeping Princess. You want to cut yourself a slice?'

'Me? Goodness me, no. Too early in the day. Besides I have a wife at home and there's such a thing as love.'

The Great White Father looked away. 'Love,' he said. 'What's love? Will a man lay down his life for love? A soldier does it for a soldier's pay. Will a man go hungry for it? So he will to pinch and scrape and make a million. Will a man for love swim when his strength's gone, duck under a hail of bullets or cling for days to a ledge of rock? He'll do the same to keep a whole skin. Will a man for love obey a foolish order? He'll do it to earn his daily bread. Love. What's love? Is it a word? If so it falls off the end of the tongue and vanishes—dissolves to the air that made it. Who's got love? A mother for her baby? So has a mathematician for his equation, a physicist for his demonstration, an astronomer for his theory. Can you see it, hear it, touch it, taste it? Does it live on after you're gone? Can you see where it was? No. No to every question. Yet without love a human isn't a man. Without love an animal has no young. Without love the world is full of carcasses and dead stones.'

Blue Hills ignored these sentiments.

'What do you do when there's no one around?'

'You mean besides testing the girls?' smiled the Great White

Father. And went on, to save Blue Hills the trouble of thinking up a reply, 'I dream of things to come.' He was silent a while. 'And the blessings of the past.' Opening two more cans. 'Like the time I fell twenty feet off the turbine landing.'

'How was that a blessing? Did you fall on your head?'

'It saved my life and that's a fact.' The Great White Father was able to fall flat or on his head against solid objects with no ill-effects. 'Now all I'm fit for is ease and pleasure, low company and high living. My ambition is to be the local emperor of rollicks, bollocks and beer till a man more worthy of the title comes along. Life is only a short glass, Blue Hills, better fill it up. Because though there's a grin in every grave, there's no sound of laughing. What did you come for, Blue? About your transfer?'

'I didn't get it!' Blue Hills burst out. 'I put it in writing, but the Good Shepherd wrote No. I watched through the window.' The Good Shepherd had to rubber-stamp the Python's decision.

'Tough,' murmured the great man. 'But what is, is. I was born, I think, from a dream of strong drink around several campfires—'

Blue Hills was gone. In his place sat a young innocent lad clutching his first can of icy beer, his mouth open ready for burps, laughter, profanity, his ears open for instruction in the ways of the Great White Father's endless struggle against the total enslavement of man.

'—In order to have me my venereal Dad and Mum got blind, blotto, bloated, buried, canned, cockeyed, crocked, embalmed, high, lit, loaded, lushed, owled, oiled, ossified, paralysed, pickled, pie-eyed, plastered, potted, pissed, schickered, soused, sizzled, stewed, stung, stinko and stiff. And from enslavement to Puroil I will lead my groggy troops into enslavement to the delights of women and the bottle. In short, to inertia. A vast underground movement of inertia. To exist, to be, is all. Inertia will save us—our ability to live at the lowest pitch. This will save us from all the Puroil brainwashing in the world. Cunning, solidarity behind me—not behind the guards in that detention camp—sharing evenly all the windfall benefits we find, these are our safety factors.' The boy drank it in—words, beer, the lot.

SET-UP The Glass Canoe strode into the control room wearing a large list of his symptoms pinned to his chest like medals. Seeing the Good Shepherd coming round a corner he flicked his hand at the Sump's solar plexus, winded him, then stood back with hands on hips, having judged the Good Shepherd's entry well. The Sump, seeing the open target of the Glass Canoe's chest, retaliated lightly with his fist. You never hit the Glass Canoe as hard as he hit you—he might land you one. Just as the Good Shepherd came in the door, what he saw was the Sump's fist in the Glass Canoe's middle, and the Glass Canoe doubled up with a great show of agony, like a footballer trying to get a member of the opposing side sent off.

'What did you do that for?' he roared righteously, winking at the Sumpsucker. Seeing the wink, the Sump didn't know what to say. He was disarmed. The Glass Canoe knew this and intended his hesitation to be taken for guilt.

'Hey, Shep!' full of good humour, 'your supervisors have started to bully the workers.'

'So what?' said the Good Shepherd genially. He hoped it was the right thing to say and in the right tone, and passed on quickly. How could these men persist in wasting time on what amused them instead of devoting themselves to the company that nourished them?

'That had him in!' laughed the Glass Canoe to the Sumpsucker as if they were conspirators together. 'He didn't know what to make of it. Hey, I passed the widow's place yesterday and her front lawn was full of forty-four gallon drums stacked two-high.'

The Sump made no answer, but peered at his chest, trying to make sense of the Glass Canoe's symptom list. He failed. The words were written upside down so the Glass Canoe himself could read them if he glanced down his chest. The symptoms of his disease were the aims, ambitions, resolutions, promises and cautions he wanted to bear in mind in his rise to the top.

He got tired of toying with the Sumpsucker and strode off outside into the propane-rich air. Over by the steam generators where some contractor prisoners were making patterns in light-gauge aluminium, an Italian face bobbed out under a grey safety hat and an arm plucked at his sleeve.

'Come here, Aussie. Come here.'

The Glass Canoe surveyed the man over and under. Italian, greasy, short, forty, no boots, only sandshoes, torn shirt.

'Come.' The man gazed into his face sincerely. If he had seen the upside-down symptoms he gave no sign.

'What d'you want?'

'You will break my arm.'

'What?'

'Please.'

'OK.' He grabbed the arm in two hands, lifted his knee and braced it against the arm, looking into the man's eyes. The man smiled expectantly. He dropped the arm.

'Don't be stupid.'

'Please, Aussie. Mister. Break the arm. I go hospital, get compensation. No work for six weeks, my wife sick, I look after. Please. Not be frightened.'

'Give us it.' He took the arm, lifted his knee, strained, bent the arm a little but couldn't break it. The Italian's face was a little whiter and the smile not so wide.

'Please. Try again.'

He tried again, sweating. No good. Something was holding him back from the effort needed to break the arm. 'Here. Get down lower.'

With the man crouching low, the elbow propped on a metal ledge and the hand flat on the concrete, the Glass Canoe lifted his heavy boot. With a peculiar kindness he took out his handkerchief, made it into a pad and placed it under the elbow.

'So you won't get too bad a bruise.'

'Thank you.' The man's smile was back. The Glass Canoe lifted his boot and brought it down on the middle of the forearm. No break. The man's eyes were on him, warm and brown. This time he grabbed the railing, jumped into the air with both feet off the ground and crashed his right heel down on the arm with all his weight behind it. There was a crack-crack as both bones broke, one after the other. The man rose, his face dirty with approaching shock, and tried to smile. The smile came unstuck and wouldn't sit square on his face.

'Thank you,' he said. He walked off to report the injury.

The Glass Canoe sweated, but steadied his misgivings by looking down his chest and reading his symptoms, which he repeated aloud like a prayer.

THE STRONG AND THE WEAK It was after dark, the Samurai lay half asleep in his room hoping for a few hours' sleep, loathing the approach of ten o'clock and the nightly journey to detention. He was tired to the bone, he had worked a hard night shift on the latest start-up while many went down. His right arm ached where the boys had thumped him; the ache was there every day now. A dark patch that might have been a bruise showed under the skin.

From his window, even with the blinds shut, the flicker of the flare from Puroil could be seen, on and off, a nervous heartbeat. If the plants were upset and pressure had to be relieved by jettisoning gas, the hundred-foot flames made a pretty picture as far away as the Blue Mountains.

In his confused dream he was wandering in a local park, followed by the band of cheeky horses that lived there. He took refuge in the Men's, just in time to help a clean old man who was rolling in pain and embarrassment on the floor. He helped the clean old man back to the toilet seat until he was relieved of the pressure in his bowel lines, lifted him up, wiped his bottom as you would a child's and cleaned it out with water and soap. An old custom from the Khyber. Joking in his dreams. The clean old man giggled helplessly. The Samurai grew rougher in his actions, he hadn't meant to tickle him.

'You are a pervert, aren't you?' said the clean old man, putting his face up near the Samurai's. The man's helplessness, insolence and ingratitude touched a nerve in the Samurai's self-esteem, arousing a memory of his violence to a similarly helpless boy years ago. He had stoned that boy mercilessly in his own garden simply for looking soft and weak and girlish. He twisted the arm of the clean old man until he screamed like a woman. The horses shuffled restlessly outside, bumping their huge rounded hindquarters on the bricks of the lavatory wall, producing soft thump sounds.

Was his present service to man a continual effort to atone for one silly act of cruelty?

He still had the man's arm. It was the stiff arm of a statue, but his own hands were losing their grip on it. It grew swollen and heavy; fattening, lengthening. Was it possible a whole life could be lived in the shadow of a man's guilt over one tiny action? The arm jerked out of his grasp as a glow filled the room. He woke in a sweat, dragged himself over to the window and parted the slats of the blind. The evening sky alight. The flare was a mile high. He was awake, this was reality. A sunrise in the south.

Wearily he remembered the hot spots he had discovered and reported on the regenerator days ago. The so-called engineers must have come to their senses and crashed the plant. This was unusual: they got into less trouble from the absentee controllers if they let a failure develop and the plant crashed with great loss and damage than if they gave the order to bring the plant down before the fault blew out. Initiative on the spot was severely punished; the experts in Europe took no one's word that a stoppage was inevitable. The Samurai wondered if there had been a sudden burst of defiance from his cowed and weak Australian superiors.

The bright column of fire darkened. Clouds of soot from crashing boilers and clouds of catalyst siphoned from the pressured vessels by collapsing pressures elsewhere in the cycle filled the sky and were illuminated by the burning gas. The plant was down. What if the bosses had really taken the initiative for once instead of running for cover? He lay back on the bed and went to sleep immediately.

Mogo wasn't as lucky as the Samurai. He had a fifteen-mile drive home and he too had worked all night with only a break at two to eat his sandwiches. On the way home the heater was on in his car and he nodded off to sleep and ran off the road.

He had a sleep in the hospital and broke out in time to get to work. Some of his mates joked about the bandages on his head:

others sympathized. He told them all to save their breath. He wanted nothing from any man. He wouldn't even fill in compensation papers. He still worked while others slept.

Blue Hills, on the turbine platform when the plant collapsed, fell to the grating in shock and put his shoulder out. They took him to the hospital he asked for. The Good Shepherd, as soon as he heard about it, jumped into his car and set out for St Joseph's to visit him. When he got there Blue Hills was sitting up in bed, shoulder and forearm bandaged, very pleased with himself. For some reason he felt a hero. The Sister, dressed in long, cool, pale-blue robes, with a crucifix of gold on a chain peeping out from the folds as she walked, spoke to him in a voice that sang in his ears like the silver bell at the Home Beautiful.

A CLOSE MOUTH   Far Away Places was alone among the glitter and extravagance of the amenities—*Personnel to use this facility only during authorized breaks*—but he was not unobserved. The Samurai rounded the corner of the grey building in time to see Far Away lift a bottle of soft drink to his mouth and take off the top with his teeth. Strong teeth. Was it possible a man with so little on show, a man regarded as insignificant by everyone around him, could have secret strengths? And the self-command never to display them? Perhaps the prisoners weren't all as pitiable as he thought.

A CONVENIENT WINDOW   The Samurai found the house. No answer to his knock, so round through a gate in the white-painted trellis, past a wide-open window. Not past. Back and looking in stupidly. She was sitting naked before a dressing-table mirror, cuddling and stroking a small furry animal with an attractive hand equipped with five petal fingers. The animal said not one hard word to her. Even as he watched, that hand-flower opened one petal, then another. Like a pink rose opening.

'Mrs Hills,' he said by way of opening.

'Yes,' she answered, looking at him in the mirror.

'I'm from work,' he said idiotically gazing at her white buttocks overlapping the stool on which she sat.

'Come in.'

'Get something round you.'

'Come in.' He climbed through her window.

'It's about your husband.'

'I have no husband.'

'Blue Hills.'

'He lives here—if you call it living.'

She stood up facing him, her hands still protecting her furry pet and soothing its excitement at the coming of this long-expected visitor.

'You're welcome to undress.' And seeing he was not entirely at ease, she said, 'This isn't his room. He never comes in here.' She had mistaken his hesitation.

'Excuse I,' she said delicately, stepped up to him and with swift fingers flied him. She had left her pet to its own devices and seeing it lonely he comforted it. It was the least he could do. He didn't feel too badly about it; he reckoned that if she was as easy as this, there must have been others. Since he was one of a number the guilt was divided. He was wrong. There had been no others, though for years she had pretended there were, ready for the day when a live man would lift her window sash and climb in.

After tea, he got round to telling her why he'd come, but it was too late then for her to visit the hospital, she said.

Night came, as if in decency to cover her shame. Outside the stars were cold, the moonlit flowers just as cold. The trees grew silently in the yard; and heavy, to keep their roots underground.

Next day he left the house after having quarrelled over breakfast.

'We're through,' he exclaimed mildly as he climbed out the window. He didn't mean it. He had no other entanglements and was glad of something that was made so easy for him and required so little thought.

PRIDE OF PLACE Oil drips had been splashing down for months from the American butterfly valves which had never worked properly: the leaks had been notified by the cowardly prisoners—who stood to lose their lives in fires—but were disregarded.

'They've always had a small leak in the hydraulic lines,' said the Python to the Good Shepherd. 'Tell them to wake up to themselves. They've never seen a good fire.'

'Neither have I, thank God,' said the Good Shepherd, who obeyed his superior in spite of his better judgment. 'Only the fire on Signal Hill.' It was a movie fire, bad enough to be banned from the new operators' induction course.

One fine day in May—the morning a stray cat had its kittens on a sugar bag behind the instrument panel—the drops flashed and Puroil had a nice fire on the flue-gas header. Mumbles in gloves saw the fire, yelled at the Grasshopper to phone the fire station. But the Grasshopper's East German dignity was too tall for humble phone calls.

'Get an operator, Mumbles! I'm going up!' he shouted bravely, walking slowly towards the distant fire.

'God almighty. I've shot better Germans than you,' roared Mumbles after him. He was one of the Tobruk Rats and very proud of having survived its siege. Even the cat looked up when prisoners started running for fire hoses. Mumbles was cheated of the premier position: it was a point of pride to be first out to a fire so the Wandering Jew would be impressed. Mumbles lost valuable seconds phoning.

The prisoners were often more realistic. Oliver Twist the delegate was first to the water connection, which was some distance from the fire and the point from which the hoses were run out. He let others have the honour of holding the fog nozzle.

THE MAGIC OF NIGHT Certain hours of the day possess special qualities. Consider the magical period between 2.30 and 5 in the morning. Primitives think this belongs to the night, but sophisticates such as shiftworkers live for years with the undeniable fact that this is part of an ordinary day. Workers must be up and doing; up reluctantly and doing as little as possible.

The Great White Father returned one day at 3.45 from the Home Beautiful to carry out some menial tasks the Super had set him. He was one of the few who were never seen exhausted from anything but drink.

He came upon Reflux just inside the door. Reflux was having one of his night-shift spells. He stood full height, head slightly bowed, eyes closed. His arms were raised sideways forming a cross with the rest of his thin body and bent at the elbows until his closed fists, led by the knuckle of his first finger, pressed at the base of his nose. He was a television antenna. More than that, he was imitating the Garfish, who could be seen in this position inside the pay office until the glass was thoughtfully painted over to stop the crap looking in. After that only his own staff could see this ritual.

'Is he going to be all right?' asked the Two Pot Screamer, walking round him, inspecting.

'He's in tune with the Infinite,' pronounced the Great White Father.

'Look out,' alarmed the Humdinger, 'or he'll floor the lot of you.' Everyone was glad of the diversion. The Great White Father stood off a few paces and examined Reflux.

'Floor me? What weapons could he possibly muster against me?'

'Brains,' said Humdinger slyly. Reflux was noted for his one-eyed approach to plant operation: whatever went wrong, his remedy was always either more or less reflux.

'Small arms?' questioned the Great White Father. 'Against—' tapping his own skull—'against the nuclear deterrent?'

'Night shift's got him. He's eaten too many pies in his lifetime.'

KISSING MATES The control-room door opened and let in a blast of sound.

'The header's alight!' yelled Loosehead. 'Ant's up there.'

The Great White Father ran to the door and disappeared a hundred feet up the boilers in a cloud of smoke.

The Enforcer came out, the Sumpsucker close behind.

'What's up?'

'Fire!' Men left to look. The Great White Father climbed the vertical steps like a tall monkey, looking for the Angry Ant. The siren wailed. In a few minutes the Good Shepherd was down from his company residence to join the search for his lost sheep.

After they put the fire out and the fire truck arrived, several prisoners and the Good Shepherd reached the Great White Father on the landing bridging the tops of the two tall boilers. The Great White Father worked rhythmically on the Ant, pushing and blowing, giving him the mouth-to-mouth treatment. It took a few minutes.

'I can see why you ran up the stairs,' said the Humdinger. The Good Shepherd looked uncomfortable when he heard the boys pretending.

'What's the Ant like to kiss?' pursued the Humdinger.

'Sweet as a nut,' said the Great White Father. 'Reminds me of a widow I knew at Richmond. Whenever I visited her and a plane went over she'd drop whatever she was doing and rush over for a smoush. No matter what she was doing, no matter what she was eating, no matter whether she had her choppers in or out. Always affected her like that.'

'Has he been chewing garlic sausage?'

'I like garlic, but he's got his choppers downstairs in his locker,' said the Great White Father.

'No, I haven't,' said the Angry Ant righteously, reviving completely. 'No. They must've dropped out when that stinking bloody smoke started to choke me. That's when I started to toss up my goodies.' Grinning at the Great White Father, whose mouth folded in distaste.

'And I thought your breath was like that naturally. Better wait for daylight to look for your teeth.'

'Perhaps we could help him downstairs,' suggested the Good Shepherd, anxious to stop the talk.

'Never mind,' said the Great White Father bravely. 'Friends have no germs. Only strangers have germs. Females have fewer germs than males. I'd much rather kiss a woman than kiss Ant. Wouldn't you, Shep?' He dug the Good Shepherd in the lower ribs.

The Good Shepherd watched as he led the way, ready to support the Ant if he felt dizzy again. The air was full of flue gas, pouring from the leak below, which had flashed. The flue gas contained 7 per cent carbon-monoxide, but the men's noses didn't detect it. There was also a small amount of vanadium: they were unaware of its effect. In the distance the hydrofluoric blow-off from a neighbour chemical plant was caught in the lightest of breezes from the west, and was bearing down in a thick, horizontal discoloured column towards Puroil. The local industries tried to keep their noxious and pestilential blow-offs till night time to avoid being seen and reported by residents of the surrounding suburbs on whose houses and through whose windows the vapours, acids, ash and soot fell.

The Good Shepherd remembered the last time he had overheard the Great White Father giving advice to one of his tribe. 'Better not tell the Sumpsucker the steam pressure needs upping: tell him the trouble's due to the difference in ambient temperature—then he'll fix the steam pressure.' He wondered how many ball-ups were averted by the good offices of men like him, cheerfully circumventing the idiocies of those above. He sighed, as much as the poisoned air allowed, and mentally erased such thoughts. The Company was somehow bigger than the individuals of which it was composed, wasn't it?

Was it? His Christian Good Shepherd instincts started to prepare for conflict, but before they could make a row inside him, something else stronger in him made those instincts lay down their arms. That stronger thing was an amalgam of loyalty and reverence for the established order. Render unto Caesar the things that are Caesar's.

The Great White Father was capable of internal conflicts but he had a governor inside him that automatically resolved them in favour of people, not companies.

THE ARMOUR OF FEAR The Trout appeared at 4.30 in the control room. Unshaven and red-eyed.

'I've been sitting in the car all night over at Riverditch and the noise of this plant is terrible,' he wailed. Like most of the aspiring executives he wailed and complained to the prisoners with zest and abandon, but minded his language very carefully in the presence of those nearer him in the Puroil scale of values.

'Don't you fellers know the company is up for big fines for smoke and noise?'

'Tell the Sump. Don't bother us,' said the Angry Ant. The vertical split separating department from department meant the Ant could defy anyone from another department. The Spotted Trout had no business talking to an operator.

'It must be cold in the car this time of morning,' said the Great White Father kindly, and the Trout left, miserably, and went to complain to the foreman about a man peeing out on the utilities section of the plant. It turned out to be the Beautiful Twinkling Star hosing down his unit. Grease, birds' droppings, rubbish, had to be hosed off the concrete with cold water that dribbled from hoses. Using the fire hydrant with free salt water from the river and 180 pounds pressure he could have done the job in half an hour, but he'd been standing hosing for four hours of the night and was nowhere near finished. The job would have to be done again tomorrow and every day.

'Consider the Trout and be wise!' declaimed the great man. 'Encased in the armour of fear!' He took a breath. 'Puroil is the concretion of the fears these men have exuded and is built up strong in steel and concrete because men are weak and afraid. They have built round themselves a fence, a protection and now it is become a prison. No one can get at those Puroil protects—only Puroil!'

The foremen in the office heard, but stayed put, waiting for him to go away. Lifting his voice high above the outside roar of turbine and compressor and venting steam, the Great White Father of the operators sang:

I'm only a turd in the Puroil cage,
A pitiful sight to see!

It was no use trying to shut him up.

THE BLOOD MARKET The Samurai met him in the car park. 'What's the price of blood, Cheddar? How's the market?'

Cheddar wasn't going to take the trouble to answer, but the Samurai might not have understood silence, so he brought out a few reluctant words.

'The ass fell out of it.'

The Samurai could hear the misery of a man who has suddenly lost profits.

'What's the story, Cheddar?' Try as he might, he could not keep the sympathy out of his voice.

'Well,' it came out with a rush, 'after I jacked the price up, suddenly there was millions of people with my blood disease. About two hundred people in the metropolitan area reckon they have it now and more every day. They all want to be in it and sell their blood, so what happens to the price? The bludgers. Not a thought what happens to the price. They spoil it for everyone. Now I've got to try and live on wages alone.'

'I'm sorry to hear so many people are sick with it.'

'Sick? They're not sick! I'm not sick!' His pale yellow skin glistened transparently, like sweating cheese. 'All it does is cut a few years off the ass end of your life and who wants to get old?' The Samurai was about to ask him why he didn't go off work and try for the invalid pension, but he remembered the amount invalids and pensioners get.

'How did the other two hundred get to know of the market for crook blood, Cheddar?'

'I know how. The Python got to hear of it and he's got a daughter with a blood disease. Not as bad as mine, but interesting enough to scientists. Well, you know the Python. He got his daughter to sell her blood and from her the news spread everywhere.' His horizons momentarily widened. 'Even in eggs and fruit and fish—and diamonds—they have orderly marketing so the producer won't go down the drain, but these nongs couldn't think of that.' The horizon narrowed right down to normal focus. 'Fifty cents a pint. It's not worth growing the bloody stuff.'

'They might stumble on a cure, Cheddar. I hope so.'

'I hope so too,' he said viciously. 'That'll teach 'em to spoil someone else's business.'

'They didn't think.'

'The Python didn't think, either, when he tangled with me.'

NAT'S GIRL They had stripped her from *Playboy* magazine before it was banned. Now she was stuck halfway up a wall in the plant laboratory, every inch of her tan flesh promising juicy bites to sex-hungry men. However cold the winter, she never once complained or asked for clothes.

She was what all men desired: lovely, good to eat, helpless. All you had to do was grab her—she was light as a feather—jerk her horizontal, move her arms and legs to the positions you wanted. She saw many interesting things. If her impressions could have been salvaged somehow from the glossy paper, some that are now industrial dukes, princes and section heads on the earth might have cause to fear.

Ambrose often locked himself in the lab on night shift and by the light cast on Nat's Girl from a neon tube across road 15, masturbated into several sympathetic rags while he gazed over the whole of her body.

Loosehead, who had more imagination than he was given credit for, one night in similar circumstances constructed out of 14-gauge square mesh wire a life-size dummy woman and clothed her with rags from the clean-rag boxes. He stuffed the dummy with rags, too, and lay down on the floor with her, similarly fixing his eyes on Nat's Girl, whose parted lips and confident eyes he imagined so close to his own flesh.

He left the dresser's model in a corner behind a door. He wired the door handle back to the wall so his Galatea would not be discovered. However, next time he came in for a short private orgy he found she had been interfered with. He had to replace some of her soiled rags before he performed his pitiful, convulsive act.

The Samurai came to consult with Nat's Girl. He walked with his judo walk, feet hardly leaving the ground, steps short. A smile sketched itself on his face with the merest lifting of lips and crinkling of eyes.

'I'm dangerous, girlie,' he said to Nat's Girl. 'There's two hundred pounds of dynamite here with an inch and a half fuse.' Nat's Girl made no comment.

The Glass Canoe came to see her, but he would treat her as an oracle, trying to tell her his troubles and asking for her advice. '...but if I try to teach the other boys what my aims are so they will know me and what I am trying to do, they will understand me and know I am right. I can start to be happy, then.'

Because of his own nature, the way he was made, he would never be able to understand the Samurai's attempts at complete honesty.

'To lie is to dream,' the Samurai was fond of saying. 'You have a choice: let yourself lie and you enter a dream world where everything consists of words, and is unreal.' The Samurai didn't understand that the Glass Canoe could do no differently because his circuits were arranged in a particular way.

The Samurai got the pleasure of duty done from some of his pronouncements. Nat's Girl heard him say to one of the Kaffir-kickers: 'We are brought up to believe in personal integrity, a fair go for others, the value of the individual, good manners...'

The Kaffir-kickers would be puzzled by this emphasis on the rights of others and vaguely dissatisfied. The social air they breathed in Europe had taken one thing for granted, so obviously, so trustingly, they were hard put to express it. It was like something you were always used to and never conscious of. It was respect for authority. And obedience. This was something he hadn't mentioned.

Here again, the Samurai didn't have sufficient patience for people who had come from lands of acute class-consciousness and respect for betters. He didn't realize this, though, and carried on with his theoretical statements of what he thought should be: the precepts he had grown up with and which he took literally. His circuits, too, were arranged in a particular way.

Bubbles, creeping into the lab for a sleep one dark night when the plant was down, remarked apologetically to Nat's Girl, 'We're never all down. There's always a few up. We take turn about.' She smiled back at him, her smile eternal as paper, illuminated by the cold glare of neon.

A MALIGNANT GROWTH The Samurai went to see Mrs Blue Hills when her husband was next on duty.

He had intended this to be a call of passion combined with a special concern for her welfare, but she met him at the side door like an old friend and started right away making tragic noises. First it was about her sin. She had a religious ornament round her neck which he had to kiss before he was let loose on her body. Kissing the medal somehow made it all right. But this time even that holy action was insufficient.

'Don't kiss my lips,' she urged, as he unbuttoned and unhooked her, allowing her flesh to find its level. 'I must talk. They have discovered Mother has cancer of the breast, she's had the lump for years and we were always telling her to leave it alone, but she would fiddle with it and squeeze it and knead it like dough with her fingers. We used to joke about it and my husband said she was making bread.'

The Samurai was robbed of incentive by this mood of hers, and felt the gorge of distaste rise in the thick column of his throat as his blunt fingers touched her white, fine-grained skin. On and on she talked, refusing to turn off the light. The Samurai eyed the blinds for cracks that might let in darkness and men's eyes.

10
THE BEST THINGS IN LIFE ARE FREE

WET DREAM Next night a fire in the reactor riser where catalyst at 600 centigrade met waxy feed at 75 centigrade and travelled together one hundred feet up in the reactor. The catalyst persisted in escaping from leaks in the expansion bellows and inducing oil to follow it. Given the chemical composition of the old and the temperature of the catalyst, fire was the only possible outcome in the open air.

When the plant was safely down, its usual state now, prisoners were split up and distributed over plants of which they had no knowledge. This was to reduce overtime and increase the efficiency of the work force.

The Samurai went to Eel wharf. He helped tie up two barges, connect several fat rubber hoses, then went down on a heap of rags on the concrete floor of the darkened amenities room. He dreamed of Mrs Blue Hills.

He woke miserably, water lapping round him. Water covered the floor. The Grey Goldfish had left a pump running and put his head down; half the river was up on dry land, unsubsidized and duty-free. The amenities block was an island. It took two days for the water to subside.

ECONOMY PLANT And two weeks to get the plant back up. More tankers re-routed.

Hooked in as it was as an integral part of the catalytic process, the power recovery section, the money-saver, made the whole complex of plants vulnerable. The American idea was to tack it on the end of the plant so that disturbances to it, though they put the money-saver out of action, would not crash the money-making end of the process. This was known to the European designers, but they preferred the more ambitious, in-balance design. Installed in a modern refinery, where every other plant on the refinery grid was new enough to be reliable and where a closer, more threatening grip on the workers was possible, it could have worked.

But at Clearwater! Uneasily joined to plants which had been scrapped years ago but still ran, and of a size the humble prisoners at Puroil had never seen, trying to get going under staff policies and Union policies appropriate to an old-style shearing shed or convict compound, the complex had no chance. Every new thing a graft on the old.

An old bitumen plant was churning out three thousand per cent of design production. Four valiant old boilers had been scrapped once a year for ten years: they were still producing. Seven years before, they had been sold for scrap for next to nothing, but someone found they needed them and Puroil bought them back for an additional fifty thousand dollars. Puroil took more outside contracts for steam. A new hysterical direction came from above that in an emergency, if the steam flow was jeopardized, the men had to jettison process plants and sell steam. High costs? What did it matter? The consumer paid.

Middle-aged humorists in Melbourne, following orders from overseas, dictated a staff policy for middle management which meant that engineers who were relied on to prescribe for the ills of failing plants were pitchforked into and out of different types of plants too quickly for them to master the operation of any one plant. Plants have personalities inbuilt by designers and suppliers of equipment and foibles that cannot be taught at universities only learned on site. The reason for this policy was to give these men experience on various types of plants; this varied experience was to help them rise in the Puroil organization. Some might say the aim should have been to make the highest possible profit rather than provide careers for employees. Here again the American practice was to keep an engineer on one type of plant for ten years at least. In this time his salary was not tied to his breadth of experience but to his value to the company. After ten years he might be earning as much as the manager; his plants ran steadily and efficiently for long periods and made fantastic profits.

The men Puroil attracted were usually mediocre. This couldn't be helped: brilliant men did research or went back to the universities. Hierarchical organizations were most attractive to cunning conformers like the Wandering Jew, who ignored Clearwater and kept his sights on Head Office and the Board of Directors.

With the lowest prisoners, the policy had been at first to employ almost anyone off the street, then more recently to be severe on the old hands and to employ young men with better paper qualifications. Another rough graft that didn't take. The new men wouldn't nurse failing equipment the way the oldies did: they expected everything either to work or to be fixed immediately.

The ideal plan would be to employ operators who did their own fitting, instrument and electrical work—all gathered into one company union and called 'staff'. This was impossible: each craft wanted to stay separate from all others and preserve its own identity.

At the tail end of the power recovery section, just before the stack, where hot flue gases had given up most of their heat to the boiler tubes, these gases did one last duty in an economizer, where at no extra cost they heated up the boiler feed water before its entry to the lower tubes and so on to the top of the boiler where the gases were hottest, over a hundred feet up, by which time most of the water was steam.

It was five in the afternoon. The plant was getting up again after the last fire. On dayshift, ominous bangs and rumbles had come from this economizer and two men imported from Europe for the start-up which had been proceeding now for eighteen months were looking at it and listening and guessing in a foreign language. They would shortly take steps.

THE EXAMPLE OF OLDER MEN At the same time in the amenities room, Ambrose had been trapped into looking at a sheet of paper on which was sketched a plan of the control-room circuit lines and drains together with a phone number and several words like 'Micky Muncher' and 'Leg Belly is a Crap House'. This opus was pasted on the concrete wall. Seeing him coming, several seated prisoners looked fixedly at the paper and chuckled. Ambrose stopped, looked, hesitated, looked again, chuckled timidly, searched their faces, almost decided to ask them what the joke was, thought better of it, and single-handed laughed his head off at the diagram. The others laughed louder; this accelerated his stupidity. Soon he was helpless with laughter, even pointing to bits of the diagram with his finger and enjoying the fun piece by piece. His tormentors obligingly roared each time he pointed.

MEANWHILE... At five o'clock, the Grey Goldfish and One Eye had taken the rowing-boat across the river to get set for a little prawning. They loved a feed of prawns and the price was reasonable. They would leave empty kerosene tins and several nets on the bottom, in sight of the wharf. When it was dark they would row over quietly and commence operations more interesting than lining up hoses of discharging barges. The tide would be just right.

On the stroke of five, the Beautiful Twinkling Star received the first news that he was being transferred to a lower job.

At the same time the Python was locking his office desk ready to join the peak-hour traffic. He made sure there was nothing on his desk: anything could be incriminating given the circumstances. He pocketed the desk key, not like others who hung theirs on a hook under the desk. Head office auditors had a habit of descending suddenly on a Termitary, grabbing keys, impounding the contents of desks, humiliating anyone who broke the slightest regulation. Fortunately they came only once a year and usually descended first on the pay office and the cashier. He often chuckled over stories of how these incorruptible pimps, in the interests of their own careers, had come into the offices, running their fingers round picture rails for keys conveniently hidden.

What could be so important that it must be made a matter of life or death to lock it away and to hide the key? One or two desks and cabinets, yes. But all desks? And a paper clip would open them. All for a precious line or two in the auditor's report: 'Three desks unlocked, four keys found after superficial search. Please comment.'

One year an office boy, having heard of these procedures, broke up several razor blades and stuck the pieces into the timber of the picture rails in the pay office and accounts office. This was a bonus to the leader of the audit team, who got himself good marks first by reporting the injuries to his team's fingers, and again by reporting the carelessness of his assistants in not getting up to look for keys instead of searching with their fingers. The organization man can make capital from anyone's mistakes—staff friend's or labour enemy's.

The Python cleared away everything. He was thinking of a solution to Puroil's labour problem. A labour problem exists when a management is under pressure to reduce its establishment, and this pressure came from Head Office staff division without any regard for local needs of new and untried plants or different labour attitudes. Aloud he said, 'Sack the lot! They'll come crawling back for jobs!' That was his solution. That attitude was behind every dealing he had with the lower orders. As a man rises in the world, the lower orders begin just below his own status, so they seem to be multiplying and becoming more complex and unwieldy all the time. Unnecessarily numerous.

He left his office and walked the corridors of local power. Every room empty. Where was the power? If the leaders were not there, and not there in Melbourne, London, New York, Hamburg, Paris, where was the power? Or was there nothing? Was it only in the minds of its prisoners? Was it, unknown to the world of prisoners supporting it, was the whole vast enterprise in angel gear? He shivered.

At five o'clock, at the northern end of the control room, Far Away Places was talking into the foremen's office to the Good Shepherd when a shiny brown hairless hand came round his body into his overalls—touching his bare skin—and flied him. He stood there gaping at his superior, every button of his overalls undone, everything on show. The Glass Canoe had got him again.

But what was this new feeling? There was an echo on his bare skin of the touch of his tormentor's fingers. If he hated the Glass Canoe, why did he like the touch of his hand?

A PRETTY PICTURE At a minute after five, the economizer burst a tube. The two foreigners took steps—long ones—in the opposite direction. The Two Pot Screamer was watching them from the top of a stack of catalyst boxes. Lying belly-down, just to feel a little pain there. He had a nest in the catalyst shed. The foreigners flew. They seemed to know what to do when danger, smoke and loud bangs filled the air.

Ambrose carried on laughing. He didn't recognize the sounds outside as anything but noises. He didn't know the sound of safety valves. His audience left him. The Humdinger ran to the economizer, bypassed the feedwater, isolated the economizer, grabbed a piece of angle iron, climbed up beside the safety valves and seated them with a few shrewd blows. The foreigners came back slowly, full of diagnoses and orders. In their excitement they spoke their own language until the Humdinger casually hefted the angle iron under their noses, testing its weight.

'Talk your lingo in the dykes, mateys!' he bellowed. Men of their standing, spoken to like that in Europe, would have lain hands on the man, struck him in the face, toed him up the trouser. Unfortunately for their egos, they could not do that yet in Australia.

The Grey Goldfish heard nothing. The battery button was turned off. One Eye cocked his head. 'Dirty weather up at that big heap of crap,' he said, and looked at the Goldfish for a confirming grunt. The Grey Goldfish didn't lift his head. One Eye understood. He let it pass.

The Python pricked up his ears, listened to the noise of the safeties, and grinned. He was not on the plant. It was a great advantage not to be on a plant when something blew up. Nothing had changed inside humans in the recorded past. He was glad it was happening to someone else.

The Glass Canoe was no chicken, he would have gone out with the Humdinger if he hadn't been occupied inside his own head with the Glass Canoe. Why, he asked himself, why do they fight against me? Do I ask too many questions? Do they take it the wrong way when I fart-arse round with them. It's all in fun. They must know my bark is worse than my bite, by now. I don't mean them any harm. His mood had changed in a flash since he flied Far Away, it needed no outside stimulus. His internal chemistry was under no one's control. Its sequences were random.

The Beautiful Twinkling Star for once didn't rush out to help. They squash me and bypass me and tread on me because they know I won't complain. A tiny voice whispered in him, Why are you taking on the whole world? Are you daring extinction? This world isn't made for the kind man. Wake up to yourself. Get thee behind me, Satan, he answered. But inside him the whispering continued. A battle had started on a lonely field in his brain. Whatever the outcome, he would be the victim.

What a beautiful picture. A burst economizer tube, fleeing foreigners, a Grey Goldfish with battery disconnected, a Beautiful Twinkling Star demoted and resentful, a Python grinning maliciously, depraved Humdinger heroically saving the day and standing up against foreign domination, Ambrose laughing at a non-existent joke, and Far Away Places ignominiously flied. Advance Australia!

A GAME OF CHESS The plant was down two weeks. Another week and it had struggled to its knees.

In a filthy corner of the locker-room, chess was the game between Canada Dry and Humdinger. The chessboard was of paper spread flat on an upturned carton. The chairs they sat on were not burnished gold but battered sheet-iron and had been rescued from an old building torn down to save the wages of two canteen workers. The locker-room was filthy because the present shift had taken over from No. 1 shift, notoriously shy of the broom and the mop.

'When you going to Canada?' asked the Humdinger, as Canada Dry was lining up an attack with both knights.

'Next September.' He had been saving for two years to go to Canada. He had enough cash to get there, and back as far as Hawaii.

'The Enforcer will think twice before he goes over to the fractionator again. See the slurry all over his shirt?' Canada Dry had forked his king and rook. He moved his king.

'That would be the first time he ever went out on the plant. I'm waiting for him to come out with an opinion on the running of it.' Canada took the rook.

'Get that up you,' he exulted calmly. The Humdinger moved a bishop back to the queen's square, the knight was trapped in the corner.

'They had a good night last night,' said Humdinger. 'Got down in the start-up hut, rags on the tables and the heaters on. Some log crept in, though, and emptied a pint of piss on the heater bar. The stink! Like when we did it on the steam lines in the boiler house. Full of ammonia as a baby's nappy.'

The boiler men were noted for their disinclination to leave the boiler house. Their bed was behind the back wall, they defecated on a shovel and threw it in the combustion chamber together with their lavatory paper. You could murder a man there and get rid of him completely through the explosion door.

The Humdinger cooked socks in the tea urn, he couldn't leave that habit behind, but his most spectacular bit of foolery was to come up behind Captain Bligh who was holding a billy of milk by his side and talking earnestly to the Two Pot Screamer, and drop his donger in the milk.

'Like a lizard drinking,' he said admiringly and Captain Bligh looked down for a second then threw milk, billy and all as far as he could. The Humdinger was too cheerful about his vileness for anyone to be angry.

THE HUNGER FOR WAR Stretch appeared briefly with his hollowed-out plant manual in which he hid war novels. He was nervous about being discovered breaking the reading rule despite the fact everyone did. When Slug or Enforcer came round, he turned a page and pretended to be reading about impulse and reaction turbines. He wouldn't have known one from the other, but he knew that page of words well and could answer a quick question on it. When the covering page wore out, he had to read the preceding page. In this manner he was learning something, even though he was doing it backwards and had started from the middle.

He had no sympathy for chess and the Humdinger despised him. He went away restlessly. He was one of those who shone at training schools and wrote long and erudite handovers for the following shifts, but if you walked down to his plant and asked why he was doing something, he couldn't answer.

He found a locker-room corner and got into his paperback. He was back on the Eastern front, his mouth watering as he chewed through a delicious story of German and Russian soldiers competing with each other several decades ago in torturing temporary prisoners spectacularly in the snow. What were once men were cutting off live men's toes with wire-cutters, shoving barbed wire into places where it would cause discomfort, cutting out eyes, crucifying men with barbed wire, cutting off hands, testicles, fingers, noses. By now the survivors were respectable family men; friends, not enemies. Stretch read, swallowed hard the saliva this story brought into his mouth, blinked so he wouldn't miss a word.

War was keeping a man awake: performing, years after, a valuable industrial service.

THE EASY WAY Into this peace a voice called, wavering, 'She's going down!' Men got to their feet, ready for flight. Strange noises outside.

'The boilers are rocking,' yelped Mister Puroil, who belonged to the pump-house where emergencies of this nature never happened. He left quickly on his company cycle for the safety of the tank farm.

'They are, too,' said Humdinger, looking out the high window. 'Look! There's the Count. Up there pulling levers again and she's coming down round his ears. Get on it, will you!'

There he was, fifty feet up, working the pressure-tapping levers one after the other. The noises inside the boiler, fearsome to the others, meant nothing to him. He'd never bothered to find out anything beyond his own immediate routine. He was there for a weekly pay packet and to follow orders. A dead loss.

'She'll be wearing pink pyjamas when she comes,' sang the Humdinger, running out to the control room. People were rushing about, trying to arrest runaway levels and failing pressures. This was the time when the turbo-expander machines usually tripped. But not this time. Instead, one of the machines took the easy way out and blew itself up. The bang stopped the Count in his tracks, but the pieces of casing and fragmented blades were on the opposite side and descended in a shower on the plant plot for distances up to a hundred yards. The rotor core, twisted and bent, fell to the grating. The rest of the machines surged and tripped, the plant collapsed.

Blue Hills, on the turbine landing, went to water and fell to his knees. The breath left him, his chest pained heavily. For what seemed like minutes, he couldn't breathe.

Ten minutes later a party of visitors under the guidance of the Spotted Trout descended on the place.

'Due to the latest technical improvements, this is an extremely silent running plant,' he extemporized. What the hell was wrong now? Several of his party made remarks about metal lying in the quadrangle.

'Is there a cleaning problem here?' asked a young accountant who would never have tolerated metal fragments on his office carpet.

'Just a moment,' said the Trout. He asked the nearest prisoner. 'What's all the bloody mess?' The Humdinger looked him over.

'I've seen bigger boobs than you,' he said loudly, glad to have an audience. 'But I don't know where. Can't you see the bastard's blown to bits?'

The Trout didn't want his visitors listening to this sort of talk.

'And in here,' clutching his loud-hailer and diving into the control room with the charmed rats after him, 'is the latest in radio communication between control and the operator on the job.' They were just in time to see the Glass Canoe perform a savage Gotcha on Stretch, who squealed and leaped like an arrow for the ceiling.

Outside, the Beautiful Twinkling Star was left posted on the worst jobs. But no complaining. He would never let his one-man side down by squealing.

Under a tarpaulin in the regenerator skirt, a body moved restlessly. Itchy with catalyst dust, the Rustle of Spring settled down for a night's sleep. It was quieter now.

AN APPLE A DAY 'What's the matter with Herman the German?' the Enforcer asked Stillsons in the silence of the controller's hut.

'Osteo-something.'

'They say his hand's off at the wrist.'

'Do they?'

'Isn't it?'

'It is.'

'Why doesn't someone tell me?'

'Why don't you keep your ear to the ground?'

'What are you shitty about?'

'I'm not shitty.'

'Yes you are.'

'No I'm not.'

'Yes you are.'

'Not.'

'Are!'

'Not!'

'This osteo is spreading, is it? Can he do his work without a hand?'

'He's still as good as any six men.'

SIXTY-DOLLAR CAT The Great White Father brought home a cat in a cardboard box; he'd rescued him from a rich doctor's house. The doctor's wife had been boasting of his cost and pedigree and the Home Beautiful deserved the best.

This cat was a ball of white wool, rolling in play on a harmless floor, pretending to be angry, advancing like a dragon on your shoe, a lion swatting a teasing piece of rag while men roared. White?

'So none of you mob treads on him.'

'What if we see double?'

'Don't tread on either of him...Many of us were made for the price of a seat at the movies and a bite to eat, or a chocolate malted at the milk-bar, a gin and lime at the pub, or a few cigarettes and a bottle of cheap steam on the golf links, but this cat cost sixty dollars!'

PICTURES FROM AN EXHIBITION Humpy was out on the turbine landing. It was night shift and in the dark the flue-gas header glowed cherry red under its thick grey sleeve of glass wool. Drops of oil splashed gaily down from the hydraulic connections of the great butterfly valve on the southern end.

The Samurai gazed without speaking at Humpy up near the turbines. What was he doing?

Big Dick ran out from the shower holding two handfuls of his prized possession and waving the rest about. He loved to be looked at. The Count followed him: he couldn't take his eyes off Big Dick. He'd seen nothing like it in the cold land of his birth.

Out in the panel room, Captain Bligh was doing the rounds, cracking jokes, singing, anything to make a noise and keep the prisoners awake. The Boardrider puzzled him, head in hands, an open plant manual before him. Captain Bligh got down on his hands and knees and crawled along the deck into range, looking up under the Boardrider's hat. The eyes were just open. The Boardrider had been alerted by the sudden stop in the flow of Captain Bligh's nagging words.

On the turbine platform Humpy watched as the oil drops smoked and crept slightly downhill toward the glowing section of the header. He looked round for a steam hose. Yes, there was one. And yes, the valve was shut and only hand-tight. One of those multiple-type gas and steam connections.

The Samurai went out into the panel room. The Glass Canoe talking interminably. He was getting thinner: another attack coming on. He usually lost condition before his illness struck. The Samurai tackled him.

'Do you only talk about yourself?' he asked sourly. Was it a weakness in him to detest weakness in other men?

The Glass Canoe didn't reply. I'll shut up, he said to himself. But he resumed the conversation when the Samurai was gone. Had quite a serious session with himself.

The Samurai, as he turned an eye towards the turbines again and Humpy, reflected that everywhere men carried tragedies round in their lumpy chests. He thought of Mrs Blue Hills. She had dropped her bundle again when he went to see her. Lamentations filled the air; she was so worked up that beads of sweat sprinkled her face and at one stage she shot a small fairy.

'Why does the woman always pay?' she wailed. The Samurai sneered at the commonness of the mind that could vomit forth such stuff in moments of agony.

The best things in life are free!' he shouted at her. He didn't know what to say. Besides, on night shift, at any hour of the twenty-four, his mind was furry and intractable like a strange, disobedient, untrained animal. He couldn't make out what was wrong with her. He couldn't make head or tail of her complaints. The visit ended with him having to do what he had no taste for.

Her tongue was probing, but tasted stale; she hadn't showered, and stank of urine. He felt guilty because he disliked her. If only he believed in God, or something. He could speak! He could be a trumpet to blaze forth to the world its failings and its ills. He could hold forth the patent medicine of ideology and compel the world to taste and try.

Humpy, twenty-one and bent like an old man, waited for the oil to flash. He was happy when the flames tore upwards: he had the steam hose ready. He spun the valve, aimed the nozzle at the flame. A fierce jet of vapour shot towards the fire and immediately ignited, right back up the spout of vapour to his hand. The gas at seventy-five pounds had overcome the fifty-pound steam and he was feeding the flames with fuel gas. His stomach on fire with fright, he turned off the gas and looked for a steam hose without any other attachments.

The Samurai saw the blaze, ran and doused it, bumping trembling Humpy out of the way with an expert hip.

The Samurai phoned Mrs Blue Hills when he judged that Blue Hills was on his way to work. She was still upset and he thought it best to ask her to meet him. Calm her down. He smuggled her into his car and went out to a motel at Riverditch, local haunt of marriage strays and passionate office lunches.

The cataclysm that burst on his amazed body left him weak and exhausted. All her woes and miseries and petty hates gathered in a storm of sex and rained on him. His body seemed to swell under her assault. He felt like a whale threshing about in a sea of tiger sharks. She was teeth and tears, feet and heels and fingernails. And all the time her story of tragedy and wasted love and misunderstanding and mistakes poured forth. She referred to Blue Hills as Rumpelstiltskin. She referred to him continually.

He went home and snatched a few hours' sleep in the afternoon, but woke around five, sick. Mrs Blue Hills must have given him her husband's cold.

Trying savagely to go to sleep, he did drop off into a dream of a world of fantastic order: a world where there was no waste of men or materials, not even of love.

He was threshing about still when the Great White Father broke in on him drunk. He had left his Home Beautiful for a day in a fit of night-shift horrors. He was shouting drunk, and seeing the Samurai looking sick, was full of panaceas.

A PARALLEL Down on the plant—though it might have been on another, harsher planet—the Glass Canoe grudgingly gave Far Away Places a hand with a large, tight block valve. Abusing him all the time.

'You sure you're not using our lavatory? A man like you, rotten with disease, ought to be careful.'

Far Away didn't mind, he was glad to have the big man's help. The valve was dangerous and hot; the air rippled and shimmered above it. There was not a safety poster in sight.

Far Away admired the eruption of energy each time the big man took the strain on his heavy wheel key. The top of his overalls was open, tanned chest showing, the red-brown tits set in a dark hair-mat moving along with the slabs of muscle underneath. Those hairs—they were so shiny. The man's body was in beautiful condition. Far Away Places eyed the sweat running down his neck and gathering in bright crystal drops under his chin. Was he resentful of this man who had tortured him and even now was abusing him in time with his pulls on the wheel key? Side by side with resentment was admiration—for the Glass Canoe's strength, the electric energy, the rhythmic flow of his efforts on the heat-stiff steel.

What a sly thing is a man! This admiration for strength co-existent with resentment for ill-treatment was like a population's half-willing, half-unwilling subjection to a strong leader.

THE COMFORT OF INDIFFERENCE None of the various grades of prisoners was aware of it, but while the hours and years of their detention passed, the captive moon swung round the tiny earth, the tides slid in and out obediently and the piece of galaxy in which our solar system nestled comfortably swung slowly in the nothingness that enveloped all existence and this nothingness tugged gently at all that had substance; prying loose, looking for weakness, drawing all things to it.

And perhaps, although it may not be considered in good taste to mention the fact, we might remember that the tiny earth which entertains us as guests, or lice, upon its surface while its present chemical state endures somewhere between the unbearable heat of the past and the unbearable cold of the future—this nice little home of ours is dying under us. We are now clever enough to measure by just how much our day is lengthening, and just when we shall draw the moon in to us as a ring of rocks and dust, and when we shall fall unnoticed into the sun. And cheerfully set out this information for children to understand, in books with coloured pictures showing the future final disaster. Just like a fairytale.

We don't know when we came here, or where we came from; we're having a free ride through space and call it life. And we are now aware that the earth is indifferent to us. She is not complimented when we set aside areas of natural beauty for ourselves, nor concerned when we wreck our surroundings. Her fate is sealed. We may as well plunder, exploit, bomb, bulldoze, alter, shift, drain, kill—anything—for all she cares.

QUICK RESULTS Nevertheless, despite the obliteration to come, we carry on as if life is important. If we don't, our attitude and behaviour become conspicuous.

The plant was readied again as if gasoline was important. Safety was discussed and circularized as if human life was important. The Spotted Trout did great strokes proving to hosts of innocent people how safe the plant and how kind Puroil was.

Three weeks—and the plant still starting up. If they had sense enough while the plant was down to do all the work notified as faulty or dangerous instead of rediscovering it when the plant was on the way up. But the pressure was on the brass from Melbourne, London, Europe to skimp on maintenance and show a quick result.

11
THE COLOUR BAR OF MIND

MUCK A saboteur at work. In every book in use in the distillation plants, ethylene, cat cracker, pump-houses, utilities, the word MUCK appeared in crude capitals. It was in and on books, overalls, drums of products in the yards, on the bodies and doors of trucks. On tanks.

Alone in splendour sat the Great White Father. His Home had not been defaced by MUCK. Oblivion was not muck, it was a solid product and of infinite use for as long as history extended. 'Not that our life and graduation as humans was a cosmic joke: it was simply a mistake. There is an ingredient in us we cannot use. This ingredient looks upward to a life without greed and hate. And greed and hate are necessary to keep our digestions balanced, our bodies in the pink, our identity separate, private property intact and our economy healthy. We are a spoilt batch—a monkey batch, the distillation boys say. Our life, for which we are not properly equipped, is better spent in the oblivion of alcohol or drugs. Death will come sleepily, the shock cushioned, a pleasant continuation of drugged sleep.'

He was talking to himself. His long, brown, confident fingers played with a small pearly button from Cinderella's blouse sleeve. It had come off while he was performing his regular test.

'I want a state of mind among them. Where all is permitted.' He was an idealist. 'They've been pushed so far back on themselves by the society we inherit that the only place they can hope for freedom is in their minds. Organized capitalist society is one without opposition or alternatives, its members have as little power over their government as the members of totalitarian societies. And their children are still taught pathetic nonsense about the ballot box being a remedy. What I have here is an underground movement opposing the official government of their lives, the federal, the state, the country, the local council, the union, the company, their next employer. What they want is to go on living, not too keenly, not too laboriously, with as little thought for anyone else as possible. Keeping their heads down, hoping the nasty things happen to others. Minding their own business when they want to and not having anyone pry into it. The only way is to teach them to enter the kingdom of oneself. Oppose everything, not outwardly but in their heads. Never oppose themselves.

'They are prisoners of their own image of themselves. Half the time you see them doing things they've copied from other people, and you think it's a mannerism, then after a while there's nothing left but mannerism. They've become the thing they copied. That's where I step in. I'll make them love this little taste of indulgence and oblivion so they'll think of nothing else, and treat everything else as so much illusion. No matter what happens to them—they may be redundant next week—they will feel self-sufficient, not because they can hold their heads up in this silly world, but because they are in my world, inside their heads, and there they are princes. Princes of the blood, with me their king. That's what they miss: the colour, the natural subordination to a king whose authority is unquestioned and whose orders coincide with their desires. Democracy is a treadmill for them, a grey, colourless place in which those favoured by birth and brains and a different metabolism forge ahead and take by brute force of intellect and personality the prizes of the obvious world; they need not equality, because they can never be equal, but a purple and gold monarchy. The purple in their mind's eye: the gold in the amber of their beer.'

THE ENFORCER It's like being in the lodge. When you're here at Puroil, you can't afford to speak of anything but the job or the weather or something harmless; nothing that would cause dispute, no political discussion, no religious arguments. Not that this lot or any lot of worker chappies could say anything worth listening to: if they had anything in their skulls they wouldn't be working here. I can't afford to let my tongue wag, either, or some bright spark will be quoting me and I'll be up on the carpet getting the boot right up the arse and when the next promotion comes, little old Enforcer won't be the pea, he'll be the peanut. I think I'm a decent person and a fair person and a kind person. But right now I'm sick. It makes you want to throw it all up rather than put up with this ugliness. Puroil has a decent, fair record, and it's always been kind to its people. Why do they always go against the company? It's almost as if they wanted to keep fighting the boss. As if they thought the company hated them and they're always trying to get back. But the company doesn't hate them; we take every care of them. As far as humanly possible. Puroil is good to the staff. We are civilized here; after all, it's a big company, old enough to have its little quaint ways. That's why all this ugliness—this stoppage nonsense—hurts so much. I almost wish I hadn't heard the rumour. It reminds a man there is a terrible side to life. Like having a viper in your bosom. Just because the company rejected all their silly demands. Still, you can't afford to talk too much about controversial things, someone's only got to dob you once and your name's Mud. Once they've got it in for you they never forget. Neither do I; there's still four people working here that I owe something. It doesn't matter to me if the Corpse gets the sack, I'll get him. I'll get him.

He had reached the wharf and rubbered along, peering inside the fogged windows of the amenities hut.

ADRIFT Blue Hills had walked a little way from the plant in the cooling air when he saw the Enforcer struggling in the darkness with two or three shadowy prisoners right on the edge of the wharf compound. The light was bad: safe enough for working, but not for defending yourself. Blue Hills was humane enough to go to his superior's aid, several mild pokes about the body were sufficient to show the assailants the Enforcer was not alone. Fearing the light, the prisoners backed off into the shadows and Blue Hills, breathing with difficulty because of the tension of the moment, turned to face the intended victim. He knew it was a member of the commanding class and expected only grudging thanks. The men were undoubtedly going to throw the Enforcer in the polluted river. With any luck he would have impaled himself on the shore debris of stray timber and bottles. Unfortunately, Blue Hills had left himself wide open by leaving his plant.

'You're a fair way from the cracker compound,' grated the Enforcer. Blue Hills tried not to puff, he didn't want to show he was in need of air. They might work him towards the gate if they thought he was cracking up.

'Following the crude-oil line,' lamely.

'Better follow it back again. This is as far as it goes,' said the Enforcer. 'I'll let it go this time, but don't let me catch you off the job again, night shift or no night shift. The Company has rules and I'm here to enforce them.'

Blue Hills slunk away, although he didn't feel like slinking; he felt more like calling the Enforcer a pommy bastard. He didn't. It was better to creep off with your tail between your legs.

'Go on! Shake a leg!' called the Enforcer.

Blue Hills hurried some more and bent his head forward in penitence. It was no joke to be forty-five with fifty not far away and them looking to get rid of the oldies. At that age it was much safer to be in chains than to be free.

'Bloody colonial crap,' muttered the Enforcer in a low voice. The word colonial was taboo, but you could still think it or say it quietly.

Next thing he was flying like a bird. His former assailants came from the shadows, came at a rush and bore him off his feet, bore him over the last few yards of solid ground, over the steel retaining wall into the river. He didn't land with a splash, but with a thump on a small black barge which moved off immediately into deep water. Two other avengers with company rag round their heads were pulling on a rope from the end of the wharf and soon the barge was moving fast by the wharf, out into Clearwater Bay. At two in the morning the bay was a lonely place. He would be lucky if he got back by daylight.

Blue Hills looked back, but one of the assailants threw a piece of shale after him and he took the hint.

'That'll teach the Enforcer to come snooping around,' said one.

'The other barnacles on the bot of progress at least ring up to alert you before they come,' said the other in a tone of grievance.

'Not him. He carries the whole company on his shoulders.'

'There was no barge pole on that thing, was there?'

'No. The current's got him now.'

'Don't go telling Blue Hills you saw him there. He's learnt nothing from the Enforcer's little lesson. He might put us in.

It was true. Blue Hills didn't understand that some men are not swayed from their duty to the company by any amount of mercy, pity, humanity and helping hands, but will look for an opening to gain from the weakness of any man stupid enough to help them. Gratitude had no place in manuals of official conduct and was represented by no entries in the company's books.

STILLSONS SAYS ALL RIGHT, MUM Poor Stillsons. They transferred him from the new plant to the old. He couldn't believe it the first day. He had no wife or girl or men friends; the company was the sum of his expectations.

On the second day, returning to home and mother, he went to his bedroom and made a small model of the cracker in corks of different shapes, linking the columns with sharpened match sticks. When the main vessels were connected, he went to Mum's sewing basket and took her little blue tin of pins, the one with black paper inside to keep the pins from rusting.

He carefully stabbed pins into the cork columns. The fat regenerator took most of them—it was a champagne cork: he picked it up in the street one day and wondered what it was. He'd never touched a drop, he had to ask Mum what it was for.

'Your dinner's on the stove, son,' his mother called.

'All right, Mum.' Why was he nearly in tears?

'There's tea in the pot!'

'All right, Mum.' He hadn't cried since he was a boy, since his father had given him a few licks with the old horse-whip.

'I've set the alarm for the morning.'

'All right, Mum.' How could they do this? There was no more loyal staff man than Stillsons. He wished them every harm that terrified him on the job. He resolved to work and work and work, to atone for whatever wrong he had done. He had no idea what it was. Could it be for not putting up a sign about the sewage leak? Why didn't they shift the Sumpsucker? They couldn't imagine for a moment he was a better man.

A RISING LINE The Beautiful Twinkling Star had a failing: he found it too easy to see both sides of a question. 'I can see where it must be very difficult for the company.' This was his way of asking for moderation in Union claims. The industrial agreement was up for renewal. Men were letting their heads go, asking for more leave, less hours, more money to be written into the Union's draft log of claims. 'Just where do these concessions and rises end?'

'Never,' said the Samurai.

'But look how bad things were. And how good now. What more do you want? This is our station in life, we can't get everything we want.'

The Samurai drew a line on the floor with the toe of his boot. A line with a rising slope. 'Here's us now, on top of the slope. What about a hundred years time? Do the next hundred years carry on at this level? No. We go up, still.' He continued the line. 'We're a long way short now of where we'll be then. This isn't the end of the world. Where's your opposition to improvement?'

'Improvement, from a company point of view, would be a decreased wages bill. I can see where it must be very difficult for the company.'

'They'd have us work for naught if they could.'

A QUIET WEEKEND The Samurai went off night shift that Friday morning fairly tired, but pleased the plant was going. All that could happen, if the plant continued steady, was that the company would start to reduce the manning scale of the plant. They would do this just before the agreement, then with a great show of compromise restore the manning scale but strike out half a dozen items on the Union's log of claims to balance their generosity. Then when the agreement was signed they'd reduce the manning anyway. Still, it hadn't happened yet.

He decided to have a weekend in the country. At half past seven he rang several old friends, all young women, before they had gone off for work—all his friends were someone's employees—and persuaded them to meet him that evening at seven, with the promise of an idyll in the country. That gave him time for ten hours' sleep. Mrs Blue Hills would still be there when he got back. He felt he had to get away from Sydney and the smoke for a bit and get some dirty water off his chest.

He took three of them and got back to Sydney at ten o'clock Sunday night. He was completely shagged out and much quieter in his mind. Ready for the treadmill.

CONDITIONED One Eye worked a doubler that day, off night shift, and felt very seedy. His beard grew, his clothes commenced to stink, he was uncomfortable. At nine in the morning he had a visitor—didn't know who it was. The sun blinded him after the pleasant dark of night shift, his cups of tea tasted bitter on the tongue.

'Fine morning!' called the Wandering Jew from out of the sun. He was a little startled, himself, to be confronted by this wreck of a man.

'Go and get yourself well and truly upped!' rasped One Eye, the whole weight of his fifty-one years, a long night shift and an extra eight hours on his back.

In a moment of rare understanding the Wandering Jew said, 'Sorry, I can't hear you,' and turned and walked back to the blue Mercedes. What was the point of disciplining this poor devil? He would probably see who it was when he looked out of his hut window, then he'd be sorry enough. He went back to his office in the Termitary in time for morning tea and felt good. The cracker was going, the refinery was healthy.

One Eye looked from his window, it was just as well to see who you yelled at, just as the Wandering Jew slid behind the wheel of the glittering Mercedes.

'Jesus wept,' he said aloud and wondered if he would see his sixtieth birthday out on the refinery. Then he remembered his plan for the sack and was glad. Night shift must be getting me, he thought. For a moment there I was crap-scared of a boss.

YOU TALK LIKE BIG BROTHER The Good Shepherd was asked by the Whispering Baritone about the men's feeling on current issues in dispute between management and men. As he looked at this good man across his desk, he was filled with loathing. Here was a man who could be left posted on bad jobs with no complaints, a man who wouldn't stick up for himself. These engineers and scientific bodies thought they could get ahead in this jungle by virtue of their master of specialties; he, the Whispering Baritone, was there to tell them they were fooling themselves. How had the Python got where he was? Not by Boy Scout actions that belonged to a world of childhood and dreams.

What could you do with a man like this, especially if you were one of the new, smooth class like the Whispering Baritone, neither an owner nor a prole, but constantly on the lookout for your own interests; not tied to fixed principles or doctrines, only to what will benefit yourself most, a man who had never suffered and was on the alert to see he never did?

The Good Shepherd had been trained from childhood not to be greedy for himself, trained so effectively that a certain selflessness had become part of his nature. His main mental hazard was his inability to see why others wanted to be selfish when he didn't.

The Whispering Baritone's funny feeling about nostrils bothered him again. Looking sideways at the Good Shepherd he could see certain hairs protruding from the man's nose, hairs that should have been trimmed. It was true that nostrils seemed to be for breathing, but why did they have to be large and so dark inside? And hairy. The Baritone couldn't bear to look at them. He worked away at the flaking tips of his fingers. The flesh under the flakes was new and clean, like a baby's.

'There are a few reclassifications we've decided on,' he said casually, knowing a casual tone would pierce the Good Shepherd, who liked to think the greatest care and soul-searching had gone on before a man's livelihood was taken from him. Reclassification was a euphemism for dismissal. This was usual. When the men made demands the company tried to scare them first. If they persisted, this meant they might mean business. They couldn't possibly sack men out of hand. The time wasn't right. The rest of the unions had to be crushed first and this hadn't been achieved. The Good Shepherd was part of the hierarchy himself, he didn't want it otherwise, but sometimes he wished either he had no part in it or that he had the entire authority, so that decisions would rest on him and if they had to burden some soul, it would be his. To think that it burdened no one—that was dreadful. He could never get it into his head that the threatened dismissals tactic was a try-on.

'Don't be so down in the mouth. You might ask me who they were,' mocked the Whispering Baritone, using the past tense in speaking of bodies that he hardly recognized as human when they were employed at Puroil, but having gone or being under threat of going, ceased to exist.

'Don't forget that though the public looketh on the outward appearance, the employer looketh on the heart.' He told the Good Shepherd some of the names.

'Why One Eye?'

'The Old Man didn't want him sacked, but I thought it best; the person spoke in an insolent manner to him. It will be your job to tell him.' The Baritone enjoyed this.

'He's the best man in the pump-house! You won't replace him out of those available.'

'Rubbish! There are replacements.'

'You speak as if anyone could walk in there and do that job.'

'An unskilled job? Of course.'

'And I tell you it would take you as long to learn that job as it took One Eye. There's equipment down there that needs to be personally known before it's operable.'

The Whispering Baritone laughed. 'That's up to engineering. Don't bother me with that.'

'There'll be trouble over this.'

'Not unless you make it.'

'Who are the others?'

The Baritone tossed the paper across the desk. 'Read it.' He went on, while the Good Shepherd gasped at the names on the paper, 'There is in all civilizations a colour bar of mind. The people you take so much thought for are beyond education, they lack basic intelligence. Throughout the Greek and Roman civilizations it was universally assumed that a large slave population was required to perform services unworthy to engage the activities of a civilized man. In other words, a civilized community could not be self-sustaining. A comparatively barbarous substratum had to be interwoven in the social structure to sustain the civilized apex. Nothing has changed. The substratum is still required; a slave population is needed for supplying the mechanized manpower for the continual building and repetitive work. The submerged population is still submerged, modern conditions of industrial employment are not significantly different from those of ancient slavery. Why? Because the history we know is the history of kings and wars and movements of nations. Those slaves had a good life and enjoyed their diversions and were protected by the state. Bread and circuses the same as now. Show me the difference. The only efficient way to govern them is to actually reduce them to the status of a lower species. The ultimate aim is to make them animals—then ruling them is easy.'

'Surely you're one of them yourself!'

'I was. But like some—*some*—slaves of those days, I have risen, and some day I will be a manager and walk calmly forward on the plateau of full citizenship—equal with the best!'

'And what happens to the ones we can't get at—the pensioners, the sick, the mentally retarded?' the Good Shepherd asked bitterly.

'Vermin. They have no place.'

'You talk like Big Brother.'

'Big Brother? Tell this to your slave friends: the man who does the work put before him need never worry about Big Brother.'

What a reasonable sentiment! How absurd it makes the fears of a few of us for the totalitarian future! The Good Shepherd passed over it easily; it reminded him of duty, honesty, obedience, loyalty. Solid Christian virtues.

Dear Reader, please read the sentence again. It is apparent we can't rely on the Whispering Baritone or the Good Shepherd to comment further. The Baritone is shuffling papers as a sign he has finished talking; the Shepherd is taking his time, not going to be hurried. After all, he has to do the dirty work.

Did you read it? Isn't it nicely put? The work put before him. Could be tending furnaces, early morning rifle practice, designing a new gas nozzle, making lampshades. Anything. And Big Brother will never bother you. But how is it that good Christian virtues are such a help to him?

GOTCHA To his great surprise, the Corpse was caught walking off the job early, going through the blue gates without ringing off, buying gasoline for his car and bulk detergent to cut and sell to his friends, then in again to ring off. This gave him a start getting out of the car park. It also broke company rules.

In the course of a casual conversation, the Enforcer alerted the Black Snake, who told Luxaflex, who mentioned it to the Brown Snake. The Corpse had been doing this for months before the Enforcer found out, and could have carried on till retirement before the pay office caught him, although he walked out past this office every day. There was a routine to detect late comers, but not early goers.

The two Snakes waited and caught him. He drew six months on day work. Vicious words flew round in the Corpse's head, but he kept them in.

THE GLASS CANOE It's all over. I thought of trying to stop the rot, but after a certain point you have to let them have their heads.

Vote carried. Unanimous. Twenty-four-hour stoppage, only they haven't decided when. Mind you, there's no intimidation there, but you could back the wrong horse if you went against the mob.

The man that's in command of himself all the time and knows what's going on inside him has it all over these types; they don't know what they think, they've had no training looking inside themselves. Like I had after the invigorating experience in hospital. Face it! That's the secret, it's the only way. Once I was in darkness about myself and bad things happened; now I'm in the clear and I know what I'm doing. You never think when you're a kid the peculiar things that are going to happen to you later on. That picture of me standing between the big guns on the deck of the old cruiser *Weemala*, I even had that on the dressing table at home when I castrated myself.

I remember thinking what a fine sailor I made in the old bell-bottoms, and the tunic fitted tight over the chest. I was a big man then, none of this fat. Not many men would be game to face up to the truth about themselves and get to the root of the matter straight off. That's the one thing the doctors criticized me for, and I still don't agree with them. I was right to do it; I have no doubts about it any more. Even Rita understood. She didn't say a word, a man was lucky to have a woman like that to stand beside him while he tried to get to the top in this jungle. There's still time to make something of myself. Not that I have those stupid ambitions any more: a man's aims must have a lot in common with the things he is capable of. Straight edge secateurs.

I've never told any of these people about it, not because I'm running away from the memory of it, but you have to keep something to yourself. Doctor Rosenblum agrees with me there.

Secateurs. Done a bit of pruning, Doc. Give us a few stitches and something to stop the bleeding, please. Too many people forget their manners with doctors; they don't have to do a good job on you, it doesn't hurt to speak to them as nicely as you would to a bank manager.

I thought the secateurs would act like the thing they castrate the sheep with, not breaking the skin but cutting the cord inside the scrotum. How is a lay person to know secateurs would cut off the whole scrotum? Stones and all. There was still a bit hanging. I would have to go and prove how much nerve I've got by finishing the job in front of the doc.

If I told these sort of people that work here, at least I'd get a laugh when I tell them I can't ever be hurt by a knee in the groin. I might do that, just for the laugh, they know I like a bit of a joke sometimes.

On that cruiser, the first few days, I was so sick after they gave me that dish of spaghetti I had it coming out my nose. That was probably where I learned to appreciate a good joke; after that it was my specialty to feed the new kids spaghetti. And when they got me in the diving suit and left me with the thing shut and screwed down tight and I nearly suffocated while they went off and had lunch, that probably set the style for my own pet practical jokes. I've been lucky so far, no one knows I've got claustrophobia from that diving suit thing, if they did they'd probably get me in the plant lift and switch off the current when she was between floors.

Poor old Far Away Places slipped on the top landing today, he was lucky I was there, I saved his life for sure. I just managed to grab him, the poor silly old no-hoper had tears in his eyes with fright trying to thank me. He was more upset at being saved than he was when I had a go at him in front of the crew down in the control room. I just had to abuse him, I was so relieved at being able to save someone's life, I've always wanted to feel I saved someone from dying. I don't think he would have jumped.

I felt so pleased with Far Away that I started to tell him about my operation, but a funny thing happened. He started to get all frightened and screaming and yelled out: 'Don't tell me about it!' That's something I might ask Doctor Rosenblum when I go in to have a chat next week, it's no use trying to get any sense out of old Far Away; poor devils like that have no idea why they do anything. It isn't as if I had an urge to confess everything; maybe he thought that was it. I didn't. Just wanted to tell someone, that's natural enough. I can't see what harm it would have done him to listen. It isn't as if I was psycho and would have cut his throat just because

I'd told him a secret. I'm not like that, I never have been and never will be. I ought to know exactly what I'm like.

I'm glad we'll be out for twenty-four hours, it'll give me time to study up next week's lesson in the correspondence management course. It's our fantastic unity that beats the company every time.

A MARATHON When the Kraut left for a rival company building refineries in Queensland and found his pro rata long-service leave was not calculated at the rate that would have applied if he had been taking the leave he swore for four hours till the office staff went home. Swore in German, but repeated himself a lot.

He couldn't get it into his head that there was justice in the principle involved. His service period had gone ten months into that year, so he received ten-twelfths of the base holiday pay he would have got when the twelve months period was up, except that if he had taken his annual holidays he would have received his shift penalty rates—the same pay as if he had been at work—but because it was at the end of his service with the company he didn't receive the benefit of penalty rates.

It seemed to the Kraut that he had worked shift for ten months without the benefit of it in his holiday pay, but his attitude was out of order. The company's policy was exactly as he had been paid, so where was his grouch?

He accosted his Union delegate. 'If I was on my leave, I get this shift money. Why not for the ten months of this year? What does it matter I'm leaving? I worked the shifts!' And his mouth working, too, after the words had stopped.

'They told you what their policy is: you don't get it. Besides, you're going up there to be a foreman, aren't you?'

THE VALUE OF EDUCATION One of the items of value in great demand by the money-hungry prisoners was lead; not the most portable, certainly, but when the cyclone wire of the main fence was unclipped, the wire pushed aside, and the lead thrown to the ground, the operation was over. The odd car that stopped early in the morning to lift its bonnet was hardly noticed. Security was at the main gate then. If a man were to leave the car door open as he tinkered with the car, it was simple to drop the lead in through the door on to the floor of the car and drive off. Just a few small parcels, not much value, say a hundredweight, but when it's done seven days of afternoon shift and seven nights of night shift, the money mounts up.

Nothing like this was possible on day shift: small objects were noticeable then. Day shift was the time for whole pumps or compressors, ladders, lengths of pipe. Narrow pipe inside wider.

Poor old Bourke Street Freddie was very fond of lead and copper. He was in the sinker business during working hours. The company was under the impression he was employed in the mechanical workshop in the remains of the blacksmith's shop, but this was incorrect. He collected lead and sold sinkers made from the roofs of the older buildings. Even fishermen who had bought some last week were suckers for sinkers.

Bourke Street was illiterate and could be told anything, but he was only once tricked over lead. Loafing round on day shift, men like the Humdinger taught him to play noughts and crosses in a special way. They taught him to win by making a line of noughts or of crosses with a bend in it. After losing four out of five games against him, the Humdinger would get up and say with a straight face, 'He's too good for me. One of you lot better take him on.' Bourke Street, who was never taught modesty as he was never taught to read and write, would lord it terribly over everyone because of his superiority in this fascinating game. The Humdinger had even better sport when after a string of losses and with a boss approaching, he would accuse Bourke Street Freddie of cheating. He would get up like a prophet of old and roar deafeningly at his workmates. He could never be made to understand that the business of Puroil, in the eyes of men like the Good Shepherd and the Wandering Jew, took precedence over any personal interests or attainments of the prisoners.

In his nearly empty mind there was another fact floating about, bouncing off odd corners of the few other unrelated facts in his head: it was the notion of equality. 'You're just as good as him,' the Humdinger or the Glass Canoe would whisper to him as the Wandering Jew or the Python came into sight—usually by the back door, hoping to catch men idle.

And Bourke Street would disgrace himself, talking a babble of empty words with no rhyme or reason to the executives, who took themselves seriously. When he saw something had gone wrong he would offer them sinkers, taking them in handfuls from his pocket and extending them under the noses of these men who had the power of employment or separation over him.

When others decided to move in on his sinker business, he was up against men of superior education and was lost. The men who had been through school right up to the age of fourteen years put it over him easily. Those few who had gone right through high school were even more proficient at making a fool of him. Cunning, selfishness and dishonesty were not hindered from coming into flower by education.

He was seen one Sunday on the roof of an old building behind the workshop, carefully removing the lead flashing put there in the good old days of peace and plenty of lead, by two characters from the refining end, who sneaked round under the building on the side towards which Bourke Street Freddie was rolling the lead, waiting for it to fall into their arms. And it did. The poor wretch took his time getting down, walked round to claim his prize, but no lead. For months, every day, his rounds of the refinery included a sorrowful look at the place his lead should have been.

He came to a miserable end. His body was found in a storm-water drain in Waterloo, a blackened Sydney slum, several weeks after he was killed for his holiday pay. This pay was given out in small brown envelopes and Bourke Street Freddie was always proud when he had a few extra dollars, always holding it up for people to see. Some kids who found the body let their secret slip to a teacher at school. They'd mentioned it at home, but their parents were not the sort who took notice of kids or approached police.

They made that teacher's life hell ever after: they'd enjoyed having a corpse of their own to play with after school. Usually they only had dogs' bodies and cats'.

GOVERNED BY STRING Rain. The air was warm and drops of liquid descending in heavenly reflux to earth fell on everything that happened to be in their way.

Some of the younger operators and visiting student technologists found puzzling the sudden speeding-up of the steam turbines supplying feedwater to the boilers.

The operators, who had been in a state of darkness concerning this, commenced finding others to blame. The Samurai came in. He listened to their agile attempts to pin some absent person with the blame for the speeding machines, and to the attempts of the student scientists to find the explanation in the unskilled workers' handling of the plant. The Good Shepherd walked through, listened, then looked for the Samurai and beckoned him over. The Samurai regarded him gravely, didn't move. The Good Shepherd remembered it was he who was after help and went over to the Samurai.

'Is there anything to worry about in this turbine business?'

'Nothing more than usual in a dump that cuts its maintenance staff to cut costs instead of getting all the maintenance it needs so plants can work at maximum through-put all the time.'

The Good Shepherd knew this very well, but wasn't going to say the company was wrong.

'Why are the turbines speeding? There seems no reason for it.'

'See out there?'

'The rain?'

'You know what happens when it rains?'

'I can't think of anything that would make this sort of difference to the plant. Except power dips, but they trip the electric machines, not steam turbines.'

'The rain stretches the string holding the turbine governors. They speed up.' He looked away and rubbed his right shoulder lightly. It was tender.

The Good Shepherd thanked him. How was it those people milling about blaming each other didn't know? Did they spend all their time inside, or go about outside with their eyes shut? How was it Engineering could have such protection from above that stupidities like this could remain unremedied? String holding the governors, solenoid trips wired up, blocks of wood holding in key compressors by blocking mechanical trips, drop-shut gas valves jammed open with bits of wire, buckets and tins placed under oil drops on plants operating at high temperatures, contract labour brought in to do quick and slapdash maintenance jobs on equipment they'd never seen before just to keep the labour establishment figures down to the maximum prescribed from elsewhere. Cutting costs.

12
THE GREAT SOCIETY

NO BENDING A great society is a society in which men of business think greatly of their functions.

'It shouldn't be too difficult to get their guts,' remarked the Python. 'Dismissals, overtime, manning scale, the new wage agreement, there's plenty to beat 'em over the head with now. They'll probably help us by thinking up a few ridiculous grievances we can use against them, too. It's like a game the kids play—yes, like No Bending! You yell out No Bending! while you poke 'em in the gut to make 'em bend, and if they bend they're out.' The Python was careful to say this sort of thing to a man like the Good Shepherd, who would never repeat what he heard. His goodness, his honesty, thus had their market value: they kept him docile and obedient and ensured Puroil its money's worth. A splendid arrangement. In this way the religion of the Gentle Jesus has its value in industry.

NO COMMENT Puroil had brought in men from local engineering firms to extend an eight-inch line from one side of a three-foot vessel round to its other side as a return line to carry a gasoline caustic-soda mixture from one bundle of mixing elements to another. Why did it leave one side, project itself twenty-five yards away and curve round a concrete pillar before returning to the other side?

'Why is this?' asked the Good Shepherd.

'It's on the plans,' said the men from the igloo. The igloo was the construction office, a wartime nissen hut of corrugated iron which looked like lasting long enough to be used in World War Three.

Was there an operational reason? Support for the vessel? No one knew. Years later, men were still pointing it out to new men as evidence of the crazy operation of which all were sneakily, slavishly part.

'It allowed for an extra 150 feet of stainless steel pipe on the plans, mate, so we had to put the 150 feet somewhere. We couldn't just forget it and credit 'em with it,' said a clerk of works to the Samurai on the next shutdown a week later.

A NAIL FROM THE CRUCIFIXION The dismissal threats produced a counter threat. Let's have a stoppage. When the stoppage ultimatum was given to the management, the reaction was usual. Stand them down, don't wait for a stoppage. That's how it always started, then the advocates of this policy, like the Python, allowed themselves to be talked into negotiating. This time, though, when the Python brought out the hard line, no one persuaded him to drop it. Even the Whispering Baritone, misinterpreting the fury of the Wandering Jew at the men's threat, kept his tongue still in his twitching cheeks. His tic was bad.

'I want you to tell them that anyone concerned in a stoppage at this refinery will be stood down,' the Python said to the Good Shepherd. There had never been stand-downs before.

At the meeting with the men, the Brown Snake stayed coiled in his chair while the Good Shepherd passed on the executive decision to the delegates who called it a threat and went away and called out their men immediately.

The Whispering Baritone took great pleasure in drafting the notice of the stoppage, careful to mention that no specific reason had been given by the operators.

On the cracker the notice couldn't be put up, there were no pins. After vainly searching, Captain Bligh directed that it be nailed up. None of the men would touch the paper. We're not carpenters, that's a carpenter's job with hammer and nails. He drew a blank with the fitters, too. They wouldn't touch something that concerned operators. Eventually, he found a great nail on the ground outside the control building and nailed it up with that.

It was only a few minutes before Big Dick wrote near the nail: One of the Original Nails used for the Crucifixion. It was a very large nail.

When the parties were before the authorities and the workers duly warned back to work, there were a few things said about the ultimatum given to the helpless workers. Nasty things. Not even judges can be relied on to refrain from sarcasm at the expense of the employer, though the employer's profit is usually safe in their hands. They feel themselves in a position parallel to that of the employer rather than to the humble, unwieldy multitudes of workers who do, after all, get under the feet like so many cow-cakes in a paddock.

'You'll have to deny this threat you made of standing them down,' said the Brown Snake.

'Deny it?'

'They misunderstood you, that's the line. The Commissioner said the threat caused the stoppage, so we must make it appear there was no threat. It was only word of mouth, so it's your word against theirs. Because of the court's criticism, it is obvious the time isn't right for bulk dismissals: only One Eye is to go. We'll get a stand-down clause written in to the next agreement.'

'But it wasn't my word, it was the decision of all of us, and besides, they'd already decided to have a stoppage.'

The Brown Snake yawned. There was no problem here. He was tired of these amateurs, men who couldn't tell a convincing lie. How could they hope to hold a job requiring a sense of responsibility?

What was the Good Shepherd to do? Resign rather than lie? Spend hours, days, in soul-searching conflict with himself? How delightful if we could say yes. But it wasn't so. If he had resigned for that reason, the Company would have been hurt. Loyalty to his superiors won, and for their sake he scarred his soul, which he thought of as immortal. He stood up on his hind legs, lied like a man and the men jeered.

VIRGIN SODS UPTURNED The Great White Father was visited by many prisoners in need of more than sex and beer and refuge from the forces of a society which had nothing for them. He knew they were beyond his ministrations.

'The body,' he said, looking at their empty faces, 'has a wisdom we know nothing about.' He was about to drag in a reference to the Glass Canoe, whose great body was designed for emergencies it would never meet in our phase of civilization, but the man himself was at the back of the drink hut, moody, sipping his beer. The Great White Father thought he knew how such a man was feeling, imagining himself blocked off by a few tinpot executives who could say when he worked and when he didn't: men the Glass Canoe could crush without ferocity with one great brown shiny hand.

'We are the body of the company. Sometimes we are the first organisms to sense coming danger or ill-health. Some day there may be a new way of organizing places like this so we won't have to have stoppages, but in the meantime our civilization is founded on mutual distrust; our world is full of cops and screws, talebearers and auditors, bosses, dobbers and governments.

'It's a great inspiration to me to see you all listening with your mouths open—the better to drink your beer. You know what we are. We're the crap. We don't argue with that. To them up there we're a crowd of zombies with numbers—we look sideways at them in their nice coats and ties and what do we see? We see them looking sideways at us. They're just as worried about us as we are about them. We're here in captivity, we always will be. They pay us not to walk the streets; they pay us to keep out of mischief, because there's so many of us that if we got into mischief we'd end up rocking their old employment boat and shorting their profits and maybe cutting off a few heads for a laugh. But we're not interested in that sort of thing'

'Why shouldn't we think about it?' came a voice from the back. The Glass Canoe had risen to speak, but found his position false in that atmosphere and sat down again. He said weakly, 'It's better to die standing than live on your knees. And that's what we're doing.' Something in him wanted to be accepted by both sides.

'Better still to sit down and have a drink,' suggested the Humdinger.

'I know how it feels,' said the Great White Father. 'Sometimes the worker feels like a big gun, loaded and primed, ready to go off. But there's only one target. Sometimes it feels as if a man is just rotting away in peace—there's no chance to be put through your paces, nothing to fight, but there's one target. Men are not made for peace, you say, just as our bodies are not made for sleep. Feet are the only part made to take a man's weight. And feet are for charging the enemy, and there's only one enemy! Who is the enemy? Who is my enemy? Who is your enemy?' He stopped, stooped down, lifted a can and sank it. 'Your own brother is your enemy! The only target is your fellow man. He is your primal competitor. And more than that when you *are* led into battle by one set of leaders against your enemy-target-brother who has another set of leaders, the leaders of both sides have a funny knack of stepping aside at the last moment to leave you face to face with your target-brother. You fight him, you kill each other, and who survives? Leaders. They live to lead another day. Then what happens? The emergency and the hate are past, the fights over, the dead buried, words forgotten, vows broken, revenge forever unsatisfied...as we sit down to sup with our enemies and go to bed with the dead and enjoy it.'

Another can at a noisy gulp.

'We are the eternal rabble. In our name shame comes. We never benefit. We are the same before as after. We kill ourselves, our brothers, for what? Not for ourselves, but for those skilful enough to make a profit from our wars. We never profit, we have no skills to make money from death and conquest and spheres of influence. Standard of living? Maybe it falls if we get beaten? It's more likely to rise. Was life any worse before the airplane and the TV set and the megaton bomb? We could go back there any time and we wouldn't take more than a day to get used to it. But who wouldn't get used to it? The bludgers that have all the things this world can give them—things we make—the free ones that toil with other people's money and go to bed on the wealth that we and the machines produce.'

'Sounds a big red rag to me,' said the Glass Canoe.

'No, mate!' shouted the Great White Father. 'No! That sort of thing is bull! That's changing one set of masters for another more efficient at keeping you in your place. And what's our place? At the bottom, the arse of the pile; we're the undiluted, eternal crap. No. No isms. The only way is our way. The vast underground life of prisoners, working when you have to, but not too hard unless you feel like the exercise, taking time off, pulling the whole thing back with a steady pressure, the whole juggernaut!—having a drink when you feel like it, like they do up there!—jumping on a bunk with a free and easy sheila when you feel like it!—just like they do up there!—eating as well as you can...The whole edifice of civilization is built with our bones cemented together; the streets are paved with our brothers; we are like little coral animals whose skeletons make the foundations on which islands rest! We have only one life. Let it be as easy as you like to make it, there is no other.'

He sat and drank again. Somewhere in his great eye-sockets a tiny team of nerves worked shoulder to shoulder and squeezed a drop of saline solution along his tear ducts into the corners of both eyes. As soon as he was aware of these drops his sinuses seemed to swell and he knew motion had taken him by surprise. He blew his nose strongly and dismissed the tears.

BOURKE STREET FREDDIE When the Two Pot Screamer heard of Bourke Street Freddie's death he made up a few verses and stuck them with Puroil resin to the wall of the drink hut.

Bourke Street Freddie, dead a week
Ignored the crown and anchor board, the cry
Of 'Heads a dollar', the hated smell of soap,
The glowing forge and ring of steel on steel.

Storm water in the drain with care arranged
His bones, conveyed a graceful, swaying motion
To burst stomach, water-whitened legs
And all his private skin the water changed.

His arms were broken backwards, eyeballs gone,
Children poked his pubis with long sticks,
One foot was missing, dogs had licked his blood,
But this man was our brother, and is home.

The Great White Father liked it, but criticized the feel of the last line. I asked the Screamer about the reference to crown and anchor and it turned out he'd lost all his money on it himself, the money he was to go into the hotel business with, ten years before. He didn't know whether Bourke Street Freddie had ever played either crown and anchor or two-up. And there was no blacksmithing done any more. Bourke Street had had to become assistant to a young fitter, there was no provision for getting qualified in another trade once yours was redundant. I thought it rather sad.

THE EXPANSION OF HATE Later that day a teenage contractor was seen inside the Puroil prisoners' locker-room. Twenty dollars missing. The boy was caught in an hour. For the following twenty-four there was a crazy mess of rumours as to his nationality. The Two Pot Screamer took notes like mad. The nationality of the thief depended on the present retailer of the rumour. It was easy to pick out those who hated Scotsmen, the Irish, Estonians, Hungarians, Germans, English, Welshmen, South Africans. The only ones not mentioned were those nationalities the speaker had never heard of. The limits of their knowledge were thus the limits of their hates, or to put it another way, hate expands with the available facts.

THE LIMITS OF SYMPATHY Everyone spares a thought for the man who is disabled through no fault of his own. Scene: the Humdinger in the bed hut, the light on, the Old Lamplighter wanting conversation.

'Who's that poor man with his arm off?'

'Arm off? I don't know anyone with an arm off.'

'From the elbow down.'

'Thick-set joker, bullet head?'

'Sort of hefty, yes. Always eating apples.'

'Herman the German. But he's only got one hand off. Disease in his bones.'

'He's got an arm off now.'

'An arm?'

'At the elbow.'

'Poor bugger. Must be spreading.'

'Will it go right through him?'

'I hope not, poor sod. Listen, are you going to keep your mind on the job or not?'

COINCIDENCE The Enforcer was put into hospital one night with broken arms, skull fractures and bottle cuts. Three men who did this sort of thing for hire waited for him near his garage which he reached by driving along an unlit lane, asked him for a light and proceeded to do him over. A bottle from behind, a tyre lever from in front and a man with heavy boots to work on the sides. It was eleven-thirty at night and no one heard his yells.

'Someone must have hated his guts,' commented the prisoners. 'Probably the neighbours did it.'

The assailants beat him up from fifty yards behind the house right round to his front veranda. The first blow with the tyre lever broke his right arm. The second broke his left. By a curious coincidence he was disabled for six months exactly, the same length of time the Corpse was on day work. The funny thing was, the Corpse didn't hire them. He'd been talking in a pub about the bastard that dobbed him in, and a little man who said he was a psycho and feared by the police thought he'd do the Corpse a favour. It was a love job.

HALFWAY UP A WALL Nat's Girl, watching them all from her perch halfway up a wall, smiled. She had been taken in every conceivable position; every inch of her body had satisfied some seeker as a sexual object: there was no waste on her. Hair, nose, ears, feet, eyes, hands, elbows, buttocks, neck, thighs, breasts, heels, navel, toes, lumbar region, instep, ribs, tongue, shoulders, teeth, knees, chin—everything. Every square inch. There was as little sexual waste on Nat's Girl as there was economic waste on any of the sheep, cattle or pigs bred for man's other satisfactions.

She made no moral judgments. A man's a man, that was her starting point. She watched as the Samurai came in to her little room while the plant was steady—it wasn't going and nothing could be done until the skeleton staff of fitters bolted a few large flanges.

He had had a dreadful interview with Mrs Blue Hills. She was looking for him on the weekend when he took off for the country with girls and was determined to be very bitter about it until she was able to make him suffer, then she would turn in mercy and forgive him. But not until he showed some signs of suffering and remorse, though what this meant for her or what satisfaction it was remained obscure.

To cap it all, he had a visit in the lab from Blue Hills himself. Words had flown like erratic birds from Blue Hills' mouth: words hurt and strange. The Samurai listened like a priest. Blue Hills was sure someone had been seeing his wife. The euphemism hurt him as it issued from his shapeless lips. What he wanted to say was that another man, who hadn't had the expense of marrying his wife and keeping her in food and clothes for fifteen years in return for household services and infrequent sexual intercourse, this other man who had been spared the drag side of his woman had now come along and was being given as much sexual intercourse as he wanted, with none of the other irksome duties like being with her all the time and taking her out and seeing her when she was not fit to be seen and smelling her when she was not fit to be sniffed, and being set up for his rare sexual trick with an impatient scarecrow in pins and curlers.

'What should I do about this man?'

'If you can't satisfy your wife, she's got to get it somewhere. If you can't, leave her. Get someone you can satisfy and that can satisfy you. That's all I can say. Now beat it.'

Nat's Girl smiled down from her elevated position at this male wisdom.

DOUBLE BUNGER In the control room the Samurai heard WHUMP WHUMP! and didn't move an inch. Sure enough, as he turned his head, there was the grinning face of the Humdinger peeping round behind the metal panels on the end of the middle console. Soft thumps on those panels produced sounds like the surging and tripping of the banks of turbo-expanders. But others hadn't seen the Humdinger.

There were people everywhere inside ten seconds, milling round in the control room, running for the door. Panic. Those wanting to rush out and do something couldn't get out the door for bods running in. Dutch Treat was nearly trampled to death in the doorway. It revived the Samurai's spirits a little to watch the ignorant and fearful scatter.

Who was it? What was it? Some looked across the yard to where the Sump was supervising the removal of empty polymer catalyst drums so that he could take them out off night shift. Most blamed the Sump. He was easy to pick on. They were still calming themselves by diverting their fear of a plant crash on to hatred of the smelly, dirty and defenceless Sumpsucker, when a hot spot on the flue-gas header blew out with a roar. The turbo-expanders tripped on low flow, the header pressure dropped and the white-hot catalyst was sucked over the top of the boilers with the flue gas, following the drop in pressure out of the hole in the header, and through the turbo-expanders.

In seconds there was catalyst over everything and men running in circles. The Humdinger cursing and swearing, putting the plant down, throwing cut-off levers and emergency steam cut-ins, none too sure that his little mock whumps hadn't caused the whole crash. He had slumped the catalyst bed so the whole six hundred tons wouldn't be lost; now it would have to be vacuum unloaded from the reactor and stripper and from the regenerator down to the air spider level, then the remaining sixty tons below shovelled. Three days for the catalyst to cool, seven days' shovelling. The catalyst was 87 per cent silica and some of it as fine as 15 microns and what it did inside a lung was nobody's business.

The Western Salesman came in, jubilant.

'Shovels, chaps! Twenty cents an hour!' He wouldn't have understood if you asked him how twenty cents an hour made it all right to breathe the dust.

After all, it was an economy plant.

13
TOMB OF THE UNKNOWN INDUSTRIAL PRISONER

LIFE IS NOW Witnesses heard the Great White Father going to town on several despairing prisoners whose great cry every day for their past dozen years of detention was 'Seven hours and fifty-nine minutes to go! Come on three o'clock.' Or seven, or eleven; keeping up a running commentary on the time left each day. They wanted time to be past, wanted their lives behind them. At sixty they could be free. Delightful.

'This is life now,' said the Great White Father. 'Not tomorrow. Not three o'clock. It's not a practice for something later. Later you won't exist. This is all the life you get today. There's no more. Tomorrow's another world.'

DEDICATION A dozen sat in the locker-room to watch their leader polish off a few cans of warm beer. With his air of being a visitor to the place, never involved in work, he restored to them a hint that they might be men, not merely extensions of the nuts and bolts outside. They had this feeling only from contact with him, they were not strong enough to hold it firmly and live by it. Constant exposure to the wiles of ever-present Puroil and its concerns made them lose contact with themselves: they had not only no importance, they had no existence. Completely overshadowed and the life sucked out of them by this world-gripping monster that seemed so often stronger than governments—though owned anonymously—they had to be reminded they were men. Even huddled together in the Union meeting, where their conflicts of self-interest were most evident, they had no such feeling of sharing in the life of individuals as he gave them. They needed him as weak people need drugs.

The boilers were started again after the header was welded, the noise of the newly starting plant coming on loud and strong, when the expansion bellows blew on the same header. Expansion bellows were provided to take up expansion and contraction of the header between two fixed vertical boilers. Bellows metal was thinner, and the carry-over of combustible material that caused the previous hotspot affected the bellows, too. It was right at the place where the men stopped to take their readings on the performance of the turbo-expanders.

Taffy the Welsh, standing in this position, was nearly cut in half by the escaping gases. The roar of the rupture could be heard above the screaming turbo-expanders and the high-pitched whistle of the fuel gas in the lines. Men ran.

They brought Taffy down. He was out to it; the overalls had been burned off him, but the men did not notice that a small patch of flesh on his side was cooked till they got him down to the control room floor where several bits of cooked meat fell away from his body. There were no stretchers. Macabre, the Safety Officer, had earned good marks from Luxaflex for economy by taking them off the plants: they were half a mile away in the fire station which acted as casualty centre. Taffy was laid on the concrete floor with some flattened cartons and sleeping rag under him for insulation.

A call was made to the main gate to order an ambulance.

'You'll have to ring the fire station,' said the main gate. 'You must report all accidents to the fire station.'

'This man's seriously injured!' roared the Samurai into the phone.

'I've only got your word for that,' said the guard cockily. 'All accidents must be reported to the fire station, and the fire station will authorize us to ring for an ambulance.'

'Damn it, I'll ring one myself!' yelled the Good Shepherd, who had grabbed the phone. Parallel to his decent world was still this other world where suspicion and hate were a law of life.

'You're taking the risk that the ambulance you call will not be allowed in at the gate,' replied the man. The Good Shepherd slammed down the phone and rang the fire station.

'I'm sorry,' he muttered to the men gathered angrily about him. No one liked Taffy, but his burns could be theirs. The Good Shepherd felt they deserved some sort of apology. Inside him, he felt sick. He knew there had to be regulations. He knew the people who frame them had the responsibility of making regulations that would cope with the worst emergencies that could happen. This particular regulation was designed to cope only with the problem of dealing with malingerers with a scratched finger who demand an ambulance and a roomful of surgeons to fix it.

He went through the channels and fortunately the firemen responded quickly: he was glad the company hadn't had its way and abolished the firemen's jobs. Someone had made an anonymous call to the newspapers, who rang back and checked with the Trout. The idea was dropped.

'The sooner we get this man to hospital the better,' he observed to the men gathered around.

'You'll take Taffy to Saint Joe's, won't you?' the Great White Father asked the Good Shepherd. 'You can't take him to that other place.' He was referring to a hospital of sinister reputation where the nurses acted like sluts off the streets, dying to get out with their boyfriends, not caring a hoot for anyone. 'It's a terrible place. I know a poor devil—he was shot, I admit—he fell down between the railway lines at Banksia and grazed his arm. A pretty bad graze. They left him four hours in casualty. When they did bother to get someone in, they had to take his arm off.'

'You're exaggerating,' smiled the Good Shepherd. That sort of thing couldn't happen these days. 'Medical science—'

'They left him sitting there and he had gangrene in four hours,' the great man said seriously. 'I don't know how long he was getting to the hospital. Now he's got this much stump.' He pointed to a spot halfway up the Good Shepherd's upper arm. 'Another bloke went in, had half his stomach out with cancer and they found he was rattling all over with cancer lumps. Just after they told him about the cancer and that he was a goner, some pig of a doctor waddled in and called out in the ward, "Who's dead and who's not?"'

The Samurai spoke up. 'You might as well take him to a place staffed by people like us. Just in off the street. You need hospitals where the people don't work just for their wages—where they're dedicated. Like Saint Joe's.'

Just beyond his grasp there was a shining idea; was it the key that could open up this present attempt at civilization so that the whole vast machinery might suddenly get to its feet and work? Instead of slumping, half idle, aimlessly, as it was now.

What was needed? Dedication to what? Not simply the State and not only personal goals. He bit the inside of his lip in the fury of this sudden concentration of thought. If a man could have his personal aims and a reasonable chance of fulfilling them, and beyond them to be caught up in a larger idea. It eluded him. No matter. He knew the idea was there. Perhaps next time he would grasp it and see it face to face.

'We could work this place, no trouble, if we had people dedicated to Puroil,' said the Good Shepherd, but even as he spoke he knew they had no time for him. They could understand chronic liars, but not the honest man who suddenly lied.

The Great White Father butted in. 'What nong's going to be dedicated to some bunch of foreign bastards that don't know us except as workers they'd rather do without? No, man. You'll never get dedication in a place like this, I hope. Even you're not dedicated: Christianity made you what you were. And you, Samurai—you're not dedicated. You work because you're too proud to be a bludger like me. Don't bring in dedication: no intelligent man could be dedicated to making gasoline just for putting in the tanks of a few million stupid motorists.' He relaxed. The mood was too serious. 'Did I tell you about the last time I was in hospital? For the prostate. There I was with this permanent catheter and a big glass bottle suspended over the side of the bed. Every single visitor bumped the blasted thing; there it was swinging on the end of me and everyone that leaned over the bed to sneak me a can or two or a brandy bottle pinched the damn tube. I was in hell, I tell you. Dedicated?'

The Sumpsucker heard it all from the lavatory. There he was, busting for a pee, but every time he took it out it was an erection. Desperately he tried to pee by accident, the only way he ever managed, but it was no good. The thing knew. Tricked him every time. As soon as it peered from his trouser into the open air it shot out straight. He was whimpering. All that going on out there and he was the foreman, he should be there to take charge. Tears came into his eyes. He didn't want to do it in his trousers. Perhaps if he put blinkers on it. He grabbed a handful of rag and surrounded it. Come on, you stupid bastard! And it worked. He'd tricked it. It thought it had clothes on, and relaxed. He peed gratefully into the rags and threw them back in the rag box.

Taffy was still out.

THE VERTICAL SPLIT He was out for another ten days. It took quite a bit of sidestepping of the regulations to get some money to his family in time to buy the week's food. Company interpretations of compensation regulations laid down that no money be paid out until the proper claim forms had been completed by the injured person and a report made to the company's medical officer. This, too, was designed for the man with the scratched finger. The company advanced some money from Taffy's sick pay. Even so, there were questions asked up in the Termitary: why couldn't the man have stood to one side when taking these readings? Why didn't he report the injury himself? The auditors picked up the fact that payment had been made when the claim forms hadn't been filled out by the injured person. The men responsible for circumventing the red tape had the ever-present feeling their own jobs were in danger. It was clear to the operations people that Taffy had been in no condition to fulfil the regulations, but there it was—the vertical split. The questioners were in other departments; they had no knowledge of what sort of work Taffy did, what it meant to have some of your flesh cooked off you, what dangers the men faced every day. They had often only the haziest idea where the plant was and what it was supposed to do, although they joined in heartily with shocked displeasure when they heard of yet another breakdown. 'It's the poor types we get as operators,' they said.

SLEDGEHAMMER FINESSE Man is irrepressible. You can't keep him down, especially when his livelihood is in the balance. In the latest crash the great compressor had surged and tripped, its shaft bent. A maker's representative was flown from Hamburg to watch it taken apart. Despite all speculations about whether the plant would go, another start-up was proceeding normally.

The rest of the refinery was served by a brand-new high-pressure boiler capable of eighty tons of steam an hour; a beautiful piece of work except for its instrumentation, which had nothing in common with the instrumentation on the other boilers. None of the operators understood it. The cracker wasn't ready for steam, but just to be able to report to Melbourne that something was going, the vertical boiler was blasting away for a fortnight, as soon as the bellows was patched.

Weeks passed. The deadline was brought forward. Working at night while the expert was asleep in his hotel, fitters aligned the German compressor-turbine on its bed by bashing it with a fourteen-pound sledgehammer. The foreman fitter was told that if the machine wasn't ready by next morning he wouldn't have a job. Tolerances of eight times the maker's specifications were winked at, the machine housing hurriedly replaced in the dark.

High-pressure steam at fifty kilos was let down to the eighteen-kilo main; what was not used exhausted into the 3.5 kilo main; what was not used there exhausted to atmosphere. After the Good Shepherd had got as much equipment running as he could to use the steam, there was still twenty tons an hour at two dollars a ton wasting. This six-thousand-odd-dollars-a-week waste was one and a half times the wages of the four shifts at the cracker, but no one seemed to worry. At last steam was used in driving the great compressor. If it went well, the whole complex could get under way. The funny thing was, the rate of steam wastage remained the same.

The German engineer sent out to set the machine to rights was baffled.

'It must come down,' he said in sorrow as he watched it bounce and shake. The expatriate Puroil engineer whose main interest was in finishing the maintenance work, standing back and letting Operations division fall on its face again, said no. The Wandering Jew backed the German. They took it down, looked, and put it together. Did nothing to it. There wasn't time.

After another run of half a day the German looked at the vibration readings and said no, it must come right down: no half measures. He had never seen things done this way before, but there was no one to tell this to, he wasn't at home now. The only consolation he had was in being invited to advise two other refineries on their compressor problems. He collected two fat fees. But at Puroil, maintenance said no, don't pull it down, and this time the Wandering Jew backed them up. Probably tossed a coin. Faith, hope and confidence were used as substitutes for intelligent actions. They went ahead. Seventeen hundred tons of Borneo feed and a cable overseas to report the happy event. Nothing must go wrong.

Nothing wrong? Power dips, failing equipment, dirty pumps, machinery run to destruction, set your teeth on edge, made you think of decaying teeth in an uncared-for mouth.

HIGHER AUTHORITY On the next shift thirty-kilo spray water was put into a kilo-and-a-half power balanced operation. The Python, unavoidably present, had been cornered by Captain Bligh, who handed him the problem gratefully. 'Can't get the bottom temperature down. Gas valves go wide open.'

'Spray water,' suggested the Python.

'Right.' The Captain relayed the suggestion as an order. The Woodpecker belted the spray water valves wide open. One of them had no spray nozzle—it had burned off—its water discharged into the header in a solid jet. The fault had been notified three months before.

'She's shaking loose a bit,' smiled Captain Bligh, when the booms and bangs started.

'Are there any overspeed trips on the turbo-expander machines?' asked the Python steadily, watching the speed indicators rise.

'No. Only low flow trips. But you can trip them from here. Those red levers—' He was dying for an excuse to crash it.

'Cut out the spray water, and get an instrument mechanic.'

'There's none on shift.' They had been taken off as an economy measure.

'Call one in.' He left the plant hurriedly.

'He didn't even know there were no overspeed trips,' marvelled the men. But Captain Bligh knew he didn't know.

CEMENT HEAD An hour later Cement Head came in. His strides were long and he covered the concrete floor with deceptive speed.

'There's smoke coming out of the compressor. A noise of metal on metal it sounds like to me.' His words were directed to his immediate superior, Captain Bligh. Captain Bligh was turning this way and that, his duty to his own superiors was running about in his head, knocking against this new piece of information. Or was it information? That was what he had to decide. He turned away to cope with his boiling night-shift brain. Three in the morning. The control room packed with anxious white shirts.

Cement Head wavered about. He didn't often stay in the control room, his job was elsewhere, but this was serious. If that compressor blew up, there would be metal fragments for miles.

'They take no notice of a man,' he wailed. 'A man's been around this place three and a half years now, he ought to know when the equipment's crook. But they take no notice. They think a man's a frigging idiot!' His face was always tanned, but now it had a grey underlay.

Five minutes later, when several trivial and irrelevant instructions from one of the oblivious technologists had been carried out, Captain Bligh had time to go the hundred yards to the beautiful, sleek compressor. It was rocking. He tripped it immediately.

The high-pressure steam had nowhere to go. In the control room, hands reached for the tiny knobs and knurled wheels that controlled the giant edifice outside, which shook and roared; safety valves blew, screamed from the sudden excess of pressure. Thousands of people in bed for miles around were jerked upright by the sound. As if it reached into their bedrooms and took them bodily into terror.

LOVE A little after eleven, the Samurai was on his way to Blue Hills, who had begged him to visit the house. In ten minutes he was embroiled with the Hills family. Mrs Blue Hills started to abuse her husband and looked as if she might be thinking of hitting him with something heavy enough to keep him down permanently. And all the time she was busy making little signs to the Samurai.

Blue Hills himself began to fidget and mumble. From some of the things he said it was evident he knew the Samurai was the one who was getting his share of his wife's body. He started to assume the role of a procurer. He worked himself up so much that he came yelling and grinning and leering close to the Samurai and stooped down quickly and flipped open the Samurai's fly. Disgusted, the Samurai got to his feet and shouted, 'He loves you! You can have him!' He bolted, but not quick enough, for she threw herself at him and caught him round the legs. He didn't want to kick her off, and stopped. This gave her time to climb up his limbs and grab him round the upper parts of his body. He fought her off as well as he could, but at last, with her screaming obscene love at him, he threw her away, knocking Blue Hills over. She hit the divan and bounced off on to the floor where she pretended to swoon. Blue Hills, getting up, trod on her face, recovered his balance and trod directly on her left breast. She roared.

The Samurai was gone. Her husband began to pack his dilly-bag and dress for work. He had lost respect for her so far as to bring into the house his old working clothes, instead of dressing in the laundry outside. The smell of stale gas nauseated her despite her distress.

'Where do you think you're going?'

'Work.'

'It's not time to go to work, you fool.'

'Home Beautiful.'

She thought he was being sarcastic about their own establishment and hit him with his dilly-bag. He weathered the blows with dignity and left the house. The dilly-bag followed him and landed in a diosma bush, forcing its thin branches outwards, making a picture rather like a sea anemone trying to swallow something much too big and dying in the attempt. Was life itself the lump on which Blue Hills was choking? Or did it mean nothing at all?

With a last defiance he turned and jeered: 'You missed!' But the door was shut. And in that moment the house broke from its moorings—the path snapped—and floated out into the river behind the house, a river he had never noticed before. On its broad surface floated millions of little boxes stretching far into the distance. He was glad he trod dry land in the street. When he was gone a little way and looked back, the house was drifting past in a current that would take her away from him for ever.

MEMENTO He drank solidly at the Home Beautiful, and reported for work at seven. At three he was back across the river, this time with the Sandpiper. Strangely, he didn't feel tired. They were close enough together to satisfy the men spying from the edge of the mangroves; their molecules were mingling nicely.

'I think I must tell you,' said Blue Hills modestly, 'I have this cold coming on, I'm a bit wet and snuffly.' He wasn't even bothered about being in the open and no roof on the world.

'Come on,' commanded the Sandpiper, 'give me that cold.' She made him press his mouth to hers and moved about and jiggled his denture with her tongue, snuffled and bobbed till the poor man had to haul off to get his breath. 'I'm not your daughter! It's all right to do it! What's all the fuss?' she urged.

Poor Blue Hills. Lately he never seemed to eat. He was stale, his breath pushed away everyone who came near him, like a big fist. She wasn't finicky; men were men. You had to put up with a lot you didn't like and pretend you liked it. After a while you got pretty hard, you could stand anything as long as you got paid.

She watched him recover his breath. 'Better?'

'Yes. I feel great.'

Then the pains started. Like a hand reaching into his chest and grabbing the first vital organ it came to, like a very strong and ruthless hand, pain twisted inside his chest and throttled. He got away from her body and seemed to contract into a ball of agony. Knees drawn up and hands across his chest. He fell back and lay panting when a little breath returned to him. He didn't feel the ridged clay or random edges of shale.

'Lie here beside me, Sandpiper. I think I can die easy then.' She laughed and looked at her wrist for the time. Twenty minutes left. Plenty. They were out in the open, the way people were meant to be. Not that she hadn't seen a heart attack before, but Blue Hills was faking. He wanted extra attention for his five dollars. Pity he hadn't picked on the Sorcerer's Apprentice: she was handier with the extras.

Laboriously he fished in his shirt pocket.

'Keep this.' He held out an old black and white snapshot to her. 'It's a photo of happier days. I'm there, with an old mate of mine. I never let my wife see this photo. You keep it. It's no weight to carry. That bloke you see there was my best mate years ago.' He rambled on. 'That's the house I used to have and there's all the trees I planted. My favourite trees, before I went and got married. And there's my old orchid house. Happiest time of my life. A bit of a job to give me tucker money—go where I liked, when I liked—'

'OK, baby,' she answered, stuffing the photo in amongst the light clothing she had shed, a neat little pile beside them.

'You finished?'

'Yes.'

She started to dress.

He looked away to the low hills across the river. The house. Why not stop this fooling about and go to that house and find who belonged to the waving arm? It might be a surprise. If he lost his nerve he could always say he made a mistake. No. He'd go right to it, never taking his eyes off. It was someone waving, no mistake. Waving to him, a welcome, a real friend. The friend you get only once in a lifetime. It wasn't waving now, perhaps that meant something.

'I've had,' said Blue Hills, 'some wonderful dreams. In my life.' His breath came heavily.

'Yes,' she said. 'Yes,' pulling her dress on over her head. The fabric was patterned with startling flowers. He put out a hand to touch them.

'But I had to sleep to have them.' This statement seemed to give him some satisfaction.

'Sure you did.' What could she do to comfort him? She knew only one thing.

'You have to sleep to dream.' Dresses were mysterious. All that warm dark space up inside and the thighs smooth.

'You better get dressed.'

'All right. Did I give you the...' he paused delicately.

'Yes. I got it.' Money first you couldn't work any other way.

He began to dress. On the pink clay a red meat-ant struggled with a huge burden of food in the direction of its home. Courage, tenacity, strength. Blue Hills stabbed at it with his shoe but only succeeded in injuring it; its legs came off on the left side. However, the good half of the ant continued to tug the huge burden in the direction of its distant, unidentifiable home.

THE INTERNAL OPPONENT He rested for a while; then, seeing him better, she suggested they move on back to the Home Beautiful.

Mustering his strength, he tried to struggle to his feet, but that was the end of him. He fell back, making sounds. His breathing seemed to be obstructed, his face screwed up helplessly, a nasty sweat appeared on his forehead. His efforts to breathe, she thought, sounded like the noise of a baby feeding, a greedy baby sucking in food and air in gulps.

'What'll I do?' she said aloud. But she was a hero, and knew the men were looking from the trees, so she had a bash at the mouth-to-mouth resuscitation she had seen advertised in the women's rest-rooms along with the snake-bite and electrocution hints and the venereal-disease warnings. His dreadful, terrifying breath held her off for a moment, but she shut her eyes and went ahead puffing and stopping, puffing and recovering, turning her head away to breathe in. The kiss of life. Puff...She shuddered. I might be a wow as a cut-price prostitute but I'd make a hell of a nurse, she thought, and smiled inside, congratulating herself that she took nothing seriously.

Blue Hills seemed to revive. He tried to sit up and did succeed in raising himself on one elbow. Was this why the distant waving was not there today? The Sandpiper wiped her mouth with half the length of her forearm right through to the back of her hand.

Blue Hills mouthed a moment and finally shouted; he was dying in strength and panic, the hard way.

'I'm still strong! You can't let it take me! Look!' His twisted face thrust close to the Sandpiper's, he sat up straight. 'Look, I've got all my strength! All I ever had!' He flexed his arms, straining against the thing fighting him from inside. But he wilted first, not his internal opponent.

'Where is my strength going? How *can* I be dying?'

Next moment he was flopping and heaving. He died with a shout, a squeal, as if he had been pulled down shrieking from beneath. Blue Hills forgot the terrors in the sky, forgot all about the distant waving of the unknown person on the Jerriton hills and the beauty of the silver tanks at sunrise. He never knew there was no person waving—it was the tip of a revolving sign at a Puroil service station on top of the hill, hidden by houses. Just peeping by the corner of a red texture-brick house as its triple arms revolved in the wind, beckoning consumers. No one at all; not friend or woman or lifelong undiscovered mate.

The Sandpiper stood, then stooped to pick up something that fluttered out of her clothes and remembered the photograph. She glanced at the absurd thing for an instant before flicking it away.

Poor Blue Hills. The last memento, the last solemnity, thrown away with a sneer as soon as he was dead.

It curled in the air and returned like the miraculous boomerang, landing near the heroic ant which was, by this time, a little farther on towards its own destination.

ACTIONS WITH NO CASH VALUE They brought the Great White Father to him.

'Bad,' he said, when he saw him apparently dead, and stooped to change the expression on the poor face, smoothing away the terror and leaving the trace of a smile round the mouth. This faded, though, and the face settled into vacancy, but at least the terror was erased.

'We can't have all the boys thinking death is as bad as that, can we?' Heartily. Death had scragged Blue Hills before he'd started to live, and flung his scraggy cadaver carelessly on the clay.

'Must have gone off his rocker, eh?' said the Humdinger. 'Never seen him with the girls before.'

'Will we say some words over him?'

'If words were heartbeats, yes. He'd live. But it's too late for words.'

They all stood round looking. Hearts fail daily, millions relax and rot, millions struggle to birth. Millions of heads lean over, watching.

'Did he die before or after?' the Great White Father asked the Sandpiper.

'After of course.' Professional pride was involved. And the dead don't contradict.

It might be considered hard and unfeeling to show a cut-rate prostitute walking away unconcerned from a pitiful death. If only we could show the Sandpiper, golden-hearted at last, bestowing a farewell kiss on that commonplace brow that was rapidly losing temperature, and dropping a few womanly tears on the corpse or the surrounding clay. Not on the lion-hearted ant, though, to whom a teardrop would be a flood.

These desirable events did not happen. Perhaps if she had known that members of the public—one or two—might some day read about her, she might have trimmed her actions to suit the prevailing taste; she might have done the thing she would like to read about, but this would have falsified the actual events and her own nature.

While we're on the subject, consider how little sympathy you would expect from a high-class prostitute: no one expects to see riches and virtue together. But a cheap little prostitute—she has nothing: how tempting to expect love and sympathy, tears and gentle sobs from such a person. Look at all the old fables with which our collective childhood was poisoned about unfortunates being kicked out of palaces and given shelter in huts by other unfortunates whom the savage blows of misery and poverty had made gentle and forgiving.

How easy it is to assume the Sandpiper will want to lay up treasure in heaven by displays of beautiful actions with no cash value, while her richer sister, hardened by money, steps unconcerned from corpse to corpse, making a fortune. But—and this is the tiny grain of truth in this mountain of ore—no one expects the pursuit of money to have a softening effect. And the corollary? Lack of money doesn't have a softening effect either. This is the truth illustrated by the Sandpiper as she walked away towards her next five dollars.

They covered Blue Hills with a tarpaulin. The flies were bad.

THE VACANT NAME As he walked back to the Home Beautiful, the Great White Father reflected that today a man had died who'd had a name. Now the name was empty. Had he taken it with him? Did the man still exist because the name Blue Hills existed? Elsewhere, new names were being created all the time. Babies were being started all over the world in a daily cycle that followed the turning motion of the earth. As soon as the earth turned away from the sun and shadow blotted out the night, humans were at it. And death was busy at the other end of the production line, feeding constantly.

DEATH IS A PERSON In the drink hut the Great White Father lifted his beer to signal silence. 'My friends, for Blue Hills, who would not pretend death was a friend—Well died! Poor little man. You have to admire a hard death. Blue Hills has ridden on ahead, as they say. He has been gathered up—which contradicts my first metaphor, but never mind—he has been chosen to go straight from the Sandpiper to the enormous soft bosom of eternal nothing. To float on clouds of bliss, of which our present alcoholic haze is the first foreshadowing. Drink up.' There was a necessary pause while supplies cascaded down his throat. 'Now. What arrangements will we make? I'll take suggestions from the floor.'

The Humdinger suggested that as the body was resting on the unhallowed ground of Puroil—at the moment covered with a faded tarp the colour of the surrounding clay—it should be left there and a phone call made to the Termitary. The Glass Canoe drew attention to the fact of the footprints and relics of the Sandpiper's presence.

Gradually the mood eased, intoxication increased, and immediate action, its attractiveness, its possibility, receded. The Sandpiper had been allowed to go home. Actually she was put out over this, but they explained to her so firmly that she was upset over the death that took place in her presence, that she could see it was no use arguing that it would be better for her to be active because this would help her to forget. They would have seen through this immediately. She gave it up, but so reluctantly that they passed the hat around and drummed up the best part of what she would have earned the rest of the day. She went away with a good grace.

'I wish,' said the Great White Father, 'that we could think of some way of making our late brother's death work for our cause: the cause of rest and refreshment, ease and plenty. If we could make of his death a great moment in the history of the Home Beautiful, we'd have something to look back on, a monument, a memory that wouldn't fade of one of our sheep that wandered among the human machines and got lost. I'll never forget that moment at school, I was a kid when the history teacher taught us—

Like stout Cortes
When with eagle eye
He glared at the Pacific
And all his men
Dated each other in mild surprise...

'Just such a moment I look to, when one of you logs has come up with a recipe for it. By his death to slap Puroil in the eye, as a token slap in the eye for all who employ their fellow man as we're employed, as private, limited-liability slaves. Not like the slaves of long ago: fashions in slavery change as much as anything else. But you've heard all this from me before. These people over us, although we can't get rid of them, we can get in their way. But the boss our bosses represent, the old man with the scythe, we can't beat him. Have you mob ever thought of the inhabitants of this pretty little earth before we started brewing beer on it? Those soft-bodied pre-Cambrian bits of life, they were a delicacy. For what? What was it that thought them rich pickings? Just picture them, you beer-suckers. Each lot of animals thinks its group is pretty well intact; only a few of their number, relatively, gets picked off by their main predator. So it is with humans. Us. And what is the monster predator, nibbling at the edges of our ranks, and sometimes getting greedy and reaching in and taking a huge slice of us? Death, my cute little woman-wallopers! He's our great enemy. Employers and bosses, who have more power over us than we have over them—they are the official agents of death! Weakening us, softening us up for their boss. We are the pickings—for death! and for the grinderies and termitaries of the world. We must be nasty and unattractive to death, just as we are slow and easy and uncooperative with Puroil.'

'I'll drink to Puroil!' said Loosehead, who had missed the point completely. The great man went on.

'Death is a person. And here's mud in his eye!' He picked up a twenty-six-ounce can of Victorian beer—one of several dozen strangers on the ice—opened it and lifted one side to his wide brown mouth. All present drank to the discomfiture of death and his agents. Most of them had followed at least a few of the tall man's words. 'Let's wait till it's dark. We can carry Blue Hills in to the cracker control room and say we found him.'

'We can't leave him out there,' Far Away objected. Then, thinking he had gone a little far, continued less strongly, 'It's a problem. I remember when my old man was dying. Fortunately he died at the right time. You see, we had only two bedrooms and put my sister in with Mum because I was growing fast. The old man should have had a room by himself, but at least he had someone with him when he died. Not like dying on bare clay. With a tarp for a blanket.'

The assembly was amazed. This was the longest he had ever spoken.

'Pox or no pox, it took some poor cow dying in a paddock to get you outa your shell,' remarked the Glass Canoe derisively.

A PERMANENT MEMORIAL The Samurai rolled Blue Hills into the tarpaulin and pocketed a black and white snapshot near his body. He didn't think footprints would show, the clay was too hard and all the safety boots were the same make. The corpse would be safe in the pipe track till dark. He was surprised at the relaxed feel of it.

He mounted the steps of a tank in the tank farm and looked about. In the distance the cars of the Termitary workers streamed from the car park. They were a different race of people, leaving the place at four or five, never knowing the strange life of the refinery at night; never seeing the dawn glow in the east, the marvellous lavender-silver tanks, the pink and gold vapours and steam clouds rising with the sun behind them. Another world.

In two hours it would be getting dark. There was unfinished concrete work on the new gasoline splitter foundations. He had a nice grave picked out for Blue Hills. It was only a matter of lifting out some of the broken stone of the foundations, placing body and photograph in the hole, replacing the broken stone, sprinkling some sand and leaving it till seven in the morning when fresh concrete would be poured. After that the steel tower would go up. Blue Hills would be part of the enterprise.

Mrs Blue Hills would have to register him as missing. It would be like a bonus to her. The uncertainty about his existence would be the Samurai's protection from her. Strange, though, the corpse hadn't stiffened.

14
INDUSTRIAL JOKES

SHIP OF FOOLS Three hundred feet in the air Dutch Treat adjusted his earphones and tuned the crystal set. He had climbed the stack to be nearer to God and His radio waves. The ascent had taken half an hour, birdshit made his boots slip and crusted his hands. A watcher could have marked his progress as he disturbed sleepy birds who fluttered back and settled down after he passed. He didn't mind breathing the flue gases, as long as he made contact without interference.

He descended to the control room in case he'd been missed.

'Hey, Dutch,' said the Humdinger. 'Make contact with the Big Boss? Where'd you go this time?' Dutch Treat didn't tell him. Climbing the stack was dangerous and prohibited. 'Come on. What did He say? You can tell me. I won't tell the others.'

'Shut up,' shouted the bird-spattered climber.

'Well, you shouldn't have done all the talking.'

'He didn't say shut up. I say shut up.'

'That's not nice. Didn't He tell you about turning the other cheek and forgiveness and all that jazz?'

'God has nothing to do with forgiveness. He tells and we do,' the foreigner said sharply. He was one of those who'd never get naturalized.

'You mean He gives orders?'

'Commands. We obey.'

The Humdinger turned away. Another poor bastard looking for a boss. He turned to his own pursuits and in two hours sold a book and a half of raffle tickets and was thirty dollars richer. He would get a three-dollar bottle of brandy tomorrow and present it to the winner, someone reasonably popular. The start-up proceeded normally.

Now to fix Bubbles. Bubbles had won a conversational fight. When they got in that day he told how he'd been shacked up with this slut at the Cross with a supply of Hunter River cigarettes; he'd had so much every day of what he should have enjoyed at leisure that he had to have a skin graft. This had topped the Humdinger's story of the family he had stayed with down at Bega when he was on the road travelling in tea; a girl, her mother and her granny with advanced ideas of hospitality. The story was true. It wasn't much fun to be beaten on a true story.

He went to take a drum of water up into the ceiling of the control room, but there was no ceiling. He got a bucket, climbed on the fiat roof, found one of the holes and made it rain over Bubbles. Bubbles arose in wrath, and cursed the misbegotten Humdinger.

Bubbles went out into the dark, stuffed his earplugs in and whipped open the high-pressure steam blowdown. This little trick caught everyone on the plant—the blast was too big to be ignored. There were white faces everywhere. The Humdinger pointed out joyfully to Bubbles that they were like lawyers, they were the blades of the shears; they shouldn't be trying to cut each other, but bisecting the mugs between. Bubbles saw the wisdom of this, changed his overalls and led out Ambrose to follow a certain line up the side of the reactor. Following out lines was the first step in the making of an operator. He picked a ripe victim. Ambrose spent an hour climbing, following this two-inch line, up and up, down and down, here and there. It was the handrail. Bubbles called out the entire crew to watch. When he got to the lower stairways of the reactor, Bubbles added to his trick by running quickly to the water drench valve, an on-off tap to quench controllable fires in the skirt-enclosed part of the reactor bed, and gave Ambrose the full spray from the fog nozzles round the outside walls. Ambrose was thrown off his stride and came in dripping. They cheered him. He reddened from scalp to Adam's apple, and smoked a cigarette deeply as he had learned to do in moments of emotion. It gave you something to be emotional about. Everyone watched, amazed, as he changed into dry overalls and prepared to go up again to find out what was at the other end of the two-inch line. He couldn't be persuaded he was being had. He spent weeks following that line in the daytime until Mumbles forbade him absolutely to go up there and then he thought he was being picked on.

In reply, the Humdinger collared Disneyland and fed him a gentle line about being young, superbly built, extremely fit, a natural athlete. Disneyland lapped it up, the broad scar over his eye wrinkling with pleasure. He'd cut himself so often the skin was tissue paper. In five minutes he was running round refinery roads. It was seven and fairly dark. Bubbles replied by pulling Ambrose in and getting him to stand up straight in the control room, look up at the light, then turn round fast. Round and round he spun and of course fell over.

'You'll have to do it again and again, practise it until you're perfect, otherwise you'll never pass your advanced physical.'

'Have I got another medical to do still?'

'You want to be an advanced operator, don't you?'

Ambrose was in—hook, line and sinker.

Disneyland was still away after Ambrose had spun and fallen fifteen times, so they had to look for another victim; neither was willing to admit the other had won by these puny demonstrations of man's power over man.

The Humdinger rang in the voice of the Sumpsucker for the services of Goathead, an old long-service prisoner who came round on his bike to test for the presence of gas. When he came, grumbling aloud as he pedalled, he didn't get past the spray water tank. The

Humdinger took him, meter, sniffer, bike and all, with the jet from the three-inch hose.

This was great fun for the audience, who barracked loudly for the two men after each trick was done. Laughing beforehand to warn the victim was unfair.

'I'll need some help with the next one,' said Bubbles. 'Does anyone know how to do the three-man lift?' No answer. 'I'll ask it the other way. Does anyone not know the three-man lift.'

'I don't,' said Ambrose. Bubbles couldn't believe his luck. Soon they had one man sitting on the floor gripping Ambrose's ankles, another sitting behind him gripping his arms behind his back and Bubbles stood over them as if ready to lift the three men locked together. But instead of lifting, Bubbles bent down and searched until he found something belonging to Ambrose, a pretty little thing with a small, pink mouth and wide, glowing cheeks. He held it up between finger and thumb, showed everyone, then got out the black boot polish he used to smarten up with when he went straight from work to the club, and blacked this little thing all over.

'Beat that!' exclaimed Bubbles to the Humdinger. The Humdinger scratched his head. A light went on in his face.

'Back in half an hour.' He was seen creeping out into the night towards the gastail plant and not again for an hour. The Samurai saw him though, and Dutch Treat, who was up the stack again, climbing carefully up the vertical ladders of the two-hundred-foot absorber column, a slim, silver, dizzy column swaying in the wind. Rung by rung, up under the sleeping birds that infested the ladders and railings of the tallest parts of the plant. Clouds of birds came from the north-west every day to sleep. Thousands of starlings, sparrows, swallows. The Humdinger would get under a step with birds on it, snake his hand up quietly, grip a bird tightly and shove it into his open overalls front. He came down with several dozen of these pets, starlings and sparrows, half and half, took them behind the control panel, positioned himself behind one of the cutout sections (new instruments were going in all the time) and waited.

His luck was unbelievable. At 8.30 the Spotted Trout came in with a busload of visitors on a sightseeing tour and when they were nicely spread out through the control room, he was ready to go. Bubbles and the others couldn't hold back, they had to help make this a winner. The idea was so good petty rivalry was forgotten. Bubbles and the Samurai, who came in from doing start-up work, and Far Away Places, all amazed the Trout by taking little groups of visitors helpfully in hand and getting them strung out along the length of the control room, giving them innocuous but good-natured lectures on the parts of the panel they were facing. Most didn't know the place at all though they worked there every day, but they read out the labels on the instruments and put in words that sounded technical and the visitors didn't know the difference. Just as in the technical bits of a TV commercial, they made up additions to the table of elements.

When the gabble was stilled and the lecturers had attentive listeners, the Humdinger held his stomach against the eight-by-six hole and let the birds out into the lighted room. The panic started slowly, then accelerated like the panic of a person wakened in his own bedroom by the police.

The lights blinded the birds, who flew erratically from one end of the room to the other. There was no space for the visitors to get out; by some chance there was a gaping, grinning, ducking crowd of overalled operators at the exit end. People milled, women screamed. Men lashed out to protect themselves from the little winged bullets, which were too fast to get away from. Beaks hit faces. Clubbing hands hit other people.

The Slug took one look from outside the door and stayed out to examine the spray water pump. How could he be blamed if he was outside when it happened? Captain Bligh had a rolled newspaper in his hand and stood valiantly in the middle of the floor and batted the birds as they came from either end.

He was a hero. He missed many at first, but when the birds started to slow down after knocking their heads on the concrete walls at either end of the long room, he got more and more. Birds lay stunned, were trodden on. Feathers filled the air. Softened the concrete underfoot. The Humdinger and his crew unblocked the exit end and adjourned to the locker-room to finish their laughing. It was very pleasant to be the Humdinger. Bird lice would keep him scratching for days, but it was worth it.

The Trout managed to get his hysterical visitors out to the bus, apologizing and swearing. He explained he was swearing at the birds, not at them. Next day he reported Captain Bligh for having a newspaper. Reading matter was forbidden. He couldn't report the happening, or he'd have been in the gun for the failure of his tour.

Bubbles had tearfully, joyfully handed the palm to the Humdinger for the joke of the year and went on laughing for the rest of the shift. Disneyland came back, puffing from his four-mile run round the outer roads of the refinery.

'I'm back,' he said. He didn't know why they were laughing and didn't know how to find out without exposing himself to their laughter. Sweat beaded his forehead, collected in the scar and ran down into his eye.

'Look at my calf muscles now,' he finally said to the Humdinger. 'They're getting bigger, I think.'

The Humdinger took time off from enjoying his success and said, 'You better go round again, I think.'

He went. Hysteria resumed. The world was full of fools.

THE DIMINISHING WORKER The creator of the Home Beautiful asked a few tactful questions in the cracker panel room.

'Seen Blue Hills about?'

'Not since earlier,' said the Humdinger cautiously.

'He's gone.'

'Gone? The company must have taken him away.'

'Haven't heard anything. Keep your ears open. If there's no news, keep it dark.'

'No names, no packdrill.'

Handed down from convict days, the freemasonry of fear of the authorities kept the news of Blue Hills' collapse quiet.

'What if he got up and walked away?' said the Humdinger.

The Samurai walked in the north door. The panel room phone rang. The Great White Father picked it up.

'Yes,' regally, 'this is the Great White Father. Herman the German? No. Where is he? Out of the anaesthetic? We'll send up a party each day to visit him. Poor old bastard.' Herman was no more than five years older than the Great White Father. Hearing the name, the Samurai walked up to listen.

'I'll be damned. Off at the shoulder, eh? How long has he got, did they say? A year? Probably means three weeks. Well, we'll make him as comfortable as we can. Any relatives? OK man, we'll do our best. He'll have visitors.' He hung up sadly. Looking down he saw the Samurai's overalls flecked with good beach sand.

'Dying?' asked the Samurai.

'Looks like it. This bone disease keeps spreading and they keep chopping bits off. We'll have to get him on the beer.'

'He's a teetotaller.'

'Up to now. He won't be when I get hold of him.' Where would the Samurai pick up sand? Concreting?

'Off at the shoulder. This mob'll sack him now, but he's still as good as any four men.'

'Yes, they don't employ bloody cripples. They said so.' Perhaps he'd walked through one of the contractors' sand heaps.

THE RANGE OF FRIENDSHIP The Samurai received his usual number of thumps on the arm from the Humdinger. Lately they had been getting more frequent, both from the Humdinger and Two Pot, even from Bubbles; not to mention several of the quieter prisoners. They were very fond of him and instead of holding his hand or kissing him as women might their women friends, their contact was limited to a thump or two.

The arm, near the shoulder, was getting very sore. In his judo experience, he had seen men with bad legs from years of repeated foot contacts. He had started to turn his shoulder away or to present the other one. But they didn't seem to like hitting the left shoulder. It left his right arm free.

He couldn't ask them to ease up: that was like pleading. They were human enough to attack more if they suspected weakness. And this would only bring on confrontations, which he wanted to avoid. He tried to anticipate their friendly blows and move out of range.

NO MAN PROVOKES ME WITH IMPUNITY A week later, after his arm turned blue-black just below the shoulder where the muscle crossed the bone, he took himself along to a doctor, who told him he would have to avoid anything that might knock his arm. He should have taken the week off, but relied on being able to persuade the boys not to thump him on that muscle. He knew he was kidding himself.

Ten days after that, the skin started to break as if it had been undermined. It smelled. He had seen gangrene and knew this was the end of work for a while. The Humdinger and Bubbles looked offended when he showed them the arm.

It was better in three weeks, but had not healed in the deep wound-trench where the gangrenous tissue had been cut out. Still, it was good enough to be back at work. Thickly strapped.

He noticed a certain coolness from the Humdinger, who looked at him as if the whole thing was some sort of frame-up. Very likely they would never forgive him for what they had done.

Why was he the one to take injury from the casual, tongue-tied affection of these poor creatures? He was used to the sight of it now: the others thought it a horrible disfigurement. But the sore had transferred itself to a place inside him and was still spreading. When would he find an opponent worthy to fight? The festering inside him would only be checked by violence. Revenge. Revenge. But on whom? Had it taken only this little wound to sour him? Was he soured or merely sufficiently provoked?

NOT A FOOT WRONG He was back at work for yet another start-up. The latest crash had been disgraceful, they told him; men milling round the instrument panels; the Humdinger trying to break through a group of fitters having a conference in front of the fractionator instruments and failing to get through in time to save the column puking; starting the reactor with five instruments not working; broken-off probes still in the plugged tappings of key controls; running blind on levels; only one slide working on the double-disc slide valves on stripper and regenerator; discovering there were no other probes in the refinery to clear plugged pressure-tapping points; a violent mix-up of supervisors, technologists, engineers, foreign experts crowding round the main panel and showing resentment if operators tried to elbow them out of the way to reach controls. The only good thing had been Gunga Din, who always made sure the urn was full of water for the next brew of tea.

The Humdinger tried to get to the high-pressure steam letdown valve in time, and finding his way blocked, stood back with arms folded. There were loud bangs outside. Bomber Command saw him.

'Either they get outa my way or she crashes,' he said above the babel of voices.

Bomber Command came good and urged a dozen out of the way, saving the boilers and making himself unpopular with his superiors, but this was an exception. He kept clear after this and the next crisis saw the plant down nicely. The experts conferring were world famous in their line, but they were not familiar with the state of the plant at that particular moment. And in fact they were not discussing it. They were considering future modifications to the most recent modifications and in this gentle atmosphere of erudite technical speculation the plant as it was at that moment diminished in importance and receded to the farther limits of their horizons. Sharply rising and falling chart lines were objects to them, not disasters. The local brass were the same, they didn't so much walk around to see what was going on as stand stiff in attitudes. Leadership. Rebuke. Progress. Ambition, Kindliness. Authority.

Attitudes, no more. The Samurai shook his head. It was the same everywhere. All over the world machines replace men, the men don't take any trouble. The people above don't care about the job to be done—they despise it because an interest in it is the infallible sign of the subordinate not the manager type—they care about moving on to the next job, slightly higher in status, promotion from job to job until the final bright day when they reach management ranks, always the eye on the future in the approved cautious, self-protecting style, never on the immediate task; that was safe with the subordinate type. If they left their desks to visit the plant often, others might get at their papers, or Admin might denounce them for not being on the job. Or they might be accused of fraternizing with the enemy.

It was madness. Men who waffled knowledgeably at executive meetings, sooner saying nothing than daring to put a foot wrong; so scared of making one mistake that they made the mistake of doing nothing that someone hadn't thought of first; these were the Puroil men and they thought they were running a refinery. What made them think this? Well, the overseas bosses pour money in; equipment, foreign experts and construction crews are imported, you put in a management structure diagram, observe Puroil International Procedure, hire people to get their hands dirty, give them flow diagrams and a pay packet and the refinery runs itself. Feed goes in here and product comes out there. Madness.

TECHNIQUES OF CONTROL Gradually the lines of decision-making and control became more numerous, more tangled. Competition between departments, out of place in this type of refinery where marketing was handled by a different company, raged fiercely. Those responsible for planning the refinery's structure thought their problems solved by administrative innovations, pruning here, expansion there, alteration everywhere; arms, voices, memos flailing uselessly at disorder, without supplying on-the-spot control at the point where the crude oil and later streams were refined; without emphasizing the prime importance of the basic operations for which the refinery was built. They cut the cracker complex in half and doubled supervision: this worked one half against the other nicely. All this was very like the steam system over the refinery which was so complicated only three or four people understood it. Lines, valves, loops crossed and backtracked. A nightmare to work on.

Each supervisor had his own remedies for plant conditions; little points which, if observed, would keep the gasoline flowing in spite of the uninformed efforts of all the rest. One would surreptitiously change the pressure controller on the gas-absorber column from automatic to manual; another would open a bypass on the fractionater bottom level; one liked to run with a carbon reading of 0.3 per cent on the catalyst; another liked 0.55 per cent, just on the edge of a coke condition. There were as many panaceas as there were foremen, supervisors and controllers and they all fiddled with a good conscience and usually to opposite effect.

When nasty things happened, as always they did, the Education Officer—traditionally a spare-time post for a not too well-entrenched body in Personnel—went round with the official company reasons for failure and the excuses for the inevitable tightening-up. This tightening-up worked in the same way on the prisoners as it did on the immense valves on the process gas lines. Something that showed a dangerous leak under a temperature of 600 centigrade would be shut down and tightened cold. When it was hot again, no half dozen men could move it because of the tightening-up.

One of the new men, a cracker-expert from another country, had been on deck six months when he pulled up the Samurai over a certain arrangement of the reactor recycle flows. He had no authority—this was the refuge of such men, who gave opinions and directives no one really had to obey—but the Samurai wouldn't have obeyed. However, he gave no reasons for refusing to take the man's advice. The Boy Wonder saw this from a distance and knowing both of them, waited till the engineer stamped off red-faced. He whispered to his staff colleague.

'This is a two-stage reactor.' That was what the Samurai expected the chemical engineer to know. It made all the difference to recycle flows.

'Is it?' Six months and he didn't know. How did they spend their time? Were there so many pieces of paper to attend to, so many schedules and returns, so much in-fighting necessary to keep their jobs, that they had no time to look at the plant in detail? What was the dreadful penalty for asking questions?

15
THE GLASS CANOE SAVAGED BY WORDS

A PERSISTENT GLEAM OF SANITY There is no me. There are only memories of parts I've played in this stupid production called existence. There are only the characters I've made up on the spur of the moment, in an emergency, when people demanded I be something definite. I know there is no me. I'd still like to do everything, even the things that occur to me at odd times that at first I think are mad. I remember coming out of the twenty-four-hour sleep they gave me at hospital after the shocks. I said to myself—or someone that just got born said inside me—'Why don't you try breathing with your forehead? Thinking with your stomach lining? Singing with your eyes?'

I came out of it yelling and screaming this and they nearly put me under again, but I realized in time and quietened down. You have to keep your wits about you in case you have a sudden flash of clear-in-the-head, there's no sense making things more painful if you can help it. When you're in the middle of it and raving, you don't care. They can do what they like, it wouldn't matter if they killed you—snuffed you out in disgust.

Breathing with your forehead, thinking with your diaphragm, singing with your eyebrows. Wrong again. If you don't watch it, the right words tail off into something else and before you know where you are you're saying something different; only a little different at first, but if you don't get back to the right words immediately, after a few changes you're right off the track. And the funny thing is it is words that cause all the trouble; they dictate what I think, they dictate what happens to me, they dictate what I make happen to other people. If I could get rid of words I might get better. I might feel more comfortable. Breathe forehead, think stomach, sing eyes. For weeks I couldn't get those words out of my head. And yet they were no use to me. They made nothing happen. They might just as well have been a set of words that said anything or nothing at all. They were all over me, those words, I couldn't shake them; crawling up my arms, running through the hairy forests of my legs, popping out of my hand when I made a fist. I wish I could—or I wish the part of me that's responsible for this could—but all of me is responsible: I can't separate any of me off and say that without it I'm the same: I wish I could have expanded enough to say real things like love, fidelity, jealousy, adultery, incest, murder, theft, betrayal, pride, honour, courage, seduction, elopement, horror, rape. And yet they're not real: they're emotions that might make me feel real. No, they're not even that, they're just words like the others. But let me follow this...If I can say the word, I can do the word. Rape: I could rape someone. Murder: I could do it. When you know something the word stands for, you can do it.

I could even have a secret language with myself, so that honour meant murder, and saying honour I could kill someone, because the power of knowing the word gives me the power to do the word. What I mean is my own private meaning could be different. And no one need know...I'd better get off this line of talk. Let's get on to something harmless. You've got to keep thinking of something: you can't just stop yourself like that.

The thought I had this morning when I was about to switch off the gas when the toast was done—all the things that are *un*. Yes, that's harmless enough. Puroil's unofficial army, unanswered phones, unopened letters, unlit cigarettes—think of the millions of unlit cigarettes resting at this moment in closed packets or cartons or crates or warehouses all over the world—all the untasted tea and coffee and alcohol, all the unraped women, all the unburgled houses, all the unattacked enemies, the books standing closed on shelves unread with the words flattened like springs waiting to leap out at you (words give you so many alternatives, you either do everything or slacken off and do nothing), the unmuzzled dogs, unmasked villains, unaccountable foreign companies, unaggressive Beautiful Twinkling Stars, all the millions of un-American people in the world, the unpolitical Australians, undetected perverts, the undistinguished leaders of the country, unattainable wealth, unavoidable death, the unborn millions in every man's seed, the uncertified lunatics.

Everything in the world can be un.

THE AGE OF ANXIETY I don't know who sent it round, but I have a copy of the form they say is issued to everyone they want to raise up to the staff. You have to answer all the questions, but they give you no clues about what sort of answers they want. It isn't like an exam at school where they teach you the stuff first. You have to dig in your own head and come up with something.

WHO DO YOU BLAME FOR YOUR PRESENT PREDICAMENT? What does that mean? The predicament of promotion? Or my wife dead? Funny how I don't even miss her.

DO YOU THINK IT'S TOO LATE TO CHANGE?

DO YOU HAVE TO FIGHT FOR HAPPINESS?

DO YOU LIKE THE PUROIL UNIFORM?

WOULD YOU BE HAPPIER IF YOU WERE TALLER OR HAD BLUE EYES?

HAVE YOU FINALLY HARDENED YOUR HEART AGAINST US? What sort of question is that? They try to sound like God talking.

WHO IS THE FATHER OF YOUR WIFE'S CHILDREN? They've got no right to demand answers. Maybe if you don't want to answer you can just leave a blank.

WOULD YOU RATHER BE YOURSELF AND DIE OR CHANGE A LITTLE AND LIVE?

DO YOU REPROACH YOURSELF FOR YOUR MISTAKES?

DO YOU PRIDE YOURSELF ON BEING A STRONG CHARACTER? Talking about strong characters, the Sump is still bad with heights; last Saturday when the movies were on at Jerriton drive-in the whole shift was up the structure, not a soul below the first landing, and there he was down below, singing out for us to come down, but no one heard. He must have no guts at all, he's always saying he's a coward, maybe he is. I couldn't say it even if I knew it was true.

DO YOU THINK OUR POWER IS GODLIKE?

DO YOU THINK DISCUSSION OF OUR DIFFERENCES WILL PRODUCE AGREEMENT?

COULD YOU HAVE SAVED THE PLANT IN THE LAST CRASH?

DO YOU UNDERSTAND US?

HAVE YOU EVER BEEN HUNGRY?

DO YOU FEEL YOU KEEP GOOD TRACK OF TIME?

CAN ONE MAN SAVE THE WORLD? It beats me; I don't know what they're getting at. Maybe it's not a proper Puroil question sheet; someone might have just made it up. An experiment. I wonder if it was one of the young technologists? No, more likely the Two Pot Screamer, he's very sarcastic at times. When the company was trying to tell us that hydrofluoric acid was just a weak acid—Doctor Death said that for them—he made jokes about going for a swim in carb-soda in the bath they keep over there if you get any on you. He even drew little cartoons and stuck them on the ceilings where they couldn't be taken down till the cleaners got in. I wish I hadn't put my foot through the ceiling; I was lying on top of the console and pretending to raise the roof with my legs, but the ceiling gave way.

HAVE YOU EARNED THE RIGHT TO STAY WITH THE COMPANY?

ARE YOU AFRAID OF THE MANAGER?

DO YOU THINK THE WORLD IS SICK?

WILL YOU EVER TAKE YOUR SAFETY FOR GRANTED IN THE FUTURE?

ARE YOU SURPRISED THAT WE USE NO FORCE ON YOU?

NAME SOMETHING THAT IS REAL.

ARE YOU HAPPY? These questions remind me of the hospital. Examining everything. Carting you off doped, leaving the medical fossickers happy with your nuggets.

NAME SOMETHING IMPORTANT.

This really has me wet. There can't be anything in it. There's no reason why I shouldn't let someone else be tricked by it too. Let some other silly bastard worry about it. Old Far Away. I'll stick it in his bag. Pity old Blue Hills isn't here, I'd worry him sick.

He didn't see the eye watching him from an inch hole in the steel panel. A man stood back there, only six feet away, boots braced on green-painted air mains that branched upwards into ever smaller lines, the arteries reticulating life-giving air to the hundreds of control points all over the complex of plants.

This man smiled and watched and fiddled with himself under his overalls as the Glass Canoe pulled himself to his feet, clutching the paper, and made for the locker-room, adjusting his symptom list, swallowing a calming pill and checking that his lower parts were covered.

16
A GREAT DAY FOR FIRST THINGS

FIVE HUNDRED PAIRS OF HORNS The tea was warm and the Beautiful Twinkling Star sucked in a mouthful. There was no warning, no flicker. The electric power failed. Everything. No lights, no pumps, no electricity. After a second the emergency generator cut in and restored lights on the panel alarms, the red, amber and white sixteen-volt bulbs. It wasn't enough to see by. When in the darkness men touched each other they sprang back in fear. The rest was uproar.

To move more quickly the Star spat out the tea—it went down his overalls—and raced for the door. The power failure lasted half an hour and in that time the plant crashed again. If the stand-by boiler feedwater pumps had been assembled they might have saved the boilers. The electric pump was silent. No water. The Humdinger cut the fires by the light of a torch. The great compressor stopped without high-pressure steam, it was no use making gasoline vapours to be compressed. The whole complex was down.

When he got back inside, the Western Salesman, one of the urgers who had bludged during the emergency by looking for nonexistent work down at the opposite end, noticed the wet on the Twinkler's overalls, saved his breath till he had a good audience, then let go. 'Look who got a fright and pissed hisself!' Pointing to the wet stain.

The Beautiful Twinkling Star had never had this reaction before; never, that is, long enough for it to remain unsuppressed. Perhaps it was the aches and pains of the flu or the accumulation of the feeling that because he did his work he missed all the lurks and perks others enjoyed. Whatever it was, he lashed out.

The Twinkler had lived a clean life and worked hard and yet he was very strong. His right fist flashed at the man's middle and seemed to go through to his back-bone. 'You bludging mongrel,' he said in his polite voice. For a long time those who liked the Twinkler, and they were many, called him the Beautiful Twinkling Right, or Beautiful Twinkling Knuckles. Perhaps one of the Salesman's buttons was undone, but the Twinkler scraped his knuckles enough to draw blood. He went to his locker for the bottle of red dye. Empty. He went out to the control-room stationery cabinet and filled his unlabelled bottle from the red ink supply for the instrument charts. Unselfconsciously he dabbed his cuts with red ink. The Samurai was the only witness. If the others had seen, his credit would have been gone forever. He looked back squarely at the Samurai as if the bottle contained an expensive antibiotic.

'Is that what you dab their cuts with?'

'I dab their cuts with care and consideration and love.' The Samurai didn't pursue it.

The Twinkler was ashamed of his fistic outburst, but something in the way it was received by the others took the edge off his self-blame. As if they liked him now he was human, instead of only respecting him for his good deeds and Christian intentions. He went further. He left the plant, a thing he'd never done before, and walked down to the river, hailed the Volga Boatman and visited the Great White Father.

'What'll it be, a drink in the bar, a woman in the master bedroom, or both? There's Never on Sunday in there waiting to tell your horoscope by the way it feels.'

'Can she do that?'

'No. She feels nothing. She reads up the horoscopes in the afternoon papers.' He raised his voice. 'She'll buy a new dress for herself with your five dollars.' A cry came back.

'I never spend it on myself! That would be wrong!'

'Isn't that nice and homely?' said the Great White Father. 'Interested? You can take your pick. Old-fashioned, Fido, Sidecar, Furniture, Corpse, Lung Cancer, TV, Ballet, Carpet Snake? You can call the tune if you pay the piper.'

'No, thanks.' He settled down on a seat. No, he said to himself; I left home today with the kiss of my wife wet on my lips; I'm not likely to want the women down here. Perhaps I'm peculiar.

'Well, you are peculiar,' said the Great White Father.

'I can't change myself.' He liked the Great White Father. Envied him. Wanted the great man to like him. Was he so weak with a temporary sickness that he needed human props and stays?

'I wondered when you'd come down here for a pow-wow. Did you kick over the traces or something?'

'Sharp of you.'

He looked grateful just to sit and talk. Was that the suspicion of a tear in the corner of his eye? The great man laughed.

'Don't pat me on the back, my own hand is constantly poised for the job. It took no great sharpness. You probably shot the Slug over the top of the boilers and hit someone in the mouth. It was bound to happen to a man who keeps himself under like you do.' I have no dumb idiot child inside me, the Great White Father assured himself, that I collapse to tears and repentance at a kind word or the lack of it, thinking somewhere there is some great love for me alone.

'It's not me that keeps me under. It's the power that entered my life—my religion, to you.'

'Don't kid yourself, son. You have a lot of muscle in there'—a long brown finger poked him gently in the stomach—'and you hold yourself in with that muscle, same as you hold yourself on your path of religion. You probably call it following Christ and I honour you for it, but I tell you now it's not Him that keeps you on your path, it's you. The government of heaven is in you. It *is* you.'

'Now, now. Don't try to subvert my faith,' smiled the Twinkler, with the tolerant look reserved for the ungodly.

'Subvert? That's good. I like it when one of my men uses a good word.'

'Your men?'

'You're all my men. I claim you in the end, when you're old enough to lose the last bit of faith in your nominal masters and you find your heavenly supports are inside you. But I'm good-natured. I can afford to be: I've never really suffered.'

'I've never heard it put that way before. The best Christians I've heard of have been the ones that have gone through the mill.'

'They're the ones like you, with the big muscles in the stomach. Plenty of guts.'

'Faith,' said the Star. 'When my little girl was dying I prayed for her life. The faith that moves mountains.'

'Did she get better?'

'She died three weeks later. That was the turning point for me.'

'Did you tell God to get nicked?'

'My spiritual turning point. I realized it wasn't for me to question God's purposes. Beyond my understanding.'

'But—'

'We must submit with gladness to His will.'

Appalled, the Great White Father watched him. There seemed to be a trace of satisfaction in the voice. I can't blame him, he told himself, for reacting irrationally. What sort of God needs the death of a child for any purpose? Then he saw it. The man's goodness was the product of this turning point. His kindness, never dobbing, getting rags for others but never sleeping on the job, this was his irrationality. The product of an obscene tragedy. Time to change the subject.

'I've been through a few mills myself, but what happened was, I got ground to powder. I was in Brazil once, still young and not a grey hair in my head. We were taking cattle to the railhead, five hundred head and we had to cross this river. Well, five hundred head of cattle walked into that river and swam across and five hundred pairs of horns climbed up the other side. Know those little fish with the big mouths? Well, I had my first grey hairs that day. You see, I swam across before the cattle and when I saw their skeletons I went white.'

'What about the others?'

'The ones that were left on the other bank stayed there till they could find a canoe. I went ahead with the horns.'

He laughed hugely and drank.

'I've been through the mill, that's why I have no faiths left. I used to be a beggar, you know, down in the Haymarket. Begged all day and my man brought the Rolls for me at six. As a boy I was treated hard. Meal times I was put under the table, they threw food at me. I was the last and not wanted. Dad and Mum were camping out and had sex at the wrong time of the month and here I am. They thrashed me to make me walk. Hosed me with cold water in the winter. I was put out the back and left whenever there was a thunderstorm; they thought I might get frightened to death. I was naked, too. Apart from that I wanted for nothing.'

A WELL-AIMED GRANNY To soften Herman up a little, the Garfish let him into his office without the usual wait.

Unthinking, Herman put out his hand, but it was ignored.

'You haf called me to the office,' he began awkwardly, and smiled. 'Why is that?' trying to take the edge off the question. The Garfish shuffled some papers, hoping for a good opening.

'Is it about my arm?' No answer. 'The arm that was?'

The Garfish suddenly blurted out, 'We'll have to let you go, Herman.'

'Let me go? Go where?'

'Just go.'

'How is that?'

'Not work here'—waving his hands as if giving street directions to a foreigner straight off the boat—'Not any more.'

'Why is that? My arm?' He switched his eyes jerkily round to his empty sleeve and queerly sloping shoulder. The great round lump of emptiness in his stomach told him the answer. 'The sack.' The words were out.

'No, no, Herman. Don't take it like that.'

'How can I take it?'

'No. We have to let you go. With great regret.'

'Who regrets this? The desk? The building? The tanks out there? The company?'

'Puroil regrets—'

'Who is the Company? Is it you? Is it me? No one regrets this sack, but me only. I regret.'

'We thought the end of the week. Unless you wish to go sooner. It's up to you.'

'Up to me? Is it? I want to work! I can do my work with one hand, more work than two men!'

'I'm sorry. The end of the week, then.'

'The end of me! That's what!'

'Don't make this any more difficult for me.'

'Difficult? For you? How is this so? For me it is difficult, not you! You sit there now, you sit there next week. Where do I sit next week? And all because I can lift a pipe with one hand and once I miss and pinch my finger.'

'We can't entertain any workers' compensation claims at this stage. That's out.' His voice resumed its edge. Either these people keep to the regulations or they get no consideration.

'And where is that finger now? Burned in the incinerator with the hospital rubbish. And where is the hand, my hand, that I had for fifty years? Burned to ash! I knew every line of it, every hair, every scar. It was a good hand. And my arm to the elbow! And now the shoulder! With muscles that were ten times the muscles of other men. Because the finger bone was pinched. Because I work hard and not calling the crane driver for shifting every little pipe.'

He got to his feet. The Garfish was relieved. The fool was only worried about his finger and arm. He had no further responsibility, everyone is supposed to know the law. If a man didn't make a claim, he didn't want to make one.

'We need your signature on your refund of pension fund contributions,' said the Garfish. Let him go, he thought. He'll get over it. I'll get the signature on Friday when he leaves. Herman stuck out his hand and the Garfish inadvertently took it. Herman squeezed. The Garfish flopped about like a rag doll on the end of Herman's fist, making faint whining noises. Herman went out. It wasn't much consolation, but he'd done something in return. Why did they do this to him? He didn't want to go to law, he wanted to work. Unemployment benefits weren't meant to live on.

From his pocket he took an apple, a large, green Granny Smith. With a ferocious gesture of helpless defiance he threw it at the upper windows of the Termitary, where it struck with a flat sound. It was too hard and green to splash much.

CONFRONTATIONS One Eye met the Wandering Jew on a narrow walkway head on, and pushed him out of the way. He pushed the Manufacturing Superintendent aside from the entrance to his amenities room, barged through three visitors that were blocking a door, and accidentally elbowed a lady cleaner out of his way as he walked up to the bundy clock on the way out at eleven. He beat the first two easily, drew with the visitors—one of them tripped him—and suffered multiple bruises from the lady, who was in good condition.

It was a great day for first things.

LOVE IN HIGH PLACES The Glass Canoe came in from the darkened inner bay of the locker-room where he had been reading a morning paper and for a few moments he imagined he saw himself, tall and straight, standing over his young son. Or was it the Rustle of Spring? He narrowed his eyes and shook his head to get rid of the hallucination, but it took its own time to vanish. No, it was the Great White Father and dirty little Sumpsucker.

The Rustle of Spring had not been surprised by what he said to him way up there in the top of the reactor, nor by the things he asked him to do. In fact, it seemed to the Glass Canoe that he had been waiting for that very request. Or the boy was very quick-witted. He had been expert; he must have done this sort of thing before. The Glass Canoe was a Navy man for sixteen years and had some experience of other men—a turn in the barrel after the regulation three months at sea—but he thought Italian boys, with their poverty and good looks, were probably exposed more to older men with exotic tastes. The boy had hinted at a little present. Maybe this was a prelude to asking for money straight out. He wasn't going to pay money, not to some dirty little immoral tike off the streets of Naples. No. Mantova, he called it. Mantua. All they thought of was money. There was so much more in the world than money.

Nevertheless, as he pulled his attention back to first things and opened his plant manual at the gasoline treating section—he'd studied nearly all the plants in the complex without taking a step outside the control block—and reminded himself clearly and logically of his ambitions. Nevertheless he said quietly and reasonably, 'I like the little bugger.' As if it were a blessing he had power to bestow.

RESCUE THE PERISHING The Great White Father found Herman friendless in a nursing home and kidnapped him back to the Home Beautiful. A special hut was captured from Puroil and erected by the bed hut so that there were four huts arranged symmetrically with awning over the middle space. Drink hut, bed hut, rest hut, death hut.

Herman was now very sick. The disease was reaching insatiably into his ribs and spine. His rescuers went about shaking their heads. He was not much longer for this world. They sent the Volga Boatman for large supplies of beer and prepared to nurse poor Herman till death came to whisk him away. He was in a little pain, he said. Not much.

The girls inquired tactfully if there was anything they could do. Free, of course. But Herman was not up to it. They looked disappointed. He knew they meant well. His healthy tan, from years working in the sun, gradually faded.

FIRST THINGS FIRST A small plume of vapour appeared at the south end of the plant. A figure moved about. Congo. Must be draining gas. The Samurai moved inside and thought no more of it for a few minutes until he smelled the characteristic aromatic odour of the alkylation process. He went to the door. The huge courtyard enclosed by the rectangle of plants was full of vapour.

'Where's Congo?' he shouted to the Humdinger.

'There he is.' He pointed. Congo was sitting in the amenities room, having a smoke.

'Did you leave a gas valve open?' the Samurai asked. 'Did you leave gas on and walk away?'

The man shrugged.

'Get out and shut it. And put out the cigarettes, all of you. The yard's full of gas.'

When he saw the vapour the Congo Kid ran, skirting the white cloud. One tiny spark—that was all it needed. A metal tip on a shoe, a fitter's blow with a hammer.

The Samurai took a thick piece out of Congo and the man knew he deserved it. Nevertheless, he promised himself revenge on the company to atone for his discomfort. He had never been chipped before.

THE MANAGER'S WINGE Men like the Sumpsucker had been going about saying 'Do what you're told. Don't ask questions' on the slightest provocation. This was a hint of the awful caning the Wandering Jew had in store for every employee lower than himself in the wage scale. His own buttocks were sore from the caning he received from those above him in Melbourne, who were sore, etc.

He took rosters over a number of days to read his prepared lecture to captive audiences. He came in through a door to which the men had no access, stood waiting for silence, and when he got it began his spiel. He had never spoken to them before. He thought of them as animals: now he wanted their understanding.

'We have sustained very heavy financial losses in recent years—yearly losses which have increased rather than decreased'—he tactfully omitted to mention that the cost of the cracker construction had been charged against Clearwater refinery and that was the reason for the loss figure—'and it is therefore necessary that action be taken to rectify this if the future security of each one of us is to be assured. Unless we can prove that we can operate profitably then further developments will be in jeopardy and certain of our activities could possibly be transferred elsewhere. We are over-manned in various departments and some reductions seem inevitable. There has to be change if we are to progress, there surely cannot be any argument about this. Your basic interests after all are synonymous with our own, that is, that the future will provide us with the security so necessary to our individual welfare. What will be done therefore has to be done.'

AN INDUSTRIAL OMBUDSMAN He finished and asked for questions.

'Is the place going to be shifted?' asked Oliver Twist. 'We ought to be told now so we can get other jobs. We're not going to move to Port Stephens or wherever it is and find there's only company houses to buy. We ought to be told now; after all, we're the permanent employees, you're not.'

'What does that mean?' asked the Manager with dignity.

'Managers stay a few years, then go somewhere else. We stay till we retire.'

'Does this mean we'll get no change in the sick-pay policy?' asked the Count. 'In the old country we got six weeks on full pay and six weeks half pay after six months' service. Here we get five days a year in the award and there's no policy in writing. It seems to vary from man to man.'

'I can't pronounce on staff policy,' said the Manager, smiling at their ignorance. Didn't they know it was uniform throughout the world?

'How will they liberalize sick pay if they're economizing, you log?' said Oliver Twist to the Count.

'What about safety?' asked the Two Pot Screamer.

'Special attention will be paid to safety. I am taking a special interest in it. I hope you will send representatives to the next Safety Council and not boycott it. After all, they're your plants.' No one questioned the pronoun.

'I hope when we ask for something we need in the way of safe working,' said Oliver Twist, 'we won't be outvoted by office galahs that don't know what we're talking about.'

'I think we'll see improvement all round. I'm personally very interested in the safety question.'

'We've had things in the safety books for months. We have wooden ladders in places where you need proper steel ladders stayed to columns. There's all the safeties that won't reseat, the drains that are full every time it rains, fires every few weeks and a whole mess of things at the cracker. They've all been notified and nothing's done. They've got sixty kilo boiling water going through a rubber hose down there.'

'I'll have all this investigated promptly. If you men will draw up lists, plant by plant, of all hazards, I personally will see it gets attention. The plant must be safe.'

'If we can't get action from those directly above us, the foremen and section heads, can we come up to you, then?' persisted the Two Pot Screamer.

The Manager stopped. He hadn't meant this. He was so unused to talking to prisoners that he hadn't realized they would take this meaning from his words. Couldn't they see it was just the old line—not meant to be taken seriously?

'Well, I'll be attending every third or fourth meeting of the monthly council, so eventually I'll see all the minutes. You can stop worrying.' He looked round for the next question. He knew the effect on most of them of his economy drive. It would soften them up ready to accept the company award instead of pushing their own claims.

'Wait a minute,' said Two Pot. 'When you said you were personally interested and you wanted to know, you seemed to be saying you were going to resume the old style manager-worker contact, like we had with Gentleman Joe, the one before Glorious Devon. But every three months! Christamighty, we could have blokes dead down there and you'd read the minutes three months later! What we need is a man to combine industrial and safety investigation. Not just the Brown Snake, he doesn't do anything till we make a complaint. Why can't we have a man coming round to nip these things in the bud? Why don't you streamline your industrial set-up by appointing an industrial Ombudsman? That way you'—he almost continued 'could bypass the Union', but stopped in time—'you'd have a man in charge of industrial relations that we could trust, too. One that couldn't be suspected of being on the Company's side. One that didn't owe loyalty to any particular department. The unions together could pay half his salary and the Company the other half.' But Two Pot had stopped on the way to work for a few pots. Everyone understood and took no notice. The Manager disregarded the question. Two Pot didn't realize how little power the Manager had; certainly he was not allowed to tamper with Procedure, which laid down that Puroil was to have a Brown Snake after the pattern of Puroil snakes all over the world. None of the prisoners said anything to show they thought they should have a say in Puroil's management. All their training, all their education from childhood up had ingrained in them the conviction that they should be ruled by others.

THE STRUGGLE FOR FREEDOM One Eye waited at the other end of the building; he knew where the back door led.

'You know what you need?' said One Eye, jostling the Wandering Jew as he scurried out. The Manager recovered his balance and asked, 'What do I need?' One Eye stood between him and the path to his office.

'You need a few hard knocks outa life,' said One Eye loudly. 'You haven't been around enough to be a boss to these men.' He had avoided witnesses: he liked to feel he could get his dismissal in a man-to-man session with the Manager.

He pushed the Wandering Jew, tipped his white safety helmet over his eyes, pulled the white handkerchief out of his pocket and blew his nose dirtily on it. The Wandering Jew hoped vainly that his spectacles would not be touched, but One Eye hooked his finger in them and whipped them off. The Manager's eyes looked oddly naked, they were surrounded by skin which had not weathered with the rest of his face and seemed defenceless.

HEEL! When the lectured workers got down to the cracker, the Sumpsucker was waiting for them, his little eyes screwed up in close examination of their faces. Softly he sang the first verse of 'Rock of Ages' as he moved among them. He walked off a few paces and stood with his hands behind his back as if he were hiding a rolled-up newspaper.

'Come here, all of you!' he experimented.

'You go and have a tootie on a hot brick,' advised the Humdinger. 'Some day someone'll hang one on this company. They can't do what they like to people.'

'It won't be you mob. Or we'll wear your guts for garters.'

No one else looked up. They trooped into the locker-room, except for those like the Western Salesman and the Loch Ness Monster who hung about like dogs, looking for the Slug and sniffing for news and scraps of loose talk. But the Sump knew that though they were tall, bronzed, rugged Australian individualists, more or less, they would end up doing exactly as they were told. The new industrial agreement would tell them how high to jump. After years of taking it, the Sump was in a position to dish it out. Not one man had the heart to joke about the big black drums on the footpath outside the widow's house. The council had ordered her to move them. Sumpy had to pay for the job. She still demanded something each time he had her and catalyst drums were the only things he could get free.

VICTIMIZED The phone calls started that same day. All departments, even the day workers in the Termitary, heard the earnest voice asking them about the proposed transfer of the Puroil enterprise to Port Stephens. The voice would answer no questions, merely repeating the words Port Stephens, and 'When are the company's activities here going to be abandoned?' People started to be agitated over nothing.

Next day One Eye was called up to the Brown Snake's office, told that Head Office had reduced the Clearwater establishment by one operator and he was it. Sacked. At fifty-one.

He swore, stamped, banged the desk, called the Brown Snake

for everything under the sun, scattered all his papers, tipped up the desk and threw the Brown Snake's hat and coat out the window on to the garden beds, then did a wee on desk and carpet, with the Brown Snake coiled in a corner. As a last gesture, he ripped the phone from its mooring, spat on the Brown Snake's white shirt—a little went on his tie and on his Puroil long-service tie-chain—then pulled open the door and strode to the car park, jubilant.

He would get his proportion of long-service leave now; as for his tantrums, they would be overlooked. If they were made public, everyone might get in on the act. But he'd made sure they didn't change their minds on his dismissal.

How was it, then, that he felt enraged? Why had they chosen him for the chop? There were bludgers aplenty all over the plants. He'd got what he wanted, all right, but it was like their bloody hide to pick on him.

17
THROWOUTS

GOODNIGHT, GOD The Great White Father nearly didn't reach work, his battery had leaked acid for so long it fell through the floor of the car. He was lucky to be able to put it back in; a few old newspapers wedged it tight. That night the plant was down and the unlucky ones were in the cracker's regenerator, digging out soaked and rock-hard catalyst with picks. He listened briefly to what they told him of the latest disaster. Some fool foreman had insisted on belting steam into the system for too long, the steam condensed to water, and when white-hot catalyst was circulated the water became steam again. The resulting pressure nearly took the lid off the lot. More steam was injected to damp down the whole mess. The catalyst was poisoned with water. He clucked his tongue.

'Saw Slackie in town the other day. Back from Australia's riches in the west. They get him out there, eight hundred miles from nowhere and tell him to work twelve hours next day. That's all right. He does his twelve. Then he finds it's twelve hours a day whenever they say and they say it thirteen days a fortnight. One day off in two weeks he got, and he made the mistake of querying it. Out the gate he went and had to find his way to Perth the best he could. You should hear him curse those foreign bastards.'

'Who owns it?'

'Yanks and British. They do what they like. You say one word and out you go. Not even the Unionists were game to fight when they brought in Japanese workers—they had to be stirred up by a man who'd never voted Labor in his life. But never mind all that, all I want you blokes to do tonight is tuck me in, then come round at six and beg me to get up. And don't forget, wear double underwear on Anzac Day, the forecast is for cold weather.' Anzac Day was months off.

'Aren't you going to be careful now they're tightening up?'

'This is the time to stand up for your rights. I'll sleep tonight. So goodnight God and stay tuned to the Great White Father: he'll dream about you.'

Not all the shifts picked at the work in their usual exhausted fashion. This night, on 2 shift, they worked like madmen. The catalyst was thick and wet and only thirty tons to go. By the sort of coincidence that Puroil usually managed to avoid, the men were paired off in exactly the right way. The standard method was never to match up two men who got on well together in case they sat and talked; no, put the enemies together so they work hard. They never did, but Puroil stuck to its method. It was laid down.

The Samurai was with the Humdinger, Disneyland with Gunga Din, the Western Salesman with the Loch Ness Monster, the Two Pot Screamer with Terrazzo, the Thieving Magpie with Knuckles. There was little talking and no grumbling. Because the catalyst was wet there was no dust. No silica to breathe.

No one knew why everyone wanted to work—perhaps because the Slug was off sick catching up on printing orders, perhaps because it was the last day of the shift—but that thirty tons was down the vacuum line in two hours and the first thirty tons took four days of three shifts each.

TRAINING FOR FREEDOM On the plants men were learning the details of the new plan. There would be a pool of workers, the throwouts, who would be given training of a sort then sacked if they failed an examination. A Navy man was brought in to take charge of training. Men who had been there thirty-five years were given induction courses. No man would have any one job but would regard himself as temporary, to be moved as often as necessary. This and a few discipline adjustments were a violent change in the established job indulgency pattern.

There was a doubling of all supervision. One of the catalyst lines had blown through erosion by fine particles over a long time and this had caused the latest plant crash; doubling the supervision would stop the catalyst from doing things like this again.

A dozen men whom the company thought had a lot of influence on the rest because they talked a lot, were called up for interviews to be foremen, competing for eight places. The winners were to be announced after the industrial agreement was signed.

One of the group told to report for training in a month's time—the inference was that this was a reward for inefficiency or incompetence—was the Glass Canoe. At first he argued. Surely they meant he was for a foreman interview. It was soon explained to him. He went home dazed, forgetting an appointment under the Stripper skirt with the Rustle of Spring. He also disappointed Far Away Places, who had taken to spying on them.

Why are they doing this to him? Hadn't he had the right attitude all along? Suck to the company, rubbish the workers. Hadn't he always told the mob the company was reasonable, they'll look after us? Did they care so little that a man had the right attitude? He was ready to forsake all—all his mates—for the company. Was this his reward? Demoted. A throwout.

His hopes died.

He went for a pee. There was purple everywhere. He couldn't do it. Instead he went out into the pipe-track, like a tramp in a ditch. Just as if he'd been told not to pee with the mob.

LITTLE WOODEN BLOCKS And there was the computer. Much of the stock and accounting work was already handed over to the machines. The company was leaving it until the last moment to announce its redundancy plans and the clerks' nerves broke first. Without benefit of Union advice, a party of them climbed the stairs to ask the Whispering Baritone where they stood. They imagined that if they didn't call in the Union, Puroil would think better of them.

They knocked at the Baritone's door as he, Luxaflex and the Garfish were messing around with little wooden blocks of different colours, like a set of children's numbering rods. They were working on the problem of where to put the clerks so they wouldn't get in the way of the machines. Pixie hadn't been invited: he was on the list for re-training. The Garfish answered the knock, being the junior of the three. He closed the door and reported.

'Clerical bodies. About redundancy rumours.'

The Baritone nodded. Clerks. The new solidarity. How easily he remembered their reluctant determination, their almost convinced defiance. And the dawn of gratification in their eyes when the company backed down in face of full Union membership. Their new confidence. They started to call him the Whispering Baritone openly and with louder voices.

'Hold still,' said the Whispering Baritone to his helpers. 'Don't say anything. I want to talk to the poor devils. They'll stay still if we don't alarm them. Come in,' he invited, and the white shirts choked the doorway, gaping at the coloured blocks. No one wanted to be first to speak, the leaders always got the worst punishment.

'Now, ladies and gents, don't be afraid. This has been coming a long while. Our way of life can't last for ever. We're working on the problem right now.' He beamed at the little wooden blocks, then back at the shirts. 'I can't pretend to know what's in your minds when you see us here planning your future. It must be a mystery to you, eh? To see top company executives playing with bits and pieces, enjoying themselves working out ways to save the company money; you probably think we're going to get the money we save on your salaries, but that's not it at all. We won't get a penny more. It's not for us, it's for progress. We can't hold progress off any longer. We'd like to keep you on, but your skills are simply not needed. The lower reaches of management are on the way out—that's a fact of modern life.' His tic seemed to be better, his neck didn't twitch, he was completely at ease. All he needed to heal his body was the restoration of the power he always knew should be his.

'We welcome the day when the machines take over the whole management function; no one will be more pleased than we will when he can hand over our desks to the programmers. Redundancy is a disease and its spreads. We'll suffer, too, but it's a historical fact that you must suffer first. I know we could afford to keep you on, but what would the shareholders say? They demand the business be run efficiently. Maybe we'll replace shareholders with machines some day, eh?' That was a funny one. He gave it the laugh it deserved.

'Never forget. We've nothing to fear but fear itself! The change will be gradual. So work hard and maybe you can avoid being the first to go. Be obedient and do your best for Puroil and you can rest assured only the dead wood will go first. Gradually, that's the key word. You won't feel it. Re-training.'

Who would train them or where they could possibly be fitted in, he didn't know or care. A purely academic question.

With these words the Second Industrial Revolution caught up with his panicky audience. At that moment a bulletin was on its way to the official leaders of this rabble, containing the first redundant classifications. The warmth and monotony of work and home and work and home again had never seemed so desirable.

The top people watched silently as the bottom people shuffled silently out. They would forget their solidarity now and work like slaves to be the last to go. Fear, like a monstrous sore planted by a rabbit exterminator, stood out hard and crusted on their faces.

THE MAN WITH THE POWER High in a corner of the Termitary a man in a small office with a commanding view of several car parks and fat warehouses took a paper from a document wallet, drew a line through some typed words and added some words of his own.

'Delete Zone 5, Insert Area Blue.'

In houses and pubs for miles around, and down on the job for the twenty-one days' detention of the twenty-eight, something went out of the lives of the male prisoners and their domestic prisoners—women and children who waited for them to bring home the means of subsistence. Even their domestic animals—the prisoners' prisoners—suffered. Their golf club had no name, their common bond was in doubt. Men who thought of themselves as natural-born Zone 5 men became suddenly men with no name. In time the wound made by this man's pen would heal and when they all felt themselves born-and-bred Area Blue men they would forget, they would huddle together in the warmth of Area Blue-ness; but for the present they were unsettled, they were savage to one another, they kicked their cats and dogs and withheld their dependants' food money a little longer.

THE WANDERING JEW ADDRESSES HIS EXECUTIVES 'What Puroil needs right now is a good dose of tough-mindedness. If we are going to hold our own in this uneasy world we will have to sharpen our ability to face hard facts and act with intelligence and courage.

'In the years since the great depression, a fuzziness has crept into our thinking. Australian business has fallen prey to a cult of human relations that worries excessively about people's feelings. The cult has come between us and our old-fashioned ability to get a job done. We think less about how to do a good job than about how to be a good fellow. Frequently, business failure can be laid directly on the doorstep of human relations. I have seen executives exhibit such sentimentality and tender-mindedness when they needed hard-headedness, that businesses have had to close down, putting a lot of people out of work.

'Throughout his history, man the animal has been trying to achieve an intellectual and moral veneer. I believe that a large part of the job of education must be to toughen and thicken this veneer, not to encourage people to crack it and peel it off, as popular self-centred Freudian psychologists would have us do. I suspect that some of the principal causes of increasing mental disease lie in morbid introspection, lack of strong moral considerations, and leisure that we have not yet learned how to use.

'Australia cannot afford the pampering luxury of human relations. The Marxists are tougher-minded than we are. Unless we can restore our toughness and our ability to get a job done, while suspending a little of our concern with human dignity, time will run out on us.'

The executives still sat. What had the Wandering Jew meant? No one wanted to be first to speak in case he said something that exposed his flanks or vulnerable underparts to attack from his brethren. For a distressing number of minutes nobody moved.

It would have been an error to be first to go. Like disagreement. Argument. Disloyalty. Rebellion. Subversion. The Python made a sudden movement and an engineering man, thinking he was rising, almost got to his feet, but saw his mistake in time. At length, like the suspicious and primitive warriors they were, all sat forward on the edge of their seats and after much feinting, rose together. Honour was satisfied and no one had his neck stuck out. They separated in silence.

THE WILL OF THE PEOPLE At the Trades Hall the prisoners obediently sat on thick timber chairs polished a shiny brown by the bottoms of countless thousands of toilers. They looked placid now. Not like yesterday. They had stopped work at midnight after a stormy meeting the day before. Somehow they got the bit between their teeth and men who never even raised their voices to a foreman stood blustering and yelling and demanding that clauses be removed from the company's award offer. The men's application was rough, ill-typed and sort of doggy: the company's answer was well set out, neat, official-looking. An impartial observer would have no hesitation in predicting a triumph for the company. The package was better.

Perhaps the militancy of the day before had been a last skirmish before the surrender, the final defiance after the fright of the Manager's Winge. The Federal Secretary of the Union was not sure which way they'd jump today. Whatever happened, the Union couldn't afford stoppages that lasted any length of time. Fines of a thousand dollars a day would mop up Union funds in a few weeks.

The executive wanted to keep the peace rather than look too closely at grievances. They'd never even been to the plant to look at it. They lived off prisoners' wages just as industry did. Their organization was the same pyramidal hierarchy as Puroil's.

'Puroil is busy with their computer system and they want to get everything squared away, preferably in round figures, before the bulk of their work goes on the machines. They haven't shifted an inch from their proposals, that's what I'm here to tell you. The overtime ban must go and the company's draft award be accepted. The Brown Snake, when we told him of your stand, said the challenge of a twenty-four-hour stoppage is accepted. But, he said—BUT! and this I must emphasize to you all. The company would have listened without a stoppage.' He paused impressively.

There was no answering buzz of surprise or complaint or rebuttal. The men went on breathing, smoke continued to pour from their cigarettes, upwards, to form a solid blanket of incense over all. It was ridiculous. Two hundred and fifty men pulling in two hundred and fifty different directions—there was no resultant that made sense. A small group, three or four men on each shift, could have whipped them into shape and told them what to want.

'Some despots are successful—this you must understand. Fighting does not always bring victory. National Steel, now. They did no good, brothers. After a strike of three weeks they came back with three dollars less. Therefore, I recommend you accept the company's proposal. But if you do not, then rest assured, you have the Union behind you.' He didn't say which way it would be facing.

He sat down, but because of certain lies he had been caught out in in previous negotiations, got no cheers.

A white-headed man, small and clerkly, who had been taking a backseat, prepared to speak to the docile workers. But the Glass Canoe had the wind in his tail. He had nothing to lose now. There was no stopping him. He challenged the Advocate.

'Who's he? Is he a lawyer? How do we know he'll represent us when he leaves here?'

They didn't. No one knew what he said to the management under the weight of their hospitality. The slap-up dinners and the booze put on for inspectors of boilers and equipment were fresh in the prisoners' minds. The Chairman answered with dignity.

'It's true he's not a lawyer.'

'What are ya?' bellowed the Glass Canoe.

'I'm an economist,' said the Advocate redly.

'He's a Bachelor of Economics,' supplied the Chairman, grandly.

'I'm a bachelor, too, now me wife's gone!' the Glass Canoe roared. He sat down. There was hubbub. The Glass Canoe started to weep. His own reference to his beloved OG had hit him hard. Now she was dead he realized he loved her deeply. She had never liked him calling her OG, even though he protested the letters stood for Old Girl. He was lying, of course: actually they stood for Officers' Groundsheet. He heard some stories about her once dating back to her wartime service in the Women's Auxiliary and mostly believed them.

The tears dropped from his eyes, but there were no encouraging pats for him or rough male voices shyly saying, 'Cheer up.' He was too dangerous and unpredictable a man to be pitied. No one had even let on they knew his wife died.

'Our main concern now is to decide whether or not to go to Arbitration, bearing in mind the delays in getting a hearing and the money we lose while we're waiting. Now, the original judge is sick—judges get sick—and we have been left with a new judge. He's a friend of mine, I've known him for years, but even he will not sympathize with what you have down here on paper as your demands.'

He cleared his throat and put on his sternest look.

'No judge will give you less than the company offers.'

The chairman stood. 'Do you want me to leave the chair to move or from here?'

A general grunt signified the depth of the men's feelings.

'Very well, then, from the chair. Yesterday we threw their award out completely, but whatever the reasons we give for the stoppage, I move we accept the company's latest decision on the consent award. I know we value our right to say as we like and we've said it. But there's nowhere we can go from here.'

It was as quiet as that. And still the men hadn't said a word. Except for the twenty who seconded the motion. The men on the platform felt easier.

The Glass Canoe stood, he was a different man. This mob was weak as piss. 'I'm for it, chaps. We tried to squeeze the lemon and this is all the juice we got. I'd like to say about yesterday's meeting, I was an observer—I admit that—I had no intention of voting no-confidence in the delegates, so I hope there's no misunderstanding there.' This confession meant nothing to the crowd: they didn't know he'd tried to rubbish his own delegates to get back into favour with Puroil. 'Well, no one can say we didn't try. Anyone who speaks against this is a fool. The money's still good.' They worked one day more in each twenty-eight than the law provided, and were paid penalty rates for this day, but they persisted in thinking of this money as simply part of their normal pay, rather than money for extra time.

The little white man stood. 'We'll try to retain the one and a half per cent retrospectivity for you that we got via the metal trades. So don't worry. All in here'—he thumped and brandished the company's schedule—'all this still stands even if we accept now with our tails between our legs.'

An unidentified man fidgeting in the body of the hall half-rose to his feet and said half aloud, 'We're all piss-weak.' Those near him heard clearly enough, glanced mildly at him and puffed mildly on their cigarettes and pipes, as his bottom sank back where it belonged, but those farther away, eager to be diverted by any interruption, leaned their heads towards their neighbours, nudged and asked, 'Whadesay?' from the side of their mouths. 'We're all weak as piss,' was the usual mild answer. Radiating outwards like spokes of a wheel, this interruption persisted until all were satisfied they had heard the remark. From a distance, the nudge, the heads leaning inwards, the pause, the repetition further out from the centre, went on. From the platform, the leaders of these mild men observed the ripples spreading outwards. Wind on a field of wheat. The message didn't reach them till after the meeting.

Another man stood. 'We're not fools to disagree with this motion at all. Look at Union history! Imagine what it's going to be like in the future. Here in this thing we've accepted redundancy with no fight and stand-downs when they're slack and a pool of rejects. I say get a good barrister and spend some money and take our chance in court. The only reason the company offers us one cent is because if they say they can't afford to pay anything the court can examine their books. I know we'll end up with the same-sized slice of the cake because whatever we get, prices go up. But prices still go up even if we get nothing. I say fight!'

He got only murmured support, just as no one gave more than murmured opposition. They'd made their gesture of defiance. They were weak. They had got used to eating three meals a day. Every day. If anyone had to stick his neck out, let it be someone else. Yesterday's ardour had scared them. Yesterday they had been defiant, powerful, and knew they should be punished for it. Yet they were still getting the money promised. Who cared about a few rights? They crumbled. Each had in him a small traitor who wanted to eat, drink, make love and be left alone. They didn't know that their Union's Federal Executive was not willing to spend money to back their case in court. Once in court, a rival Union was waiting to step in and claim half the members at Puroil. They had no chance either way. The company and the Union wanted the same thing: acceptance and no fuss.

A GRATIFIED SMILE Just for the fun of it, when they were back at work the Humdinger let go a rumour.

'When the plants are running well, they're going to let a few germs go in the water cooler and in the food from the canteen, so we get crook and have our sickies when times are good. Then when the plants play up we've got no sickies left and we can't stay away.'

He repeated this to the Murray Cod, Quick Tip, the Elder Statesman and the Western Salesman; all good talkers and tried and true alarmists. The Humdinger sat back and watched his bullet being fired over and over into the soft receptive bodies of prisoners helpless to defend themselves against rumour. He felt powerful, like a politician who calms a population with lies, then smiles as his lies are repeated as truth, are believed, and finally come to be accepted as axioms men live by.

The Samurai spent a day in bed sweating out a chill and was startled when the Brown Snake didn't pay him. Even the time off for his arm hadn't mopped up all the sick days he hadn't taken in the past few years. In his office the Brown Snake sat thinking how clever he was to put the words *More Information Required* on the Samurai's application for pay. He knew the ones who wouldn't be bothered explaining to some office joker. And if he did complain the words could easily be changed. He smiled. It was so easy.

A DECENT CHAP The Wild Bull of the Pampas had lost his neck—instead of eighteen inches he had fifteen and a half—and three stone besides. The danger flag was up.

No one contradicted him or tried to calm him when he rattled on and on about money and how was he going to manage and he could only put away ten dollars a week. He was single. Soon he would be in hospital again, the doctors would pump him up the extra three stone with calming drugs and he would cease to worry about money for six months. It never occurred to him to do something about getting more money. He was too decent a chap for that. He hated the notion of combining against his employer. He even hated trade unions. He was a lab man and jumped at the company's offer to include lab men on the staff. He could get away from trade unions for good. What were they but Communist fronts? It as good as said so in the papers. Outmoded. Unnecessary in a planned economy.

The thing that bothered him now was that the company had the whip out to staff men and were putting them off if they got an inch out of line. Overtime was gone, the number of tests doubled. And the shrewdies who wouldn't have a bar of staff status were not only under the Union's wing and talking back to Custard Guts the lab chief, they were getting so many doublers they were starting to pick and choose. How would he make ends meet with no overtime? The low types—reds and unionists—were laughing behind his back. He was one of those called up for foreman interviews and had helped persuade the others to get on the staff. On top of it all, there were only four plant men made foreman, the other four came from outside and didn't have a clue about the refinery.

The company must have something in mind for staff men, something to make up for all this. They would announce it at the right time and everything would be made right. Just a matter of patience. If you have staff privileges you must expect to earn them. The company expects a staff man to have higher standards and not just complain. Besides, they only made you staff status if you were a decent chap.

WITHOUT REPRISAL You're nothing but a number, now.

The phrase became a sort of greeting, an open password, in the grounds of the Puroil Termitary and Grinding Works and beyond it into the pocket-handkerchief lawns and cell-like rooms of the worker-spawning laboratories, dormitories and marshalling yards known as suburbs.

Some prisoners still relied on charms to ward off the company's all-powerful displeasure and the cold winds of separation. 'Someone told me I'd be a foreman before long...' 'I'm an old digger, they'll look after me—I go the company's way...' 'The Enforcer is my brother-in-law—they wouldn't sack me. No, I can't tell you why.' The old fictions.

The good old days had never seemed so precious and so remote as now when they appeared to be gone for ever. Instinctively the men should have huddled together, in fear, in anger, in a mood of action. What they did was divide, every man for himself, and were an easy prey for the triumphant managing class, who still lived among them—their houses dotted here and there—without reprisals, though in the main they tended to gather in suburbs they wished to call their own, safe from the smell of the product and poverty.

BRASS BUTTONS Yesterday Kramden had been a company-oriented trade unionist; today he was newly appointed safety officer. They dressed him in the black uniform of a fire officer. Macabre had been outed. In the shake-up they had made him responsible for plant safety but given him no authority or initiative. All he could do was recommend action to the safety council, who opposed action if it cost money and only acted if the fuss made by the men rose to danger level on the fuss-meter. The new man was quite content to be told what to do. The company had what it wanted; a man who followed orders, didn't clutter the air with his own opinions, and could be left holding the bag if something happened.

Yesterday Kramden had been flipping cigarette butts into sandboxes full of paper and laughing at the blaze; today it was a safety hazard.

'Get the proper rubbish tins for those papers or I'll have your smoking permit!' he roared at some cracker men.

'Let the company put tins there.'

'You apply for them. You want us to do everything for you!'

'Take the smoking permit, then, and Puroil will have you for rocking the boat.'

He wore the uniform proudly and strutted as poor Macabre never did. But then Macabre was never dressed in a uniform, with shiny brass buttons.

The sixty-kilo boiler water had to burst the rubber hose some time and it chose a moment when the Gypsy Fiddler was holding it, directing it down a drain. He was scalded from chest to knees. When they carried him in Kramden abused him and Calamity Jane refused to treat him. She never touched men there.

Next day the plant plot was crowded with big yellow signs: safety hats must be worn at all times.

THE CONFIDENT-AUTHORITATIVE MANNER Far Away Places had a few lungfuls of acid from the alkylate plant and went to see Doctor Death about his cough in his own time. Sometimes he couldn't blow a whole tune on his mouthpiece for coughing.

'I make a weekly tour of the refinery,' said Doctor Death. 'There are no bad drains or fumes anywhere in the whole complex of plants. We have an unusually high degree of freedom from noxious gases and dusts.'

Far Away coughed a little, trying to direct the droplets of moisture away from the placid expanse of Doctor Death's beautiful suit. He was trying to cough softly, so as not to appear by his actions to be contradicting the physician's statements of faith in what he had been told by his chief contact, the Spotted Trout. There were no tours of the refinery. A lie in these circumstances, though, was no worse than a lying word of comfort and good cheer to the about-to-be-bereaved relatives of the terminally ill.

18
THE FALL

TEXT FOR THE GLASS CANOE 'A man's internal development marches a little way on before his achievement and his achievement is a little ahead of his reputation. A man needs all the self-confidence he can muster not to believe of himself the things others believe.'

He wrote it out on a piece of cardboard and read it before going to bed, every night for three nights. After that, writing was not good enough: he printed it. It took several attempts before he got it done as he liked it. The cardboard was glossy white one side and bare the other; the box he took it from had contained his dead wife's last brassiere. The bit of brassiere box was appropriate because the thing it contained had in turn contained a woman's breasts, pointing steadfastly forward. Tilted slightly upward. Parallel with his own temporarily revived ambitions and his hope in the future that recurred like an illness. So he was in the training pool. He wouldn't let it get him down, he would overcome this obstacle, too.

HOSPITALITY The Humdinger stood cursing. Both gauge glasses had blown on the high-pressure steam drums, the Samurai had isolated them. Two years before this, the Humdinger had read up his boiler manual to go for his ticket.

What's the first thing you check on your boiler? Answer: The level in the gauge glass. What do you do if there's no water in the glass? Cut the fires. It is of the greatest importance that those in charge of a boiler shall know with absolute certainty the height of the water level in the boiler. He got his ticket. No trouble. The company was eager for men to get boiler tickets, so his three hundred hours which he hadn't spent on or around a boiler was winked at and signed as a fact, and they gave him a letter to the examiner, mentioning half a dozen boilers he'd never seen.

He looked at his instruments. They showed levels. But he remembered all too clearly times they had shown levels when the boiler was empty; he remembered panics when there were no levels on the instrument panel and no time for men to climb one hundred and forty-nine vertical rungs on ten different ladders to the gauge glasses, but there was still water in the boilers. How much? No one knew. It was as much as his job was worth to cut the fires without orders, though if there was an explosion he would lose his ticket immediately.

In his examination he found the inspector knew nothing of the boilers he worked on. He was asked questions on the Lamont, the B & W, Cornish, Lancashire, Scotch Marine, Locomotive, the Vertical, Colonial, Yarrow, John Thompson, and Stirling. Even the Jackass, of which there was still one in New South Wales. The principles were the same, but he found it strange that the inspector didn't recognize boilers that operated for months or years at a time, twenty-four hours a day. He was given questions on morning duties, banking the fires at lunchtime when steam demand was low and closing the boiler down at knock-off time. He laughed. He tried to say something about hot carbon-monoxide gas being the main burner on his boilers, with hydrocarbon gas auxiliaries, but the man thought he was being funny. He tried to say these boilers were integrated with a cyclic reaction and regeneration process and their high-pressure steam was vital to a huge compressor on the other end of the process, and that the hot flue gases, besides providing steam, did a second duty in driving turbo-expanders which provided air for the regeneration process and also air for its own combustion chambers, but the man started to talk about grinding up coal.

He waited. The Samurai found the Slug and demanded fitters. No fitters. The one maintenance man was a mile away on an important job. The sight glasses needed many bolts undone before new ones were fitted. For this job spanners were used, and no operator could even carry a spanner at that stage.

He cursed Puroil, the Slug, gauge glasses, boilers, the inspector. Then, as if in answer to a prayer, he saw him. The very same man. Supported by Puroil men, the Python and several others.

Macabre, disgruntled, had made a phone call giving a list of unsafe conditions. The Humdinger didn't know of the phone call. The Python did: the inspector had spilled his guts after he was wined and dined in the manager's private dining-room. No PR room for this man, nothing but luxury was good enough.

'G'day,' said Humdinger. They stopped. They hadn't come to look at his boilers.

'What's going on?' said the Python.

'The sight glasses are gone on the boilers.' He pointed up.

'You've got panel indication.'

'Yes. There's a level here.' Pointing to the instrument.

'OK, then,' said the inspector.

'But I can't operate a boiler without a gauge glass.'

'Who said?'

'You did.'

'Me?'

'You did. You tested me for my ticket.'

'This is different. You've got instruments.'

'But you said I must know exactly. These have been wrong before.'

'You've got instruments. What more d'you want? You men get everything these days. When I was young we had nothing.' The Humdinger was licked. He thought he had a cast-iron case.

'Can I have that in writing?' But his superiors turned away.

'No action required,' smiled the Python. And the men holding up the visitor laughed and laughed and steered him outside where he looked up at the dizzying tangle of steel, then helped him back to the car. On top of the structure Far Away Places relaxed the grip of his finger and thumb and resumed his pee. He'd had to cut off the flow halfway through in case the Python spotted him.

CRISIS MAN The new man's initials were SK. It was the work of only a few seconds for the Two Pot Screamer to christen him SKlation. Escalation was a new word then.

And it came true. No one knew if the man was like it before he was christened or if the new name forced him into this mould, but whatever was going when he came on the scene got rapidly worse. If the boilers were playing up and SK came through the rear door as the bosses always did, the trouble developed into a crisis very quickly. Things just naturally went bad when he was around.

He was brought in to make up the number. A revision of the establishment figures in Melbourne showed that One Eye need not have been dismissed, but it was too late. The new figures were to take account of expansion. After a week he went up to the Python and complained he didn't have enough to do and everyone else sat round all day doing nothing. He left shortly after the other prisoners heard of this.

WORDS UNDER THE SKIN The Congo Kid had been going on for quite a time in the amenities about English atrocities during the '39 to '45 war. His listeners had no facts and his fire and ferocity on the subject were such that no one was arguing with him, but waiting for him to run out of steam. While he was going well, the Gypsy Fiddler was quietly getting up his head of steam; he had seen the bombing of Berlin from the ground and was always particularly impressed by his memories of the unfortunates splashed by phosphorus bombs; he had seen old men and children running round like chickens with their heads cut off, too much in agony to scream, taking refuge in fountains when they could find them. Water covering their burns took the pain away, but the moment they got into the air the phosphorus burned into their flesh. Living fire. And the rooms and cellars full of jellied, roasting children, their flesh and fat running together in the fire; he himself shot children who were nearly in halves, not yet dead and still screaming. Weeping as he fired. At age sixteen he shot dying women; the one he remembered most took his burst in the chest and gave birth to two babies in the last moments of dying. They were extruded from the woman's body into the street and dried where they lay on the concrete.

He was ready to talk. He had never burst out with this to British ears, but he was heartened by having another man attack them. He was aware he would be met with the charge that his own people were first to use phosphorus and the argument would be futile, nothing but a balancing of one horror against another. But sometimes futility doesn't count. If it did, they wouldn't have stopped to worry about Puroil's new repressive measures that threatened their peace of mind and their pay packets: they would have kept their heads down and their mouths shut, like better slaves in worse parts of the world.

The hunter in us that seems blooded from birth, and, lacking a weapon, uses stones or words to kill, was hot on the scent in these two men.

The Glass Canoe was upset. His temporary emotional revival had passed. His naval experience had not prepared him for this sort of attitude to the war he'd been in or to the nation that suckled him. He was an Australian to the backbone but British at heart. He was trained not to look too closely at individual deaths and the details of dying. A man bought it or he survived: you didn't make a song and dance, about each little wound. You should aspire to higher things and do whatever you thing is right. Bad things were done, but not by our side. God's with us after all and He can do what He likes. The country goes to war for the good of the people: running away never solved anything. The flags had been blessed in church and the padres held services every week. They would have known if we were fighting wrong. They weren't nongs; they would have refused to use the words God, duty and freedom. We always win for the reason that God and right are on our side. That is our

British faith, everything is lost when that's lost. These people are not like us. What's Congo? A Belgian, a European. Not the same, they don't have our training. It's not healthy to linger over details. War is war. You try not to think of it but you must make decisions.

He was right at the bottom of a trough. He had taken some pills without caring which sort they were. Any pills would do.

Suddenly he was no longer depressed. His great heart lifted, his strong will bent towards them. He looked round at their childlike faces. Compassion glinted in his eyes.

'I'm one of the guilty race, Congo,' the Glass Canoe said.

The lucid tone, the calm voice got the attention of every prisoner. With the right approach they could be spoken to like reasonable adults. There was a lot to explain to them, such a lot they needed to know. He shifted his great buttocks eagerly on the metal chair. Before he spoke his hands sketched vigorous, inarticulate plans in the air. All his great energy showed in the smallest motions of his hands.

'It's easy enough to curse England. Leaving us out here like a shag on a rock, but I don't apologize for being British.'

'Australian, you mean,' a voice said. It didn't matter who it was.

'British,' he insisted, intense and determined, but with the kindliness of absolute conviction. He could speak now. Words had been conquered; they were plastic, usable. 'Where else in the world but in a British country can a man get an education that makes him a writer better than Shakespeare and speak all languages—'

'You can, can't you?' Another voice interrupted. He didn't bother to look; he knew there was nothing behind the voice.

'Of course. It's never popular to display that sort of accomplishment. That's why I never mention it. But it's silly having other languages. Look at you, Congo. Belgian. What's a Belgian? Why not one language? All we need is a sort of brain-washing educational machine to convert everyone to English. I'm working on the details now.' He saw the wonder in their faces. 'I got the Wandering Jew to help me, but although he's a great engineer, he's put me in charge of the project.'

'He put you?' Another voice. He was surrounded by leafless, branchless trees; words issued from stumps.

'Actually I forced my way to the top. He didn't know I was an engineer.' He was grandly silent. The others waited, not sure when the violence would start. He spoke on, knowing his was the one voice that could save them. 'People have no imagination. No genius. I ordered a million copies—'

'Only a million?'

He showed no resentment at the interruptions, only a vast patience. The others began to get the idea and waited for a chance to hit him with a question.

'—a million each day, of *How to Win Over Friends and Influence*, to be distributed to every human on earth. You see, wrong ways of thinking are really symptoms of mental disease and this can be controlled by controlling the words fed in to the brain. Words are the great stumbling block.' He nodded, satisfied with himself. The fight against words had been worth winning. His hands pledged their loyalty: they must be rewarded.

'Look how pleasant the air here will be when we cover the refinery with a plastic dome and pipe gases and smoke out to atmosphere. It will be so good you'd want to live here and never leave.'

'So the smoke goes out to poison the rest of Sydney,' said the Humdinger, offering him a cigarette to take the edge off his words.

'Oh no. We'll be moving the refinery to the top of the Blue Mountains. One of my projects is to build the tallest distillation column in the world, so all processes can be done in the one spot.'

'There'll be money in this.' Even the Gypsy Fiddler was game to have a go, now there were other bodies to hide behind.

'Ah, yes, millions. But it's all for charity.' They were all with him now, he could feel the strong bonds of his words pulling their wills, making them show mateship. Waiting for his words.

'Did I tell you about my operation? You'll never guess how heavy I am. Forty stone. Don't look it, do I? I've had all the bones in me replaced by steel. This arm. There's steel in it. Nothing can hurt me. I've got plans for a machine to do the operation on applicants I select and soon we'll have the steel for their bones reduced in weight. I don't mind being the heaviest, it's no weight for me to carry, but the ordinary man would be weighed down by forty stone.' This was living. He had reached his rightful place in the world and they acknowledged it naturally.

'I'd like to have the operation,' said Dutch Treat. 'Where can I get it done?'

'You'll have to wait till you're selected.' He blew out smoke calmly, with precision. He was no man: he was a god. 'I've had my age adjusted, you know. I'm twenty-five now and always will be.'

'Any other inventions?' They felt closer to each other now there was a fool to bait.

'There's my car. I run it without gasoline.'

'That's tough for the refinery.'

'We're switching to plastics to make houses that never need painting. Never need cleaning, either; all dirt drops through the mesh floor.'

'How do you do all this? All this genius must come from somewhere.' Even as he said it the Humdinger wanted to step back to duck a fist, but the Glass Canoe didn't turn a hair.

'The clinic. I go back to get shots of power. Actually it's a lubricant for the steel, too. Special nurses give me the shots in the backside. Pretty, too, those nurses.'

'I'll bet.'

'Yes, I wouldn't have any ugly ones touching my backside. Trouble is, they take my blood at the same time.'

'What, steal it?'

'For the blood bank. I have a sort of composite blood that can be used by all blood types; they fill their blood bank from my bum and they think I don't know.' He chuckled. 'I let them go. It's for the sick and those not as fortunate as I am. I don't mind giving it away, just like the Great White Father gives grog away.'

'I wouldn't mind having some of the money you give to charity.'

'I've thought of that. I'm having a fund set up so everyone in the refinery will have his wages made up to a thousand dollars a week.'

'I wish every millionaire was generous like you,' said Bubbles.

'That's the trouble.' He was serious. 'They can get away with all sorts of wrong doing and wrong thinking. But I've fixed that. I'm having a new surgical law passed. The law is too literary, too many words. There'll be a little operation, a small capsule in the head of each citizen. No second chance—there's far too many people on earth. The first wrong doing and the head blows up, immediately. No fuss. No formalities.'

'There'll be bodies everywhere.'

'Won't matter. Seeing automatic punishment will help others to be intelligent and do the right thing.' They tried not to look at each other. The first one to laugh might snap him out of it.

'How are you getting on, batching? You going to get married again?' The Humdinger tried to get him back to ordinary things.

'I've got it all teed up. Marrying a young girl who's never seen a man before. She holds a VC from the World Health Organization.'

'VC? For Valour?'

'Virginity Certificate. I don't want a woman whose personality has been warped by contact with other men.'

'How about your boy?'

'He's written a pop song called "My Dad". The revenue it's bringing in for Australia is so huge he's getting a knighthood.'

'With all your money you could buy Sydney,' said Bubbles. 'I'm the agent for it, actually. Interested?' The man was harmless. Off his head. Someone ought to make a phone call.

'Sydney belongs to me. Whoever sold you the agency put one over you.'

'When do you go for training? In the throwouts,' said Congo. Any idea of sympathy for a sick man was over his head. The cruelty had started. Some edged towards the door. But the phone rescued them.

'Hey,' called Cheddar, smiling greenly. He never quite forgot his own woes. 'There's a phone message from the main gate. People waiting to see you. Trucks full of crates of champagne.'

'It's OK to let them in.'

'Champagne?'

'For the whole refinery. Just a little gesture of appreciation to the workers.'

'They'll nail your hide to the blue gates for this,' said Congo with relish.

'They can't touch me. I could jump from up there'—he pointed to the top of the reactor—'and not feel it. These steel rods are powerful as any of the steel out there.' He pointed to the steel structures as if they were rivals he had surpassed. 'And I can see from what you say about the British that we should go and jump off the top. So I'll jump for all the rest.' He was Christ.

'You can't be British,' said Congo. 'The British would get someone else to do it.' This provided a laugh for the rest. The Glass Canoe was surprised at its jeering tone. Someone must have made a joke he didn't see. He went out toward the reactor lift. They started to speak of something else. When he got to the top and looked down, there was not a soul watching. He expected them to be out there to see. He went back. As he came down the structure his elation began to diminish.

'I told you I was going to jump off the top. No one watched.'

'Ha, ha,' said several, to get rid of him. The joke was paper-thin; any moment he might start swinging.

'Why don't you go up to the main gate and get the champagne?' prompted Humdinger tactfully. The Glass Canoe had always been a dead bastard but you couldn't see him come to harm.

'Champagne? What champagne? What you talking about, champagne?'

'Forget it. Forget it.' He walked away.

The Glass Canoe shook his head. Poor Humdinger. Soft in the head. All that filth he goes on with has got to him. There's always been a vital connection between moral health and mental health.

'If you're going to jump, who don't you?' said the Congo Kid. 'You British have no guts. You fight like rats—when you're backed against a wall and forced to fight. Here they've put you in the throwouts and you do nothing.'

The Congo Kid was an unknown quantity. He had towelled up the Woodpecker, it was true, but he hit Woody from behind, and besides, it was only from being called a bastard. Funny people, Europeans; a man should be able to call you a bastard. The Glass Canoe shook his head massively, the British lion shaking off flea-bites. Something they said had lodged in his mind. He was slated to go for training in a fortnight; he, who'd once done a top operator's course. A reject. And he only ever tried to please them.

He went up to the top of the structure again. Life wasn't so important; a man should be able to take it up lightly and lay it down just as casually. Our civilization doesn't teach us what the ancients knew and that is how to die. And what to die for.

At the top, on the landing above the seventh floor, he looked down. The Samurai was watching from the regenerator top, but no one was out below. He tried to remember if the Samurai had been in the amenities room. No. The Samurai turned away and went on walking over towards the top of the boilers on the connecting landing and down the steel ladders to the concrete bed in which the whole plant was set.

The Glass Canoe looked out over the refinery, away west to the squat crematorium stack, the misty, hazy concrete of the city skyline, round to the sand hills at Botany, and back to the activity round Clearwater; rubberworks, brickmakers, tanneries, gaol, the Puroil tank-farm and the huge suburban vista right through the age-old river basin to the western hills. Now my own life is folding up, he thought, what would be more natural than wanting to take a few others with me? He wrestled with the thought of getting half a dozen of the boys up with him, herding them into an angle of the safety rail and tossing them over one by one, then jumping with them. What a temptation to strike a man! But he would be no better than the Congo Kid; he'd do something like that. As if he couldn't stand to do the deed without dragging someone else into it out of spite. No. He was better made than that.

To the east, he saw a couple behind the shed on the land belonging to the Clearwater boat club. He could see several men on Clearwater wharf, watching them. Presently the man put the girl across the seat of the propped-up motor-bike and mounted her from behind. When he had been making certain movements for a few minutes the men suddenly shouted 'Hey!' He saw their faces split apart with the action of shouting but couldn't hear the sound of their voices—the cracker plant was not going but steam was roaring from vents—and he saw the couple assemble themselves hastily into more usual order of dress and speed away on the motor-bike. Life went on two wheels.

The Glass Canoe could not find it in himself to smile at them. Instead his heart, full of himself, burst out into words—that did not, however, seem to him to issue past his lips into sounds.

'Handsome heights! Embrace me, I reach out to you! I am your equal. Metal! You can't hurt me. See! I fist you with steel hands. My nerves are dulled, my skin thickened. My head well protected by a great steel case. It refuses to be dented. Try and make me bleed! I heal quick as lightning. I fall many times to tempt you; in every way I try to make you smile at me and nod. Still you look the other way. The whole world looks the other way. Every single thing in this world ignores me! You plants, sitting at my feet like pupils listening to a teacher, drinking in the milk of the word, you are dead! I am life and I laugh at you! I am greater—one step and I am over you. This is my proper height, this elevation is my proper view of you. No longer do these things around me embody part of my life and my history. They are become cold, wasting objects, feeling nothing, reflecting only the light reflected from my body. I hate the world! Nothing loves me of its own accord.'

He knew he didn't need to jump. There was no compulsion inside him. Simply that he was capable of it. Knowing it made him a whole man. Not all the threats of Puroil to put him among the rejects could take that from him. He looked down, without thinking, to check if he was naked.

THE FALL Far Away Places came round the reactor and there, in front of him, was the Glass Canoe standing on the handrail, supporting himself with one hand from a light standard. He was bellowing loudly out into the space between the rows of plants.

Far Away could see him now as he saw him that day when he came upon him with the Rustle of Spring under the stripper skirt.

There was still the hole in the backside of his overalls. He took his own hands out of his overalls, crept up behind him and seized one side of his bottom in two hands, making a thick horizontal steak of flesh bulge out. His teeth almost met in the Glass Canoe's left buttock.

Sudden pain sucked the Glass Canoe's breath away, threw a black screen behind his eyes. He could no longer see his steel audience. Arms and legs jerked, out of control, he wanted to pull air into his chest. Involuntarily he pushed forward to take in air.

The instant the Glass Canoe was airborne, Far Away Places ran and scuttled, jumped and stumbled down stairways, across landings, round vessels, through manways to the shadows on the other side of the main structure. He stood breathing quickly like a terrified rabbit.

He didn't see the fall, nor see the body hit. He was spared, for a while, the sight of blood.

The Glass Canoe had landed on the concrete apron, but his corpse was hidden from the control room by drums of spent catalyst standing irregularly around.

Some had seen the fall, and ran towards the spot.

THE EFFICACY OF WORDS He talked as he fell. Even in dying he would not be silenced. Talking to himself. He had to keep issuing the words to his distribution centres, even if they got no further, just as they were minted in his brain. As if they had some value.

MOTION OF A BODY The actual manner of the fall was not without a certain interest. When the body stepped forward into the atmosphere, it left the support of the metal it had so lately defied and abandoned itself to the mercy of gravitation. From an upright position the body fell forward into a flat position, like a diver entering the water with a belly-buster. This attitude was maintained only down as far as the last railing, for at this point the boots struck metal and imparted a spin to the body—the last thirty feet was traversed in the motion of a propeller—and it spun many times, landing flat, in a face-down position. His right arm was pinned beneath his crutch, as if he were readying his member for insertion in the earth, mother of his mineral-fed flesh.

THE LOVE OF SOLID OBJECTS On the ground the dying flesh of the Glass Canoe spoke out of its agony. No sounds came from the big brown lips.

'This is reality, these ironworks, gauges, furnaces, vessels, valves, compressors, turbines, gratings, concretes, just as much as the soft pith of a man's body coating once brittle bones.' Even then he knew his steel interior hadn't shattered. It was flesh had let him down. 'Steel girders are precious, I want to cling to them. Through them I heard the vibrations of the earth. I stroked the handled wheel. These things exist. I felt the friendly steel. I want a piece of iron, the wood of a living tree, the side of a firm house to cling to! Don't let me go! Stop me from dying! Keep me with you! And with the sunset and surf and purple hills. And the clear, clear, clear, clear...' It was the last word. The next was to have been 'sky'. It had been called for—ordered, if you like, selected—but between the stock of words at his command and the actual attainment of sky there fell eternity.

THE COLOUR OF ETERNITY The Glass Canoe. His head was on one side, turned away from the reactor and regenerator and the turbo-expander landing to the open side of the quadrangle.

In this position he looked at the world out of the corner of one eye, as if it were somehow behind him, as if he had momentarily turned his head from the important things lying under the skin of the earth, the minerals and elements from which he sprang, to the fleeting, fading constructions on its surface and the mocking infinity of sky.

Out of the corner of his eye. Not worth his consideration. Irrelevant. With head turned, eyes open to the sky. A fly, on thin legs, stepped delicately on his eyeball.

But the blue above him shrank rapidly, bordered on all sides by a roaring, rumbling wave of black. The blue of the sky became smaller, the blackness growing and roaring, the sky quickly diminishing now and black nothingness triumphant until the blue of day was tiny as a pinpoint and when it flickered out the world stopped.

TWO MYSTERIES No one could make head or tail of the bite marks, which showed clearly.

No one could account for the sand that came from the mouth. When the head—flopped on one side—was still, and the eyes fixed, this fine white sharp sand spilled on to the concrete.

THE INSUFFICIENCY OF EYES The Beautiful Twinkling Star looked out the window, to check if there was reason to worry about the Glass Canoe. He saw the fall and the other man on the landing. Others saw his body give a start, as a fist clenches. When he retracted his head others looked out.

'Don't look,' he advised, so they crowded round. The Glass Canoe was in the air. All the eyes in the world couldn't stop his fall or send up a beam to support him. Several swore they saw a spark struck from the last steel rail. They were too late to see the other man running over the structure. Only the Twinkler and the Samurai saw and recognized Far Away Places.

BITE MARKS The Samurai had seen the fall and was first to run down to find the body. He could see no brown of overalls or tanned skin—the catalyst drums were in random groupings and hid the Glass Canoe well—and he was up to the spot before he knew it. There had not been much blood, but what had come from the Glass Canoe's cracked head had been gathering in a tiny depression in the concrete apron and only started to flow when the Samurai was about ten yards away. Then it flowed quickly and spread to a foot-sized pool just under the rubber of the Samurai's left boot. He slipped in the blood and disappeared from the view of those following.

From the direction of the wet gas compressor came the Slug, but while he was yet a long way off, he howled to the approaching multitude, 'The Samurai! Get first aid!' Thinking the Samurai was the only fallen body. He hadn't seen the Glass Canoe. One that trailed the field broke off and ran back and spread the word that the Samurai had fallen.

The rest disregarded the blowing and breakneck babble of the Slug. Some glanced at the Glass Canoe and saw he was dead, then went on to help revive the Samurai. Others gathered round the dead body and stood in a circle, looking down, heads leaning inwards like a Salvation Army street-meeting at public prayer over the fall of sinners.

The Slug's lower lip billowed loose and swung from side to side as he moved; a slim channel of dribble flowed from each corner of his mouth. His hearers were concerned when a liquid level built up behind the middle of that slouching bottom lip: this liquid was likely to spray out over them along with his aspirates.

Far Away Places slipped round to the back door of the control block and walked through after the prisoner had phoned for the first aid man. He walked out to the solemn ring of men, just as the red fire truck pulled up on the concrete apron. As he got to the body and the blood he heard a man say, 'What do you make of a dead man with bite marks on his bum?' He put a hand to his mouth and innocently bared his teeth. Unthinkingly he closed his powerful jaws on the fat knuckle of his index finger. The Samurai watched the teeth with a mild fascination. Big, beautiful, strong-grained teeth. Looking up, he saw the Samurai looking straight into his eyes. Guiltily he put his hands back in his overalls and resumed comforting his private parts. He could piss with the rest of the crew now.

The Sumpsucker walked up from one of the southern units and while still a few yards away called out: 'A group of five men or more constitutes mutiny.' No one answered.

He waited his chance to get even. When they were all inside with cups of tea and breaking out lunch packets he came to the door and sent ten of them out on jobs. There was no set lunch hour. They complained, but not loudly. No one chipped him about the widow's catalyst drums, which had overflowed two deep on to the footpath outside her house again.

Dutch Treat was detailed to go and check for leaks on his fuel gas lines. He was glad. This was something like. It didn't matter that the job was useless: he had a boss on earth as he had in heaven. Someone told him what to do, right down to the smallest details. It didn't matter what the orders were, as long as he had a boss. Without orders he wouldn't do a tap of work. He was happy.

THE CONVERSION OF QUICK TIP   Men were gathered round the time clocks waiting for their turn to go down and tend the machines. It was ten-thirty and a fine night.

Quick Tip stumbled in, precarious on his pigeon toes, elbows and knees moving in his broken-down boxer's gait; his face, battered smooth, alight with joy.

'Oh boy!' he said. 'What a night last night. Got home early Mum and me from the RSL round half-past ten. Both full and plenty of go. Oh boy! Like a second honeymoon.'

'The Glass Canoe snuffed it,' said the Outside Fisherman. Why not tell him? This was more important than what Quick Tip and his missus did between scabby sheets.

'Go on,' said Quick Tip. 'You don't say. Anyway, I didn't know she had so much go in her. Or I wouldn't have been spending my time lifting the skirts of every bit of stuff I met up with. It makes me wonder if I been having it on my own, if she's got that much go. It was mouth, teeth, legs, bum, fingernails, the lot! All night. She slept in till midday and only got up for the midday movie. I even got her a cup of coffee, I was that amazed. It was all I could do to get in to work tonight.'

'He fell off the cracker yesterday, on our day off.'

'Yeah. Tough. And I put the hard word on her tonight again and she come across. She's a beauty! And here she's been under my nose all the time and me spending dough just to get a bit of variety. She's so tired now, she's not bothered about burglars like she usually is, but I forgot to feed the Alsatian, so we won't have anyone breaking in.'

'They had to use a bucket to get him off the concrete.'

Others joined in, to bear down Quick Tip's story by weight of numbers and make him take notice of theirs.

'A squeegee they used, to rake him up.'

'And a wet mop.'

'Red ink everywhere.'

'Who pushed him?' asked Quick Tip, reluctantly.

'Just fell, far as they know.'

Quick Tip went down to his plant, still trying to talk about his domestic joy, but they went with him in a cluster, burdening him with all the nasty details. He resented having to listen, but had to give in. They were quite prepared to repeat his story and make him a star, as he wanted, but not until after the fall of the Glass Canoe had been exhausted. They followed him, attacking him with details until he gave in and became a spreader of the story of the Glass Canoe.

Night pressed softly down over them, yielding to light, but always pushing softly against it. Let the light retreat one instant and night plugged the hole immediately.

PROCESS CONTROL While the prisoners were outside making their first appraisal of the plant right after shift-change to see what sort of mess they were left with, Bomber Command tacked up a new regulation on the wall.

'In view of the fact that toilet facilities have been used by some operators in a time-wasting manner, it has been decided to institute a system of passes for those wishing to use the toilets. Cubicles will be kept locked and application must be made to the foreman on duty for permission to enter. It is hoped that it will not be necessary to keep records of the amount of time consumed by visits of this nature.'

The off-limits chit became famous quickly. Even the local rag mentioned it, but Puroil was too powerful an advertising patron to allow the metropolitan dailies even to hint at it.

The management had nothing now to fear from the Union and was not deflected by the isolated actions of those who, like the Humdinger, had to dramatize the whole thing. He put a loosening medicine in the tea, so there would be a rush for the permission-chits. Fortunately nothing bad happened on the plant while all the men were queuing with their chits. The Sumpsucker was duty foreman and was suspicious of the crowd of men who asked for passes, but he drank the tea and lost his suspicions. Halfway through the signing of the passes he shouted to the man inside to get out, and told the rest, 'You'll all have to wait. It's my turn for a chit.' There was only one cubicle.

The Humdinger drank the tea, too: if some suffered, all had to suffer. He was one of three caught short, but because of his nature he revelled in the predicament. Next day, in the Rustle of Spring's bedroom, where the catalyst shovels were kept, each shovel was flat on the concrete and was decorated with a huge Henry the Third.

THE SMELL OF BLOOD Two days after the fall a brown and white mongrel dog same sniffing around and stood near the place where the Glass Canoe landed. He was a cheerful-looking dog, with prick ears, a good chest and a quick step. He was mostly white, the brown was distributed in patches over his face and in a saddle on his back; there was a nice crinkle to his tail. He just stood looking up and around.

It never occurred to any of the Glass Canoe's workmates that he had a dog at home. They knew about his wife's death and heard he had a son and his wife had a baby, but he'd never mentioned a dog. Animals often came in the refinery and hung about a few days. Sometimes they were fed a few scraps before the dogcatchers got them.

After a while he sat down. No one thought much about it until Far Away Places noticed the dog hadn't moved for a long time. He guessed it was waiting for the Glass Canoe and knew why it was sitting on that particular spot. He half-expected the dog would refuse to eat and was surprised when he hoed into some scraps of meat Far Away gathered from the rubbish tin. Yes, he would eat, but not move.

While Far Away was out there, Rustle of Spring suddenly popped up near him from behind a catalyst drum, and made urgent signs. He hesitated. The pretty boy made unmistakeable motions with both hands then and Far Away glared at him until he gave up and went away. Couldn't these foreigners do anything without money?

Three days later, someone tried with a bucket of detergent to scrub the smell of blood and the stain off the concrete. The dog didn't go away. They used kerosene, they tried acid. No good.

'How can that mutt know where the splatter was?' asked the Humdinger plaintively. He was a bit wary of a dog that loved the Glass Canoe.

'You wouldn't say it was a mutt if it wasn't the Glass Canoe's dog,' said Far Away Places.

It was the starting point of an unspoken change of attitude to the little dog; men started to act as if it had been purged by its master's death of guilt by association. A lunch was specially bought for the dog each shift. A full meat lunch. He ate three times a day, but didn't move from watching that spot. Rain or shine, night and day. Men started to pat him. Supervisors who asked for the dog to be removed were met with a certain opposition.

Dying, if it didn't make the man acceptable, at least rehabilitated his dog.

THE COMFORT OF ROUTINE Five days later, a shiny in the pay office was rushing about trying to find out why the Glass Canoe, number 1208, had not clocked off on the afternoon of Thursday of day shift. Had he worked overtime? If so, there was no endorsement on the time card. Time card? It wasn't even filled in and there was a week's pay to be made up. The Garfish knew, of course, and told Hanging Five in time to make up the severance pay.

Even so, the absence of the clocking imprint on the bundy card and of the daily figures on the time card set certain automatic machinery in motion and resulted in two memos being sent to operations office deploring these omissions. Two more days it took for the news of the Glass Canoe's death to penetrate this far. Weeks later, some of the Termitary workers heard of it. A joke, of course. Only fools lose their balance and fall from buildings. Non-staff people always exaggerate. What was anyone doing up there anyway?

No one called to pick up his car, which stood in the car park, diminishing. Gradually, men who needed spares were stripping it, just as worms were doing to its owner in his silk-lined maple container in another park. Both being stripped down to the chassis. One by his brother man who had been his competitor all his life, waiting to overthrow him; the other by the tiny internal competitor he carried about inside him, waiting just as remorselessly to reduce him.

SCARS Taffy the Welsh was back. Except for the scars of the grafts he looked much the same. He wasn't, though.

Look what they done to me! he said constantly in the secrecy of his own head. His was a peculiar mentality: his hospital fees, doctor's fees and wages for the period had been paid—what more did he want? Didn't he realize an accident is an accident? Why couldn't he consider nothing had happened? Wipe out and pass on. Forgive and forget. That was the proper way. Instead of this hell fire of revenge burning in his body.

What was it made a man cast handfuls of fine catalyst dust every day into the lube oil tank serving the turbo-expander machines? How could a foreign enterprise leave such a tank as this with an unsecured hatch? All he had to do was lift the hatch and throw in his powder. For all the company knew, everyone was doing it. Puroil shares weren't on the Australian market, there was no popular shareholding in the company; how could they leave out of account the hostility of the natives they exploited? Did they imagine giving them employment in *their* enterprise would buy them body and soul?

And when a man was disfigured on the job, how could they bear to let him come back amongst the machinery that had injured him? Did no one ever consider an industrial prisoner might be human enough to exact revenge? Look what they done to me! Taffy whimpered to his shaving mirror, and every time he washed his hands or had a pee he passed the wall mirror, saw his reflection and made silent vicious vows to the only god he knew.

SURELY NOT From their position high above the world of Puroil prisoners in the topmost one of many mysterious holding companies, the world board of seven directors sent two of their number out from Europe on similar but separate missions to put the boot in and to give special instructions to the Wandering Jew. New plants were to go up, more vacant acres sown with rich, money-yielding process plants. The overseas controllers had great faith in Australia's future and what it could do for them. It wasn't a shareholders' decision: shareholders had no say. While the group profit was maintained throughout the world, they didn't know or care about Clearwater. The growth and continuance of Puroil, not the maximizing of profits, was the aim of the managers and boards, the professionals. They got no profits, but they did get bigger empires the more the company grew under them. The story put out was that they were to give a verdict on whether to carry on at Clearwater or to abandon operations; and to answer the question: Why did the plant still have teething problems after three years?

None of the prisoners below the rank of branch manager was allowed to see the big boys, they were smuggled in and out at night for fear of too close contact with the lowest prisoners or the unpremeditated ferocity of an opportunist.

After they had sneaked out again, the local hierarchy let it be known through quiet chats with the sullen prisoners that Puroil Refining Termitary and Grinding Works would not be closing. And on this bright Saturday, Bomber Command was back at the cracker, full of joy, to spread the counter-rumour. Few noticed that he had lost his craze for Gotchas.

The Two Pot Screamer said, 'I'm glad they've abandoned that stupid rumour. If Puroil left this refinery they'd only have to build another one elsewhere in New South. They can't ignore an expanding market. All the other companies are building refineries as fast as they get the money.'

Bomber Command said nothing to that, but went on. 'And there's to be a big shutdown. A lot of new equipment going in, to make this place work. Even an electricity station just for us to make sure we don't suffer from every little electric storm. Just quietly,

I'd take a look at the stand-down clause in the new agreement if I were you. With this new pool of operators, they can keep the ones they want and you-know-what with the rest.'

Stand-down clause? Surely good old Puroil wouldn't lightly use the power they had of starvation or plenty over the miserable prisoners. Surely not. Was this what the Good Shepherd meant when he said the honeymoon was over?

The news ran like poison through the veins of the company.

19
THE PARTY

A SECRET MUSIC The shutdown lasted for months. Strange rumours spread of a new order more fearful than anything they'd known. At the height of these rumours, the Great White Father decided a party was overdue.

'Coming to the party?' That was all it took. He sent men out into the highways and byways of Puroil with these missionary words on their lips and they returned in the fullness of time, dragging in their wake the dregs of humanity to the feast.

It grew from nothing, and when the time drew near for it to start, it seemed to tower above everything; no one wanted to talk about anything else. It was a pillar of refuge on the horizon of industrial prisoners who had nothing more rewarding to look forward to than these periods of blank happiness, drunken hysteria and artificial camaraderie.

'Look at us,' the Great White Father said. 'It needs alcohol to get us together with affection and cordiality. Alcohol and the way we go on with women, they are the two great things that bind us together.' It was unusual to hear him speak with his mouth turned down at the corners. He went to the death hut where Herman was, and put an opened can by him.

He set the day for the start of the party as a Monday, since for the usual day-working bodies Monday was a work attendance day. A Saturday or Sunday might bring wanderers through the mangroves to stumble on keg and incapable drinkers; wanderers who could wrest keg, cans and women from their rightful owners and take them off to another part of the mangroves to enjoy them.

'It should be pretty well over by Friday,' he remarked comfortably to the Volga Boatman, and rang the silver bell. All over the refinery certain men heard a music others didn't.

He was seen leading a goat along the Pacific Highway on the Sunday. The sighting was widely reported, but mystified everyone who heard it. One man even photographed it, but all who saw the print proved conclusively the photo was a fake.

WHERE THE RACE IS NOT TO THE SWIFT For flags they borrowed a carton of scrap rag—bits of women's dresses, all colours—and ran them up between the huts. They hung in tatters and flapped drunkenly, but to the prisoners they were Mardi Gras.

The ice-making machine was borrowed from the main lab and connected to the illegal power loop at the Home Beautiful, but this had to be arranged on the Sunday because Custard Guts the lab boss couldn't be relied on to be generous in the week, when he was there. Big Bits was one of the early starters, mixing whisky with beer in the same glass. The older drinkers knew the score with him—he would be first to start and first to finish—and only watched him to make sure he was shepherded away as soon as his eyes got glassy; it was not safe to be anywhere near him when he started heaving.

By midday Monday they were organizing foot races. Bubbles, the fattest man there, won the marathon which was run over a course in excess of forty yards. It was a boat race, of course; the others held back, developed lameness, stumbled. Big Bits, already far gone by then, didn't have the idea at all: he kept trying to race ahead and it took the efforts of several dozen race officials—all claimed to be officials—to trip and push him out of the race. It was unthinkable that any man but the clumsiest and fattest should win the marathon.

Big Bits was persuaded to carry on drinking to drown his sense of failure; these younger fellows couldn't get it into their heads that they were not supposed to win. All they ever thought about was beating the other man. You can't have a friendly atmosphere when people run around with this attitude. They didn't blame Big Bits; they knew the pernicious influence of family, school and industry was still upon him, with its estranging emphasis on competition between man and man.

The best race was the five and ten yards dash; this was run from anywhere and it was left to each runner to decide where he came in the race. It was one race, not two.

Big Bits successfully drowned all sense of failure. By the end of the foot races he was observed to have a never-ending stream of vomit erupting like lava from his overburdened intestines. From some instinct of cleanliness and decency he attempted to fit his hand over his extended mouth, but the stuff escaped past his fingers.

'Whisky is an emetic,' said the Great White Father wisely.

Big Bits' fumbling fingers found, for a few moments, a button grip on his wide-stretched lips, but two smaller streams, back-pressured by this grip, issued from his nostrils.

The Great White Father led him kindly outside, where he sat on the step and continued this exercise.

THE WILD BULL OF THE PAMPAS A little after lunch a great new diving champion was discovered. It was the Wild Bull of the Pampas. Alcohol had different effects on him, depending on the temperature, the time of day, the season of the year and whether he was due for a psychiatric check-up or had just had one. This time it took him in the legs. He wasn't content with the rigours of the ten-yard dash, he had to go straight for the river. Through the swamp, over stumps, knocking down saplings and bouncing off larger trees, nothing stopped him—merely deflected him—until he reached the river bank, ran off into the air and by a superhuman effort fell forward and entered the emulsion of oil and water that was Eel River, head-first. He was under the water two minutes. This was unintentional; the river was shallow, the soft mud deep, and he spent those two minutes pulling his head and chest out of the sucking mud into which he speared himself. The Volga Boatman refused to go after him with the boat because of the blue-black mud all over his body, and the smell. He liked his boat ship-shape. No one was very surprised when he came back black, clothes and all, heavily wagging the water away, nor was there any prejudice against him on account of his colour.

A GENTLEMAN'S GAME The Donk, a cricketer himself and the mainstay of Sullage City Diggers, insisted on a game of cricket. The only place this game could be played was in the space between the huts, and there was quite a bit of interest in it for a few minutes, mainly because there were no proper balls: empty beer cans had to be used instead. With half a fence-paling as bat. It was contrary to the spirit of the Home Beautiful to have a wicket or to bowl from any one place—those ideas gave a rigidity to the game that any drinker would deplore—but after the thing developed a trace of bitterness evidenced in the aiming of the cans, it had to be banished to the pathway between the Home Beautiful and the river. This was very narrow and gave the batsman the assurance that he could not be hit by cans coming from an angle. Until they took to the trees and hour by hour carried the game farther from Home.

HAIL AND FAREWELL A small conference in one corner of the drink hut reached a decision. These were the planners, the long-distance drinkers, not the Big Bits type who grabbed beer cans as if they were a last refuge, but men who drank a bit and talked, and thought a bit and ate, and could keep it up for days.

'We'll just go up there and kidnap him. Simple,' said the Great White Father. 'Three should do it. Including one to drive the Mercedes.'

'Why are we doing it?' Angry Ant said.

'It's never been done before,' explained the Great White Father.

'How will he take it?' asked the Humdinger.

'How can he take it? He doesn't know by sight which shifts we're on and he won't be game to tell anyone what happened. If our mob leak it out there'll be talk, but his best defence will be to shut up and ignore it. We don't elect him Manager—our talk can't hurt him. Probably won't even reach him.'

The Humdinger, Canada Dry and the Angry Ant stood, shook their beer cans for the last drops, and finding none, departed gravely for the refinery. It took them an hour, but it went well, they said. The Wandering Jew looked a little knocked up, there was a wrinkled look about his suit, and the blindfold he wore was a piece of some Sydney housewife's old dress salvaged in a rag drive and used by Puroil operators for wiping oily hands or for insulation against concrete.

The Great White Father shook his hand—by force—and announced to him: 'We're going to see you have a good time, young feller. Where's Volga?' Volga rose and approached his leader.

'Put out more rags, Volga. Here's the Wandering Jew.'

'He has the blindfold on.'

'He'll appreciate them all the more later.' Volga ran up some more rags on string and poked extra bits of coloured rag into crevices and on projecting nails round the huts. The place was gay. The Great White Father called his flock together.

'Ladies and gentlemen,' he said. 'I say ladies because it's well known that four per cent of the male population is homosexual…' He waited for the laughter to evaporate.

'Before we're all completely molo, we'd better say a few words in memory of our fallen brother. Charge your glasses or pierce your cans and we'll drink to the Glass Canoe. But first, a few words.'

The gathering did not keep proper order and some of them, reverting to their natural undisciplined habits, made no pause in their drinking, but at the signal they all stood.

Unfortunately, the first few words of the Great White Father's historic speech were lost; he turned and saw an old grey rabbit sitting calmly on a hump of earth in the swamp as if waiting for him to speak. The side of its face and its left eye were pushed out in a great sore; the thing had been infected with myxomatosis and was not long for this world.

'There's a poor devil of a rabbit out there in the mangroves. Got a dose of myxo. We'd better kill him out of kindness. If we don't kill him, he'll only die, or some unprincipled shopkeeper will cut out the sore and sell him. Will you do the honours, Volga?'

Volga darted inside the drink hut, they heard him standing on a seat and reaching into the roof; presently he came out with a sawn-off twenty-two, fitted with a home-made silencer. Big and clumsy.

The Great White Father took the rifle, aimed, looked round and seeing his congregation silent, decided to speak.

'Hold it,' he said quietly. 'Just keep still. I want to talk to the poor little feller. He'll stay quiet if we don't alarm him.'

The bemused party was quiet as their host addressed the dying rabbit.

'Now, now, little rabbit. Don't be afraid. This has been coming for a long while. You can't live forever. If the dogs don't get you and you don't starve to death we're here to eat you up, only for that rotten sore over your eye. What do you think of when you see us here, lapping up the grog? It must be a bit of a mystery, eh—all us big people making a row and enjoying ourselves? Drinking out of cans—drinking gallons and pissing pints? Any other time you could go your way, but look at you! You're diseased. You're on the way out. The sight of you could put us all off the grog. Why? 'Cause we did it to you, matey. We poisoned you and we have to put you out of your misery for our own sakes. It'll be quick. You won't know what hit you.'

With these words, a bullet was on its way towards the waiting rabbit and eternity caught up with him before he heard the report of the gun. The rabbit flopped and jerked and lay still on the little mound of earth he had hopped to. The audience heard only the faintest whup. It was a handy weapon.

The Great White Father looked round with great compassion at his own people, a compassion not unmixed with a certain humour. He began to smile. Before he knew it he was grinning broadly, the grin became a chuckle, the chuckle turned quickly to a laugh, and the moment he hit the full broad notes of an uproarious laugh the puppets around him laughed too. Some of the girls had turned up; the Sandpiper had ideas of taking some of her regulars out into the paddocks, much the same as a beast of prey cuts out stragglers from a flock of sheep. The Sandpiper laughed. Everyone roared. At nothing. At the Glass Canoe, at themselves, at the rabbit, at the Wandering Jew, at being human, at the beer cans, at Big Bits, at the Wild Bull of the Pampas, at the whole idea of the party.

So the Great White Father's first words were lost in the general din.

WHO CLOCKS OFF EARLY? '...so the great operator goes home. And we consign to Rookwood his craft of ambition, promotion, pills, and a vision that saw the grand design, the noble acres of Eel Flat sown with brand-new plants. Pumper, panelman, delegate, golfer—he stood up at every Union meeting. Now ended his brief span, a one-man band of all the talents has gone down.

'We heard him in debate, ear-splitting or prophetic, up one day, the next completely down. We saw him by shock-treatment unsoured—the energetic come-back, the dustcoat in his sights. Here was a man in whom great issues brought to light genius to grapple them. On a poised rail, danger drew steel and height struck fire from him: the black tide of death filled his impetuous mouth with sand.

'Who clocks off early? A man whose strength and strong bent for suicide will stand for ages yet to come; a myth, his stormy heart now stopped and destiny fulfilled, our Glass Canoe is shattered and gone home.'

THE RECEDING UNIVERSE That fine sharp sand—why did it spill? Was it only to give the Great White Father a line to speak in a funeral speech?

All drank to the memory of their fallen fellow-worker, their mate, their tormentor. But the emotion and the beer had been too much for Big Bits. He had made a come-back after his stomach's gesture of rejection, but not for long. He did not settle back to drink like the rest, but sought support from the post of the rough veranda built on the drink hut. He had the wild impression that this post was in danger of falling away from him and with it the universe and that he was supporting both, unaided.

'She's going! She's going!...There she goes!' he shouted. But it was he that was going, losing his grip and falling flat like a length of timber on his back. Even on his back he was concerned for the post falling and the universe receding from him and did not seem to notice how long the one took to fall or the other to disappear. He lay like that for a long while, unable to move. At last he drifted off into an uneasy, dream-filled sleep. People just stepped over him.

A NAVEL SALUTE When more of the girls came, the Great White Father got them dancing to music from someone's transistor. He got the Wandering Jew fixed up with the Sandpiper, thumped him heartily on the grey-suited back—leaving a handprint in beer—and roared in his ear, 'Have you got the right knack o' dancing yet?' The assembly doubled up at this old joke, but the Wandering Jew didn't get it. Some enjoyed the dancing; the fabric of the dance and the sheen and irritation of the music settled round their limbs as a taut lacquer; their surfaces became alien and set.

The Great White Father's joke was carried a few days later by the Wandering Jew back to his secretary, who deciphered it for him, then spread it through the office where it was seized upon by irresponsible persons and torn to shreds.

Embarrassingly, the Old Lamplighter took one of her rare fits during the dance and had to be held down. Her arms and legs kept going, however, as if she were still dancing, and she continued to drink from the blue and gold can she held; no one could take it from her grasp. Beer slopped everywhere. They had to take her away into the bed hut and stay with her. She was quiet in a few minutes, brought up everything, got back on her feet and began all over again.

Into the party ran the Sandpiper, dragging Far Away Places by the hand. For the last half-hour her body had been home to him. The Great White Father rose to salute them.

'Here's a toast to the heroes of Australia's latest navel engagement!'

Innumerable eyes lamped round on the Sandpiper, who was cheerfully dressed in a pair of gaping, unbuttoned overalls, and on Far Away Places, who had put on her pink swami Woolworths briefs, forty-nine cents' worth and cheap at half the price.

After a while they went bush again. He was an ordinary little man and she a hearty trollop with a dirty tongue, but hand in hand into the branches of the mangroves they seemed innocent as boy and girl and clean as kids on a beach.

THE ORGANIZATION MAN The Wandering Jew was frightened at first, but the beer relaxed him.

'Who is the leader of these rebels?' And the Great White Father answered him.

'Revels, man. Revels.'

'What's behind this notice I see glued up to plant walls everywhere?'

'Puroil 1852 or the other one?'

'The other one.'

'Ah,' said the Great White Father, and recited, rolling the words out, 'Men that were once bludgers and thieves are now become eminent foremen and controllers. Some are Suction Heads now who before were rabble-rousers and whisperers of rumours, still with the same evil faces which now shine with sweat above white shirts and semi-stiff collars. Those there are who run and hide when no man approacheth, only the Wandering Jew. And this, too, is a matter for wonder, for this Wandering Jew is not as other Jews but goeth about unpersecuted, rather persecuting others; and persecuting in the name of the only free men: the far-off anonymous shareholders and owners of the world. For no man can be free whose livelihood is on the line every time he takes a stand for his own opinion, or insists on having his self-respect whole or retaining a little human dignity. Even an animal is allowed to pee in peace; even a dog is allowed to finish his dinner undisturbed.

'Things there are that were once men, crawling under the plant structures, carrying their heads forward like rodents. From the sagging belts around their guts swing the shrunken heads of their victims. Honest men wait in hiding for them to pass by, carrying lumps of mild steel.'

BLOOD BROTHERS 'Did you write that?'

'No. We have an author in our midst; a maker of notes, a scribbler, a signwriter, a stealer of other men's lives, lines and lies.'

'Who?'

'You're not advanced enough in drink for me to tell you. He's writing down everything that happens here. All the stupidities. I bet your understrappers don't tell you those things. Anyway, let's think of something cheerful. I'll sing for you, and you'll appreciate it when I stop.'

He sang, to the tune of 'Safe in the arms of Jesus':

Safe in the arms of Puroil
Safe on the weekly staff
Sitting astride a pension
We can afford to laugh.

His voice a pleasant bass. The Wandering Jew, under his blindfold, tried to gauge whether these men were desperate enough to harm him. They had been a little rough getting him out of his car, but probably no more than necessary to persuade him to go quietly.

'Did Simsy come to the party?' asked the Humdinger. 'He was supposed to be going to give us a quote on that heap of junk up in the Puroil yard—that cracker thing.'

'How about swearing in the Wandering Jew as a blood brother?' asked Loosehead, who got brilliant ideas rarely. The others winked at each other and said enthusiastically, 'That's it! Reckon he deserves it. When he's a blood brother he won't be giving away any secrets.'

On the spot the Great White Father thought up a ritual of splendid mumbo-jumbo, somewhere between that of the Masons and the Knights of the Southern Cross, two secret societies whose rituals were widely known. When it came to the final swearing of brotherhood, they actually cut into his arm with a little penknife the Great White Father had on his key ring, and pretended to mingle the blood from his arm with some beer from their cans. They pushed him to his knees.

'There we are. How about if we raise our brother out of a state of darkness now?' yelled the Great White Father. And in reply the assembly, except for those lunatics still playing cricket in the distance and whose wild shouts could be heard, responded with a completely valueless mass affirmation of brotherhood. With a flourish, the blindfold was lowered so that it became a sort of scarf round the Wandering Jew's neck.

'Now you are one of my twelve. Go not in the way of the brass and avoid the haunts of the trusties, the ambitious, those for whom the word of Puroil is enough.' This was a strange thing to say to a manager, but no one minded.

With rough ceremony, he was yanked to his feet by the scarf, blinking in the strong daylight, and forced to shake hands with the entire crew. Each gave him a bone-crusher grip.

'What are you going to do when the mangroves come down?' he inquired in retaliation. The silence was thick. Only the Great White Father was unmoved.

'It'll happen some day, boys and girls. We'll move some day, plans are being considered.'

But this idea was almost too much for his simple flock: they found it hard to defer worry. They also found it hard to defer drinking and the Great White Father wisely gave the order that anyone found with an empty glass would be thrown in the river.

'Let's have some entertainment,' he said. 'How about the Sandpiper singing for us?'

She obliged with twenty-one verses of Abdul the Bulbul, Emir, in the locker-room vernacular.

The Wandering Jew, well on in liquor now, sang a little Termitary ditty. 'I wish I was', it was called, and the verses went from 'I wish I was a little Eskimo', through 'I wish I was a fly upon the wall', to 'I wish I was an automatic lathe', and as last verse, 'I wish I was a chair in the typing pool'.

The assembly picked the words up quickly enough to join in the refrain. He considered giving them the Rugby Union song, but reflected that they were more likely Soccer or Rugby League supporters, being industrial prisoners of the lowest grade. Even sport had its class distinctions.

'Thank you, Wandering Jew!' shouted the great man joyfully. 'A man who can drink and sing a song is not all bad. Feel free to wander among us, but remember, that way lies a ducking in the mud of Eel River.' He pointed the way of the track to the river. The Wandering Jew made a vague sign that meant he would behave, but after wandering about watching the party-people he found he could not approach them. There was a barrier still up in spite of the levelling alcohol, so he gradually made his way back to the Great White Father and eventually these two sat down together in a place where the sun angled down between a gap in the branches overhead, and drank steadily and talked.

'Why is a man like you so thin? I expected a man five by five with fat, not seven by two of bone.'

'It's worry over my next drink. It's because I never eat. It's because I couldn't do my falling-flat trick with a belly—I'd roll like a barrel or rock like a seesaw. How did you get on with my flock?'

'I make them uneasy.'

'Yes. You see that here Jack's considered not only as good as his master, but likely a damn sight better. To these people, riches and power are corrupt.'

'And if they had the chance at my job?'

'They couldn't stick it. They don't have your need to impose yourself on the world about you. You have drives they know not of: drives to avoid poverty and subordination. They don't. They have fewer fears and fewer wants than you. It was their condition of wantlessness that made me despair of their ever bettering their condition by their own efforts. I came to the conclusion that democracy was not for them. They aren't capable of competing on equal terms with the rest of the world. The good God above simply made them a little slower than their brothers, a little duller, a little less worried about survival. Your urge to survive and, having survived, to get ahead, awakes no echoes in them. They hear the words, but there is no answer inside.'

'How did a man like you come to be occupied with people like this?' asked the Wandering Jew.

'The poorest and humblest and nakedest are more comfortable to be with. They have no extra skin for a man to penetrate. No veneer. And the life I live, like this, with no worry and plenty of grog and being the Great White Father to the little people in my little pond—it's very satisfying. I refuse to compete. I have only one life, my friend, and it's not going to be taken up with futile things I don't like doing. I'll go down with them into the past. They know there's no place for them in the future.'

HERESY IN LOW PLACES 'Why have you let the micrometer and the nickel-alloy tools and tension wrenches be replaced by the sledgehammer?'

'I don't follow.'

'Months ago I saw fitters working on your German gas-compressor up there at the cracker, aligning the machine by bashing the bed at the turbine end with sledgehammers.'

'You're pulling my leg. All you've been saying is a leg-pull.'

They both laughed.

'And all this effort and conflict to put a bit of gasoline in the cars of citizens so they can wander aimlessly round thinking they're seeing Australia every time they get beyond the suburbs.'

'You talk as if it's childish,' chided the Wandering Jew. Not that he cared. Technological progress was here to stay. He thought in these terms, as if progress were an edifice men had decided to construct.

'No, I don't mean that only Puroil is puerile: I mean the whole vast undirected effort. A means of making an internal combustion engine is found, so one is made. This is ridiculous. Where is the thought of what will happen when it is made? This thing is fitted to a body with wheels and there are no laws that say it can't be given to a private citizen. So it is given. Fantastic. We change ourselves with every change in our technology. A way is found to make any number of unrelated things—so they are made. Crazy. Automation will help us, they say. But who is us? These poor devils? You and me? Or a few people who are only too keen to get rid of human components? We are allowing these random things, these inventions springing up like mushrooms in a night, to dictate the course of our own history, when we have the means to direct it now to any ends we wish. If we can think of any. We sit back as if all this were the will of God and nothing could be done. As if everything new were a gift from a spirit world. Superstition. My quarrel is that because a thing is discovered, use is made of it. I know that in the course of using the artefacts, new artefacts are made or needed or hinted at, but why allow this random, mushrooming growth to dictate the movement of history? Methods of invention have been invented. You can slow the machine down or speed it up, give us longer or shorter lives, make us different people from the genes up, but not just allow everything to happen by chance. Chance isn't the only sort of god. We can build the sort of world we want, and if we make mistakes, start again. Climates can be altered, new rivers gouged out. We could act like gods, get into history and make it for ourselves rather than watch and wait in fear and trembling. We're in the game, we're no longer spectators. The future cannot only be made and predicted, it can be planned. Totalitarian? Perhaps. But at least a dictatorship by people: what we have now is dictatorship by blind events.'

ARE YOU ONE? From these promising beginnings might have come a few words which in the hands of some young pampered genius might have been fashioned into a key to unlock the secrets of the future, or an ignition key to start the rusting, neglected engine of hope, but unfortunately for these vagrant, irresponsible, unsubsidized wishes and unfortunately for the peace and goodwill of the establishment, one of the less civilized of the drinkers chose that moment to rush up to the Wandering Jew and yell at him, 'We're not inside the barbed wire now, you're just crap out here!'

The Great White Father didn't demand an apology from the Outside Fisherman for this breach of etiquette, for he believed men say exactly what they mean even if they mean different things at different times, and he encouraged them to stand by what they said, no matter how stupid it was.

'Take it easy, Fisho,' he said. 'If he's crap outside the gates, what are we?'

'That's all right,' the Wandering Jew assured his host. 'I am not affected by either tact or brutality.' He said this so grandly that the Great White Father looked at his glass. Empty again. He signalled to the Ant for a fresh jug. The Outside Fisherman, not yet startled by his audacity in yelling at the Manager, had staggered away to bury his teeth in the Sandpiper's neck. It was years since his own wife had an unwrinkled neck, it was such a belly-warming pleasure to mouth a young girl.

Out of the blue, Ambrose said in a loud voice to the Wandering Jew, 'We're all against homosexuals here.'

'What's wrong, Ambrose?' asked the Great White Father.

'This nice chap is one,' he declared flatly. His beer rocked in a sort of counter rhythm to the motion of his body.

'Attention, everyone,' yelled the Sandpiper. 'We've found one!' Movement stopped. The Humdinger took the Wandering Jew by the shirt-front and glared into his glassed eyes.

'Are you one?' he roared.

'No!' shouted the Wanderer.

'He's not one,' said the Humdinger and released him. Everyone was relieved. The party flowed again. Ambrose wasn't satisfied, but the Wandering Jew lurched a few steps to the north-west and Ambrose lost sight of him, for he could only see straight ahead.

SELF-PITY The Two Pot Screamer, referred to earlier by the Great White Father as a stealer of men's lives and lies, had taken a few notes, but alcohol had overtaken his writing-hand. His body was propped by one wall of the bed hut, notebook clutched weakly in his left hand. He had sense enough to put it into his inside pocket, but not enough to catch sight of a sheet of paper that dropped from it.

Another man did, who had slyly taken care not to drink too fast. He picked up the paper, unfolded it and read:

THE TWO POT SCREAMER IN CASUALTY

They bring him in after a shanty fight
His one enormous bottle wound still bleeds
A nurse's voice complains beside the light
His dying peace disturbed by natural needs.

His mother bled once, from her pain he came
Beautiful as life. I ask you how
He came to be abandoned in the rain
Wrinkled, fragile, incontinent as now.

His mother knew no love before he came
She probably conceived against a fence
Did some weak human love grow just the same
In him whose life was caused for fifty cents?

To this man dead for fifty years I wish
Forgetfulness of every lifelong fear
It was a kind of love formed him from flesh
Best we pretend that he was never here.

He looked at the poet's drunken face, puzzled. Two Pot never talked about himself. It was a queer feeling to read a man's private thoughts. This effort wouldn't get published, either. Didn't he mind? What made him keep applying his pen to bits of paper? He was about to put it back in the Screamer's pocket, but had a second thought and put it in his own.

DISNEYLAND USES HYPNOSIS 'What about a demo from Disneyland?' called the Humdinger.

'Yeah!' chorused several urgers.

'Come on, Disneyland. Pull 'em down and let's see you give the girls a bang. Hey, Sandpiper!'

But his plans foundered. Disneyland wouldn't take them off. They were all at him, but couldn't separate him from his pants.

'I don't think he knows about girls,' said the Sandpiper. He wasn't insulted.

'I know about girls. You kiss 'em and marry 'em,' he said. 'I seen it all at the movies.' The Great White Father questioned him and found that all he knew about sex was what he'd seen at the movies. What they didn't show he didn't know.

'Never mind. I taught him hypnosis, didn't I, Disneyland?' said the Humdinger.

'Show us the old hypnosis, Disneyland,' echoed the urgers.

Disneyland stumbled forward into an open space and discarded his glass, looking for a victim. The Wandering Jew backed into view.

'Hey,' said Disneyland, spinning him round by the shoulder. 'I'll hypnotize you!' He fastened onto the Jew backwards and tightened his thick young arms round the Manager's chest.

'Breathe,' he blasted into the Wandering Jew's ear. 'Breathe in and out as fast as you like!' There was nothing the Wandering Jew would rather do, since Disneyland's grip had nearly collapsed his chest which was quite unused to the tight clasp of his fellow man. He breathed in convulsively; Disneyland's grip pushed the breath out; he breathed again and so on, in and out, the process was in motion as taught to Disneyland by the Humdinger. Presently the Wandering Jew blacked out, falling like a sack of wet grain at the feet of Disneyland. The party roared and cheered.

'You forgot to hold him up, you nong,' said the Humdinger. But he beamed with pleasure.

A sack of wet grain? That was a second thought. Actually the Wandering Jew fell like a sackful of dead cats and this was the original phrase, but there was something there that troubled me—what was it? Perhaps it was the feeling of rigidity about sacks of wet grain, or the lack of dignity in sacks full of drowned cats, or the disgrace for the local manager of a vast foreign industrial enterprise in being compared to either.

DO NOT BEND, FOLD OR MUTILATE The Wandering Jew came round and resumed his vertical position. He tried to get back into the conversation, but couldn't quite remember where he'd left it.

'Do you believe in destiny?' he asked diffidently.

'Yes,' said the Great White Father firmly.

'How?'

'The destiny of a slotted, punched card that one day suddenly finds itself alone—and important—traversing the labyrinth—'

'The what?'

'The guts of the processing machine, to pop out at last—the card of destiny. The card the machine was set for.'

'You're having me on.'

'Sure enough. But don't forget the word destiny applies just as well to the Glass Canoe or poor Blue Hills as it does to the Wandering Jew.'

'Is that really what they call me?'

'It's a kind of immortality.'

'But why a Jew?'

'A Jew is anyone on good terms with money.'

'Who are those other men you mentioned?'

'Punched cards that went astray. Replaceable. Not to worry.'

FEED MY LAMBS Perhaps it was due to the presence of an unusual bacteria in the air or to the strange feeling of freedom involved in gulping beer in a swamp that was neighbour to rich industrial land containing or capable of producing the technological marvels that are a matter of daily boredom to our sophisticated publics; perhaps it was because he felt he was losing the faculty of distinctively human speech—whatever it was, the Wandering Jew found himself walking silently among the party members with beer in one hand and biscuits in the other. The beer for himself, the biscuits for the Great White Father's flock.

He smiled weakly, half-drunk. No drought here, yet the flock was being hand-fed. A stray pellet of sentiment—who fired it?—struck him. Was this all he could do for his fellow man? His own defences mobilized and rushed to his aid, like antibodies roused from their kennels by the sound of strangers at the gate. Why do anything? He smiled again and those he served gave him, entirely free, curious looks.

As he passed among the multitude he committed certain errors of judgement, ever and anon dropping biscuits or the crumbs and poorer relations of biscuits into the beer of his fellow man. Many disciples cursed him, but the glow of perfect charity that filled him made the sounding brass and tinkling symbols of their complaints seem as nothing. Had he not heeded the command of the Father when he said, 'Feed my fish?' He peered into their glasses, dropped crumbs into the depths, and half expected to see mouths devour them. Conveniently equipped with tails, of course.

One man was prone. Face up, mouth open. A fly fished tentatively from his lower teeth, apparently unaware that closing jaws could place him in jeopardy.

As the natural current of air drew him down, he gripped the teeth with suckered feet and wrapped his wings close about him. As the air blew out, his wings flattened of their own accord in the draught and he had to hang on even more grimly. Getting a meal was difficult under these conditions, but not impossible.

With care and compassion, the Wandering Jew—representative in New South Wales of the wealth and might of overseas controllers and in the Home Beautiful a feeder of the Great White Father's flock or school, of lambs or fish—the Wandering Jew aimed a goodly crumb, taking care, as Galileo did in his celebrated experiment, but for a different reason, to select a crumb that would not allow the factor of air resistance or wind direction to deflect it from its proper path—into this open mouth with the dual desire of delivering the man from the attentions of the fly and of giving nourishment.

He parted his fingers, the crumb descended. Earth's gravitational properties normal. The fly saw it coming and took to the air, then returned undaunted to the pickings. But crumb descended past teeth, past tongue, into the gullet and tipped the uvula in passing. Things happened quickly. Breath was sucked in sharply, fly was inhaled and portcullis of teeth shut with a snap, chipping a tiny piece of enamel from a bicuspid incisor.

Crumb, breath, fly, enamel—all were trapped. Not for ever. With the casual air of a doctor treating someone else's ailments, the Wandering Jew waited for the mouth to reopen, and when it did, poured in beer. From his own glass. Greater love hath no man.

Motives and aim were good. Beer followed crumb past teeth and tongue and swamped the uvula. But he reckoned without the stomach, which did not need beer.

In the twinkling of an eye (that space of time, we are still assured, which will be occupied in resurrecting and assembling the dead of the past million or so years, depending on whether we date the emergence of man from the time he or it first stood erect, first used words, first used weapons or first killed for fun. Any of the typically human actions. Although if the agent of this miracle of synthesis is in any doubt on this point, the time may be exceeded. But this is enough of that. Our Maker, Killer and eventual Re-maker must not be thought of as being in doubt. The question: Why, if we are to be resurrected, kill us at all? occurs naturally, but to presume such a Person capable of doubt, this is blasphemy)—in the twinkling of an eye, the Wandering Jew was privileged to see the first recorded vertical vomit.

Geyser. Gusher. Blowout. Words rushed to his aid, waiting obediently to be said. Another instance of Australia's riches in natural gas.

The flow subsided, there was no need to cap this well. The man was still unconscious and the fly dead. And there, all over the shoes of the Wandering Jew and the bottoms of his trousers, which he should have worn rolled, was the material that had given this man his name. The Wandering Jew had met Big Bits.

THE SANCTITY OF MARRIAGE Beer had been flowing into the drinkers and, after processing, out again into the surrounding swamp; frogs, in their mucky pools, barked less often and were limp.

Ambrose came slowly back into circulation.

'If he's not one, is he married?' he demanded of everyone he bumped. 'Is he? I'm married. I'm not one.'

He was persistent, so the Great White Father got him off the Wandering Jew's back.

'Are you married?'

'Soon,' replied the man born to be Branch Manager, and to silence Ambrose the Great White Father stood on the step of one of the bed huts and addressed the multitude on the sanctity of marriage.

'Marriage is rightly regarded as sacred. Marriage sanctifies the single-bed sinner, it puts on the straight path the dodgy lodger and blesses the union of those who tire of the back seat of the car, the fence behind the picture show, the bottom of a boat, the beach at night, golf course, office carpet. Marriage loosens the nuts and tightens the bankroll, it conjures storms from a clear sky and children from careless conversations. It is a gift from heaven that must be paid for in instalments, of which each day is one and yet not one, for the balance owing never diminishes, only cancels very suddenly. With a word. Or the lack of a smile. It is a bonus from life in which two can be a world, and that world coloured with the beauty of gods and ringing with the music of distant galaxies—or the voice of prisoners bickering in a cell.'

He hadn't meant it to sound serious, but he caught his conscience inadvertently on a little snag left in his memory by the rupture of his own marriage.

WELCOME, STRANGER Some strangers called in late that afternoon, men who wandered along the river bank and were fascinated by the game of tree cricket they saw. The cricketers kept their alcohol level up by frequent trips back to the keg, but always returned to their game. The strangers wandered up the path to the source of this refreshment, which they could smell at a distance, and mentioned a drink.

'What about it?' called Canada Dry, who stood up, all seventy-seven inches of him, ready to repel the invader.

'Let 'em drink.' The great man gave the nod.

'Who pays for this bounty?' slurred the Wandering Jew, and the great man answered quietly, for his ears only.

'They all chip in. I foot the bill for the extras. I'd rather give the beer away than sell it, and these are strangers. We'll fill them up so they don't remember a thing and Volga will transport them downstream under the bridge where they can sleep it off.'

The Wandering Jew started to wander off innocently away from the main party, but everywhere he strayed he stumbled over bodies in pairs on the naked ground. Far into the mangroves there were the unmistakeable flutters and grunts, thumps and slaps of love. Man pressed woman back into the earth everywhere, compelling her to the horizontal of sickness, sleep, death, love.

Did he envy them? Would he have shared their poverty just to have these working wives on the floor of a swamp? Not likely. The suave daughters of the better classes had been available to him ever since he was released from a highly private Public School in Melbourne. There was nothing to envy and nothing to fear: these people thought only of their bellies and what depended from them.

Perhaps it was good they had this man to look to, whose words some took for saint's words, who probably kept his dirty fingernail clippings and jars of his bottled breath.

By five o'clock another keg was running dry and the trusty ones were off to get another. This time the keg went slower, for many were indisposed. The Wandering Jew insisted he had to go, otherwise there would be search parties out for him—which wasn't strictly true—so they reluctantly agreed.

'Don't go yet. We're just beginning to like you,' protested the Humdinger, but the words had a sound of good-bye. The Great White Father knew that the Wanderer wouldn't stay the night, so he was blindfolded again and the Volga Boatman took him round a little farther than Clearwater wharf and led him off through thick rushes to the back of the saltwater pumphouse and so to the cooling water tower, where the Mercedes was parked. The blindfold was removed and Volga waited till the Mercedes made a few kangaroo starts then lurched off up the road before he went back to the boat. The Wandering Jew said to himself over and over in the car, 'He uses his own money. His own money. On those dregs. His own money.' He couldn't get over it.

At the Home Beautiful the two strangers had started a fight which raged over the clearing into the trees and so to the water.

They were retreating under weight of numbers, though they were putting up a good show.

Many merrymakers had to report over the river for work and the latest rumours on night shift, so Volga was kept busy after ten o'clock. This helped keep him fit and work off the beer, and with the Great White Father and other steady drinkers he stayed at the Home Beautiful. The last keg lasted all night, but was a little flat by morning. New faces appeared then, ready to give the party another shove along. The luckiest were those whose weekend was Monday and Tuesday and didn't have to report to Puroil till Wednesday.

Next day the Great White Father knew it was impossible to live with the Jew on any terms but his own; positions-vacant ads were in the papers and bulldozers started clearing-work at the southern end of the Puroil mangroves.

The holiday roster was reorganized and Canada Dry's holiday trip was off. He had arranged for mid-winter, an unpopular time, so he was given mid-summer because he was single. All the married men with kids who had been sweating on mid-summer were given mid-winter.

20
THE LITTLE THINGS

INDUSTRIAL RELATIONS, SEEN FROM BENEATH Provided it has continued for some time and is widespread, liberalization will not be easily stopped. Simple repression is not the answer. The men hadn't changed. Their conditions of work were harder, they had lost the right to stop work—agreed to it themselves. The company hadn't changed, either; the company so wasteful of men and materials, content to allow the waste to continue in its system of replacement parts of both items; the company that trusted in numbers and didn't value the valour of its slaves; the company which was so far away.

The Two Pot Screamer watched the Samurai slyly from around corners, wondering how long this man could keep inside himself the fury that was stirred and boiled up fresh each day by the jumble, the tangle, the idiocies, the sneaking out from under, the endless don't-care. Men like him meant their hate, it wasn't just for show; they kept quiet, letting it grow and gain in strength, bottling it up, keeping it in to raise the pressure.

He procured a chit and went to the lavatory, where he proceeded to make copious notes.

The Samurai was still smarting under the indignity of being unpaid for the day he was sick. In his disgust at this and at the wage defeat, his dismay at the wreck of his arm scarred by friends, he was making the company pay for regiments of unpaid sick days. He was convinced that the Brown Snake had marked his sick form 'More information required' knowing that a man like him wasn't going to crawl along to his office with excuses and beg for the money.

The Samurai wasn't as badly off as the Outside Fisherman, who had three days off with 'humanoid arthritis in back', as he put it on his sick form. No pay. He hadn't had a day off in two years.

Why did a little thing tip the scales and cause the Samurai to do bad things? Others took more than he did from Puroil. Perhaps when you've always had it good, little things loom large.

The Samurai was varying his vengeance: one day he would depress the gasoline conversion so that the yield on his shift, instead of being a thousand tons a day, was eight hundred; and he would so adjust other plant conditions that it was impossible for those who followed him to do much about it. Other times he would adjust the end point of the gasoline, altering the quality. For now the plant was going well. He heard them come every morning, the white hosts of technologists and project and process engineers, and even the Good Shepherd was heard to say, 'It's going well and we don't know why.' They were hoping it was permanent.

The gasoline make was down, for the Samurai could play on the control panel like an organist plays his rows of keys and stops. There had been a zero error of two on the feed-flow instrument for twelve months. They were processing seven hundred tons a day less than they thought. Heads fell in accounting and stocks department because of the discrepancy, but no one on the production end knew. The fault was regularly notified, but it didn't have priority. No one bothered any more about the five hundred tons a day of steam at two dollars a ton which exhausted to the stack. Every new man who started suggested installing condensers so that the expensively demineralized water could be recovered and used again, but all suggestions were rubbished.

And every day five tons of catalyst fines—too fine to be trapped by the regenerator cyclones—were released to atmosphere. At a dollar a pound.

THE LOST LEADER The Samurai went to sleep thinking of these things. If there were no overseas control, would he sabotage them no matter what they did to him? It would be different, having your own people making money from your efforts. Why was it different? But he had always had this idea that he would rather have a friend hurt him than a stranger, rather an Australian make money from his working life than a foreigner. Was he crazy? Or was he just taking a little further the dim feelings of every Australian? Obstinate, irrational, vengeful. National.

Who would channel the emotions of these people—his politically backward countrymen—who would find a political outlet for their fears and greed? What leader would arise to show them what to want?

Those around him were willing to submit to his leadership, but he had never wanted to make the effort for them. What they demanded was what all the world's inert masses wanted—someone to lean on, someone to do their fighting for them. A mighty leader he was in his dreams—or was he an Admirable Crichton who could rise to the occasion in an emergency, then sink to his place when the battlefield cleared? Or was he no such thing?

Now and then in his life he had a feeling that made his hair crawl and the suspicion of emotional tears spring into his eyes. What was it? Yes. It was that all his life had been a preparation—everything that happened to him was training for a mighty engagement—half waking and half asleep in his lonely bed, he roamed over the remembered fields through which his imagination had taken him for years. How long was it? Ever since he was a boy and had walked out at night to the high back veranda of his home, to the square corner formed by the safety rail, and gripped it with his strong young hands and looked out over the winking houselights and street-lights, way beyond the undulating suburbs to the lights of Sydney, multi-coloured and cold in the night air. Unwinking, steady; for the air was clearer then. But waiting. Those lights, that city; always waiting.

Waiting for his voice.

THE TRIAL He drifted off into uneasy sleep. The lights were always kept on, he was a murderer in the condemned cell. Capital punishment had been deleted from the criminal code, but that made no difference to his dream: death as a punishment was still in his head. They had moved the execution apparatus into his room. How could he escape now? Escape? Desperately his mind went over the details of his trial, he began to exercise control over the outcome of the speeches—that was all they were: dead forms of speech read out lifelessly—made by his counsel; the bored, sarcastic interpolations of his judge; constantly going back in time to amend details of his crime itself, until he had tailored the crime, apprehension, imprisonment, verdict, trial, everything to suit his dreaming self. Then he escaped from under the shadow of the gallows and soon was wide awake. No, it was not right yet; he went back to sleep to change the whole dream.

He lay there in a disturbed bed. One man alone in the world. Free as a man is free whom no one claims. What was his future? Would he marry and see himself continue in children? Or be content to influence the children of other men? And was his seed capable of living again? Why hadn't he gone back to that doctor to get the verdict? Why bother about it at all? Plenty of time to discover your seed is dead a few years after marriage. It wasn't right from a woman's point of view—not fair—but who was a woman? His body fidgeted, his mind seethed.

Sleep was gone.

FACSIMILE How many men were cursed with this habit of anxiety? If he was a man with dead seed, that was the sort of man he was. Why couldn't he stop caring? Here he was, one man at war with one of the largest corporations in the world. How was it that one man could be allowed to cost such a body thousands of dollars a day in reduced production and no one competent to stop him?

No technological audit department to point the finger? No fellow workers with sufficient knowledge of the plant to spot what he was doing, go behind his back and make capital from his downfall? In the pay office a man could lose his head for a ten-cent mistake, but on the production end the plant could be run wastefully for months, everyone knew and no one cared.

All the men needed was unity and a certain strength to be able to beat the constant downward pressure of the agents of the free men who employed them. But why help to beat them? For apathetic, wantless boobies who wouldn't fight. For men who didn't want to be at work anyway.

He was moving towards the place where he was about to say 'To hell with the prisoners, there's a reward for working, too!' Was all this internal fuss and noise nothing but a prelude to conforming and shutting his mouth like everyone else?

Maybe taking revenge wasn't enough. What did he get from it but satisfaction? Defeat was ahead in a world where every man was for himself. The world wasn't right, something was out of balance.

Hours later, he slept. The day he woke to was a copy of every other day except that, following the laws governing its eventual destruction, it was minutely longer.

DIGNITY A deputation approached the Great White Father. Loosehead and some others had worried for days about the conclusion of the great man's speech on the fall of the Glass Canoe.

'We feel,' he began, then feeling ashamed of hiding behind the plural, said boldly, 'I reckon you should have said—The Glass Canoe is shattered and sunk.' He stood silent, waiting praise or rebuke.

'What did I say?'

'Shattered and gone home.'

'Shattered and sunk, eh? Sunk? To end a speech? If it was a comedy sketch, yes. But sunk? No, Loosehead, I don't like it.'

'But wouldn't it be better? Glass—shattered—sunk? It sounds as if that's the end, nice and neat.'

'It's a good point, Loosehead, and I'm glad you listened, but

I like the end of a speech to sort of trail away. Dignity. You know? Sunk is too quick, too sudden. Like pulling out a bung.'

'But I had a theory.'

'I don't care what your theories are, Loosehead. The sound has to be the thing that hits you in the belly, not the sense. When the Bible said "Rejoice with me for I have found that which was lost", the silly bugger should have said, "Rejoice with me, for I have lost that which was found." Hear it? That's the way to roll words off your tongue. "Our Glass Canoe is shattered and gone home." Sonorous! Full! Rich! Resounding! Memorable!'

'You sure?'

'Dignity, Loosehead.' And he rolled the words out as if they made sense: 'Abide with me, for I am shattered and gone home.'

'Dignity. OK. Dignity.' Loosehead went away with his followers, repeating the word like an incantation.

EXIT FORMALITIES The Great White Father saw to it that Herman the German was sent off well. He shaved the man himself, combed his hair, and nourished his last day with a little pilsner.

All the girls were there sitting in a half-circle round Herman's bed. He saw their faces dimly as choristers and angels. Never on Sunday held his hand and the Sorcerer's Apprentice his knee. Perhaps a little above the knee. The Humdinger led the prisoners in a few garbled verses of 'Abide with Me' and Far Away Places assayed an emotional version of 'God be with you till we meet again' until tears ran down the faces of prostitutes and prisoners. Only Herman was tearless.

His washed face shone. He was back in Bebel-Strasse, Hamburg. Angels in chorus sang:

Wir tragen dich hin, verschwiegen und weich,
Eiapopeia ins himmlische Reich... And solemnly:
Ein' feste Burg ist unser Gott...

Hayricks, heavily thatched farmhouses, the joyful, jumping dogs, a holiday once with the family in the Harzberge and everyone warm in thick coats and fur hats. Wonderful days and your chest full of the cold crisp air of the Alps. He felt it now—although it was a warm day—that cold crisp air in his lungs as his body failed him for the first time. Before he could be surprised at this, death eased him.

The Great White Father took the body to his house in his own decaying car and got a doctor to sign the papers. He made out Herman had been bunking there. The doctor asked no questions. Every week among the aged and neglected he saw worse than this: after all, a significant percentage of the population had a standard of living that put them in danger of malnutrition. This man at least had someone who would see that he got a burial.

The hat went round for Herman's funeral, no one knew or bothered about his bank account. Men from the four shifts went to the crematorium, including half the shift on duty that day. Each man put on his absentee report by arrangement, 'Attending funeral of Herman who was sacked because he lost an arm.' They didn't get paid.

That afternoon and for a few days after that—the Cremmo waited for a pile of corpses before lighting the furnace—whenever a man looked up in the direction of Rookwood and fancied he saw an extra black puff of smoke he would say speculatively, 'That might be Herman now.'

Herman's son turned up looking for his Dad's bankbook, but his landlady had burned the old papers to keep the room tidy. She'd known him for years and was quite fond of him, but business was business. She let the room the same day, when Herman's rent still had a week and three days to go. She made a profit and the thought of it softened her eyes and relaxed her mind. She spoke quietly to the other boarders and didn't take a headache powder all day.

SURPRISE! When the big shutdown was nearly over and the Wandering Jew had his new towbar, patio rail and barbecue equipment—made on the job—the Python organized a night raid, caught several fitters doing foreign orders and sacked them. With their usual ability to recognize an important issue, the operators declared their support. The Sumpsucker heard them talking. 'Don't forget your Union agreed to the no-stoppage clause.'

What no-stoppage clause? This was a surprise. Righteously they raged in a dozen amenities huts. First a stand-down clause, now a no-stoppage clause. How can the Union itself say they can't go out? It was different with the other trades, most of them had clauses in their awards banning strikes. But their awards were forced on them, they hadn't cut their own throats.

The Two Pot Screamer from his pleasant cloud of genital pain—he'd been to see the girls—told them to go ask the Samurai. Men from the scattered plants sent ambassadors to speak for them.

'You remember how we went out—to show the company we meant business? Then pulled our horns in and accepted everything they offered? Like whipped dogs? And three weeks later there was a Union meeting. Not a summons meeting. No fuss. Just a meeting. And the Chairman got up with three little points. Remember?'

Some vaguely recalled a meeting. None knew what had been said.

'I'll tell you. That third little point was a request from the management that in the event of any stoppage we'd see the plant was manned. That's all. Fair enough? Oh, one other thing. The company reserves the right to say how many will be left on the plants when we have a stoppage. They know plant requirements—we can trust them in a little thing like that, they reckon.'

He paused and examined their faces. They seemed to be following him.

'You remember me standing up? And pointing out what this meant? No? Well, it might be better if you did. It means no stoppage can be more than a token stoppage.'

'Why? We can stop. We have the right.'

'The right means nothing. If you have to leave a crew on the plant, production goes on. The company doesn't feel the pinch. The idea of stopping work is we make them suffer. If we vote stoppage who stays on the plant? Those the company picks. Will you be one?'

'Oh,' said several.

'But,' said another, 'we can reverse the decision of that meeting. There were only a dozen there.'

'That's where they got you. They held up the printing and

signing of the agreement until they got the word from the Chairman and included it.'

'Why did he do it? Why did he sell us out?'

'You're the Union. You're the ones have to do the thinking. He's not a leaning-post. You have to go to the meetings and think before you vote. You lean on your leaders at your own risk.'

He'd said it all before, he knew they wouldn't change. He walked away, trying not to show his disgust. They were surprised that so much business had been done at that little meeting.

21
PAYBACK

PROFIT When the shutdown was over, repairs done and new equipment installed, the cracker got off the ground. Several new columns had been added as further refinements to the process. Reflecting their overseas masters' increasing elevation above them, the tall steel columns towered higher over the heads of the humans who tended them, and since to look up it was necessary to tilt their heads far back so their safety helmets fell off, they removed them first. Not that the columns looked down and saw the humans; they looked steadfastly, proudly, far over their heads, towards structures similar to themselves.

The birds were glad of the extra columns and came there in greater numbers to sleep at night. Someone with nothing better to do started a campaign against them and squeezed out sticky jelly to snare their feet and clog their feathers. They fell to the concrete apron, fluttering and exhausted, and were gathered up in empty tin drums to die together, their bodies tossed into a mass grave.

Down at ground level, men were called in one by one to be shown by their foremen the reports the foremen had written out about them, before they were sent on to the Python. The men's eyes were infallibly caught by the new metal board on which were posted their names on coloured magnetized blocks that could be moved anywhere on the board. Or taken off. There didn't seem to be much of a pattern to the reports, except that men over thirty-five all did badly. These little things seemed to be accepted as the price of progress. On the cracker, new air-blowers, pressure valves and a certain electricity supply were keeping the process going steadily just as the company had hoped three years before.

Six months went by, a year, eighteen months of constant twenty-four-hour-a-day production. The prisoners kept their heads down, hoping these technical changes would benefit them.

Someone scratched the words *Unknown Industrial Prisoner* in the concrete near the base of the gasoline-splitting column. The concrete was swept and kept clean by an unknown hand. Later a bronze plate appeared with the three words engraved on it; the plate had four legs brazed to its underside and was cemented into four holes in the concrete. No one was game to show ignorance by asking who did it, or initiative and dig it out.

Gradually, on the cracker, the supervisors supervised and no prisoner was able to get his head down on night shift. The much older plants, without the attention given by management to the cracker, still retained sleeping rights, but had to be more careful. Bubbles started to work, and surprised everyone. Bomber Command stopped his Gotchas, and men moved about in less fear for the safety of their genitals. He could no longer be persuaded to show his dirty black and white photographs, but dozens of new men were being recruited, mostly ex-Navy, and little bundles of even more exotic photographs—in colour—began to be circulated.

One day, six months after the start-up, a Sydney newspaper printed a tiny paragraph showing a yearly profit figure for Puroil Australia. It wasn't much, only three million dollars. The Humdinger tore it out and pasted it on a notice board at the cracker. It lasted half an hour. Bomber Command personally scraped it off.

A year after the start-up—that is, after a year of continuous running—two morning papers published a yearly profit figure for Puroil's Australian operations. They'd got it from their London offices; the figures weren't available in Australia. Seven and three-quarter million dollars. This time the prisoners got a supply of cuttings and glued them up as fast as the foremen and supervisors tore them off. The financial editors of both papers made peculiar remarks about the company's heavy depreciation figures and large provision for tax.

At the same time the Actor, in the role as Education Officer, was delivering prepared speeches to the lower reaches of management, hammering home the point that Clearwater was still losing money and radical new changes were about to take place in staff policy. No one was game to ask what the word *loss* meant—and the Actor wouldn't have known—but it meant that although the cracker was nearly paid for and making an increasing profit, some of the items of cost such as maintenance and wages were higher than the company wished. If they had been lower, the profit figure on paper would have been higher. Therefore there was a loss of profit.

Down on the cleared clay flats, for months heavy trucks had been delivering thousands of tons of beach sand, graders spread it out into rectangular plots of three to five acres, just the size of the dozens of new plants.

On the cracker the great compressor struggled on. Every day for eighteen months vibration readings were taken and heads were scratched, but it held together. The cracker was going so well the company applied to the Department of Labour and Industry for a deferment of their regular pressure-vessel inspection. An inspection meant a shutdown and a shutdown meant an interruption to production.

During this idyllic eighteen months there were eleven fires. One was funny. The Gypsy Fiddler was standing sunning himself not far from a slurry pump with leaking seals. Maintenance had been under pressure to fix them, there had been no asbestos seals, only teflon, so teflon was used. They leaked white vapour. Fifty yards away, the Samurai saw the vapours change to blue, then flash. He charged forward past the Fiddler, grabbed a dry powder extinguisher and put the fire out. When the Fiddler turned and saw what had been happening behind him, he fainted in terror. He said it was his blood pressure and begged the Samurai not to report him.

The worst fire occurred when part of the plant was bypassed so that a quick cleaning job could be done and some repairs welded. Several bundles of heater tubes were isolated and one of the foreman-pleasing prisoners, the Western Salesman, insisted the operation was depressured and gas free. Everyone wanted to believe it, so the tubes were opened while a welder was working below. Hydrocarbons under pressure spewed out and down as far as the welding torch, ignited, and the whole thing flashed while eight men were on the tube landing. Four went over the side, three climbed higher but were burned, and one was set alight while they watched. He was in hospital six months and even after he was on his feet had to go back for twelve months for more skin grafts. One of his hands was a claw.

There were several more small fires at intervals of about a month, half of them in wet weather when the drains filled and hydrocarbons floated on the water. The refinery siren could be heard ten miles away and began to worry residents of nearby suburbs who complained querulously about possible danger to themselves. It was reasonable in the circumstances that an order should be conveyed by word of mouth—it was never put in writing—that no future fires were to be notified to the company fire station. The firemen would blow the siren automatically and this was undesirable. Instead, the foreman on the job was to take charge, use the portable foam and powder dispensers and only make a fire report if it looked like getting out of hand. Anything was preferable to bad public relations.

Thieving hadn't stopped. Stealing from each other was so frequent that gradually all the men on shift equipped their lockers with U-bolts and padlocks. Men walked out with bags so heavy they could hardly carry them. Whole welding sets, oxygen cylinders, stocks and dies, hammers, wrenches, gauges, blowtorches, grease-guns.

Several were caught and in amusing ceremonies removed in the charge of plainclothes police. One arrest attracted so much attention—two men had been taking metal scrap meant for the scrap merchant—that all classes of prisoners watched police chase them over fences, buildings, plant structures, through workshops and excavations, before they were caught and kept on the ground by a few judicious short kicks to the body. Just as, two hundred years before at Tyburn, pickpockets plied their trade in the crowds watching pickpockets hang, two others, while justice was seen to be done, helped themselves to a truckload of wooden crates covered with expenditure symbols such as 6^{A}/352/1/16/7/02/9/0/001. They hijacked the truck and drove down to a cluster of spare construction huts near Eel wharf where they could look at their finds and hide them till they got transport. One man's share was a hundred thousand flyscreens; the other got two thousand white safety hats decorated with the Puroil emblem. They hid the screens, to get them later. The safety hats they took to the water's edge. Standing side by side, cursing and laughing, they pitched them into the river one by one. The tide took them out into the bay, all two thousand of them. White petals bobbing on the waves.

On the other hand, those who had little accidents began to cover them up. Several vigorous fitters who pinched fingers or barked knuckles began to be called accident-prone—their foremen said so in monthly reports—so the rest took the hint. Many twisted backs and sprains were masked by days off in bed with flu: doctors' certificates were easy to come by if you picked your doctor.

THE SPOTTED TROUT   The Trout had to go, too. They cut the training officer out of Personnel; might as well get rid of the PRO. Admin had to do its bit to economize.

'What's this?' The Whispering Baritone had the Spotted Trout on the mat. His fingers stabbed irritably at a yellow expense sheet.

'Scotch, of course.'

'Whisky?'

'It's the only Scotch I know.' Here was a man who couldn't make an engagement presentation of a cheap vase to an office girl without stammering, blushing, sweating and probably dropping the blasted thing—telling him how to do a PR job.

'It's not good enough.' He was red and flushed and the thin, flaking fingers trembled. 'Too high. We can't sanction these expenses.' He used the company 'we' and loved it.

'Damn it, man! I must entertain. That's why I'm employed! I have people in—I must give them a drink. Do you want me to invite only teetotallers?' He knew the Baritone was one and mentally curled a purple lip.

'These expenses must be reduced. You'll buy cheaper drink and less of it.' Firmness.

'Oh for god's sake!' shouted the Spotted Trout. His face took on its purple round cheeks and neck, shading to mauve under the roots of his hairs which stood up singly like tall trees in a thinning forest. 'How cheap can we get? This is a great company not a tinpot Parents and Citizens Club. I can't give decent people Australian whisky. If the drinks are cheap, what do they think of our products?'

'That's not your concern. I want these expenses down.'

'It can't be done. There's not an ounce of padding in it. I've been absolutely above board. The amount I'm allowed is ludicrous. What are you running here? A five dollar brothel?' His own honesty hurt him.

'I'll teach you to shout at me. Get out. I'll have your cheque posted.'

'What? Are you sacking me?'

'Obviously.' The Whispering Baritone felt easier. He had the whip hand. His fingers no longer trembled.

'The Colonel was right! You *are* a refugee from a male whore-shop! No wonder the company's going to pot if they keep poofters like you!' He stamped out.

He drove out savagely past the guards at the gate and didn't slow down for inspection. Damn the company to hell! He took out his anger on the car. He didn't really believe he was sacked. He found out the following day when he tried to get into his office.

They gave the PR job to the Actor. Something to do in his spare time. The very next week he sent a story and glossy prints to the local rag about the most recent construction at the refinery, including a mention of several new stacks over three hundred feet high to take away noxious gases like sulphur-dioxide. That did it. He was six weeks in print trying to explain away the noxious gases.

REPLACEABLE PARTS After eighteen months the prisoners remembered a new industrial agreement was due to be drawn up and in order to give themselves a better bargaining advantage began to canvass the members of other trades; the engineering unions, transport men. It seemed a good idea, a combination of all unions on the job. Men smiled at each other and raised their voices a little to foremen: if they got a combined shop they might get a decent rise in the new agreement. All they needed was a good, honest leader, a man who would take the kick if things went wrong, a man who wanted the best for his mates but was not greedy for himself.

There was no such man.

Then from over the sea a decision came and the Australians were confronted with the future. This time there was no Wandering Jew to cry on their shoulders. Every prisoner got a circular letter about reorganization, changing conditions, Clearwater's future, surplus numbers, different standards of skill, and redundancy. Some got two letters: the second was an invitation to discuss with Personnel a suitable date for separation. There would be a cash settlement. Most were over forty. They had two weeks to decide whether to take a lump sum and go, or hang on and take a chance. All but one went. Those over fifty got an early pension, suitably reduced. The retiring age had dropped ten years.

At the same time, it was made known by word of mouth that anyone else who wished could march up to Personnel and ask what his price was. If there was a price on your head it meant you were next on the list to go. If there was no price, a note was made of the fact that you had inquired and were probably not anxious to stay. Labour was given fourteen days to take advantage of the golden handshake; after that it was the greasy boot.

The first week ninety-seven men were paid off, operators and fitters. Those active in the combined shop negotiations went, those active in the Union, those over forty, their names recorded on an unofficial honour roll in the reactor lift cage as Killed in Action. After the golden handshake, those left didn't work any harder: they simply weren't so open about bludging. Cunning was rewarded, and youth.

The Congo Kid was ropable. He went up to Personnel, asking how much they'd pay him to go. He wasn't on the list. He went higher, he went to his Section Head, he went to the Python. The answer was no.

Congo banged the table of his Section Head. 'You are fools! This is a stupid decision! In my frame of mind I could easily put a tank over or blow up a pressure vessel!'

Now, now. Don't talk like that. The company wants you,' said the man gently. He had no discretion in the matter; the prisoners' reports had been sent to Melbourne for processing and lists of throwouts had come back.

'Why should you want me? I've had 149 sickies this year!'

'You're worth a lot to us. You're young.'

'Worth a lot? I've been stuck on the gasoline treaters four years. How can I be worth anything?'

'You have the potential the company wants.'

'I tell you I don't even do the work I'm paid for! I do nothing all shift so I'll be able to do a double shift on overtime and even then I do it on my back!'

'The company needs you.' Congo couldn't break down his defence. There was no golden handshake for the Congo Kid.

From the other side of the world came a solution to the maintenance problem. Ideally, Operations should have had its own maintenance staff, but there was a great gulf fixed between Operations and Engineering divisions, and Engineering had won all the battles they'd ever fought. The solution was staring them in the face all the time—make the operators do their own maintenance.

Management, master of the situation, announced this plan to the prisoners as part of the new industrial agreement. The operators were to get a substantial increase if they agreed to carry a kit of tools. A skeleton staff of qualified fitters would stay, more or less as instructors and to do the jobs their five-year apprenticeship qualified them for. The operating prisoners would do the day-to-day jobs, the foremen would decide what was too difficult or dangerous. The few remaining fitters would work alone, no longer would they have assistance to carry their tools. It was the Puroil European idea. In a few years only fitters and instrument mechanics would be taken on as operators.

The promised increase in wages was not specified. Instead, the planned amount was multiplied by four then put round as a rumour. This was, after all, the procedure used by the Union when they used to fight for an increase in the days before they got too weak, before their future was in hock to the hire-purchase companies. The days had come again when prisoners wanted to cower into corners at the approach of executives. As if the days of a thousand lashes had returned.

Half-heartedly they listened as their Union representatives reported their meetings with the company, nodded their heads in disgust as the delegates urged them to accept the company offer. When the State Secretary of the Union came out to address them, urging them to accept, one man asked, 'Why should we?'

'What else can we do?' he asked.

'We thought you might tell us,' said the man.

'I'm here to take instructions from you.' He knew they didn't know what to do, he wanted them weak.

'What about Arbitration?' asked a voice.

'No. The company states frankly it doesn't want to damage the cordial relations it has built up over the years, but it won't budge an inch. Take the money and the retrospective payments. Arbitration could leave you worse off and it might take a year to get a hearing.'

His eyes were sharp, he wanted to squash this talk. The predatory Union was still waiting to catch him in court, to claim half his members. He had to look after himself first.

They had come from the country and all over the suburbs to huddle together in the warmth of industry, and now their security was gone. Five years before, any of them could look forward to retiring at sixty: now they would be lucky to last till forty-five.

To encourage the rest, the company called up two dozen men this time for interviews for an unspecified number of foremen's jobs. The Western Salesman was jubilant. 'I'm one!' he shouted joyfully.

'Thought you were,' said Humdinger sourly. 'He looks like one, doesn't he?' No one answered. Instead several rushed off to make tea for the Salesman.

The operating manning figures settled out at fifty-five fewer than before. It was no use ringing newspapers now. Another war had started, no one wanted to know about semi-skilled labour. Dozens of young prisoners, usually straight out of the Navy, newly married and up to their necks in hire-purchase, were being taken on before the oldies left. Hire-purchase prisoners will do work a free man won't touch. Besides they had no tradition of operators never doing tradesmen's work, they were used to working with tools and used to obeying orders without thought or question. As long as there was more money to be had they were with the new proposals. The older men sounded like old women, and they told them so. It was a time of change, wasn't it? What was so good about preserving the same old conditions?

The training officer, brought in from the Navy, was outed. Puroil had no further plans for training prisoners. The company no longer wanted to pay them to keep off the streets. Let someone else bother.

In the meantime they had two weeks' grace to go up to Personnel to see if they were useless enough to get a redundancy payment or valuable enough to get nothing. After the deadline they were on their own. In various notices, signed and unsigned, the company warned them against going to Arbitration. The only reason the company didn't sack them on the spot was to keep the refinery running till the government inspection could be put off no longer. The new agreement was timed to coincide with the shutdown. If the men rejected it, the shutdown would be prolonged, and if there was a stoppage, they could stay out as long as they liked. That was the threat. Not one could last more than a week. Outside the gates men were walking the streets looking for prisons to take refuge in.

One of the men to get two letters was the Great White Father. He wouldn't go up to haggle over a lump sum.

'Let them come for me. If the Wandering bloody Jew wants to arsehole me, let him do his own dirty work. One day they'll be so efficient they'll run out of consumers to burn their silly product.'

A HEALTHY ECONOMY It was another recession year, but dividend payments were high and profits rose, though understated because of loopholes in depreciation laws. At Puroil, too, after the installation of new equipment and a stable electricity supply, profits rose: the cracker was running. Puroil's reaction was to crack down even further, to keep profit rising at a faster rate. The next figure was expected to be double the last. Extensive oil fields were discovered in Australia; the price of petrol rose.

In no way was technical change benefiting those directly concerned in the change. In the mines, manpower fell and productivity rose, but those working at the coal face were no better off. Natural-gas production rose, operating crew numbers fell; dividends increased, but the operators still chased the cost of living. Car production per worker rose, so did prices with each new model. Wages didn't. The general standard of living was rising, but rising so much faster for the élites that the poor were getting poorer. Yet on paper it was progress. There was no equality of sacrifice. Labour productivity was increasing steadily, wages were a decreasing proportion of the value of production. Manhours were falling, but there were no price reductions, no decline in the cost of living, no automatic increase in the standard of living, no automatic absorption of the unemployed into industry. Productivity growth is not the same as progress, and seems to yield worse conditions to the ever-increasing mass of humans at the bottom of the pile.

A few hundred years before, men were driven off the land into industry. Now industry was driving them out. What was the next stop? In the waterless inland there were dams unbuilt, roads unmade, yet there were oceans of water underground, enough to irrigate a hundred million acres for a century. But after the roads and dams were made and the water piped up, what then? Constant wars to sop up the surplus?

And in privileged parts of the world private speculators were threatening the currencies of great nations, reminding uneasy populations that what happened once, forty years before and could never happen again, could quite easily happen again.

One segment want profits, the rest want a wage. Is that all? Is this the whole purpose of industry? Paid prisoners, no more? Where does the community come in, or is industry the whole community? Is there no place for the feeling that each can give his share of service for the well-being of all? But there is no ideology that can induce these desirable feelings in the country's human components.

The total proceeds of the country's production are distributed unjustly, but these total proceeds are so small compared to the effort available to produce them: two causes for anger.

Large-scale industry, as time goes on being concentrated in fewer and fewer hands, can't be left to itself. The community sees its advertising everywhere but its account books nowhere, yet everything it does in the privacy the law allows affects the lifetimes of every man, woman and child in the community, all who by their consumption of its products support it.

22
ESCAPE ROUTES

HOT SPOTS The hot spots on the outside skin of the catalyst regenerator were bigger. The Samurai came in from his weekend off and demanded to know what was to be done about them.

'There'll be no decisions made today, hot spots or no hot spots,' said the Slug, and the Samurai wondered where he got his sudden strength. It was because of his own recent reluctance to take action on behalf of any of his fellows, and his tendency to keep to himself. Like a jackal, the Slug sensed this stand-off attitude as weakness and isolation; he had no means of understanding a man who could lay down his arms for a while, then take them up again when he felt like fighting. He interpreted everything he saw in terms of a man doing his utmost to his own advantage, only ever stopped by a force outside himself. The Samurai seemed to him to have been disabled by some larger power and now fair game for any sniper. He wondered later when he noticed no one else sniping at the Samurai; then, feeling that his action isolated him from the mass of men, he quickly side-stepped back into the ranks and aimed no more darts at the Samurai. The Samurai didn't trouble to argue about the hot spots.

'For the sickies they didn't pay me,' said the Samurai aloud, as he commenced to take his usual slice off production. The hot spots didn't seem to get worse. They were promptly forgotten.

ANOTHER PART OF THE FOREST In another part of the refinery, the Governor of the colony was arriving to open a new plant. Clerks wore dustcoats and directed traffic, eager middle-responsibility persons thrust their way forward to be nearest to the vice-regal car. The Governor would never know them or ever want to, but the great thing was to be seen there by Puroil people. In some mysterious way, known to all primitive people, there was virtue in being physically near the great and revered personage. Magic flowed from his body, his garments, his Rolls Royce, to the lower orders.

Eventually he was conducted to a place a little above them where he stood and spoke nonsense to office workers who knew nothing about the plant. Looking round at the attractive lawns and the native trees and shrubs, he was pleasantly impressed. The Whispering Baritone saw him look, and knew that the money spent on gardens was worth every cent. Word would get back to London from this man who, after all, had the power to dismiss State premiers and dissolve governments. Some two or three men who would operate the plant were there, insignificant beside the throng who escaped work for an hour to hear the Governor. Taking advantage of this diversion, other enterprising prisoners were at the stores like rats. Voracious, enthusiastic, undaunted rats.

The Governor described the energy tensions that create the illusion of a solid substantial company. He used words such as co-operation, team-spirit, unselfishness, harmony. He avoided words like orders, discipline, dismissal, obedience, lower costs and retrenchment.

OVERHEARD IN A LOCKER-ROOM 'Did you hear about the Python?'

'What about the mongrel of a thing?'

'Someone flattened him.'

'What with?'

'Lump of pipe. Back of the neck.'

'Is he a good Python?'

'What?'

'Is he dead?'

'No. Just knocked out. When they took him up to Calamity Jane, she found needle marks on him.'

'Needle? What sort of needle?'

'Hypo. Someone had been at him with a hypo.'

'Is he a narcotic?'

'You mean an addict?'

'Yeah. Hooked.'

'No. Someone was at him.'

'Did you get a letter?'

'No. You?'

'I got two. Don't know what I'll do now. I'm a bit old to go looking for a job.'

The Samurai listened in silence and thought of Cheddar Cheese and his lost market for blood. In his mental eye he saw Cheddar taking some of his blood back from those he gave it to, filling a stolen hypodermic with his own blood and jabbing massive doses of it into the Python while he was unconscious. He must have wanted to get even before he left. He had been invited to go up for the golden handshake. Leukemia-pity was out of fashion now; since the tobacco companies rode out the lung-cancer scare it was all heart disease and organ transplants.

CHEDDAR CHEESE Cheddar heard them, too. Pulling on week-old socks after shaking out catalyst dust. To himself, quietly and reasonably, he said, What none of you ever say is I'm dying. I read in the Puroil house journal how some joker ran round a football field four times in under four minutes and what did he get? Time off to do his Certificate then three years at Cambridge. I'm dying: that's not such a popular achievement. I suppose they reckoned I'd get time off shortly. Now they're making sure of it.

He looked at the envelope on his locker shelf. The letter lay inside it, its typed words ready again to leap out at his throat the moment he opened it.

180 DEGREES Night shift and the Twinkler down in the mouth. The Great White Father patted his head. The Twinkler had taught the Western Salesman his own job, so they gave it to the Western Salesman. What made it worse was that they'd taken SK back who knew nothing, and made him a foreman immediately. His first action was to confiscate all newspapers, even those belonging to the other foremen. Several almost told him what to do, but remembered times had changed and kept their mouths shut. He threatened to report any further breaches. SK would go far.

'Fancy them demoting a good man like you. Poor little Twinkling Star. Being good isn't enough. You have to survive and if you do it right you survive whole. You come through, at the end of your life, with a whole skin.' He laughed uncontrollably. 'That's the joke. Survive! A whole skin. Die of natural causes.' And in a quieter voice, 'Die because of death, the Great Defender who never misses a tackle.'

The Beautiful Twinkling Star said sadly, 'And death shall have no dominion.' He thought he remembered it was Isaiah. One of the prophets, anyway.

'Not bloody much it won't,' replied the Great White Father harshly. 'The whole stinking universe'—he shook a fist at the sky and the myriad galaxies not completely masked by the structures of the refinery, 'is the dominion of death.' He belted the good man between the shoulder blades. 'That's why we laugh at the whole shebang! And give it the sign!'

He gave the sign with all fingers, viciously, to every part of the night sky.

'This life is nothing,' said the Star. 'It's a trial for the life to come.'

'I believe it! For Oblivion!' he shouted. But there was a look of sneering about him. 'It was a rotten joke for your Bloke to pull. We should never have been put here,' he snapped angrily, with fierce and unshakeable conviction.

'God is love,' said the Beautiful Twinkling Star softly, with calm and unshakeable conviction.

FUNKHOLES The Brown Snake was supposed by the prisoners to be about to be liquidated by the young graduate Industrial Officer he was showing around. That was the usual pattern; you prepared the rope, constructed the scaffold and placed the noose round your own neck so the hangman's work was easy. Only the lever remained to be pulled and you couldn't do that with your hands tied.

But he slipped away into a safe hole. The Puroil Sales company, a separate entity, had made room for him for the three years he had to go till retirement. He wasn't even faced with the usual reduction in salary which would have forced down his pension rate. He knew a few secrets. Pixie wasn't so lucky. He was dispatched, trembling, to a re-training centre in Victoria. Oliver Twist, lacking a powerful patron, started to worry. He was forty: the company would be looking for reasons to let him go free.

The Garfish, who laid the ground-work for the no-stoppage clause and the pool of operators and had written the stand-down clause into the award, was robbed of the Industrial Relations job. The young graduate walked straight into it. The Garfish shook his hand, smiled, and promised every assistance. Like hell. He regarded the job as his own funkhole. He'd keep trying for it, even if it meant letting things go sour for Puroil so the new boy would get the chop.

They called him Crack Hardy. They meant you might as well crack hardy as put in a sickie. It was a common gambit: you start off hard and ruthless and when you finally smile or become generous you get more credit for it than the man who is sunny all the time. He picked it up in psychology lectures.

THE KILLER Why didn't they take their action openly? Revolt, strike, direct action. But it was the money, the time-payment instalments, the mortgage on the house. On the sly, you could get your own back and still get your money. And it was their friends. You couldn't team up with your friends: they would run and tell the boss.

Sabotage hurt them both; it hurt the company and it hurt the men. But that self-inflicted hurt was better than getting no money. Strikes meant you lost the lot, and there were bills; the baker, milk, groceries. You had to eat every day. They had thrown away their right to refuse work with every gadget they bought on time payment.

Usually, they would do their little sly sabotages one at a time. It would be like ordinary things going wrong and there was plenty of it; the company cared no more for the equipment than the men. Carelessness, it looked like. But what if men happened to do all their nasty little acts at the same time? There wouldn't be enough men to go round to keep the lid on.

And the last-minute addition to the previous Agreement just before it went to be printed—the clause agreeing never to leave the plants unmanned; sufficient men to keep them running; that was the killer. It looked so reasonable when you read it. But it meant the men were powerless. If you couldn't threaten strike, you couldn't get your case heard right away—you might wait years to get the thing heard before a court. The meaning of it was starting to seep into the minds of the men.

MUCK REPLACES ETERNITY 'Who is it keeps writing DNR everywhere?' asked the Ant. Someone was getting at the men's overalls stencilling the sinister letters on their chests, on their white safety helmets, on their time cards. He watched the lined, smiling face of the Great White Father and tried to hide the admiration he felt. It was hard to imagine he was marked down to go. If he didn't take the lump sum in the fortnight, they would sack him for nothing. Funny how people twelve thousand miles away had so much say.

'It used to be ETERNITY, then it was MUCK. Maybe it's the same joker but he's lost his faith,' said the Ant.

'Could be the same. Maybe he's working out details now—a new do-it-yourself religion. All the way from ETERNITY to MUCK to DO NOT RESUSCITATE.'

Far Away Places, writer of the word MUCK, stenciller of DNR, was standing on the topmost point of the cracker, looking west.

'The sunlight loves me,' he said to himself, feeling its blessing on his face. His cough wasn't so bad now. At home he often thought his favourite apple-tree must feel like this in the sun. Cared for. Warm. Loved.

He played sweetly on his piece of trumpet, imagining that the tunes he made floated out over the huddled, cowed houses and broke gently in pieces, falling in blessing on each one. Like the sun. He looked with profound distaste at the columns and plants beneath him. The whole enterprise *was* muck. Not absolutely necessary to life. And the humans. What was the use of them all?

FOR SALE 'The Colonel's in the news.'

'The slob in the pay office?'

'Yes—the male whore-house man.'

'Did he do in the Whispering Baritone?'

'No. He's a sculptor.'

'A what?'

'What are they when they're at home?'

'Chisellers. You know, big bronzes—'

'And a big bronze to you.'

'Up on pedestals. Only he's a welder. You know, bits of this and that and give it a name.'

'Has he got his welding ticket?'

'No. That's for welding pipes and joints and patio rails. This man's an artist, you don't need tickets to be an artist.'

'You mean bits of half-inch plate, a bike chain and welding droppings? That sort of thing?'

'That's it. He's won a competition. Thousand dollars. For a hundredweight of welding scrap.'

'What name did he give it?'

'Unknown Industrial Prisoner. Says here it's symbolic of the intense pressures on modern industrial man and the sense of compression and isolation in a confined space.'

'Why do they think so much of bits and pieces? They can come here any day of the week and give sculpture prizes to everything in the place—scrap or construction. What's so special?'

'They never see any of this. This is all strange to them. They live in another world. They'd run round like mad picking up scrap all day if they came here. They see all sorts of things in lumps of metal and rods and steel points nearly touching. The feel of steel gets 'em, too, I think. And how heavy it is. All that. The colour.'

'Christ.'

'There's tons of it here.'

'Where do they live if they never see lumps of steel?'

'They only go where it's civilized.'

'Whaddya mean? The whole guts of their civilization's built on lumps of steel. This is where it all starts!'

'They only see the big buildings and the finished job. Big offices, nice cafés, art galleries, everything nice for 'em.'

'But we're only a few miles away. Why can't they come and have a look at as much steel as they want, then they won't think there's anything special in it.'

'I keep telling you—they're in another world!'

'But a few miles...'

'Might as well be another planet.'

'They don't want to see this end of the works.'

'That's their trouble, all right.'

'Why should they? The Colonel gets a grand out of making a statue of us. We're the industrial prisoners.'

'Puroil might give him a scholarship or time off or something.'

'No chance. They only help athletes. Good, clean amateur sport. Got to watch their image.'

'It says here they're going to put it in an art gallery.'

'Good. The Colonel can go and stand alongside it. Some rich bastard might buy both.'

THE MOMENTUM OF SMALL BODIES At the Home Beautiful the Great White Father walked outside, stooped right down and put his ear to the ground. The Angry Ant looked puzzled.

'What are you listening for?'

'Ants.' He listened for a while. 'Your friends the ants. I can hear ants down there running about. Feet crunching. Hordes of 'em. Potential warriors.'

'You touched in the head?'

'They may be our future enemies. Don't laugh at 'em. A stray mutation. Anything might happen. They're the sort of thing our bosses are trying to make out of us. You ever watched ants?' He didn't wait for an answer.

'You watch 'em. They're just like us. For every two ants working, there's two hundred running round in circles. You watch 'em. There's plenty of activity all right, but they go nowhere. Up this way, rub noses with someone they know, then back here, round in a circle and talk to someone else, then back again and so on and so forth, just like shinies walking round with bits of paper in their hands.' He straightened up and stretched his long body. 'I've just thought of it. The way to put right the present imbalance of the forces of nature.'

'What?' said the Ant. It was hopeless trying to keep up.

'What?' said the Sorcerer's Apprentice, who had just come out of the bed hut, leaving her guest behind.

'I know how to fix the world,' he raved. 'Get the whole three thousand odd million to line up at the same time all over the world and at the signal run fifty yards west. All together. Think of the momentum the world will gain!—from the weight of all our bodies going west. Over 130 million tons of flesh and bone rocking a 6000-trillion-ton planet!'

BELOW SPECIFICATIONS He, too, had a private life. Who was he? Who were these unfortunates he had tried to help for so many years? They had to be told again and again they were men and life was living today, not saving for tomorrow. If he could make their present misery easier. But day in, day out, they were seized, cut up into units, incorporated into the bodies of the predators feeding on them, digested, then at last discarded as excreta.

What would become of them when the last of the great sprawling refineries was automated as they were at that moment in America and other parts of the world, and the gates closed on the unskilled workers, the men not so blessed with the will to survive, not so bountifully provided by their Maker with memory, intelligence, powers of expression and concentration? Where would they go? He was not so stupid as to assume that education could lift all men up to survival standard: the general level of intelligence was falling. These men and their mental and spiritual descendants would still be at the bottom of the pyramid. And if their composition was below the standard required to exist and be usable by the state, they were still men. They had families and they had children; some of the children would be unskilled workers and a few might climb higher in social esteem and earning rate, as the Good Shepherd climbed higher. But fewer and fewer. If they were born poor, they would probably stay poor in this lucky country.

How ugly their lives were, but they were men. It was easy to think of them as expendable items in a company's cost structure, yet they were men.

Why was life so terrible to them? Life was magnificent! All because of the tiny spark that provided the difference between men and the other animals, by which men invent the contents of the cans stacked high in the drink hut and by which they shout defiance at death while they have an arm round the old grey fellow and mock the sharpness of his blade.

He slowly swallowed several pints, enjoying every drop, savouring the gassy sharpness on the sides of his tongue. He himself was not so far from the closer hug of that grey old chap. He thought of death as a vast sea lapping the shores of the world, larger than the land and largely unregarded by the teeming life on the land.

He was alone for some time that day and sank into a mood of quiet self-pity. Waiting for the axe to fall. To think a little bastard like the Wandering Jew could pass on commands from the other side of the world and kick him out.

And once, after many waves of amber had passed over him, he stood in the door of the hut and called out aloud to all of them: 'You are my children—the extensions of my nerves, my arms, heart, brain, and all my awareness—through you I feel the world. Don't change—be your own selves.' But in the quiet of himself he knew they hated each other, competing for the available jobs and the overtime. The company hated having to employ them, but was itself composed of individuals split into stockaded departments which thought of themselves first and the rest second. Neither men nor masters thought of the community, and why would they? At any moment they or the community might dissolve in economic or military disaster. They had no morale or ideology to live by beyond personal survival. Was this all their civilization amounted to? Was this why they desperately ransacked past cultures—trying to find something they'd forgotten? Something to live by.

Afternoon drifted into the mangroves like a gas.

GORDIAN KNOT (INTERNAL) The Samurai was thinking moodily to himself. The boobs higher up had offered him a foreman's job. He was to go up for an interview in a week's time. He would be on holidays, but there was no point in telling them. The word had spread among the prisoners and instead of finding men ready to oppose him because of his possible defection to the white-shirted enemy, they were lying down in the dust before him and the other prospects like mongrel dogs. He could accept this job, carry on for a month or two, then with the benefit of his new status get a job with the refineries that were rumoured to be putting up their equipment new and not trying to economize by cutting corners on standby plant and less instrumentation. But were they different? This was Australia and now; the country was being developed by foreigners, the natives were no different.

Or he could leave the whole thing, leave the crowded city and go. Where? There was nowhere to go. Only copies of Puroil.

Into the control room came the Wandering Jew and several understrappers escorting an extremely tall, white-haired, magnificently suited gentleman. From house journals the Samurai recognized the Australian chairman of directors. The party stopped near some reactor instruments and explanations were eagerly offered by the lowest-ranking engineer. When the Samurai got near them the talk got mysteriously quieter. It stopped.

'Did I hear you say the reactor feed system was OK?' he asked.

They ignored him and went to walk on. He barred the way with his body. Flesh and blood opposed the might of money.

'Your hot and cold feed system is entirely at the mercy of the foremen in another section, and until you get gasoline coolers that'll work in a warm climate instead of only in Europe, it doesn't matter what your feed system is. Through-put is being kept down by a cooling system that's only suited to a cold climate and it's been that way for five years.'

He was facing the inhumanly elegant chairman and looked into his eyes. The black pupils of the colourless eyes looked down on him, but instead of seeing a tiny reflection of his own face he saw a moving line of hooks from which hung live sheep travelling towards a slaughterman who slit each throat. So this was an abattoirs. A sheep confronted the chairman of the abbatoirs. What was the point of talking about refining processes? This man didn't want to know. If the cost figure was too big he'd sacrifice a few sheep to propitiate the seven foreign gods. The eyes looked away and over his head, searching for other eyes on a level similar to their own.

Why should this make a difference to the Samurai and to his hate for the company? Did he hate the company? Of course, why otherwise would he be still holding down the gasoline make? But was it the company he hated? Was it only a personal grudge?

Was it the fact that he had only prison to look forward to? Or was it the collective stupidity that still made a mess of what could have been an even smoother production process? Without answering his questions, he solved the problem of what attitude to take.

He walked outside and pinched in an air line, a slim copper line encased with a dozen others in a metal track, through which air signals travelled to control points. It was so simple to pinch one of them flat with a valve key.

WE ARE NOT AMUSED The Great White Father walked into the cracker control room and hailed the Samurai, but the Sumpsucker, seeing a third person, tackled the Samurai boldly about the notebook he'd just slipped into his pocket. Besides, the Samurai might soon be a foreman and a competitor; he could afford to be on his hammer.

'What's on all those notes you write?'

The Samurai looked into his eyes and through them to the landscape in the Sumpsucker's head, a country teeming with breasts and buttocks, armpits and pubic hair of all colours and the word *Yes* endlessly repeated, with here and there a Puroil advertising poster for dignity—and announced, 'A book, Sumpy. I'm writing a book on the company. You're in it. We're all in it.' If he could tell what he had seen.

'They won't like that. You better be careful. You can't do what you like with the company.' The words spewed out in a babble. They laughed at them, but Sumpy saw nothing to laugh at.

'I wonder what your slant is,' said the Great White Father. 'You're not against this'—he waved an arm round at the evidences of progress—'this rubbish. You're for it. You try to get it to work better. You're a company man.'

'I'm an industrial man. And yes, I want the filthy place to work. I want the whole army of industry to work.'

'There you are, then. You're one of them. Production is your god.'

'You, too. You help them.'

'How?'

'Taking the mob's attention from grievances—making them forget. Oblivion. Stupor.'

'A side effect. My way is like religion, which offers Eternal Life and gets its followers to train for it now. I offer Eternal Oblivion and my followers can *have* it now.'

The Great White Father announced to his disciples a further refinement to the comforts of the Home Beautiful. The Humdinger had once been a Navy cook in real life but he had also been a telephone technician for three years. He swiped a phone and ran hundreds of yards of wire down to the drink hut.

'We are in communication with reality,' said the leader. 'You lift and dial and the world will say hello.'

23
MAKING LIFE BEARABLE

DAYMARE The Samurai on his way home with holiday pay in his pocket pictured Blue Hills' wife in his room stabbing darts into his photograph—the pathetic black and white snapshot unframed on a landlord's mantelpiece—and tearing his clothes to shreds. These mental pictures seemed to reach down into him and stir something hot and violent, as violent as his hatred of the inanimate thing that employed him.

When he got to his room she was there. But not torturing his picture or damaging his clothes.

THE LEOPARD 'Why?' It was hardly a question, more an accusation. 'Why don't you want to see me?' And the inevitable, 'Don't you love me?'

Unwillingly he dragged out words and held them up before his face like shields.

'Sure I liked you. When you were someone else's wife. Now he's gone. I'd be more satisfied if I'd killed him, but he went of his own accord. He's gone; you'll never belong to me, you were his bedmate too long.'

'You don't understand,' she said in a low voice, and when he made no answer, 'I don't understand you.'

'I'm not interested in whether you understand,' he said as calmly and savagely as he could. 'I was only interested in you when I was taking you from someone. I don't want anyone for nothing. I can't get a kick out of it.' He was pleased, he had put it more brutally than he thought possible.

He felt a warm sense of power as she quietly cried. Her soft body, even now hinting future flabbiness, was bowed under a great weight. Power was his, he felt it through every limb. This was the way to become one with the gods—assuming the power to destroy.

No one provokes me with impunity, he repeated to himself. The words had a slightly hollow ring, but not enough to make him pull them back. And the worst thing was he felt she was taking no notice of what he was saying, merely assuming he was using words as she would have used them if she wanted to hurt him. She did not take the words, examine their literal meaning and take it that that was what he meant. To her, words meant nothing; they were merely signals, or sticks to hit with and show anger.

'I won't go away. I love you and you'll have to put up with me,' she wailed in her best accents, making a successful attempt to look dainty. There was a little of steel in her voice, though.

'Aren't you afraid I'll kill you?'

'You don't understand. If you don't want me I'd rather you killed me. If you murdered me it wouldn't be like murder. I could die with your hands round my throat. And if you shoot me, stand up close and let me look in your eyes as you do it.'

'Don't be stupid. You enjoy the idea.'

'It will show that you care if you can't bear to let me live.' She knew he didn't understand.

Words. Killing her would only be necessary if she didn't go away when he wanted her to and take her place in his past. Not forgotten, but in a spare room in his mind, to be looked at and remembered when he felt like it. Oh yes, he had himself under control.

'Doesn't it mean anything? I love you, I love you!' Now she was using love as a club, beating him over the head. 'I love you, I love you!' Trying to bludgeon him to his knees. He should have shut her up with kisses, stopped her mouth with something. Instead, he answered her.

'I'm not looking for people to love me! I'm looking for people I can love! I want to lose myself in a great cloud of love, not wait like a woman while others grovel to me.' He had caught her disease of words, elevating a little sexual pleasure into a philosophy and a way of life.

'When you were in me you said you loved me. It was a lie,' she said bitterly in a low voice, hoping to get a foot in the door by changing her tactics.

'I told you the truth, but not all the truth. This is the rest of the truth—leaving you behind. It's finished.' But it was useless to make a wall with words to hold back her tide. She plunged right on as if his words had no substance, right through them.

Finally he got away from her. Once outside, he remembered it was his room he'd left.

A REVOLTING IMAGE He drove about in his car for an hour, hoping she'd be gone when he returned. As he headed for home, he passed Puroil a few hundred yards away. He stopped the car and looked at the scattered piles of steel that were coherent plants with flow schemes and feed-rates and product lines; men were moving about on the ground and on the structures. They were tiny from this distance and moved slowly, laboriously. Aphids perhaps? Insects living on the money plant and being milked by stronger insects?

No. Maggots. Maggot men moving in the body of the company.

FUNGOID GROWTHS He drove on further, stopped and looked again at the refinery structures. This time the men were invisible. He held his hand up and the whole complex refinery was hidden by his little finger. A microscope—or rather a telescope—could have made the men visible; but now it wasn't only that the men impressed him as maggots, but the plants themselves—the mass of silver tanks and tangled columns and vessels and tanks again—were great lumps of grey and silver fungus sprouting from the earth. How small they must be from Alpha Centauri.

He turned his eyes westward to the hills, the Blue Mountains. Tree-covered. Fungus of a different and more ancient type, but more deeply implanted in his blood than the steel he saw to the east.

If only he had—owned, clutched to his breast—part of this ancient land. For his own. Possessions were illusory, death was always near, but if he could have a share in this land. Not for eternity, just for life. But no. Possessions were not him. He dismissed ownership.

A DANGEROUS MAN And what of the men born to be dwarfed by this steel that mushroomed overnight and compelled them to attend it until it was strong and capable and clever enough to do without them? What had he given them? A wire toastrack he formed with his own hands. That was all. What would become of them?

They could not chalk up to their credit their part in the enormous quantities of gasoline made on the plant: no one could. The oil was simply lying underground, waiting to be taken, changed, used, burned. Once the refining plant was assembled, the rest could just as easily be supervised by machines. The plant itself made the gasoline; humans were plant accessories.

And yet, when he was dispensed with, and others like him, how was society to cope? They must be kept off the streets. He had never been on a bread line and did not know despair. No residual shackle scars itched his ankles. And precisely this sort of man was most dangerous: more likely to take violent action over a few petty inconveniences, a few slights. Men had been beaten to their knees before without effective retaliation, but they had been men to whom this servile position was familiar: men like the Samurai and a whole generation after him would be fighting guerrilla warfare in the streets long before they considered sinking to their knees.

POLICY SPEECHES Something had to be done to wake them out of this torpor. Through whom could it be done? Not through the toilers: they were a pitiful lot. They needed the pain and discipline of control, they invited control of their lives down to the smallest detail. By themselves they were capable of nothing. No leader in the world could get them together.

Only through those who moved the world would unity come to the prisoners. A new wave of oppression would bottle up the working people—their ranks growing as more and more felt the lash of privation and realized they were what they were: chattels at the disposal of others—and the resultant pressure under this repressive lid would blow the pot sky-high. With new nations growing strong around her, Australia was dreaming off to death. Repression, poverty, even terror: that was the recipe.

The whole kettle would blow up. These somnolent chattels would be forced to become political beings. They would begin to be alive—in hate, it is true—but alive nevertheless.

This internal pressure and hate would strengthen the country's arms. It would begin to save itself, as a drowner makes superhuman efforts, hitting out at anything in his way.

The Great White Father was alone. It was two o'clock. The last of the day shift had gone over the river to report back in time to shower, dress and go. The three o'clock starters had not yet come. For once there were no out-of-hours visitors. The sixty-dollar cat stepped delicately in from the mangroves.

He spoke to the cat. 'There's others more wretched than us, cat. When you look around and see 'em all, you allow yourself to feel well off. But we're not well off. We're still prisoners, our life's vile, not one day of our sentence has been commuted, no matter how many golden handshakes.'

The cat walked carefully over to him. He sat on the step of the drink hut and scratched the cat's chin. He got up and fetched beer, laying out a saucerful for the animal.

'Wet your whistle, cat,' he advised. 'The great thing is to try to make life bearable. That's all the Home Beautiful's for—to make the day bearable for my brothers. Such a motley crew we are, cat, but brothers. Our samenesses are more important than our differences. In spite of what the Samurai thinks, it's better to have a drink with a man than to found new civilizations on his corpse. I can't see men as coral polyps, dying in order to build the edifice a little higher with their bones. There is no common good that ought to deprive one single man of life.

'I'm a heathen, cat.' The cat cocked an ear, but did not look up from his pilsner. His tail bent over, nearly touching the ground, moving from side to side. The tip was bent upwards and waved a separate wave. 'I'd just let poverty and disease and injustice go—they'll always be with us. I wouldn't try to alter a thing: all systems woe. A few beers, a soft bunk, away from guards and bosses where a man is only a man. Breathing, sleeping, living. Meat, beer and women.'

The cat licked the saucer out and turned his affection back on, rubbing against the Great White Father and making cat noises. In the distance the roar of bulldozers flattening the mangroves, this time on the Home Beautiful side of the river.

AN ACT OF VANDALISM On night shift, Saturday into Sunday morning, Cheddar Cheese entered the Termitary block and starting from the top floor and working on his knees or in a crouch so he couldn't be seen above sill level, and using a screwdriver, he jemmied open the metal filing cabinets in every office. He worked in the pulsing light of the refinery flare.

With great patience he transferred part of each set of files to every other office, in an elaborate criss-cross pattern so that no cabinet held the files it should, but all held some of each. He didn't even read them. He started to halve the contents of the individual filing folders and mix them up with one another but only got through a third of the offices with this refinement of his method. He decided to rip out telephones.

He took four hours on this job and got back to his plant at five. He felt no elation. Nothing made him happy, not any more.

At seven on the way out, the wind was so fierce it filled his mouth, he had to turn his head to breathe. He looked at the Termitary grimly and made a filthy sign at it with his right hand; in his dilly-bag, hidden in a pair of dirty socks, was a brand-new wrench some other thief had concealed under a pallet handy to the locker-room. In one shift he had slammed the company that gave four years to a man who ran a mile in four minutes and nothing but a golden handshake letter to a man dying of bad blood. And he had made a small profit. It was the best day he'd had since he got even with the Python.

Man is a fighter, a destroyer, a savage beast; more vengeful and cowardly, more ferocious and ruthless than the great cats. Cheddar felt more of a man that day.

24
SABOTEURS

RECKLESS WEATHER It was Sunday, the sky blue and no clouds: harshly brilliant weather. A keen gritty wind whipped through the streets, raking away leaves and pedestrians. Sunday drivers responded to the bright day with speed and to the fierce, dry wind with feverish irritation and inflammable tempers. They swerved towards dogs and pedestrians to make sure the road was clear for them and overtook with the recklessness of anger. The erratic Experimenter in the sky had concocted a skull-penetrating wind that blew in its message of immediate hate and selfishness-on-sight and was laughing nastily down on the mess.

The Great White Father had glued the Wandering Jew's letter to a board in the drink hut and was carousing in splendid loneliness, raising can after can to toast the golden handshake invitation, while the wind blew overhead. Several customers and drinkers had called in, but the Home Beautiful was peculiarly empty this weekend. Sunday pleasure or freedom for the Monday-to-Friday millions: work as usual for the shift-working thousands. That vicious wind swept sand, dust, soot, men—all before it. On refinery plots corrugated-iron sheets on shelter sheds and field lavatories clanged and rumbled, flapping like paper. Over flat refinery acres the wind rushed, blowing through scattered plants and mazes of lines, hurrying in fear. Its pursuer never came in sight.

Steam plumes, gas leaks swept straight north; flames were torn at right angles from the mouths of the flares. Under this assault men tried to keep their lives at their usual low-tension level of monotony.

A POOR ATTITUDE TO AUTHORITY The Congo Kid was due to go off at three. Monday and Tuesday were his weekend. It was time he did something about getting revenge on this company and these stupid Australians. On the polymer plant he opened the gas drain from the butane accumulator. There were so many leaks, another little plume of gas wouldn't be noticed. On the alkylation plant he opened the hydrofluoric-acid drain from the spent acid vessel and as a final touch cracked open the hydrogen-sulphide valve draining the line into the sulphur plant. That would keep the bastards busy; they couldn't get near one for the others. He walked quickly away holding his breath so the hydrogen-sulphide couldn't get him. Everyone had access to all plants. Even contractors walking from one job to another trudged unsupervised past the most dangerous processes. They didn't know what the different-coloured paint denoted.

No Australian bastards would ever correct him again. No sir. The wind took the gas, the acid vapour and the H2S away from the control hut. A pity. Never mind, the wind might change later. Some of the gas was heavy, and condensed in the atmosphere to liquid, finding its way to the drains.

A SMALL PROFIT Captain Bligh, keen for Puroil's sake, sent all the hopeful overtime seekers home except the Gypsy Fiddler, who got a double shift watching the gas tank level. In three years the level instruments had not been fixed or replaced. For half that time a man had been kept back on overtime every shift, three shifts a day, seven days a week. Local management couldn't authorize the expenditure necessary to put in new instruments; it was easier to blame the workforce for absenteeism when the overtime figure was questioned. There were reams of cost breakdowns up in the top office but what they proved was anyone's guess. There was no breakdown of individual amounts. The subterfuges, inaccuracy and cover-ups at the point of origin of the figures made nonsense of accountants' conclusions.

The Donk had applied for a day job. Shift hours were getting his wife down. She'd rather have him out of the way in the daytime and home minding the house at night. It was so bad after eighteen years that either he got a day job or he'd have to leave.

No day jobs, they told him. Was there a price on his head? Could he get the handshake? No. He had to resign. On this fine raw Sunday, since he didn't get an overtime shift at double time he missed the bus on purpose to be late up at the gate and get sixteen minutes' overtime. You didn't get paid for the first fifteen minutes until you'd done sixteen. On the way up, going through his own section—the usual short cut—he carelessly whacked a piece of pipe against a concrete pier.

In doing this, he flattened the low-pressure tapping line to a pressure differential controlling valve on the alkylation end of the slurry loop. The valve opened wide to try to bring down the resulting high differential recorded in the differential pressure cell. Since the return flow to the fractionator was much greater, the side flow to the alkylation heat-exchangers was starved. If no action was taken, these coolers would plug completely in half an hour. Unplugging them required the plant shut down.

Donk carried on, walking as slowly as he could. He might stretch it to twenty minutes. At double time, that would be eighty-five cents.

He, too, made a profit that day. And in his bag he had the foam-rubber mattress on which he'd slept so many overtime hours away. He wouldn't see another night shift.

AN UNREASONABLE LITTLE FELLOW Dadda was back in town. He chose this Sunday as a nice time to get even with the company that put the police on to him.

True, they were obliged to tell the police where he was, but way back in his mind there was a little unreasonable fellow insisting they ought to protect their own. In his work for them he had saved far more money than his wages cost them. Other little men in his head more reasonably insisted that the company owed no loyalty to anyone, but the first little fellow took no notice of what was reasonable. They didn't have to back up the lousy coppers, he grumbled, forgetting that the coppers were in existence to back up Puroil.

There were too many people coming and going through the blue gates at three o'clock for the guards to know who was who: he walked straight down to the oil interceptors, lifted out the skimmer plates and threw them in the main interceptor. He felt a twinge in his left arm when he picked up the plates: just another souvenir of Puroil. He got back to the gate and clocked out the first card he picked up so the guards would hear the bundy clock bash and not be suspicious; by that time oil was spread down Eel River about a quarter-mile.

He didn't have to wait. He knew what would happen.

They need someone to teach 'em, he said to the little unreasonable fellow in his brain. To teach 'em they ought to treat us like we were all one lot of people together. It's a pity more of us didn't slam 'em when we got a raw deal. He rubbed the slight bump on his left forearm where the broken radius had set out of line.

DRUNK AND INCAPABLE Loosehead had been to the Ex-Servicemen's club before coming to work and his way of working off the beer was to go looking for something to do. He didn't want this work to be picked out for him by the Slug or Captain Bligh: he wanted to choose it himself.

Something troubled him. Had the feed nozzles up into the reactor bed been tightened or left undone? He climbed up inside the reactor skirt and belted all the nozzles with a four-foot length of two-inch pipe, trying to sing at the same time. The singing, however, came out broken at the joints, like cries from a zoo. He couldn't hear it for the roaring of the process.

He loosened the joints of the flanges that clamped the flow

orifice plates in position, but didn't know this. He intended to tighten them—he was given the job to do a week before, and dodged it.

The fierce heat which dried the sweat on his skin as soon as it formed helped him get some of his wits about him, but only enough to make him realize he was drunk. When he was tired of hitting, he sat down on an upturned four-gallon drum, waiting for the heat to dry him out.

VERY PRIVATE ENTERPRISE When plants were shut down, process lines were blocked off with round flat discs of steel called spades or blinds. These were inserted between flanges and bolted into position so nothing could pass along the isolated pipelines. They were left on platforms near the flanges where they were used. There was no regular check of them, naturally.

On this day of days, the Thieving Magpie was congratulating himself that four days' work was finished and every last spade had been taken where it would be some use. He wasn't able to move those of the largest kind: the forty-eight-inch stainless steel blinds needed block and tackle, and he'd taken all portable block and tackle. He got away with sixteen hundred-weight of mild steel in those four days from Wednesday to Saturday. That was on the credit side. Debit to his account the slight damage done to his car springs with an extra four hundred pounds in the car each day and the extra gasoline and still he came out with a large profit. And the beauty of the thing was he had no capital outlay. He fingered the silver cross on the chain round his neck, brought it out and kissed it for luck.

ETERNAL FIRE There was a place in the petriment lining inside the regenerator where Slackie had once bashed and bashed with twenty pounds of mild steel bar three feet long. The lining had come away from the metal skin months ago, then later cracked and the fire in the regenerator got behind the lining. It was daytime and the hot-spot could not be seen glowing, but the metal was raised slightly in the beginnings of a bubble. Beyond that skin of steel was a world of whirling fire that the company wished was eternal.

THE VICE OF MEMORY The Kraut, down on holiday from Brisbane, picked this weekend to visit Clearwater. He was only ten in April '45 and four years too young to die as a German soldier, though not too young to die as a civilian in the famous thousand-bomber raids then in vogue. When he crept round the Puroil fence it was almost like being on a mission through enemy lines, a situation made familiar in countless movies. It was broad daylight when he untwisted the wire stays the Thieving Magpie had left in the cyclone fence. The original wire was ten-gauge and too stiff for fingers: the Magpie had replaced it with sixteen-gauge, nice and easy to bend.

He lifted the bottom corner of the wire panel and crawled over the narrow roadway to the export valve controlling steam sales to all the factories round about. It was a green valve—air failure to shut—so he bled the air off the diaphragm and left the bleed open. The valve shut obediently. He crawled back, fixed the wire and crept up the roadside drain to his little rented car.

Swearing commenced immediately among the Sunday staffs of the surrounding factories. At Puroil, someone saw the rise in steam pressure and cut firing a fraction. The drop in steam sales was recorded only out in the pipe-track near the valve shut by the Kraut, so no one in the refinery would know until a customer rang up complaining, or till a reading was taken from the recorder at the end of shift.

'If I can't get the money out of them, at least I'll cost them some,' he commented as he drove away. He would like to have seen fire and smoke and heard deafening explosions. Only disasters could match the loss of the shift-penalty proportion in his severance pay.

GOOD INTENTIONS The Loch Ness Monster wanted to be helpful. He envied the men who could walk about and fix things, knowing what they were doing. This big valve, now. What a screamer! He read the inscription on the plastic strip: High Pressure Steam Let Down to Medium Pressure. Wonder what that means. He'd only been on the plant twelve months.

Just look at that vibration. A sort of collar, vibrating on that stem there. He walked a few paces and came back with a brand-new aluminium ladder, propped it against the huge valve and spun the vibrating collar down hard to the bottom of its travel.

He went away happy. He would go and make tea for the Aussie lads, just for the pleasure of announcing: 'Tea up!' It always amused them. Now and then there came into his mind the horrible moment when he had been sent up top to put one side of the new regenerator pressure control slide valves on handwheel control and he had shut off the air to both sides. The valve slammed shut, the pressure nearly blew the top off the vessel and everyone screamed at him. That was the worst—the other lads yelling. He never let this thought stay long. You can't afford to dwell on the unpleasant things of life.

The collar he'd spun down on the high-pressure steam letdown valve shouldn't have been loose, but equally it shouldn't have been spun down. It was now acting as a maximum stop, the valve couldn't open further.

A RESCUE The Maltese Falcon had cleaned that ladder. He watched now from behind a stanchion as the Monster left it by the high-pressure steam valve. As soon as the boy disappeared he rescued the ladder and hurried with it over to the trench inside the fence. He had to paint his two rented houses later and his garage with the three Hungarian boys in it: it would be very handy. And it was such a good price.

He smiled at that. The way things were left about. All he had to do was come by at eleven, after knock-off. Afternoon shift was always best: you had darkness for cover. Day and night shift ended in daylight and that was no good at all.

COMING TO THE BOIL Despite an increase in circulation partly due to the Donk, and despite a rising level, the slurry oil at the bottom of the fractionator was too hot, so the Count was told to go out and shut a bypass round the coolers to force more oil through the coolers and bring it back cooler to the column. Out he went when his cigarette was finished and shut the valve to the coolers.

By this mistake he allowed the coolers to plug, which they

did very quickly, for the water entering the coolers, expecting to be converted to steam, was disappointed and stayed cool, causing the waxy slurry to set in the tubes. Since this instruction was given towards the end of dayshift and no one bothered to check the temperature of the outgoing uncooled slurry the temperature rose past the allowable 105 Centigrade to 150, rapidly to 200, then gradually to 280, 300, running down to a storage tank whose contents were perhaps 70 Centigrade, and which was supposed to contain no water.

Unfortunately, when the tank-farm men reported no water, they meant that no matter how they drained the tank they could not get the water out. This was not quite the same thing. But pumping and tank-farm boys were different sections of Operations and kept their secrets.

The danger was that the hot oil would make steam from the water and blow the top off the tank, and that the oil would flash when exposed to air.

THE VICE OF OBEDIENCE Ambrose was thinking. His wife, on her twenty-first birthday, had made him a present of a confession. She had been his friend's girl for three years, and married Ambrose when he gave her the heave-ho. So it was true what the men said, his mate had trodden the arse off her for three years. How did they know? Could they tell from his face? It was a mystery. He was worried.

'Phone for Ambrose.'

'Ambrose!'

'Where's the poor silly bastard gone?'

'Here I am.'

This phone was one of several on the interphone circuit, but also with an outside number, so it could be rung from outside without going through the switchboard. The Spotted Trout on the other end said, 'This is the Python. I want you to shut off steam to the ethylene plant. This is an emergency. Right away.'

Ambrose said nothing, waiting to see if the Python had finished with him.

'Do you know where the valve is? Out in the pipetrack at the south battery limit. Right away!'

The Trout hung up his phone at the Servicemen's Club and went back to his whisky. Curse the company! The PR job would have suited him till he retired. Now he would be selling wine and spirits or machine parts again. Each ethylene plant crash cost Puroil several thousand dollars and worsening relations with the polythene manufacturers on the other end of the product line.

But what about the cracker? He had been so hasty he had overlooked the obvious plant to attack. Tomorrow, that was the ticket. One call a day. He enjoyed his whisky. He felt bigger, more of a man than he had felt for years now he was hitting back. He'd taken it for too long. Just a matter of picking a different nong each time. There were plenty.

Ambrose trotted happily out, saying nothing to the others. They rubbished him every chance they got, why should he always go back for more? He forgot his safety hat, of course, and came back for it, but he got to the steam valve and shut it. It was stiff, and when he finished and stood up, he saw the ethylene flare shoot up flames a hundred feet high burning to black smoke the jettisoned ethylene from the crashed plant. He didn't know that, he was trying to think what he should do about his wife. Perhaps he should keep quiet, not worry her. Women had a lot to suffer. Everyone said so.

ONE THING AT A TIME The Corpse made a habit of whipping tank valves shut at the product tanks and opening them again, denying that he'd touched anything; hoping to cause a steady number of untraceable troubles. Today he performed his few little shut-offs against the cracker, back-pressuring the final gasoline-treating section, not causing much trouble. Getting back from day work to shift hours with its extra money wasn't enough to blunt the edge of his resentment.

The trouble came when he had shut off once and looked round to hear the first rumbles from the slurry storage tank. This was such an urgent matter that he left the gasoline tank shut off. As he got near the slurry tank he could see the heat vapours rising from the unlagged sections of the line. He ran towards it.

TAKING STEPS 'We're back-pressured from the treating unit.'

'Get someone to get the gasoline away.'

'Stretch is here. You know what to do, Stretch?'

'Sure.' Off he went with great fearful strides, glad to be away from that end of the plant.

'If only,' wailed the Humdinger, 'if only I had closed-circuit TV monitors here instead of operators, to show me the position outside on key valves! Eyes don't have to walk outside.'

THE VICE OF CONFIDENCE After a short time of gaping at the plant and trying to follow process diagrams, SK had diagnosed one difficulty no one else had seen. His theory was that the pressure differential over the feed nozzles was too low. This was the cause of all the trouble. Fix that and you fix the lot.

He tried to interest others in this idea, but no one took any notice. He would fix it.

SKlation had no idea what he was doing, but he was not aware of this fact. He had the idea that any man who could drive a car, find his way to work and sign for his pay was equal to anything. He'd risen to foreman, hadn't he? He looked round to see if anyone was watching, and began opening valves. All you need is confidence.

LIVING BY RULES Stretch loped in.

'Can't get it away. Our pump's going but it's just not getting away.'

'Get on to the pumpers in the tank farm.'

Stretch went looking for a phone, came back.

'Can't get on to the Corpse. His offsider says he's outside but as far as he knows everything's all right.'

'That's no good. Get him out there to see what's wrong. Then you better go back to your unit and try and do something about all that gasoline.'

Stretch went away.

'You sure he knows what to do?' a voice asked.

'He's been on it three years. He ought to.'

'The Corpse's offsider won't go out.'

'Why not?'

'They've been told one of 'em has to stay by the phone all the time. The Python rang up Friday and couldn't get an answer for an hour, so he brings in a new rule.'

'How will they get all their tank dips—and do their blends and product movements?'

'Easy. Make a new rule.'

A SURE FOOTING The Boardrider picked his way expertly over oil-covered metal gratings and green slurried concrete. Over at the base of the reactor he saw SKlation working on feed valves.

Feed valves? Automatically he walked towards the reactor. Admittedly it was out in the open and there was no guard on it, but safety at this spot was so vital that surely no one would mess round without proper knowledge and definite orders. Still, SK was a foreman now. Plant knowledge accompanied promotion automatically.

He changed direction and headed back to the control room. His section was OK; this mob didn't pay you for doing more than your job, nor would they accept less than their own price for a gallon of juice. They gave nothing away, neither would he. Bugger SK. He turned his thoughts back where they belonged, to his dream of the Wave—the Wave gathering and curling for ever, never breaking, on an ocean without shore.

THE STORM BIRD The hot spot bubbled out. The bubble, though, was not quite ready to burst. What it needed was a sudden increase of pressure in the regenerator. Inside that bubble the regenerating fire blazed, burning coke from catalyst, to make it active again; productivity, prosperity, riches were in that fire. There was also hate. Unconfined, that fire could burn, maim, destroy the delicate humans tending it.

On the other end of the plant, Stretch lay on the ground. Congo Kid's gas had got him.

The air bleed from the instrument standing under the skirt of the regenerator was whistling. Rustle of Spring was having a Sunday indoors and the high-pitched whistle sounded very like the call of a storm-cock indefinitely prolonged. It pierced right through to a very special Sunday nerve until he decided not to put up with it.

He fiddled with the instrument, the piercing noise died down. What he did, although he did not know this—the tiny knobs looked so innocent, so remote, so unlikely to be important—what he did was raise the setting on the instrument. It was a low-flow cut-in on the regenerator air. When the air flow (which was not now registered anywhere because of a three-month temporary break-down of control-room instruments) fell to a point set on this outside instrument, an air signal was sent automatically to a steam cut-in valve, and steam poured into the regenerator to keep the catalyst in that vessel aerated.

The instrument setting was low, for safety, because the total air flow was not known, but Rustle of Spring soon moved the setting high enough.

ACUPUNCTURE Stillsons, in the shelter of his mother's house in a nearby suburb turning slowly into a slum, watched from his bedroom window, waiting for it to be time to go to work again. He noticed the flares were big. The ethylene flare was huge.

'Plant down,' he judged aloud. He lay back, relaxed for a while. He couldn't resist the pull of the plant, though, and sat up to look at the thick orange flame turning into billows of blue-black smoke.

He checked the time. Only seven hours twenty to go, and he'd be back there, safe inside the blue gates. He hoped the cracker would go down, too, now they'd shunted him off it. Humans are ferocious beasts; no one gets the kindness he deserves. He took a pin from his reactor cork—in his little model cracker—and jabbed it into the top seam of the fat regenerator cork. This was the champagne cork he'd found in the street: it had a nice round bulbous top, just like the regenerator.

THE RIGHT TO BEAR ARMS IS THE RIGHT TO BE FREE In his shooting days, One Eye used to head out for Nyngan and points west to hunt the harmless kangaroo. The skins had a little value for making toy koala bears.

In his more vicious moments he'd often wished a man could take a rifle to the footie and pot off players that dropped passes and missed tackles and stood around flat-footed. A man lost money on that sort of play. And referees, too, they needed a boot up the ginger. What was more to the point, his dry-cleaning business that he'd set his heart on for so long had failed. That was how he put it to himself; not that he had failed.

This fine Sunday, after the home team had been beaten again, he did take the rifle with him when he decided to roam round and look at Puroil again. All a man could see from outside the fence was the big plants, like the fearsome-looking cracker, high as a stack. He had never been down to that part of the works—a man couldn't leave his own section—and he knew nothing about it, although his daily job required close co-operation with it. The good old days had only finally vanished when that damn heap of crap had been built.

He fitted the silencer his son had made at Technical College and aimed at the guy wire holding the battleship boiler stack. He didn't hit it with any of his shots. What he hit was several hundred yards beyond—the high-pressure tapping line on the regenerator pressure controller.

On the way home on Highway One he thought he saw the Kraut. Funny. He was supposed to be in Brisbane.

SUFFICIENT REASON Since the high-pressure tapping was gone, the automatic instrument registered low and shut itself to keep the pressure up to the setting the Humdinger had on his panel instrument. But the actual pressure wasn't low—shutting the valve simply gave the pressure nowhere to go. It was a slow-acting valve. The pressure rose.

Just as silica-alumina was the catalyst in the company's industrial production process, so hate was the catalyst in the company's industrial relations process. With a grateful pout, the regenerator bubble burst and the hatred of years boiled over. A bellowing column of sound followed, and catalyst at over 600 Centigrade spewed in a stream of fire out into the courtyard and, carried on the wind, towards the mangroves.

The Great White Father, drunk on the doorstep of the drink hut, hardly noticed the darkened sky before he was covered in grey catalyst. He was only on the edge of the column of dust, and didn't get burned.

But this wasn't enough to reduce the pressure. The cunning vessel decided to ease itself in a more direct way. Just below the bubble was the southern seam; this bulged and opened. The top valve was now shut. The regenerator seemed to blow apart then. It swelled with its internal pressure even as it spewed white-hot catalyst. A long minute, then it collapsed in on itself. The great round sides fell inwards.

THE POSTURE OF DEVOTION Land of Smiles wasn't moving. The mouth was open in its broadest grin; the wide-spaced teeth, etched neatly in nicotine, dry from long exposure. He could breathe in and out shallowly, but the legs had left him.

He had been examining the eight-page lab results sheets, and not seeing them, when the crisis commenced. Now they were in long foolscap shreds. Between his continually moving fingers the shreds were twined and twisted; some hung, split and ripped between odd fingers, others waggled back towards his stomach, improperly severed. He seemed smaller, somehow. It had not occurred to him yet to get up from his kneeling position.

Even when the Congo Kid's liquid gas leaks travelled up the drains into the open trenches under the control-panel consoles and caught fire from the catalyst, Land of Smiles was unable to move.

The Humdinger didn't know about the fire inside the hollow console until he rested his hand on the metal while opening pressure valves. Gunga Din came good under fire. He could do nothing for his own plant but let it die a natural death. He brought bucket after bucket of water and drenched the Humdinger's panel, to keep it cool enough for him to touch.

AN ITEMIZED LIST The ethylene plant crashed on steam failure.

Neighbouring factories stopped all steam-driven processes.

The regenerator collapsed and the process stopped. The Glass Canoe's dog perished.

The Humdinger threw the feed cut-out and put steam into all high-temperature processes.

Heat from the open regenerator lit a fire in the reactor bed, where the nozzles were loose and hot oil was escaping. Loosehead was killed by the heat before his body was charred.

The slurry tank blew up and flashed. The Corpse was knocked flat for a while.

Slurry rundown was stopped and allowed to set solid in the lines and the fractionator column rather than feed the fire.

The turbo-expanders tripped, and the high-pressure steam turbine. The gas flow stopped and there was nothing for the compressor end to compress.

The high-pressure steam had nowhere to go—the let-down valve was jammed shut by the collar the Loch Ness Monster had spun down. Every safety valve blew, but this was not sufficient relief and the Humdinger brought the boilers down. The rest of the refinery plants followed, they depended on cracker steam.

There was no ladder to use to get the let-down valve open.

There were no blanks to spade off gas lines and other dangerous flows. Fuel gas was isolated on block valves and control valves that always had let by: blanks were vital to plant safety.

The process flows that had to be let go to drains went straight into the river, together with oil from the drains and interceptor and the black crude that couldn't be accommodated at the crashed distillation plants.

The white-hot catalyst lit the gas from the opened butane drain.

The Rustle of Spring, though not touched by catalyst, was cooked in his bed by the great wall of catalyst all round him, heaped up high round the concrete regenerator skirt.

The Humdinger bribed two men to go the long way round and rig up hoses to play saltwater jets on the fuel gas tank.

The Humdinger got Far Away Places to turn on the cold-water jets inside the reactor skirt. This put out the fire there and cracked the red-hot riser.

The northern part of the control hut was wrecked: amenities, foremen's office, locker-room. The Humdinger worked in great heat, despite Gunga Din's water, and was too busy to put his fingers under noses. Catalyst was banked against the north walls and had come in the locker-room windows.

The fire in the console was knocking out the instruments one by one. Gunga Din started sloshing water over the Humdinger, to keep him cool.

No other men could be found—all had gone to the windward side of the catalyst to potter on their plants so they couldn't get any orders that might take them into danger. The Humdinger shut down everything he could from his panel. He got Land of Smiles out of sight, dragging him behind the sixty-foot panel. When most of the noises had stopped or steadied out and the streams he couldn't send to storage were dropped out to drains, the Slug came back ready to give orders. Men still slipped where he trod. Then the cars appeared from the direction of the residences. The Puroil fire wagon was at the blazing tank. Inside half an hour there were white shirts everywhere with lists and company-issue pens to catalogue the bulk dead. There were twenty separate adverse reports on the water on the panel-room floor. Nothing could be done, except to play saltwater on the banks of catalyst and wait for it to cool, and concentrate on the blazing tank. Three operators and eleven white shirts were overcome by H_2S fumes, but none died. The oil on the river didn't catch fire, though traffic on the bay was coated for weeks and seagulls drowned in thousands. The firemen contained the blaze of the tank. The fire could have been a lot worse.

All in all, Sydney was lucky. Without the wind blowing flames and hot catalyst away from the main refinery area, the big tanks would have gone up and half Sydney with them.

The Gypsy Fiddler, out of sight, was coming back gingerly from his hideaway to windward of the danger area, into the strange quiet of the cracker area. The air compressor was still running on the last of the seventeen-kilo steam pressure and just as he got near it, the air-driers changed over. They were on six-hour cycle, drying and regenerating. They changed with a roar that was usually heard above the crashing roar of the cracker on normal operation, but in a surrounding silence it was like the crack of doom. The sound of bombs and shocks of war hadn't toughened him, they'd left him weak and scared. The Fiddler dropped dead. There was not a mark on him and when his skull and body were cut up in the post-mortem insisted on by the company's insurers, there was no evidence of carbon-monoxide poisoning from the regenerator catalyst or any other injury. No compensation.

The Maltese Falcon gave up hope of getting his brand-new aluminium ladder, but three days later when the fuss had died down he came by the fence and there it was, still in the trench. He said a little prayer of gratitude. He hadn't sunk so far as to lose his early religious training.

SKlation had let so much feed into the reactor that it coked up the riser and reactor bed. It would need to be drilled out. He hadn't learned a thing. His confident ignorance was another hazard built-in to Puroil's future.

The Corpse was dismissed because of the tank shut-off. It was discovered by his offsider and a tank-farm foreman on their way to the burning slurry tank. He was defiant and swore they'd never sack him, but when Luxaflex had a talk with him mentioning the Enforcer, he went quietly.

They took Land of Smiles away to a Reception House. He was never seen again.

The Humdinger performed one more valuable service. Somehow the computer boys got in on the act, accompanying the technologists to the disaster. They'd never been down to the dirty end before. After looking at the mess they trooped in covered in catalyst and oil and went up to the Humdinger in the most natural way imaginable and wiped their shoes on his overalls. The systems analyst grabbed the loose cloth on his right leg, the programmer his left, and they wiped away. The technician waited his turn. Before they finished, a party of junior engineers came in, talking excitedly of what they'd seen. When they saw the new shoe-cleaning arrangements they looked at one another.

'Care for a shine?' called the Humdinger. 'It's free. No tipping, by request.'

They took a few steps towards him, then recoiled as he lashed out and flung away from him the neatly suited priests of the new age.

25
SUNRISE IN THE SOUTH

A SAMURAI'S RELIGION (Notes found in the wreckage of a plant locker-room.)

The longing to be dominated and to hate your rulers is essential to the health of society. Control is control is control.

War and conflict have rescued from economic depression, poverty, moral looseness and decay. Strength and vitality, though expressed in strange ideologies, will inherit the earth. War is the only end of a society, the only reality men will allow to unify them. Hatred is necessary.

Life is destruction. Life and destruction stretch before me. The reason is in myself. Everything is in me. The refinery plant is a growth in my belly. No, the plant *is* me.

Just a touch is necessary. Just a touch—to destroy. This knowledge of what I have done is beginning to transform me. Transform? Rather to build on and develop what was always in me. I feel hard and smooth like polished steel. Is there a way to put the word steel into my name?

When I think of the power of one man to change and to

destroy, then think of the power of many. Walking in a street. Men and women, faces calm or relaxed in moulds of moderate greed, weak hate, vacillating joy, poverty-stricken ambition or that familiar wantless look of the half-alive. Then—I think with a great flash of light! Imagine each human extended to the full pitch of that energy spent normally on common situations—playing games, arguing with a neighbour, dodging a boss, aiming a kick at an animal—imagine that energy available all at once, channelled in one direction. The power of one man and the power of many.

REFLECTIONS ON VIOLENCE Now he was on holiday he was more than ever bound to the industrial life he lived. He had parked on the hill at Cheapley looking down over the refinery and its industrial neighbours. How could a man hate his employer yet be at a loose end when he had to stay away? It wasn't the money—he wasn't interested in money—he felt useless when he wasn't working. He looked west to the Blue Mountains: they were no help. Rocks and trees. The refinery, for all its idiocies and frustrations, was a product of strength and vitality. It was men wrenching power from an indifferent planet. The Samurai looked away from the mountains and industrial structures, started his car and headed for his room hoping Mrs Blue Hills wasn't there again, before the regenerator bubble burst. No black smoke overtook him.

Why, he thought in that dialogue with himself that was so familiar, why do they need strength over them? Why do they need strength to lean on, to protect them? Because without it and the spurs such strength is provided with they collapse to apathy, laziness. Why redeem them? Why make them face disaster? Ah, that was another matter. The answer existed in him only as a hard lump of unexplained feeling. Perhaps there really was an instinct to survive and he had a greater measure of it on their behalf.

On a rising slope of prosperity, with widening horizons, the range of lives a man could lead becomes too great to ignore. Sudden and severe jolts to this prosperity: this was the Samurai's answer.

Sabotage, destruction, hardship, violence, blood. If there were enough men tramping the street, not all the barbed wire and police forces and national guards in the world could stop the blaze. Yes. He would go about the country, making panics. Either the government acted as a government and took the country in its fist, or repression would lead to an explosion and a government would rush in to be born, a government which would take the country in its strong fist. A firm, protective fist; a strong aggressive fist, eager to do the things fists are made for.

He was convinced nothing comes about by the efforts of the people, the beasts of burden, but by individuals. Martyrs and agitators or, if their activities have some success, agitators and dictators. The temptation to seize power rather than be put against a wall must be irresistible. He was right in not wanting to work through the wantless ones. Perhaps it was an instinct. Intuition. He had stopped thinking—and started to believe in himself and in the dark forces rising from within him.

Would there be others after him who would keep at this work of digging spurs into the softening flanks of the country? For they were needed. Nothing could last, no lessons remembered, but had to be repeated over and over in each generation. The social body had to be lashed and stung, wounded and bled regularly, before it sank back into laziness and ease, obesity and death.

How long would it be until war was given—as a great gift from the experimenters on high that we have freely called gods—to make the remnant appreciate merely being alive?

I not only don't love my fellow men, I dislike them. Is this the other side of the coin? The reverse of my mission to force them to their feet? And what happened to my idea of fighting only larger opponents? What about the small people knocked about in the coming struggles? The Samurai had travelled a little way from feeling he was set apart to be a fighter for one or two unfortunates, to mapping out a programme of destruction to bring about a chaotic state of affairs in which his unfortunates and the industry that half-heartedly employed them would be pulled into gear and made to work. There were no political clubs or parties in Australia to help him form ideas appropriate to the conditions around him, no newspapers to say anything that touched his life at any point.

The parties and the newspaper proprietors were anonymous private groups responsible to no one but themselves. Their first duty was to their own continued existence.

His programme was himself.

THE GIFT OF LANGUAGE The Samurai arrived at his room. He fished out his latest notebook and tossed it into the small carton in which the others were neatly packed. He tipped them out on his bed and began to leaf through them. It was a crazy impulse, nevertheless he shuffled the notebooks as near as he could get to the order in which he filled them, took a pad of notepaper from his little table and a Puroil ballpoint pen and started to write.

Catching sight of himself in the mirror on the opposite wall he smiled at his reflection, a thing he had never done before, but did not lay down the pen. Instead he went over to the old motto *Help, Care, Listen* that he had on the wall, crossed it out and wrote *Hate, Chaos, Leadership*. A more corrosive mixture.

Was he writing about the men he'd worked with? Did they exist? He had the feeling that now he had decided to leave them they had collapsed from inside like balloon faces when the air is gone. Were those men he knew or thought he knew, were they projections of himself? Only alive while he was with them? Extensions, reflections, enlargements of small characteristics of his own?

And the face in the mirror on that opposite wall: whose reflection was that? What aimless forces had moulded him? A man born to change his world and until now denying himself the power.

And the language. Their continual swearing—would he be able to include this accompaniment to everything they said? Or modify it? But no; it was more than accompaniment; he had worked with them, drunk with them, slept alongside them: their S's, F's and B's and FS's, FB's, BF's and all the rest were often the whole substance of what they had to say. What a pity he was not clever enough to interpret these sounds—perhaps they were the outward forms of weird, shapeless desires that welled up inside them; desires for which there were no words yet made. And their preoccupation with bowel functions, a major part of their days.

He looked at his reflection again. A writer was a dangerous man, substituting words for crimes. He put his stolen biro to paper and words formed lightly in blue tracings. Were they original words, a private language? Or simply a rearrangement of patterns he had become used to in his few years' exposure to the words that surrounded him. Patterns he was so familiar with they seemed to him his own voice.

Judge for yourself. I found this fragment, possibly his first attempt to put on paper his feeling for the refinery, in his room after the visit by those I shall mention next:

'All I see is magnificent. Cool, clean, ringing steel; smoking, redhot, radiant steel; dust and motes that paint the sunsets of the world and glorious dawns; flame with its million changing faces and fairy bodies. I look in the flames and see the endless shapes of the world; smoke and vapours rising like ghosts, moving lightly in the upper air. Rich rust, bitumen black and black, concrete warm far into the night with the tradesman's handprints immortal. The grubby mites crawling between the limbs of columns, among girders, are men like me. All I see carries the stamp of a man's hand. The men I see carry the stamp of everything they touch. And all I see is magnificent.'

He was in love with industry.

BLISS BY COMPULSION As his door flew open he tried to remember if he had left it unlocked or had given Mrs Blue Hills a key. Of course—he was trying to grapple with four men, but his greatest disadvantage was that he had for once been caught off guard and two of them held him from behind—of course she had a key, the key she used to get in before.

He judged it better to be subdued and conscious than defiant and unconscious. He stopped struggling. Who could these men be? He asked them, but they gave unsatisfactory answers and bundled him outside towards their car. They made no attempt to rob him: he had his own car keys still and his holiday pay. They pulled the door shut on the way out, locking it. This seemed to please him; perhaps he thought a locked door made his room safe.

On the way out he saw several people he knew slightly and called to them, trying to interest them in his plight, but each one in turn became afflicted with a sudden and total deafness and remembered urgent business that required attention in another direction. They even pointedly looked away from the car so there would be no likelihood of their remembering the licence number and being burdened with inconvenient information.

It was understandable. For all they knew, he was going to be murdered and no one wants to get mixed up in things like that. Even if there were no cause to fear private revenge, the ordeal in the witness box was enough to take years off their lives being made fools of by arrogant counsel and judges who had no contact with the world outside their courts, being forced to say yes or no to questions that required more words, and having to observe an etiquette and use words that had vanished from the world outside the courtroom. It was understandable.

They took him to the house of Mrs Blue Hills, put him on her double bed and tied his arms and legs crosswise to the four corners with sash-cord. This seemed to be the extent of their duties; they sat and drank some of her beer in the kitchen and left soon after.

'My brothers,' she said grimly to the Samurai. She proceeded to rip his clothes from his body with no respect for their wholeness. He watched with regret as a good shirt met its end and with amazement as she used scissors on his trousers. Her next action was more familiar. She undressed carelessly and commenced torturing him.

Night slumped down on the earth, squeezing out the last light under its vast western edge.

INTERCHANGEABLE PARTS Many little deaths later she allowed his body to rest, and threw her own carelessly across his.

'Did you blow up the refinery?' Out of the blue. She couldn't be serious.

'Are you serious?'

'It's blown up. Finished. On fire.' She got off him and manipulated the blinds.

The sky to the south was red, a premature and brilliant sunrise. Had he done that? But the air line he pinched in was not in service. He didn't know it, but the line he choked off led to an open end.

'You knew all this and didn't say a word?'

'I wouldn't care if a million factories burned.'

'Oh yes you would. You'd care,' he said seriously, thinking of economic consequences.

'I'll live, factories or no factories,' she said confidently.

'It's not a factory. Refinery.'

'Who cares? One less—a lot of smoke. So what?'

'People might be dead there.'

'Millions die in wars, famines, cyclones, earthquakes, in agony. Every way. I'm not going to bleed for them. I'd rather see twelve million Australians dead than go without one thing I want.'

'But they're men from round here. Blue Hills worked with them.'

'I don't care who they are or where they come from. It's their funeral. It'd be all the same to them if I did sympathize or if I didn't. I'm just a woman with one life to live. When I die the world dies. I care about us.'

'Why didn't I see it?'

'We're in a little fold in the hills, here.'

'Why didn't I look?'

'You sound sorry you missed it.'

'There's still time. Let me go. There might be something I can do.'

'I'll let you go if you promise to come back.'

'Promise?' Stupidly.

'Or you stay tied up. A slave of sex.'

'I'll come back. Get me some of Blue's trousers.'

'Promise?' she demanded.

'I said so, didn't I?' She prepared coffee and created music with cups and saucers made of earth, marshalling them like a general in the field, herself made of softer clay.

It was clear he had involved himself in a relationship it wasn't easy to get out of. Perhaps she thought her exploits on his undefended body had impressed him with the depth of her physical love; perhaps she considered he was now bound to her. Nevertheless, she dressed and fed him.

Just as humans are interchangeable in the eyes of industry and governments, so perhaps are men in the eyes of women. At all events Blue Hills' trousers fitted him and she didn't seem surprised. He was waiting for her to say something about Blue Hills and where he might be, but she didn't. Puroil had asked her if Blue Hills was coming back to work but were holding the pension and holiday money due to him. With the Samurai keeping her she would have the necessary economic security to allow her to enjoy the change from Blue Hills.

THE COSMIC SCALES The street was dark, the houses put to bed, their sheets of grass tucked neatly under at the edges.

The Samurai climbed the short hill and came in view of the vast industrial extension of Sydney, seeing it from the top of a large contemptuous slope. There came over him the feeling of all that air pressing down, and tiny people tightly enclosed below.

Down on the plains of Puroil, the distant traffic over the bridge at Clearwater had an otherworldly look. For miles over the metropolitant area the smoke and dust, carbon-monoxide, sulphur-dioxide, acids of all types, unburned gases and toxic elements combined to cast a light haze over every distance upwards of a hundred yards.

And it was beautiful. This same poetic haze touched the natural dawn with fairy fingers and threw a dome of unearthly colours over Sydney's miles. It filled the sunsets to the stars with red and gold magnificence. The flimsiest suburban box was pretty under its veil.

One part of the refinery was well alight. Blue-black smoke bent in the wind down over the suburbs towards Sydney like a great column crashing down on crowded houses.

As he broke into a run to get to a busy corner and bum a lift, he wondered how many dead there were. High overhead, Sirius flamed in the sky. Down on the plain the refinery flares were huge, burning gas the plants couldn't use: giant candles flickering over the low bed-huts of the poor.

His lift took him past the corner where the idiot sat every day. He was there, sure enough, reliable as Monday morning. His keepers were late taking him indoors. Strips of rag flowed from his hands, covered with knots; there were filthy stockings, rags, light rope; he tied and untied all the knots over and over again. Tie, untie. Fasten, unfasten. The actions of the man's hands, the constant repetition of simple movements—even in this state of mental incompetence the man's body was reaching out obsessively towards process work. The only bar to his placement in a factory was his insistence on performing meaningless motions of his own choice.

The Samurai watched from the stranger's car as they stopped at the lights; watched with horror. Then the eyes of this permanent idiot wandered round in the most natural way and looked into his. The Samurai had a distinct, an astonishing feeling that he was transparent, that the unfortunate was looking clear through him. When the car moved, the eyes stayed looking at the same spot. He must have seen movement round him as a blur. The Samurai, looking from the car, watched with fixed eyes the gravelled road surfaces disappear beneath him, seeing only streaks of motion.

Outside the blue gates was a small girl who lived in one of the residences and was often seen skipping of an afternoon until her mother saw where she was and called her away from the gates. Her rope was turning faster than usual. Crowds were there milling in the dark and she was excited. The Samurai, coming towards her, thought immediately of the man sitting on the corner messing with his knots and twisting his rag-ends. Was the meaning of his own life and the life of the men inside the works—was the meaning of the whole thing in a child's mindless skipping and a man's aimless knotting and untying?

He stopped in his tracks. He saw the mighty Puroil acres shrink and become no larger than the little girl and the idiot, until before his eyes there were these two masses balancing one another: a vast industrial enterprise and two negligible human units. What would happen if he could throw the rest of the humans concerned into the scale—into either side of the scale?

ILLEGAL ENTRY Puroil locked its gates—normal emergency procedure. Men who lived nearby came and clamoured at the heavy steel barrier for news from the plants. The absurd guards knew nothing, could hardly pronounce the names of the plants and preserved their usual surliness which they hoped was mistaken for toughness.

The little girl moved closer, still with her rope in orbit about her, and skipped near the Samurai. He moved away, suspicious of kids that got too friendly.

'Are you real old, mister?'

'Pretty old.'

'Wouldn't it be funny if people were born old and got younger and younger till they finished up babies?'

'Yeah, funny.'

'Then maybe I could be your mother.'

'Maybe.'

She lost interest and skipped away. He was glad. Nearby ornamental trees and bushes were clotted with birds. Acacias exploded into blossom like tiny bomb-bursts. High overhead, the last birds were homing, flying on thin bones, trusting to feathers.

The refinery brigade—a shift of two men, their equipment a water truck and a foam truck—had been supplemented by brigades from a dozen metropolitan stations. No amount of fire-fighting equipment was effective against these fires, however; they had to be isolated and allowed to burn out.

It was a simple matter for the Samurai to get in. He walked round past the company residences, along the road to the Thieving Magpie's spot, unclipped the wire and crawled in.

The slurry tank had blown, flashed and was burning itself out. This corner of the tank farm—for heavier oils—was separated by several large vacant plots from the gasoline tanks. In summer they would have gone up, but now, with the wind blowing, sprays of water on their silver sides saved them.

That night the newsreel pictures featuring the black smoke from the oil fire looked like news from a war. The opposition companies didn't send their regular scouts round to see how Puroil was going. Not for a long time.

Those on night shift were caught up in the excitement for a while, but since the supervision was away huddled together in conferences all night, they soon prepared to do as they'd always done. They spread evil rags to ease the ache of concrete. Swansdown rags.

A PRIVATE TRAGEDY The old man and woman in the furnished Plymouth had been buried in catalyst dust. They were in the path of the solid column of white-hot powder. Their corpses were uncovered a week later only a little charred, rigid in an embrace, just as male and female citizens of Pompeii were overtaken by volcanic ash and their bodies found milleniums later in the same position—or rather the spaces their bodies had occupied. To call flesh clay is mockery: clay outlasts flesh by eternities.

'I wonder if they finished,' said the Ant, who found them.

'I reckon so,' said Volga. 'They just finished and thought they'd have a little rest. Didn't know a thing about it.' Everyone was glad for them; it was considered lucky not to know when you were going to die.

They'd never had to use the Acme Thunderer, it was found blackened in the glove box of the Plymouth. Volga repossessed it and the Great White Father let it hang on a special nail in the drink hut. A memorial to married love.

Some of the stolen ivy doing so well round the walls of the Home Beautiful was transplanted near the old car, where it would grow and cover their grave marker. For as a last kindness the old couple were buried under the car in the swamp that was their refuge from a society in which they could not afford to live.

A TACTFUL SILENCE When the Monday morning tide came in and deposited workers on the Puroil shores a number of heavy men wearing hats were welcomed at the blue gates and ushered into the Termitary. They had never seen the Utopia 1852 poster and scratched their ankles unashamedly as soon as they were seated.

One asked a routine question. 'Is there anyone who might have a grudge against the company?'

There was a silence. The Whispering Baritone picked his flaking fingers carefully, trying not to break the skin. By a miracle there had never been trouble like this before. In the low life they shared, management and labour had never been able to live together, but when it came to the point how could they stand up and say that any or all of the prisoners they guarded might have sabotaged them? Where would the accusations stop? Had a rumour got round about the new plans to put all processes on the computers? Better to shut up rather than give this news to the prisoners on a plate. First the system had to be readied and the work force pared down to a skeleton crew of half a dozen. Could they admit that the mob had destroyed the symbols of their servitude—the machines—because servitude was no longer necessary now machines were so clever? Could they admit that the refinery could be run more efficiently and the consumer charged less for the product without reducing profit?

The detectives assumed it was a matter of delicacy or reluctance to name a suspect, and waited patiently. After all they weren't dealing with people on the street: there was a different method of handling men like these. As if they were equals, as the manual said, or superior officers. Respectful but not obsequious. They weren't to know the wide range of suspects Puroil had to choose from.

A mile away, the Eel River was alive with oily, spattered gondoliers paddling about in skiffs, trying to fill makeshift containers with black crude from a faraway Sheikhdom, and getting mostly saltwater. To counter residents' complaints, a few paragraphs appeared in the local rag boasting of Puroil's vast expenditure on the latest methods of preventing spillage; telling a story of loving concern for the well-being of residents, seagulls, boat clubs, pleasure craft, quite over and above the secondary aim of making a dollar. It might keep the silly bastards quiet.

The lengthy shutdown was organized to begin right away. The golden handshake time limit was extended a month; after that there was plenty of time to weed out the unwanted. Besides, there was a State election in three weeks and those who benefited in the way of campaign funds from Puroil could have been embarrassed by large-scale sackings just before the voters made their marks on the little scraps of paper to put into power the self-qualified men nominated by small private groups. Politically the people were powerless: unknown men controlled them. Industrially they were powerless: the reins were held firmly elsewhere. Even weak India insisted on local majority shareholding in foreign companies. Yet they still had some power, if only they knew. If they were prepared to have their heads broken and to bleed.

Meanwhile, technology was in existence that would shortly make their labour an anachronism and their detention financially unsound. On the other hand it was certain to make their enforced future freedom politically unsound. And yet, in public places, great masses of constitutional machinery that with a little bringing up to date could have guided the use of this technology and this freedom lay rusting, unused.

FINAL SOLUTION When the great wall of still-hot catalyst was dug away from the regenerator under the supervision of Bomber Command, who had regained his position as controller in the inevitable shake-up, the Rustle of Spring was found inside, cooked. Clothes, tarpaulin burned away. When they touched him, slabs of baked meat fell from his bones, giving off a curiously appetizing smell. Men who were prepared to be revolted by cooked human meat simply because of what it was, found their mouths watering in spite of themselves as his bones undressed.

The Humdinger, who reverenced nothing, had to make a joke of it.

'We've invented the solution to the world's hunger!' he yelled. 'Munch a man a month!'

The others made a fuss at this lack of taste, but not too much. Basically they loathed even each other; what could a stranger expect?

They couldn't get the little dead man's drawings off the inside walls, the heat had baked them on. There was the Samurai in Japanese warrior robes, Desert Head had his halo of mosquitoes, Blue Hills in a coffin marked Puroil, Canada Dry was a tall bottle-shape, the Western Salesman with a brown nose crouching behind the Slug, the Sumpsucker an obscene sketch, the Good Shepherd a bishop, the Beautiful Twinkling Star as Christ, and the Humdinger had a human backside for a face. The Great White Father was shown horizontal doing his falling-flat trick.

They found Loosehead's dummy woman. Her rag insides were gone and only skeleton wires remained. The Rustle of Spring had slept with her all this time under his tarpaulin, his only bride in this arid land. They salvaged his bones and sent them back where they came from. They made a smaller package than on the voyage out.

THE GREAT WHITE FEATHER The Great White Father hadn't gone up to the refinery on the day of the fire and was still drunk a few days later. SKlation had given him a new name. All by himself. The Great White Feather. An addition of one letter.

The name stuck. It says a lot for the adaptability of men and their willingness to accept new ideas that they could change their great man's name so quickly and led by a man everyone sneered at.

Now here's a funny thing. The Great White Feather was out of commission flat on his back for several days and in that time his followers and friends resumed their retreat from the world and work. But something was missing. The girls were there, did what was expected and got their money. The great man's voice was not heard. But perhaps his friends could have survived his silence.

It was something else. Volga rowed up to buy the beer as usual, but something wasn't right. The beer flowed in and out of the drinkers, then came to a stop. Volga wanted contributions and they gave the usual few dollars each, but there wasn't enough beer. Several argued about it; there were fights. Volga cracked a few heads together, but the arguments persisted and got worse. Some even retreated to a safe distance and accused Volga of sticking to the money.

A small group of men, seeing that the Home Beautiful was in danger of breaking up, tackled Volga about the money. When he saw they were trying to be reasonable he told them, 'We'll be back to normal when we get him on his feet.'

'Who, the Great White Feather? What difference does he make?'

'He dobs in the extra all the time out of his own dough. That's why you drink well and there's never any shortage. If it runs out he'll send me up to the pub for six dozen, say, out of his own kick. Most of the time it's his beer you're drinking.'

One of them started to suggest charging the girls a fee to practise their profession, but Volga squashed that. The Great White Feather was against pimps and landlords, he told them. Volga was going out of his way trying not to be physical.

The Home Beautiful wasn't a spontaneous movement of men: it was one man. One good man. They couldn't manage by themselves.

With a true appreciation of the ideals that led to the founding of the Home Beautiful and its marriage of bed and board, the men did what they could to revive their leader, and gave him the best of attention. Soon he was on his feet again and spending freely. Happiness returned to the Home Beautiful. Men set out fresh every day to lay hands on and to hold the greasy pig of pleasure.

They still called him the Great White Feather. Even his staunchest friends used the new name easily, without embarrassment. He never objected. Actually he seemed to like it.

A WOUND IN THE SIDE When I saw the Two Pot Screamer in the Sullage City Workers' Club he said, 'The blow-up I expected has happened. I've decided to leave Puroil and go to a quiet place for six months to put it all down.'

'All what?'

'I've enough notes for a book. No one will accept it, I know, but I can't let that stop me. Artists are like prostitutes; they'll always have a trade.' I couldn't look him in the eye.

'Good luck. I hope you find a quiet place.' Put it all down? He would select and discard as I did, according to rules established by chance 277 days before I was born.

He was single, like me. It was the only way to keep free of hire-purchase, the only way you had a chance to thumb your nose at bosses. I asked him about Hillend. He'd knocked around the gold country when he was younger. Hillend carried us through for an hour. Then I remembered something funny.

'Remember the Western Salesman?'

'Sure. With the brown nose.'

'They didn't make him a foreman. They brought all the new foremen in from outside. He was nearly in tears.' He laughed. 'Him and a dozen others. They only used 'em to keep the mob quiet while they got the new agreement in.'

'They never learn.'

'And remember the Outside Fisherman?'

'Sure. Has he retired yet?'

'That's right.'

'He was looking forward to that gold watch.'

'He didn't get it.'

'What?'

'No. When they came to add up his service he was short by one day.'

'How? He was sure he'd been there thirty years by the time he retired.'

'Two days over. But on a count-back of unpaid sick days he was one day short. He had three days off with arthritis and they deduct the unpaid days.'

'The filthy mongrel bastards,' he said loudly. The words attracted no attention in the Workers' Club.

'They haven't changed,' I said. I was thinking of the Wild Bull of the Pampas, Stillsons, the Western Salesman, Sea Shells, the Outside Fisherman, the Grey Goldfish, Canada Dry, all those with unpaid grudges against the company and all the others who knew they would be at the bottom of the pile for life. Even the equipment, weakened by neglect, had rebellion built-in. What would happen when they finally tried to run the place with six men?

'No. Thank Christ we're out of there before the next blow-up. That mob haven't learned a thing. You know what they remind me of? The Glass Canoe. The way they go on. A cycle of depression, then a torpid state when they couldn't care less, then a hotchpotch of mental chaos when they thrash blindly around with a thousand different ideas at once, then a real mania when they go for one aim like a bull at a gate.'

I smiled at his earnest tone. He went on.

'Did you hear that when they took the turbo-expander machines down they were eaten out with catalyst. You know how that stuff slices through steel? Someone put catalyst in the lube oil.'

'You don't say.' I could imagine Taffy the Welsh smiling grimly and putting his fist reminiscently in the hole in his side. 'But wait till you hear this. Remember the computer boys? That were too good to talk to anyone. Well, Puroil bought second and third generation computers so they could use the original memory discs, they put all their operations on the machines and got rid of their programmer and systems analyst. When they want advice they hire a consultant or bring in analysts and programmers for special jobs. They're not safe either. Even the gardeners. Gone.'

'The gardeners? Why?'

'Nylon grass. No upkeep.'

'I suppose,' he said bitterly, 'when the ornamental trees die they'll put up posters with trees painted on.'

PREFACE Others carry their books inside them—it doesn't occur to them to put them in print. They build up now and then a sort of word-pressure inside, and let out words at random to ease the pressure—words from their book of life—to family, to familiar strangers in pub and club when alcohol loosens the tongue. Their books last as long as life, and hold secrets of the human universe, but they evaporate.

It has been my aim to take apart, then build up piece by piece this mosaic of one kind of human life, this galaxy of painted slides, my bleak ratio of illuminations; to remind my present age of its industrial adolescence.

Well friend, I have not succeeded in putting back together those I have taken apart, for they are split, divided, fragmented, as

I am split up and divided between page and character, speech and event, intention and performance.

If the faces are familiar, the expressions will not be admitted. A man congratulates himself more or less for what he has made, but parts of others are missing and must be supplied by the reader. And I myself am missing, but this lack is essential.

ONE GOOD MAN The last time I saw the Great White Feather was a few weeks after the fire. Again he was hopelessly drunk. Perhaps the fire made a deep impression on him. Or his christening. Or he was determined to stay drunk till the moon grew hair. Or it was an extension of his falling-flat trick.

I couldn't help it—shortly I was to go out of their lives for ever—I asked the question.

'That day you were leading the goat along Highway One—what was it for? What did you do with it?'

But he was unable to speak. I believe he would have told me if he had been sober. His head was resting on what looked like plans. Perhaps he had been driven underground already. A new race of miners digging for the gold of freedom. This would be an escape story where tunnels were dug with no escape beyond the barbed wire. Escape was in the tunnel. Was this their refuge after being uprooted first from the land, then from industry? Banished from the face of the earth.

The digging may have started. If so he wouldn't announce anything till the small group round him finished their work and the tunnels and underground rooms were ready. If, in the Home Beautiful the atmosphere was so free that it seemed like liberty and equality, that was, in my opinion, because the Great White Feather did what he wanted secretly and quickly. Suggestions were accepted afterwards, and improvements; he put in his ideas first. There was no nonsense about voting, or the whole thing might very well have been voted out of existence. He provided what he said they needed, knowing they were useless at making up their minds. He served them from a great height; democracy was unnecessary. Most men would have turned the Home Beautiful into a goldmine, but not all men are stupid, selfish and corrupt when they have a monopoly of power.

As I turned away I thought of another question, something about the true function of man. Perhaps his true function is to be himself, just as he happens to be, and his whole duty simply to live. But how can that be enough? It was a rather pompous sort of thing to be talking about then. Or any time. I looked for the sixty-dollar cat, but he was off alone somewhere, hunting in the surrounding swamp for animals weaker than himself.

I ducked into the bed hut to say goodbye to the girls. They were all there, all six. There was real affection in their faces for the helpless man and they seemed to be discussing their life together and the good turns he had done them—in low voices, as if he were dying. I smiled and spoke in a loud voice to cheer them up.

'Look, I've always wanted to ask you this,' I said. 'We've got a bloke up there that pees purple. You ever seen him down here?' They all said yes. 'Well,' I said, 'what colour? I mean his—you know.'

'Lavender,' said the Apprentice and the others nodded. 'We never mentioned it, it might have turned the boys off.'

'Didn't you mind?'

'Why? He paid his money. His money's just as good as yours.'

'Goodbye girls.'

They said goodbye, but kept their voices down. I came out laughing, but I didn't succeed in bucking them up.

Just for a last look I went back to the drink hut. Far Away Places had come in and stood looking down on the Great White Feather, who now was very still. Far Away spoke to him, but he did not turn his head. Far Away watched and waited. I was grateful that he kept his hands out from under his overalls. I thought of asking him if he was going to put a DNR stencil on the great man's shirt, but decided not to. I stood on the clay outside the hut, the girls were talking quietly in the bed hut. For some reason they still whispered. I hoped no one would come or make a noise; I wanted to watch, undisturbed, the strange scene inside the drink hut. The helpless man muttered a little. I thought I caught the words 'deserted soak', but it may have been nothing of the kind. Then he began to speak in a deep, breaking voice. Slowly. 'Nothing here for strangers to see. No high mountain of home units, no harbour view, only a few huts in the mangrove-trees. But though our waterhole in the bush has been forsaken by so many of our people, and overtime more attractive than leisure and ease, a few of us still care. This place still holds me fast; and I'll look after it while I can.' He paused, his laboured breathing loud. I could see his heartbeat, which shook the whole chest.

'Get a handful of earth.' Far Away places gaped.

'A handful of my country.' Doubtfully Far Away retreated outside, took a stick and loosened some earth near the roots of the stolen ivy. He came back, both hands full.

'Let me look.' And the great man opened his eyes. 'While I live I shall love to gaze on this ancient soil.' Far Away stooped to let him look. A smile spread over the Great White Feather's face. His right hand moved and I had a sudden conviction he was about to eat part of his beloved planet. Far Away moved, but not fast enough. The great man's hand knocked his cupped hands, the earth fell on his chest. Far Away's hands were big, they held about a spadeful. 'Purple. The purple everlastings clinging to me.' The great man's jaw slackened, his words ceased.

Far Away Places bent down, watching closely. The Great White Feather groaned a bit and Far Away waved his hand to scare a fly from his face then left his hand there and wiped away some moisture from his chin.

I looked away towards the river, thinking I heard the rowlocks of Volga's boat—when he saw the girls together he'd start ringing the silver bell no matter what—and when I looked back into the hut, Far Away was stretched full length beside the muttering man, resting on one elbow, gently brushing his hair back with his right hand. Suddenly I looked up fearing, as if the branches meeting above were an unreliable vaulted roof of loose stones that might crush me any moment at the command of the Great White Father of the universe who watched our doings idly, carelessly, irresponsibly; with no interest and no compassion.

Behind me the girls padded over the trodden clay. They were not disturbed or intimidated by Far Away's devotion, but took up positions on the far side of the Great White Feather and began brushing off the dirt and undressing the unresisting body they knelt before. Shoes and socks, shirt and trousers; each took an area for herself, performing for him the services of which women consider themselves the best custodians. I couldn't see Far Away's face, but I knew he'd be put out by this competition for the great man's favour. He put out a hand to touch the expanse of white skin, but drew back slowly. Reverently, I thought, as if he hoped to touch it later.

Their heads leaned inward like girls examining a ring, aunts inspecting a new baby, wise men and shepherds over a manger or surgeons over a patient cadaver. There was a healed incision in his right side. I was surprised to see how blue the scar was on his right ankle. I didn't look at his hands.

'...more important...' slurred the great man with difficulty.

'What is, boss?' said Far Away eagerly, saying the very word that might rouse him to anger.

'...no boss—not fit to be obeyed—nothing justifies one man over another—more important...' He seemed to twitch a little under the women's fingers.

'What, darling?' asked the Old Lamplighter tenderly and the girls echoed, 'Darling'.

'...neighbour—more important—god...'

This message from a remote place was unintelligible to his hearers, who shook their heads and smiled indulgently. Had he meant one's neighbour was more important than God? Or the other way round? It had nothing to do with them; they let it pass. I didn't understand, either. Once he tried to rise, but they took this for a convulsive action by which he might hurt himself, and pressed him firmly down.

That white body on the floor—seeing it there was like finding a white glare of marble cut in naked figures on the Nullarbor. I stepped inside the door and tried to phone. It worked still. On an impulse, arising from some uncharted levels within myself, I dialled a service number and held the phone to the ear of their naked leader. Both factions watched me suspiciously, jealous of each other but able to spare a little extra jealousy for a third party. On the corrugated iron up near the ceiling joists I saw several large spiders, hairy huntsmen, edging sideways from cover.

'What's that?'

'Who's on the other end?' The clamour of their voices made an interesting contrast with their previous quiet.

'It's a Dial-a-Prayer. I don't know who's on the other end,' I told them, holding the phone still. As if with some idea of not letting herself be left behind, the Old Lamplighter started to sing, 'I'll be loving you, always', in a low key, making it sound like a dedication. Without turning a hair, Never on Sunday began in a much higher voice, but very sweetly, 'If you were the only boy in the world'. Cinderella said dramatically, 'Some enchanted evening', the Sorcerer's Apprentice started 'On top of old Smokey', the Sleeping Princess sang 'Strangers in the night', but not very well, and the Sandpiper sang very badly, 'Singing in the rain'. And you will hardly credit this but the mixture didn't sound unattractive at first. Rather like extremely involved contrapuntal church music.

Far Away Places wasn't defeated by this display of devotion; he pulled from his pocket the trumpet mouthpiece he played up on the reactor structure and started something that sounded like 'Drink to me only'. It may have been 'Lead, Kindly Light'. I could identify only the first four notes. I kept the phone in position so the object of their devotion could get the benefit of the prayer service, then held it to my own ear to check. The voice had stopped, there was silence on the line. Had there been a voice? I should have checked first. For a moment I knelt there feeling ridiculous. There I was, wondering whether there had been a connection and a voice, when it was more to the point to ask whether the object of this service could have heard anyway. I went outside, looking back. Again he tried to rise. Again, protectively, their gentle hands pressed him down.

Above the arch of trees the sun, a golden lion, roared in the sky against all that was dark and cold. Where I stood, it created a peculiar light around me—the lemon light of afternoon sunshowers. The kneeling women's hands played like twelve white birds on the Great

White Feather's body, their voices lifted reverently in the words of their various pop faiths and Far Away Places knelt too, his lips and powerful jaws pushed against his section of trumpet. As their various songs proceeded, the differences in line length, rhythm, meaning and words seemed to complicate the whole effect unbearably. Each was determined to keep her own song and determined to be heard—and Far Away's strangled tune above all. A third time the Great White Feather struggled to rise and a third time the weight of their devotion kept him under.

With my head whirling in this miniature surf of sound, I turned to go and bumped blindly into the Volga Boatman. I didn't want to have to stop and try to explain—how could I?—so I tried to slip past him. He didn't intend to get in the way but he dodged towards me. I went the other way. So did he. His eyes were fixed on the source of the chanting and mine on the path through the mangroves to the river and beyond that to the complicated world outside where dangerous ideas presented themselves as simplifications to dangerous men who had nothing to lose but a few short years of an existence they despised. Yes, mine were fixed on the path out of the Home Beautiful. Beyond that, too, where on the far side of the great empty stomach of Australia lay a new industrial frontier in the west, where more foreigners were messing about with the lives of people for whom they had no responsibility.

That strange music was piercing my head like the golden needles of a quack in whom I had no faith; it set my teeth on edge; it was swelling inside me like that benign lump of faith I had had removed years ago. I had to get away from this meaningless ritual.

The Boatman and I were concentrated absolutely on where we wanted to go. We had no mind left over to escape each other. Back and forth we went from side to side, left right left right in perfect time, getting no farther forward; each, for the sake of a tiny inconvenience, wishing the other had never existed.

Text Classics

Dancing on Coral
Glenda Adams
Introduced by Susan Wyndham

The Commandant
Jessica Anderson
Introduced by Carmen Callil

Homesickness
Murray Bail
Introduced by Peter Conrad

Sydney Bridge Upside Down
David Ballantyne
Introduced by Kate De Goldi

Bush Studies
Barbara Baynton
Introduced by Helen Garner

The Cardboard Crown
Martin Boyd
Introduced by Brenda Niall

A Difficult Young Man
Martin Boyd
Introduced by Sonya Hartnett

Outbreak of Love
Martin Boyd
Introduced by Chris Womersley

The Australian Ugliness
Robin Boyd
Introduced by Christos Tsiolkas

All the Green Year
Don Charlwood
Introduced by Michael McGirr

They Found a Cave
Nan Chauncy
Introduced by John Marsden

The Even More Complete Book of Australian Verse
John Clarke

Diary of a Bad Year
J. M. Coetzee
Introduced by Peter Goldsworthy

Wake in Fright
Kenneth Cook
Introduced by Peter Temple

The Dying Trade
Peter Corris
Introduced by Charles Waterstreet

They're a Weird Mob
Nino Culotta
Introduced by Jacinta Tynan

The Songs of a Sentimental Bloke
C. J. Dennis
Introduced by Jack Thompson

Careful, He Might Hear You
Sumner Locke Elliott
Introduced by Robyn Nevin

Fairyland
Sumner Locke Elliott
Introduced by Dennis Altman

Terra Australis
Matthew Flinders
Introduced by Tim Flannery

My Brilliant Career
Miles Franklin
Introduced by Jennifer Byrne

The Fringe Dwellers
Nene Gare
Introduced by Melissa Lucashenko

Cosmo Cosmolino
Helen Garner
Introduced by Ramona Koval

Dark Places
Kate Grenville
Introduced by Louise Adler

The Long Prospect
Elizabeth Harrower
Introduced by Fiona McGregor

The Watch Tower
Elizabeth Harrower
Introduced by Joan London

The Mystery of a Hansom Cab
Fergus Hume
Introduced by Simon Caterson

The Unknown Industrial Prisoner
David Ireland
Introduced by Peter Pierce

The Glass Canoe
David Ireland
Introduced by Nicolas Rothwell

A Woman of the Future
David Ireland
Introduced by Kate Jennings

Eat Me
Linda Jaivin
Introduced by Krissy Kneen

Julia Paradise
Rod Jones
Introduced by Emily Maguire

The Jerilderie Letter
Ned Kelly
Introduced by Alex McDermott

Bring Larks and Heroes
Thomas Keneally
Introduced by Geordie Williamson

Strine
Afferbeck Lauder
Introduced by John Clarke

Stiff
Shane Maloney
Introduced by Lindsay Tanner

The Middle Parts of Fortune
Frederic Manning
Introduced by Simon Caterson

Selected Stories
Katherine Mansfield
Introduced by Emily Perkins

The Home Girls
Olga Masters
Introduced by Geordie Williamson

Amy's Children
Olga Masters
Introduced by Eva Hornung

The Scarecrow
Ronald Hugh Morrieson
Introduced by Craig Sherborne

The Dig Tree
Sarah Murgatroyd
Introduced by Geoffrey Blainey

The Plains
Gerald Murnane
Introduced by Wayne Macauley

The Odd Angry Shot
William Nagle
Introduced by Paul Ham

Life and Adventures 1776–1801
John Nicol
Introduced by Tim Flannery

Death in Brunswick
Boyd Oxlade
Introduced by Shane Maloney

Swords and Crowns and Rings
Ruth Park
Introduced by Alice Pung

The Watcher in the Garden
Joan Phipson
Introduced by Margo Lanagan

Maurice Guest
Henry Handel Richardson
Introduced by Carmen Callil

The Getting of Wisdom
Henry Handel Richardson
Introduced by Germaine Greer

The Fortunes of Richard Mahony
Henry Handel Richardson
Introduced by Peter Craven

Rose Boys
Peter Rose
Introduced by Brian Matthews

Hills End
Ivan Southall
Introduced by James Moloney

The Women in Black
Madeleine St John
Introduced by Bruce Beresford

The Essence of the Thing
Madeleine St John
Introduced by Helen Trinca

Jonah
Louis Stone
Introduced by Frank Moorhouse

An Iron Rose
Peter Temple
Introduced by Les Carlyon

1788
Watkin Tench
Introduced by Tim Flannery

Happy Valley
Patrick White
Introduced by Peter Craven

I Own the Racecourse!
Patricia Wrightson
Introduced by Kate Constable

textclassics.com.au